Finding
Her Way

MARTA PERRY

Previously published as *Mission: Motherhood*

Special thanks and acknowledgment are given
to Marta Perry for her contribution to the
Homecoming Heroes miniseries.

⊕ HARLEQUIN® SELECTS™

PLEASE RECYCLE
THIS PRODUCT IS RECYCLABLE

Recycling programs
for this product may
not exist in your area.

ISBN-13: 978-1-335-40660-6

Finding Her Way
First published as Mission: Motherhood in 2008.
This edition published in 2022.
Copyright © 2008 by Harlequin Books S.A.

The Bull Rider's Secret
First published in 2019. This edition published in 2022.
Copyright © 2019 by Jill Buteyn

This edition published by arrangement with Harlequin Books S.A.

For questions and comments about the quality of this book, please contact us at CustomerService@Harlequin.com.

Harlequin Enterprises ULC
22 Adelaide St. West, 41st Floor
Toronto, Ontario M5H 4E3, Canada
www.Harlequin.com

Printed in U.S.A.

Praise for author Marta Perry

Praise for author Jill Lynn

CONTENTS

A lifetime spent in rural Pennsylvania and her Pennsylvania Dutch heritage led **Marta Perry** to write about the Plain People, who add so much richness to her home state. Marta has seen over seventy of her books published, with over seven million books in print. She and her husband live in a beautiful central Pennsylvania valley noted for its farms and orchards. When she's not writing, she's reading, traveling, baking or enjoying her six beautiful grandchildren.

Books by Marta Perry

Love Inspired

Brides of Lost Creek

Second Chance Amish Bride
The Wedding Quilt Bride
The Promised Amish Bride
The Amish Widow's Heart
A Secret Amish Crush

An Amish Family Christmas
"Heart of Christmas"
Amish Christmas Blessings
"The Midwife's Christmas Surprise"

Visit the Author Profile page at Harlequin.com for more titles.

FINDING HER WAY

Marta Perry

Bear one another's burdens,
and so fulfill the law of Christ.

—*Galatians* 6:2

This story is dedicated to the Love Inspired sisters who worked on this continuity series—Lenora, Brenda, Pat, Margaret and Jillian. And, as always, to Brian, with much love.

Chapter 1

It had taken ten years in New York City to eliminate all traces of Texas from Caitlyn Villard's voice. It took only a week in Prairie Springs to bring it back again.

Had she really just said *y'all* to the kindergarten teacher and her own twin nieces? Caitlyn stepped out into the courtyard of the Prairie Springs Elementary School. She was greeted by a blast of air hot enough to wilt her hairstyle and melt the makeup from her face.

"Um, ma'am?" The warm drawl came from above.

She looked up. A lanky man clung to the top of a wooden stepladder, a paint can in one hand and a dripping brush in the other. "You might want to move out of range a bit."

"Sorry." She took a few steps away, standing under the shade of the roof overhang. She had obviously forgotten just how hot Texas was in July.

Through the window she could see into the room where Amanda and Josie sat at a round table with Sarah Alpert, who was assessing their readiness to start kindergarten in September.

That was still two months away. By the time the twins started school, she would be back in New York, picking up the threads of her interrupted life. Back on the fast track to partner at Graham, Graham and Welch, one of the Big Apple's most prestigious law firms. This interval in Texas, helping her mother cope with the aftermath of her sister's death, would be a memory.

"You brought the girls in for their first taste of kindergarten, did you?"

Caitlyn blinked, as startled as if the spindly potted shrub next to the door had made a personal remark. The painter had descended—tall, lanky, wearing the scuffed boots, blue jeans, western belt and ball cap that were almost a uniform here.

"I beg your pardon?" It was a tone designed to freeze unwelcome attention.

"The twins," he said, as if she was a bit slow on the uptake. "I bet they're excited about starting kindergarten in the fall."

His eyes, intensely blue in a lean, tanned face, now held amusement. They also seemed vaguely familiar.

"I'm sorry. Do I know you?"

"Well, now, I reckon I'm just not as memorable as I thought I was." He didn't look as if he believed that, in spite of the aw-shucks expression he wore. He tipped the ball cap politely. "Steve Windham. Prairie Springs High School. Ring any bells?"

She had to dredge through memories she'd happily

buried a long time ago. "Steve Windham. I guess so. You were a senior when I was a freshman, I think."

Actually she knew, but she didn't intend to pander to the man's self-conceit. He looked far too pleased with himself already.

She let her gaze wander over what had to be at least six feet or more of solid muscle. Steve had been the star athlete of his class, and he still looked it. He'd been the valedictorian, too, and probably voted most likely to succeed.

"That'd be about right," he agreed. "That was way too many years ago, I guess."

"And after high school you became a housepainter, did you? I thought I remembered that you had an athletic scholarship to one of the big schools."

That was typical of Prairie Springs. People just settled down to live the way their folks had, instead of getting out into the world and making a mark. Being a painter was fine, if that was what you really wanted, but it was hard to believe someone with Steve's intelligence and talent hadn't had any bigger goals.

Steve's right eyebrow cocked, giving him a quizzical look. "I don't guess there's anything wrong with painting. It's an honest day's work. So what did Ms. Caitlyn Villard turn out to be?"

She hadn't meant to insult the man, and realized maybe she had been a little judgmental. It wasn't any of her business how Steve Windham spent his life.

"I'm an attorney in New York."

That eyebrow lifted a little higher. "Only now you're back in Prairie Springs. Going to practice law here, are you?"

She hoped the horror she felt at his suggestion didn't show on her face.

She managed what she hoped was a polite smile. "You'll have to excuse me. I think the teacher is ready for me to come back in."

He nodded, still with that faintly amused grin on his lips.

She hurried away, aware that he stood there staring after her, with his thumbs hooked nonchalantly in his belt.

Get out of Prairie Springs. That had been her only goal back in high school.

Well, now she'd come full circle. Getting out of Prairie Springs was her only goal now.

Sarah Alpert, the kindergarten teacher, gave Caitlyn a welcoming smile as she reentered the classroom. A slim, fine-boned redhead, she seemed to exude warmth, and her casual jeans and shirt made the situation feel less formal for her young prospective students.

She rose from her place at the low table where she'd been sitting with the twins.

"You girls can finish up your pictures while I talk with your aunt, all right?"

Amanda, the older by twenty minutes, looked a little rebellious at the prospect of sitting still, but she turned back to her picture at Ms. Alpert's firm gaze. Josie never lifted her eyes from the page, appearing lost in whatever she was drawing.

The twins were physically identical, with their straight, chestnut-colored hair and big blue eyes, but they were very different in personality. Caitlyn got them right about eighty percent of the time, and probably the teacher, with her experience, would quickly figure out how to tell them apart.

Sarah led the way to her desk at the end of the room,

where they'd have a little privacy. She nodded to a folding chair she'd put at right angles to the desk, and Caitlyn sat down.

"How did they do?"

Caitlyn was surprised to find that she had any apprehension about it. She'd only seen the twins a handful of times in their young lives, but they seemed bright. Certainly her younger sister, Carolyn, had been intelligent, even if she'd scorned the education Caitlyn had always thirsted for.

"They're certainly ready intellectually for kindergarten."

"That's good." That was why they were here, after all, wasn't it?

But the teacher's gaze still expressed some concern. "As to how they'll be dealing with their loss in another two months, I just don't know. I guess we'll see where they are then. Grief from the loss of both parents could affect their adjustment."

"I hadn't thought of that." There were, it appeared, a lot of things she hadn't thought of. Well, what did she know about five-year-olds?

Sarah Alpert nodded sympathetically. "Have you noticed many changes in them since they learned that their parents were gone?"

"I haven't—I mean, my job in New York keeps me very busy. My mother was taking care of the twins after my sister and her husband were deployed."

"Yes, of course. I know that. You have my sympathy for your loss."

"Thank you." Her throat tightened on the words.

Carolyn and Dean, her husband, both gone in an instant on the other side of the world. That was something people in Prairie Springs must have to get used to, living as they did in the shadow of the army's Fort Bonnell.

She cleared her throat. "In any event, my mother says that Amanda has been more mischievous than usual, and Josie more withdrawn, although she's always been the shyer of the two. Ms. Alpert—"

"Call me Sarah, please." The teacher reached across the desk to press her hand. "We all know each other here, and your mother and I have often worked on church suppers together."

"Yes, she said that she knew you. She wanted me to mention to you that Josie will follow wherever Amanda leads, even if it's into trouble."

Sarah smiled. "I'll keep that in mind. I know your mother is very relieved to have you here to take over with the children. You are staying, aren't you?"

Did everyone think that? She supposed she owed the teacher an answer, even if she didn't owe one to Steve Windham.

"I'm not sure how long I'll be here. My career is in New York." That sounded sufficiently vague, when the truth was that she longed to get back to her own life, even though duty demanded that she be here for the moment, at least.

"You might find something to do here in Prairie Springs," Sarah suggested. "I know it isn't really my business to interfere, but I'm concerned about the children. They've been through a rough time, and it would be a shame to uproot them at this point."

It was impossible to take offense at Sarah's comments, given the warmth and concern that shimmered in her blue eyes. And she'd brought up a good point—one that Caitlyn hadn't really considered. Caitlyn's original plan had been to take a month's leave, help her mother and the children recover from their grief and see them settled financially, and then get back to her own life.

That plan had seemed reasonable back in New York, when she was scrambling to get time off work, turn her cases over to someone else and get here in time for the funerals. Now that she was on the spot, things weren't so clear-cut.

"I can't practice law here. I'm not licensed in Texas, and I haven't even considered that. I have to admit, though, that it wouldn't be a bad idea for me to find something part-time to do while I'm here."

She hadn't imagined finances would be an issue when she'd taken a leave of absence, but then, she'd never tried to do without her salary before. She hoped she'd be able to continue working on some cases from here, but it had been made clear to her that the clients of Graham, Graham and Welsh expected and would receive personal attention. At least they were willing to hold her position open.

No one could live on her salary in Manhattan, pay off college and law school loans and still have much left over anyway. When she made partner, it would be another story, but in the meantime, her finances were tight. And her mother had given up her job at the gift shop when Carolyn and Dean were deployed to the Middle East.

The twins had the funds that had come to them on their parents' deaths, of course, but if possible, Mama wanted that put away for their futures.

"You know, I believe I might know just the thing." Sarah looked pleased at the prospect of helping. She turned to her desk and scribbled something on a piece of paper. "I volunteer at Children of the Day. It's a local charity that helps victims of war—does wonderful work. As it happens, they're looking for a care coordinator right now, and I believe the schedule would be flexible. With your legal background, you'd probably be a big asset."

"I'm not licensed in Texas—" she repeated, but Sarah pressed the paper into her hand.

"Just talk to Anna Terenkov, the director. I'm sure this is all going to work out fine."

Sarah was a lot more optimistic than she was, since at the moment she didn't see anything working out fine. Still, if she could get the job, the money would be welcome. Her expenses in New York continued unabated while she kicked her heels in Texas.

Not for long, she reminded herself. She'd do all she could for her mother and the twins, since Carolyn had named her as their guardian, but in the end, her life was back in New York.

Steve worked his way methodically through cleaning up the paintbrushes. He'd volunteered two hours of painting to the elementary school this afternoon, but he had a meeting back on post at four. The group he'd formed to get soldiers to volunteer for community projects was going strong now, and he owed it to the people he'd talked into it to show that he'd be right in there volunteering his own time and effort.

From where he stood, he could see through the windows of the kindergarten room. Amanda and Josie, chestnut heads together, whispered over their papers, while their aunt Caitlyn sat talking with Sarah Alpert.

He worried about the twins, as he worried about all those under his care who had suffered losses. The twins had each other and their grandmother, and now they had their aunt. Was Caitlyn up to the responsibility she'd inherited from her sister?

He studied her, frowning a little. He remembered her well, which was odd in itself since she'd been three years behind him in school. Maybe she'd stood apart because of the fierce ambition she'd shown at an age when most girls were too busy giggling over boys, pop stars and clothes to give much thought to their futures.

Now—well, Caitlyn Villard had grown into a beauty, if you liked women who were sophisticated, even icy. She was tall and slim, carrying herself as if there wasn't a doubt in her mind as to who she was and where she was headed.

The hair that had once been flaxen was now a rich golden brown, tousled in a way that he suspected was style, not nature. Her eyes hadn't changed, though. They were a warm hazel with glints of gold when the sun caught them.

Well, the important thing wasn't how she looked, although she was certainly worth a second glance from any man. What was crucial was whether she could take care of those children.

She'd probably used that single-minded determination of hers that he remembered to take the big city by storm. From what he could see, apparently she'd made it, despite all the obstacles there must have been for a little girl from Texas with no family backing or money.

But now she was faced with even harder barriers in learning how to be a mother to two precious children. Did she have that in her? He didn't know.

His thoughts automatically went inward in prayer. *Lord, You know what You have in mind for Amanda and*

Josie, and for their aunt. If there's a way in which I can help, please use me.

When he looked again, the door was opening and Caitlyn and the twins were coming out.

Amanda spotted him first and let out a squeal. She came running toward him, waving a welcome, with Josie scurrying behind.

He bent to hug them, holding them away from his paint stains and grinning at their enthusiastic greeting. "Hey, you two. Y'all been having some fun in the kindergarten room with Miss Sarah?"

"I made a picture and printed my name," Amanda said importantly. "And I said my numbers, too."

"How about you, sugar?" He tugged gently at a strand of Josie's hair. Josie always had to be coaxed a little. "Did you print your name, too?"

She nodded. "I printed Josie," she said. "Not Josephine."

"Girls." Caitlyn had reached them by now, and she clearly didn't know what to make of this. "What are you doing?"

He smiled at her. "The twins and I are old friends." He caught Amanda's hand as she reached for the paint can. "That's wet, Amanda."

Amanda pouted for a fraction of a second before turning to her aunt. "We love Chaplain Steve," she said. "He's our friend."

"*Chaplain* Steve?" Caitlyn's voice accented the title, and annoyance danced in her eyes. "Are you really a minister?"

He shrugged. "Guilty."

"You knew I thought you were a painter." Her lips tightened.

Obviously Caitlyn didn't like being fooled. "Sorry." Truth to tell, he felt a little embarrassed that he hadn't been up front with her. "I did know what you were thinking, but you looked so disapproving I couldn't resist teasing you just a mite."

Faint color came up on her cheeks. "I wasn't disapproving. It's nothing to me what you do."

"Come on, now," he said. "Tell me you weren't thinking that I'd failed to live up to my potential, like Mrs. Clemente used to say in trigonometry class."

Josie tugged at his sleeve. "What does potential mean?" She said the word carefully.

"It means doing everything that you're able to do," Steve answered.

"Oh." She seemed to be storing the definition away for possible future use.

"As I recall, your father was a chaplain, wasn't he?" Caitlyn had herself in hand now, and she asked the question with just the right degree of polite interest.

"That's right. I guess I could have been assigned most anyplace, but I requested Fort Bonnell, and here I am. I've taken over the Fort Bonnell Christian Chapel, but I had to redecorate, since Daddy took all his fishing pictures with him when he and Mama retired to Wyoming."

"And you know the twins how?" Her voice expressed doubt.

"They're part of my job, as it happens, ministering to those of our Fort Bonnell community who've suffered losses."

He managed to keep his mind from straying to his own loss. "Not that these two adorable ladies aren't more than just a job to me."

"I see." Her face had stiffened at the reminder of Carolyn and Dean, and he felt a pang of remorse for teasing her as he had. This couldn't be easy for her.

"I'm sorry for your loss. It must be rough."

"Yes." She clipped off the word, as if reluctant to accept sympathy. "Well…" She managed a smile and extended her hand. "It was nice to see you again, Steve."

He took her hand solemnly, a little amused. "Same here. But it's a small town, Caitlyn. I'm sure I'll see you again soon."

Her smile was stiff. "Come on, girls. It's time to go home."

"Don't want to." Amanda pouted, looking dangerously near to stamping her feet. "I want to stay with Chaplain Steve."

"We have to go." Caitlyn held out her hand.

"No." Now Amanda did stamp her foot. "I don't want to."

Josie took a step closer to him, clearly not knowing what to do at this open mutiny, any more than her aunt did. Caitlyn's expression said only too clearly that she wasn't prepared to cope with this.

He knelt next to Amanda, putting one arm reassuringly around Josie. "I'm afraid you can't stay with me, Amanda, because I have to go to a meeting. And I'll bet your grandmother is waiting to hear all about how you did at school, don't you think?"

Amanda pouted a moment longer, as if reluctant to give up her grudge. Then she spun around, holding her picture up. "I'm going to show Grammy my painting. She'll put it on the refrigerator."

"Mine, too," Josie said. "Mine, too."

"She'll put mine up first," Amanda said, and darted toward the car.

"Mine, mine," Josie shrieked, and ran after her sister.

Caitlyn seemed frozen to the spot for another instant. Then she hurried after them without a backward glance for him.

Steve watched them go, frowning a little. Those children were hurting, and he hurt for them. They needed so much. Was Caitlyn going to be able to provide that?

Or had Carolyn Mayhew made the mistake of her life when she named her sister as their guardian?

Chapter 2

Caitlyn knelt beside the bathtub, wondering how two five-year-olds in a tub could so resemble a pondful of frogs.

Amanda bounced up and down on her bottom, sending a wave of soapy water sloshing toward her sister. Josie's squeal echoed from the tile tub surround, and she scrambled backward.

"Easy, Amanda." She caught each twin by a slippery arm. "Don't fall back against the spigot. That would hurt your head."

"I won't." Amanda bounced again. This time the water splashed Caitlyn's sleeve to her shoulder.

"Hey!" Smiling in spite of herself, she splashed Amanda back. "No fair. I'm still dressed, not like you." She tickled a bare dimpled elbow, eliciting a giggle from Amanda.

"I love my bath." That might be the first thing Josie had volunteered since Caitlyn had been here. Usually she waited for a question before speaking, or echoed what her twin had said.

"What do you like about it?" Caitlyn put a plastic doll into a red boat and zoomed it toward her small, shy niece.

Josie managed a hint of a smile. "Giving my dolls 'ventures. They like that."

"Good idea." She let Josie have the boat. "You give your doll an adventure with the boat, while I wash Amanda's hair."

Josie nodded, smiling, but Amanda's face puckered up at the suggestion. What now? Was it ever possible to get both of them happy at the same time?

"I don't want my hair washed." Amanda pouted. "You'll get soap in my eyes."

"No, I won't." Although now that she considered it, she wasn't sure how you managed to shampoo a wiggly child without disaster. "Tell you what. You show me how Grammy does it, and I'll do exactly what you say. You be the director, okay?"

Amanda considered that for a moment, and then she nodded. "But you do 'zactly like I say."

It was a small triumph, but she'd take it. As she shampooed and rinsed, carefully following directions, her thoughts drifted back to the afternoon. Odd, running into Steve Windham like that.

His idea of humor had been more than a little annoying. On the other hand, his concern for the girls had been obvious. And she'd taken note of the way he'd so easily averted Amanda's tantrum by focusing her on the future instead. She'd remember that technique for the next time Amanda rebelled. And there probably would be a next time. Amanda, like her mother, seemed born to test the boundaries.

Maybe Steve had kids of his own. The thought startled her. It was certainly possible, although he hadn't been wearing a wedding ring. And exactly why she'd taken note of that, she wasn't sure.

With one little girl shampooed and one to go, she turned her attention to Josie, who submitted without argument to her shampoo. In a few minutes she was wrapping two wiggling bodies in one large towel.

"Oh my goodness, I've got an armful of eels," she declared, rubbing wet curls. "That's what Grammy used to say when she dried us."

"She says that to us, too," Amanda said. "Now pajamas, and then we'll tell you just what you hafta do to put us to bed."

She nodded, spraying Josie's shoulder-length hair with conditioner before attempting to get a comb through it. This was her first attempt at getting the girls to bed on her own, and she needed all the help she could get.

Finally they were into pajamas and snuggled one on each side of her in their pink-and-white bedroom for a story. She held them close, a little surprised by the strength of affection that swept through her.

If anyone had asked, a few weeks ago, if she loved her nieces, she'd have said yes, but it would have been an abstract emotion. She'd loved them but she hadn't known them. Now all that was changed.

"'The Princess and the Pea,'" she read. "I remember this story. Let's see if it's changed any since I was a little girl."

Amanda giggled. "Stories don't change, Auntie Caitlyn. We read one book and then one Bible story from our *Bible Storybook* that you gave us for Christmas, and then we say prayers."

She opened her mouth to say she hadn't given them a storybook for Christmas, and then shut it again. She'd taken the easy way out and sent a check, and someone, probably Carolyn, had taken the time to buy and wrap presents and put her name on them.

Amanda's innocent assumption made her feel—well, thoughtless, at the least. Surely she could have taken the time to find out what they wanted and buy the gifts on her own.

That faint uneasiness lingered through the stories and prayers. Caitlyn tucked matching pink quilts around them and kissed their rosy cheeks.

"Auntie Caitlyn?" Amanda was frowning. Had she gotten some part of the routine wrong?

"What is it, sweetie?" She smoothed still-damp hair back from Amanda's face.

"Are Mommy and Daddy happy in Heaven?"

Whatever she'd expected, it hadn't been that. A theological question was out of her realm. She wasn't the person to ask. Chaplain Steve, he'd do a better job of this.

"Well, I think so. Have you talked to Grammy about it?"

She nodded. "She says God takes care of them in Heaven, so they must be happy."

"Well, Grammy must know," she said, grateful to have squeaked through that tricky spot.

"But how can they be?" Tears shone in her eyes. "How can they be happy without us?"

She was totally out of her depth now, and her throat was so tight she couldn't have gotten an answer out even if she'd been able to think of one.

Fortunately her mother was there, coming quickly into the room to bend over the bed. She must have been waiting in the hall, giving Caitlyn a chance to finish the bedtime routine.

"Of course they miss you, darling." Mama's voice was soft. "And that might make them sad sometimes. But they know you're happy and that we're taking care of you, so that makes them happy, too. You see?"

Amanda nodded slowly. Caitlyn suspected the little girl wasn't entirely satisfied, but at least she wasn't asking any other questions that Caitlyn couldn't answer.

Hugs and kisses all around, and then she and her mother were out in the hall, leaving the door open just a crack. "Not too much chatter, now," Mama called as they started down the hall. "You had a big day today."

"Thanks for coming in when you did, Mama." She put her arm around her mother's waist. "I didn't know how to handle that."

Her mother gave her a gentle squeeze. "You'll learn by experience. That's the only way anyone ever learns to be a parent."

Something in her rebelled at that. She wasn't a parent, and she didn't intend to be here long enough to learn. It was on the tip of her tongue to say that, but she closed her lips on the words.

Her mother looked tired, too tired for the sixty-five Caitlyn knew she was. Grief, she supposed, combined with the stress of caring for two lively five-year-olds for the past six months.

"Carolyn and Dean shouldn't have expected you to take over when they were deployed," she said. "It was too much for you."

Mama shrugged. "It's made me realize I'm not as

young as I used to be, that's for sure. Taking care of two five-year-olds is a Texas-size job. But you do what you have to do. It's not as if they had any other options."

She wanted to say that they should have been responsible enough not to get in that position to begin with, but her mother wouldn't hear anything critical of Carolyn.

Well, maybe her mother wouldn't admit it, but in Caitlyn's opinion, Carolyn had been too quick to dump her responsibilities on other people.

"Listen, would it be any use if I hired someone to help out a little? With the girls, or the house, or whatever?"

Her mother looked surprised. "That's sweet of you, darling, but I'll be okay now that you're here. The two of us can handle things."

There it was again—that assumption that she was here to stay.

"You're not planning to go away, are you?" Her silence must have lasted too long, and her mother looked so dismayed that she couldn't possibly do anything but deny it.

"Not now, but I have a job possibility at Children of the Day. I'm supposed to go for an interview with the director tomorrow. It's only part-time, but I don't want to burden you—"

"Children of the Day? That's wonderful." Her mother interrupted her with a hug. "You'll love it there. I'm so pleased."

The hug strengthened. Caitlyn hugged her mother back, but the feel of her mother's arms was like fragile, yet strong threads tightening around her, trying to bind her to this place.

"Welcome to Children of the Day. I hope you'll enjoy your work here." Anna Terenkov, the founder and director of the charity, rose from behind her desk after the briefest of interviews, extending her hand.

Caitlyn blinked for a second before she stood to shake the woman's hand. She'd met executives who prided themselves on quick decisions before, but Ms. Terenkov had them beat by a mile.

"Ms. Terenkov—"

"Please, call me Anna." A smile banished her businesslike expression. "We're all on a first-name basis here, volunteers and staff alike."

"Anna." She tried to grasp a situation that seemed to be sliding away from her. "Isn't there anything else you'd like to ask me about my qualifications?"

The director waved that away. "I've seen quite enough to know you'll be an asset to the organization. And, frankly, we're in need of a capable person to step into the care coordinator position. That's one job I don't want to lay on a volunteer, and our last coordinator had to leave quite suddenly."

That sounded ominous. Anna seemed to read her expression and laughed.

"Nothing bad, I assure you. Her husband was transferred to a post in the Northeast, and naturally she and the children went with him."

"He was in the military, I gather."

Anna nodded. "Almost everyone in town has some connection to Fort Bonnell, in one way or another. Now—" she rounded the desk "—let me show you our facility and get you started."

She hadn't imagined being hired that quickly, let alone starting, but she followed the petite blond human dynamo out of her office for a whirlwind tour of the building.

Children of the Day was housed in a gracious slate-blue Victorian on a quiet side street just off Veterans Boulevard, Prairie Springs's main drag. Sheltered by shrubbery and a white wrought-iron fence, the charming Victorian looked more like an elegant private residence than a nonprofit foundation.

"As you can see, the first floor is dedicated to the organization." Anna waved at the volunteer who was seated behind a desk in the welcoming lobby area. "The kitchen downstairs is for the staff and volunteers, so don't hesitate to use it. My mother and I have our private apartment upstairs."

"Is your mother involved with Children of the Day also?"

Anna smiled. "My mother does a little bit of everything, all with great enthusiasm. You'll see where I get my energy when you meet her. She also runs the grief center at Prairie Springs Christian Church. I think she mentioned that your nieces are involved in her children's program."

Something else Caitlyn hadn't known. She'd have to ask her mother about that. At least the twins were apparently getting some professional help.

Anna led the way to the next room. "This is Laura Dean. Laura, meet Caitlyn Villard, our new care coordinator." Anna paused by a desk in the room behind the lobby.

"It's nice to meet you, Caitlyn." The slim young blonde flashed a welcoming smile. "Especially since I'm sure you're going to take some of the load off my shoulders."

"Laura is officially our secretary, but like everyone else, she does whatever needs to be done. And she does it very well, by the way."

Anna was out of the room before Laura could respond, but Caitlyn guessed Laura was probably used to that.

"This will be your office." Anna ushered her into a high-ceilinged room with windows looking onto a side lawn. It had probably once been a modest parlor, with its small fireplace and beautiful molding, but was now furnished with a computer desk and file cabinets. Several maps were pinned onto a bulletin board on the wall.

Anna waved at the small blue pins that dotted the map. "Those are places where we have programs. We provide food, shelter, medical care, educational programs—anything we can to alleviate the suffering of those touched by war." Anna's passion was impressive.

"It's a big job."

"A huge job," Anna agreed. "Those projects are ongoing, and they're already established and running well. What I need you to do is coordinate the kinds of services we provide for individual special needs that arise frequently."

"I see." She didn't, but surely she was going to get more explanation than that.

Anna bent over the desk for a moment and brought up a file on the computer. "Here's the project I want you to start with. There's very little information yet, but you'll read everything we have."

"Yes, of course."

"Ali Tabiz was orphaned and injured in the fighting. We've been contacted by Dr. Mike Montgomery, a surgeon with the army currently stationed in the Middle East. We've worked with him for a while. Little Ali may need heart surgery, and Mike wants him brought here to see a pediatric cardiac surgeon. That's your job."

So she was supposed to get a minor foreign national

out of a war-torn country and bring him to Texas for treatment. She couldn't even begin to ask the questions that flooded her mind.

"Don't panic," Anna said. She pulled out a black three-ring binder. "Our last coordinator was very organized, and we've done this sort of thing many times. She's outlined a step-by-step process with all the things you'll need to do."

Caitlyn grasped the binder as if it were a life preserver and she were sinking under the waves. "Good. I'm going to need it."

"You'll be fine. And I'm just across the hall. Come to me with any questions." She frowned slightly. "Dr. Mike is usually in touch via e-mail, but sometimes things get pretty hot where he is."

"You think that's why you haven't received any other information?" That must mean that the child was in a dangerous place, as well.

"Probably, but we won't waste time. You can start by alerting the medical facilities and personnel we normally use that we'll have a case coming their way. Once we know more, you can get the details nailed down."

Someone tapped on the frame of the open door, and Caitlyn turned to see Sarah, the kindergarten teacher. "Anna, you're needed on the phone. It's some CEO who wants to make a donation and won't talk to anyone else."

"Okay, I'll take it. Never turn down an eager donor." Anna was gone in an instant, leaving Caitlyn with her mouth still open to say goodbye.

She looked at Sarah, who stood there smiling, probably at her expression. "You didn't tell me she was a whirlwind."

Sarah laughed. "How else would she get everything

done? Don't worry—you'll get used to it." She waved and disappeared, leaving Caitlyn staring blankly at the computer screen.

She found she was still clutching the binder. All right. She could do this. She needed a job, and here it was. She wouldn't let anything keep her from succeeding at it.

An hour later she was feeling far more confident. As Anna had said, her predecessor had been organized.

She'd already made several calls, and she'd been pleasantly surprised by her reception. The physicians and hospital administrators had obviously worked with Children of the Day in the past and were perfectly ready to jump into the new project. As soon as she had some more information—

That was the sticking point. No one could do anything until they learned a bit more about the case. She checked the e-mail inbox again, feeling a flutter of excitement at a message from Dr. Montgomery. Maybe this was what they needed.

She clicked it open, and a small face appeared on the screen. This, clearly, was Ali Tabiz.

Big brown eyes, short dark brown hair, an engaging smile. According to the brief statistics attached, the little boy was five, the same age as the twins, but he looked— what?

She grappled for the right word. He was small, maybe suffering from the shortages that went along with having a war in your backyard, and there was a bruise over one eye. But he didn't look younger than the twins. In a way, he looked older, as those dark brown eyes seemed to hold a world of sorrows.

"Cute kid." The voice, coming from behind her without warning, startled her so much that her hands jerked from the keys, and she swung around. It was Steve Windham again, this time in uniform. Somehow it made him seem even taller, his shoulders even broader. Or maybe that was because she was sitting down.

She shoved her chair back, standing. "Steve, hello." She noted the bars he wore. "Or should I say Captain Windham?"

He shook his head, giving her that easy smile. "I'm Chaplain Steve to everyone. Since we're old friends, I'm just Steve to you."

She wouldn't, she decided, exactly call them old friends. "First the elementary school, now Children of the Day. Are you following me?"

His grin widened. "Afraid not. Not that that's not a good idea."

Maybe it was safest to ignore the comment. "What are you doing here?"

"I coordinate all the military volunteers who work with Children of the Day, so I'm in and out of the foundation office all the time."

"Painting at the elementary school, volunteering here, counseling the grieving—surely a chaplain's not expected to do all that."

"All that and more." He shrugged. "An army chaplain has a surprising amount of autonomy. His or her duties are what he or she makes of them, outside of regular services. I follow where the Lord leads me to minister, and He led me here."

Which meant she'd be tripping over him, apparently. He'd been right to remind her. Prairie Springs was a small town.

He nodded toward the computer screen. "Is this little guy your first project?"

"Yes."

He lifted an eyebrow. "It's not a state secret, you know. Tell me about him."

"Look, Steve, I'm not trying to kick you out, but I have work to do. I just don't see why you need to know about my project." It was her project, after all.

"If that child has to be brought to the States from a war zone, then I need to know." Now his smile had developed an edge. "I also coordinate any military involvement in Children of the Day projects—which probably will mean getting that child out."

"Sorry." That didn't sound very gracious, did it? "I am sorry. I didn't realize that you were involved to such an extent."

He shrugged. "Now you know. So, are you ready to tell me about him now?"

"Of course." She managed a smile. "I don't know much yet. His name is Ali Tabiz, and he's five years old. He was referred to Children of the Day by a Dr. Mike Montgomery."

He nodded, his eyes intent as he studied the face on the screen. "I know Mike. If he wants our help, he has good reason."

"I suppose so, but he hasn't gotten back to us with much information on the boy's condition yet. It's apparently a heart problem that may need surgery. Oh, and we do know he's an orphan."

"Poor little guy." Steve reached out and touched the screen. "What do you say we send him a message?"

"A message? Well, I suppose we could ask Dr. Mike to tell him something."

"We can do better than that." He nodded to her desk chair. "If you'll let me use your computer for a minute, that is."

In an effort to seem more congenial, she slid out of the chair and watched as he started an e-mail. But the letters that appeared on the screen were Arabic.

Her mouth was probably hanging open in surprise. "How did you do that?"

He grinned. "All the computers here are equipped to switch to an Arabic alphabet. It's necessary, given where the greatest need is at the moment."

"But how do you know Arabic?" Steve seemed to be full of surprises.

He shrugged. "I have a knack for languages, I guess. And I was in the Middle East in an earlier offensive."

"I didn't know."

An awkward silence followed, making her wonder what war had been like for a chaplain.

He frowned at the screen. "Since he's only five, he's probably not reading much yet, so let's keep it simple and say we love him and want to see him."

"That sounds good." It did, and she was touched that Steve had thought of something that hadn't even occurred to her.

"There we go." Steve addressed it to the doctor's e-mail address and hit Send. "Mike will see that he gets it and that somebody reads it to him."

"I wish the doctor would get back to us. There's not much more I can do until I hear from him."

"You can trust Mike to do what's right. We've worked with him before. He's one of the good guys."

She was beginning to think that Steve was one of the

good guys, too. But that didn't mean she wanted him taking over her job.

"I have a few more things to do before I go home, so if you don't mind—"

He nodded, getting up from the computer. "I know. It's your job, not mine."

"Well, yes, I guess that's what I mean. I'd like to show my new boss I can do it."

He stood watching her for a moment, and she almost thought there was a shadow of disappointment in his blue eyes.

"Not alone," he said. "Nobody around here is a solo act. It takes all of us to make this work."

"I'm sure cooperation is important, but—"

"But you're staff, while I'm just a volunteer?"

"I didn't mean that." She wasn't sure where this tension between them had come from.

He shrugged and started for the door, but before he reached it, he turned back toward her. "Keep me posted on Ali, will you?"

"All right."

He didn't seem convinced that she meant it. "Don't forget that I'm your military contact, Caitlyn. You'd better get used to working with me."

Chapter 3

Steve went in the side door of Children of the Day, hearing a hum of conversation from the lobby. Something must be going on, as it always was, but with a little luck he might be able to corner Anna for a private chat.

He had some information for her that might be helpful, but that wasn't his primary reason for turning up. The truth was that he was curious to see how Caitlyn was working out.

She'd been with COTD for all of two days, but if he knew Anna, that was plenty of time for her to come to a conclusion about Caitlyn.

He'd been bothered since their conversation about Ali. Maybe Caitlyn was dynamite at her position in New York, but Children of the Day ran on cooperation, lots of cooperation from all sorts of people. And Caitlyn had given off unmistakable vibes that she preferred to do everything all by herself.

Or maybe *he* was just the one person she didn't want to help her. That was always possible.

He tapped lightly on the French door to Anna's office. It was standing ajar, as always, so that she could keep tabs on everything. With her passion and energy, it was no wonder the charity had grown from a small local effort to a world-respected organization in only five years.

He popped his head around the edge of the door. Anna was talking on the phone while staring intently at her computer screen, but at the sight of him, she smiled and waved him in.

In a moment she'd hung up the phone and turned her full attention to him. "Steve, how nice. I didn't expect to see you today."

"Well, since tomorrow's the Fourth of July, I thought I'd best come by today. Have you heard anything more from Dr. Mike?"

"No." Anna's brow furrowed. "I expected to by this time."

"I figured you might be concerned. The fact is that there's been a heavy offensive in Mike's area. I'd guess that's keeping him busy right now."

Anna's blue eyes filled with concern. "Is there fighting near his field hospital?"

He hesitated for a second, but Anna would guess the worst if he didn't level with her. "It sounds that way. It may be a day or two before things settle down."

"If they settle down." Anna rubbed at the line between her brows. "We both know how bad that can be. And that poor little boy. He could be right in the thick of things again."

He nodded. Anna was right—they did both know how bad war could be, especially on the innocent ones. "He's lost both his parents, and he's facing possible surgery. It seems like the kid ought to get a break soon."

"Well, he will if we can do anything about it." Anna's jaw tightened with her characteristic determination.

"Shall we pray for them?" He held out his hand, knowing her answer would be yes.

Anna nodded, putting her hand in his and closing her eyes.

"Dear Father, we know that You know better than we do what's happening right now with Mike and all those within his care, including little Ali. We ask that You surround them with Your love and protection and bring them through this trial to safety. Amen."

"Amen," Anna echoed. She released his hand. "Thank you, Steve."

He shrugged that off. "I should let you get back to business, but I did want to ask how Caitlyn's settling in. Is she working out all right?"

Anna's face lit with a smile. "As well as I knew she would the minute I met her. She's the kind of person you can just give a project and know she'll run with it."

"That's good." Although it didn't answer his main concern about her.

"It's just too bad she probably won't be staying in Prairie Springs for long."

He blinked, staring at Anna. "What do you mean? Did she tell you she's leaving?"

"Not in so many words." Anna shrugged. "But I can read between the lines as well as anyone. The most important thing in Caitlyn's life is her career, and that's back in New York. Obviously she's here to do her duty to her family, but I'd expect her to head back East just as soon as she can work things out."

"You're sure about that?" The question came out more sharply than it should.

She spread her hands. "I'd love to keep her, but I don't think that's going to happen."

Though he didn't say it out loud, he was appalled at the news.

How could Caitlyn even think of uprooting the girls? They needed the stability and security they had right here, among friends. And her mother, Betty, couldn't possibly manage by herself.

It sounded as if his concerns had been justified. It looked as if the bright, ambitious girl he'd once known had turned into a coldly driven career woman without any heart.

Caitlyn had forgotten how intensely Prairie Springs celebrated the Fourth of July, but it was certainly all coming back to her now. Texans were just naturally patriotic, and Texans living next to a military base doubled the patriotism. The twins were determined to enjoy every minute of the celebration, and so far, they seemed to be.

They'd already watched the parade and eaten their way through hot dogs and sweet corn and cherry pie, but at least they'd found a table near the river, where there was a bit of a breeze.

It had been a good day, but Caitlyn had to admit that the heat was getting to her. She'd thought New York in the summer was hot, but it was nothing compared to Texas. The heat hadn't bothered her that much as a kid, but now it was draining every bit of energy.

She pressed a paper cup of iced tea against her forehead, wishing she could just pour the tea over her head, as she watched the twins go around and around on the carousel. She smiled and waved to the girls as they passed her, thinking she and Carolyn had probably ridden those same painted wooden horses a long time ago.

Amanda was waving one arm like a rodeo rider as her palomino went up and down. Next to her, Josie clung to the pole of her stationary horse as if she feared it would throw her.

Worry flickered through her. Her mother felt Josie's timidity would resolve itself if they left her alone. Mama certainly had more experience than she did in dealing with children, so why did it still tease her, seeming to say she should do something?

The tempo of the carousel music changed, and the horses slowed their movement. The twins were out of her view, their horses now on the far side of the carousel.

Apprehension grabbed her. The carousel was going to stop with the twins about as far from her as they could be. Would they have sense enough to stay put until she reached them? She should have reminded them before the ride had started.

The music tinkled to a stop, and people began to pour off the carousel, even as others started to climb on. She struggled against the crowd of cheerful kids and adults, trying to spot the girls.

It was irrational, wasn't it, to feel so panicky because they were out of her sight? She couldn't seem to help it, and she couldn't get there fast enough.

Finally the crowd cleared, and she hurried past one painted horse after another. There was the palomino Amanda had ridden, with the stationary chestnut beside it. They were both empty.

She turned, searching the immediate area with her gaze. Where were the children? They were her responsibility—she should have gone on the carousel with them. They could be scared—Josie might be crying.

And then she saw them walking toward her. Steve had each one by a hand, and Amanda was clutching a bunch of balloons.

She raced toward them, reaching them and catching both girls in a hug. "Where were you? I was scared when I couldn't find you."

Steve grasped her hand warmly. "They're fine. I'm sorry if they scared you."

"*Scared* is the right word." She took a breath. "What happened? Why didn't you stay where you were and wait for me to come?"

"I saw a man with balloons." Amanda's tone said she knew perfectly well she'd made a mistake and wasn't going to admit it.

"That's where I caught up with them," Steve said. "I happened to walk past the balloon man."

Caitlyn knelt so that she was eye to eye with the twins. "Listen, guys, you scared me. Don't ever do that again, okay?"

Amanda's lower lip came out, but after a moment she nodded. "Okay. I promise."

Josie nodded, too, looking close to tears.

"Good." Caitlyn hugged them. Had this been her first parenting success? At least Amanda hadn't argued. And thanks to Steve, they were safe.

She rose, blinking back a stray tear as she looked at Steve. "Thank you. If you hadn't seen them before they wandered even farther—"

"They wouldn't have gone far," he said comfortingly. He turned to the girls. "Hey, do you know how to make balloon animals?"

They shook their heads solemnly.

"Well, if I can just borrow a balloon, you'll see." He took one of the long balloons from Amanda's hand. "I wonder what I can make." He twisted the balloon in his hands, frowning a little. Finally he held it out.

"A giraffe." The twins shouted the word in unison.

He handed it to Josie, and she looked enchanted.

"One for me," Amanda said quickly. She gave him another balloon. "A giraffe, please."

"Well, we'll just have to see how it turns out." He twisted the balloon in his strong hands, frowning at it intently.

"What's wrong? Can't guarantee another giraffe?" Caitlyn asked softly.

He grinned. "I hate to promise what it's going to be. It usually looks like an animal, but not necessarily what I think it's going to be."

Fortunately for all of them, this one turned out enough like a giraffe to make Amanda happy, and the two girls decided to make their giraffes dance together to the music of the carousel.

"You're a success." Caitlyn smiled at him. "And we're lucky you came along when you did."

"Not so much luck," Steve said. "I ran into Betty and she asked me to join y'all for dessert and to watch the fireworks. I said I'd round you up."

"I see." It seemed she was destined to see Steve wherever she went. As he'd said, it was a small town. "Well, I'm still glad you came when you did. I was starting to panic. I'm beginning to appreciate every gray hair Carolyn and I caused our mother."

She said it lightly, but judging by Steve's expression, he wasn't taking it that way.

"Not easy being a parent, is it?"

"I'm not a parent. I can't ever take their mother's place."

The words came out without her thinking them through, but she realized they were true as soon as she said them. She'd do what she could, but she couldn't take Carolyn's place.

Steve stopped, turning to face her. "Is that really what you think?" He was frowning as if he'd taken her measure and found her lacking in some way. "Because that's what those children need, and you might just have to sacrifice what you want to give it to them."

Caitlyn could only stare at him in disbelief, as anger welled up in her at his stinging criticism. "I appreciate your interest, Chaplain Steve. But my family life is not really any of your business."

Without giving him a chance to respond, she grabbed the girls' hands and stalked off in the direction of the picnic grove.

It was all very well to have the last word, Caitlyn decided, but it lost its effect if you had to be with that person for another two hours.

She'd expected Steve to beg off watching the fireworks with them. That's what she'd have done, if their positions were reversed.

But he hadn't. He'd come back to the picnic table with them and eaten a slab of Mama's pecan pie and drunk a glass of lemonade, chatting all the while as if there weren't a trace of strain between them.

Now, he helped her spread a blanket at the riverbank—the ideal spot, her mother declared, for watching the fireworks.

"Thanks." She smoothed out a corner and sat down, glancing at the twins running among the blankets with a couple of friends, each one waving a flag or a glow stick. "Here's a spot for you, Mama." She patted the space next to her.

Her mother shook her head. "I was just talking to Maisie Elliot, and she's going on home now. I think maybe I'll ride along with her. I'm just a mite tired."

"Mama, if you're tired, we can go home now. We don't have to stay for the fireworks." She started to get up, but her mother was already shaking her head again.

"No, no, the girls would be so disappointed. You know how they've been looking forward to staying up for the fireworks. Y'all stay. Steve will keep you company, I know."

"I don't think—"

"I won't hear of you leaving," Mama said flatly. "Now just you do as I say, Caitlyn Ann."

"If a parent uses both names, you'd better give up," Steve said. His smile seemed genuine.

She sank back down reluctantly. "I guess you're right. We'll see you at home, then, Mama."

Her mother blew a kiss and started off to find her next-door neighbor. Caitlyn watched her go, and her heart clenched.

"She's aged," she said softly, nearly forgetting who she was talking to.

"It's been pretty rough on her." Steve leaned back on his elbows, his gaze intent on her face. "Even before Carolyn and Dean died, I could see the toll it was taking on her. She wouldn't admit it, but taking care of those girls full-time was beyond her."

"You think I don't know that?" She let the exasperation show in her voice. "Have you ever tried to stop Betty Villard from doing something she thought was her duty?"

"I know what you mean." He smiled. "Texas women are tough."

She shrugged. "I've been away too long to qualify, I'm afraid."

"Never say that." The laughter seemed to leave his face. "Caitlyn, I need to apologize to you for what I said earlier. I overstepped my bounds."

"Yes, you did."

"You're a hard case, you know that? I'm saying I'm sorry."

Much as she hated to admit it, that lopsided grin of his affected her. All the annoyance she'd been clinging to slid away.

"It's all right," she said. "I know you care about the girls. As for me—I'm still just feeling my way with them."

"It's pretty different from your life in New York, is it?"

"I'll say. I probably don't see a child from one month to the next there."

"No married friends with babies?"

She shrugged. "I work long hours. When I'm off, I guess I try to catch up on my sleep."

"That sounds a little lonely."

"Lonely? I don't have time to be lonely. The firm isn't happy unless they're getting sixty hours a week out of us."

He smiled. "Like I said. Lonely."

"You don't understand." He probably couldn't. She didn't know what the army expected of a chaplain, but it couldn't be anything like the expectations of her firm. "That's what it takes in my line of work. You put in outrageous hours, knowing that the payoff at the end is worth it."

She sounded defensive, she realized. That was ridiculous. She didn't owe anyone an explanation of the life she'd chosen.

The military band struck up a march just then, and she was glad. It would save her from another argument with Steve.

"Hey, Amanda! Josie!" Steve called. "Come on, the fireworks are going to start any minute."

They came scurrying and dived onto the blanket. "I love fireworks," Amanda said. "They're my favorite thing next to chocolate cake and going to the movies."

"This girl's got her priorities straight." Steve scooped her onto his lap. "Look right out there over the water. Maybe you can be the first one to spot the fireworks."

Josie snuggled against Caitlyn. "I don't like the loud bang," she said confidingly. "I'm going to put my hands over my ears."

"That sounds like a good plan." Caitlyn patted her. "We'll hold on to each other, okay?"

"Okay."

The feel of that little body snuggled up against her was doing funny things to her heart. Lonely. Steve thought she'd been lonely.

She'd denied it, of course, but there might be a grain of truth in what he'd said. Maybe her life back in New York was a bit out of balance.

"There!" Amanda pointed to a dark rocket soaring upward. It exploded into a shower of white stars that arced downward toward their reflection in the water.

That was only the beginning. One rocket after another shot up to the oohs and aahs of the crowds along the riverbank. Amanda stared, mesmerized, and Josie alternated between watching and hiding her face in Caitlyn's lap.

Caitlyn smoothed Josie's fine, soft hair. She wouldn't have believed it a month ago, but it really was nice, sitting here, watching the awed looks on the children's faces.

As for Steve—she turned so she could see his strong profile, outlined against the water. It wasn't so bad having him here, either.

The last spectacular display seemed to go on and on as the band soared to a crescendo. Then, finally, the lights and sound faded away. It was over.

Before she could move or speak, she heard a sound drifting over the dark water, silencing the audience. It was a lone bugle, playing "Taps." The notes hung, sharp as crystal, in the still air.

Caitlyn's heart clenched painfully, and a tear trickled down her cheek. The sound was inexpressibly sad and beautiful.

The final notes died away, and for a moment nobody moved, nobody spoke. From somewhere in the crowd there was a muffled sob.

Then Steve pushed to his feet and moved to kneel next to her.

"She's asleep. I'll take her, if you can manage—"

He stopped. Then he reached out, wiping an errant tear from her cheek with one large, warm hand. Her gaze met his, and for a moment she couldn't think, couldn't breathe. Attraction twinkled between them, seeming as bright as the fireworks had been.

Then Steve sat back on his heels, looking startled. "I—" he began, and seemed to lose his train of thought. He cleared his throat. "Sorry. I—I was saying that I'd carry Josie."

Amanda tugged at his pant leg. "I want you to carry me."

"But Aunt Caitlyn needs you," he said. "She has to have a strong girl to carry one end of the blanket."

Amanda's shoulders straightened. She'd be the strong one, obviously.

He slid his arms under the sleeping child, carefully not looking at Caitlyn. It didn't matter. She was aware of his every movement.

Was he as aware of her? Maybe it was better not to know. That flare of attraction—it was probably brought on by the emotion of the moment. It couldn't be anything else.

She stumbled to her feet, helping a tired Amanda gather up the blanket and then taking her tiny hand. It was definitely time to go home, and she would not feel regret. She wouldn't.

Chapter 4

Caitlyn's stomach clenched a little as she headed toward Anna's office. Being summoned like that in the hallowed halls of Graham, Graham and Welch was seldom a good thing. She hadn't been at Children of the Day long enough to know what it meant with Anna.

She did a rapid mental review of her work. Everything she could think to do regarding the Ali Tabiz situation had been done, and until they received the specifics from Dr. Mike she couldn't do anything more. Could she? She wasn't used to work situations in which the next step wasn't clear-cut, and that made her nervous.

She paused for just a second at the French doors, which stood ajar as usual, tapped lightly and went in. Anna was at her desk, talking, but she waved her in, never missing a beat. Anna obviously had multitasking down to a fine art, which was probably essential in running a foundation like this one.

"Here's Caitlyn now. Let's see what she has to say about it."

She went to the desk, realizing that Anna was talking with someone via her webcam. Anna pulled a chair over so that they could sit next to each other, and Caitlyn slid into place.

"Dr. Mike, this is Caitlyn Villard, our new care coordinator. She's working on Ali's case. Caitlyn, this is Major Michael Montgomery, usually known as Dr. Mike."

"It's nice to meet you, Caitlyn. Glad to have you on board."

Even against the drab background of a cement-block wall, the man in scrubs had a vitality that transcended his obvious fatigue. His even features looked drawn, but his eyes sparkled with energy.

"It's good to meet you, as well, Dr. Mike. We've been hoping for some additional information on your young patient."

Dr. Mike grimaced. "I was sorry not to get back to you sooner. It's been pretty hot around here."

"We've been praying for you. But you're okay? And Ali?" Anna asked.

"Fine, fine." He glanced around, as if distracted. "I don't have much time, since people are lining up behind me to talk to their folks back home. I'm going to e-mail you a detailed medical report that you can share with the docs you normally use, so I'll just give you the main points now."

"Good." Caitlyn grabbed a pad from Anna's desk in the event he thought of anything that wouldn't be in the report.

"Ali was injured in the roadside bomb blast that killed his mother. At first glance his injuries seemed minor, but we soon realized his condition was more serious. A blow to the chest from the blast tore an abnormal opening between the two lower chambers of the heart—a ventricular septal tear. We've confirmed the diagnosis with an EKG and a sonogram, and I've consulted by phone with a cardiologist."

That sounded serious. Images of Amanda and Josie ran through her mind. "Will we need to schedule immediate surgery?" Caitlyn asked.

"Possibly not, but it's a tricky situation." His frown deepened. "The cardiologist feels that the tear could heal on its own. If so, he'll quickly regain his strength. But if it doesn't, if the heart begins to fail, the boy needs to be where he can have open heart surgery quickly."

"So we need to get him back here as soon as possible," Anna said.

"Right. There's just no place here that has either the equipment or the pediatric cardiac surgeons who can do the job."

"We'll do our best." Caitlyn scribbled rapid notes to herself. "How is he doing otherwise?"

"His other injuries were minor, fortunately. Of course he's grieving for his mother."

Her throat tightened. Like the twins, Ali was yet another child robbed of a mother's love by war.

"He's a cute kid." Dr. Mike's face creased in a tired smile. "Half the medical team has fallen for him already, and some of the chopper pilots have practically adopted him. We have to chase them out of his room so he can get enough rest."

"We'll make sure he gets plenty of attention here, too," Anna said. "Caitlyn will arrange for a complete workup with a pediatric cardiologist in Austin as soon as he arrives."

Caitlyn nodded. At least the child wouldn't have to have surgery the minute he got here. She'd gone over and over the process to have the army fly a foreign national to the United States for treatment. She didn't anticipate too much difficulty.

"What relative will accompany Ali to the U.S.?" Her pen was poised over the pad.

"None, unfortunately. He doesn't have a soul left over here."

"But…" She paused, her mind racing through all the regulations she'd read. "Legally I don't think we can bring a child who's a foreign national into the country without a guardian to give permission."

Anna's eyes clouded with concern. "We probably can't even get him out of there without it. Mike, you know the rules. There must be somebody who's willing to be responsible for the child—a distant cousin, an aunt or grandmother, anyone."

"Here's the thing." Dr. Mike leaned forward, as if he'd like to be in the room with them. "Ali's mother was married to an American serviceman who died when the boy was three. I'm still working on finding out all the details. The mother lived in a fairly remote village, and she probably used her family name for the child to protect him from discrimination."

"Are you sure they were actually married?" Anna asked the question Caitlyn had been thinking but hesitated to ask.

"I've seen the marriage certificate—it was with her things. The father's name was Gregory Willis." He shrugged. "So, the boy's an American citizen. That has to make a difference."

Caitlyn rubbed her temples, as if that might make her mind work a little faster. This was not the sort of legal issue that ever came up at her corporate practice in New York, and she certainly wasn't an expert on family or immigration law.

"Will you send us every bit of legal documentation you can find about the parents' marriage and the child's birth? I'm sure we're going to need it to prove that Ali is an American citizen." She at least knew that was the place to start.

"Will do." Mike glanced around. "Gotta go. I'll send everything I can ASAP. Good luck."

Before they could say goodbye, he was gone. Anna sat back in her chair, letting out a long breath. "Well. That's a new one."

"I was hoping you were going to say that COTD had dealt with a situation just like this before," Caitlyn said.

"No, I'm afraid this is uncharted territory. It looks as if you have your work cut out for you."

And while she was struggling to get up to speed, halfway around the world the clock might well be ticking for a small child who'd already lost far too much.

"Aren't we there yet, Aunt Caitlyn?" Amanda, in her booster seat in the back, kicked her feet against the driver's seat.

Caitlyn gritted her teeth, making a mental resolution to switch their seats so that Josie would be directly behind her. "Almost."

She glanced at the directions her mother had written out to the Fort Bonnell pool where the twins had swimming lessons. This was her first visit to the post, and it was far bigger than she'd realized. Everything about coming here seemed strange, including the stop she'd had to make at the visitors' center to pick up a pass even to drive onto the post.

She'd had to leave the Children of the Day offices just when she felt she was getting a handle on the search for Ali's parentage, but her mother had a doctor's appointment this afternoon, and she'd promised to take the twins for their lesson.

"I'm going to swim underwater today," Amanda declared. "Hurry up, please."

"Me, too," Josie echoed.

She certainly wasn't going to "hurry up" beyond the speed limit, not with all these military types around. She passed a unit marching along the roadway, and a tank rumbled past her in the opposite direction.

She didn't think she'd ever seen so many uniforms in one place before. Funny that she'd never, so far as she remembered, come on the post when she was growing up in Prairie Springs.

Beige-colored buildings stretched down one straight street after another, seeming to go on and on as far as the horizon. Most of them bore signs in some sort of army shorthand that didn't mean a thing to her. Goodness, Fort Bonnell was a small city on its own, dwarfing Prairie Springs in comparison.

She passed the Fort Bonnell Christian Chapel on her right, one of her mother's landmarks. Steve's church. She'd called him there earlier, but he hadn't been in. She needed to involve him, as military liaison for COTD, in the search for Ali's father.

She'd confessed to Anna that she was totally out of

her depth in dealing with the legal issues of the case. She hated feeling unprepared for any case she took on, but she had to be honest. Her legal background made her at least know the questions to ask, but not the answers.

Anna had been reassuring, referring her to a local attorney, Jake Hopkins, who offered pro bono services to the charity. Unfortunately, Hopkins hadn't been in either when she'd called, so she'd left a detailed message on his machine, along with her cell phone number. Surely he'd be able to unscramble this. Maybe the answer was something perfectly simple.

She spotted the pool ahead and turned into the parking lot to cheers from the girls. She glanced at her watch. They were on time, but barely. She had a lot to learn about balancing work and kids. How did people do this every day?

She hustled the twins inside the fence, stripping off the sundresses that covered their swimsuits. Luckily Mama had gotten them ready. They'd been lathered with sunscreen and in their swimsuits, clutching towels, when Caitlyn arrived at the house.

She turned them over to the swimming teacher, a tanned young woman who seemed to have no difficulty controlling ten five-year-olds in a pool, and collapsed on a chaise under a beach umbrella with a sigh of relief.

She leaned back, closing her eyes. When Steve returned her call, it would be the first time they'd spoken since those intimate moments at the Fourth of July picnic. She'd been relieved not to run into him for a few days, wanting the perspective that a little time would give.

It had been one of those things, she'd decided. He was an attractive man, no one could deny that, with his intense gaze and easygoing grin. But she wasn't interested in him. That had been an illusion, brought on by the heightened emotions of the moment.

She was not going to think about him. She opened her eyes and concentrated on the swim lesson. Predictably, Amanda was too bold and Josie too timid, but the teacher seemed to have them well in hand.

A shadow fell across her legs. She looked up, startled.

Steve. The jolt she felt when she saw him told her that those moments at the park had definitely not been an illusion.

"Hi. What are you doing here?"

"You called me, remember?" He dropped into the seat next to her, his face relaxing in that slightly crooked smile, his blue eyes warm.

Concentrate, she ordered herself. "I did call, but I didn't expect you to track me down. How did you know I'd be here?"

He shrugged. "I just took a chance that you'd be the one to bring the twins."

"But how did you know the twins had swimming lessons today?"

"I'm the one who set up the lessons. I thought it might be a good distraction for them."

She should have guessed, but she hadn't, and she was touched. "That was kind of you. Thank you."

Instinctively she reached out to him, and he took her hand in a warm, firm clasp. His touch seemed to travel along her skin, clear up her arm.

Quickly, she drew her hand away. "I…um, I needed to talk with you about the Ali Tabiz situation. We've heard from Dr. Mike."

"Yes, right. Ali." He seemed to have difficulty gathering his thoughts. "What did he say? Is the boy all right?"

"Yes, at the moment, but the injury to his heart is such that he could need surgery at any time, so we have to act quickly."

"Then we'll have to get moving. I'll check on flight space—"

"It's more complicated than the usual situation, it seems." She marshaled her thoughts. Focus on the job at hand, not on unwelcome attraction. "Ali doesn't have any relatives there to give him permission to come to the U.S. But Dr. Mike has found out that his father was an American soldier, so that should, I'd think, make it easier to get clearance."

He whistled softly. "That does put a different spin on the case, especially if the child doesn't have any family left there. Do you know what the legalities would be?"

"I don't know enough." She hated admitting it. "Anna referred me to a local attorney who has helped the foundation in the past with immigration issues, so I have a call in to him."

"Jake Hopkins." He nodded. "I know him. Ex-military. He'll do a good job for you. Well, obviously we'll need information about the father, so I can start on that end of it through military channels. Do you have a name?"

"Yes. It's Gregory Willis. Dr. Mike is sending a copy of the mother's marriage license, so that will give us some documentation, at least."

She glanced at Steve, sensing a lessening of his attention. He was frowning slightly, his gaze seeming to turn inward.

"What's wrong?"

He jerked back to attention and shook his head. "Nothing. The name seemed vaguely familiar, that's all. Do we have any other information on the man—rank, dates of birth and death, his unit?"

"Not that I know of, but Dr. Mike promised to keep looking." Was she imagining it, or did Steve seem to know more than he was letting on? "So you think you might have known him?"

"I didn't say that." He stood, his tall figure blocking the sun. "I'll get right on it and call you later."

He turned and quickly walked away, leaving her vaguely dissatisfied. There had been something that seemed out of place in his reaction to the name.

Still, Steve knew how crucial this was and it was his insistence that they cooperate and work together. If he knew anything about Gregory Willis, he'd tell her. Wouldn't he?

"So you're Paul Windham's son." Retired General Marlon Willis—tall, erect, white-haired—eyed Steve up and down as if he were inspecting the troops. He wore western dress, his hat tossed onto the antlers that were mounted over his desk, but he was every inch military.

Steve nodded, glad he'd come in uniform to see Gregory Willis's father. "Yes, sir. My daddy mentioned you often."

"Good man, that. I hope he's well."

"Doing fine, sir. He and my mother retired to Wyoming."

He'd hoped the fact that his father had once known General Willis would ease his entry to the gracious Georgian house in Prairie Springs's historic district, and it had. The maid had shown him directly to the study where the general sat in a leather armchair with his newspaper.

The bookshelf-lined room was filled with military memorabilia dotting the walls and adorning the shelves.

One thing seemed to be missing. There were no photos of Captain Gregory Willis, the general's only child, killed in action two years ago. Gossip had it the general had been devastated by Greg's death. That could make this much more difficult.

"What brings you here today, Chaplain?" Willis apparently felt the niceties had been observed sufficiently.

Steve took a breath, sending up a silent prayer for guidance. "I'd like to talk with you about your son, Gregory."

The elderly man froze, his hands tightening on the arms of his leather chair. For a long moment he didn't speak, but a muscle in his jaw twitched, and his face began to redden.

"I don't speak of him." He grated the words out, standing. "If that's all—"

"I'm sorry, sir." Steve rose, too. "I'm afraid this is important."

Willis's face reddened alarmingly. "I said I don't talk about him."

This was even worse than he'd expected, but he knew that people reacted differently to grief. "I'm very sorry for your loss, sir."

"Thank you," he said, clearly ending the conversation. "I'll see you out." Willis turned toward the door.

He couldn't let the man shove him away before he'd said what he'd come to say.

"I've been working with Children of the Day to arrange medical treatment for a five-year-old boy named Ali Tabiz. I'm sure you know of their work."

The general jerked a short nod. He wasn't making this easy, but at least he hadn't thrown Steve out.

"The child was injured in a bombing that killed his mother, who was apparently his only living relative. But we've learned that the mother was married to an American soldier. Captain Gregory Willis. Your son."

Was he wise to come right out with it? He wasn't sure, but the old soldier seemed like the type who'd prefer straight talking.

"No." The general ground out the word.

He was taken aback at the flat denial. "I'm sorry, sir, but I've looked into it very thoroughly. There seems no doubt that Gregory married this woman—"

"That may be." A vein throbbed in his temple. "But he's not my son."

"If you mean it's another Gregory Willis," he began, but the general silenced him with a sharp gesture.

"I mean Gregory is not my son. I cut him off when he made that foolish marriage. I'm sorry the woman is dead, but it's no concern of mine."

For a moment he couldn't say anything. He knew better than to take the general's brusque words at face value. There was a world of pain, grief and anger beneath them, and he sent up a silent prayer for guidance.

"Gregory had a son," he said gently. "Ali. He's five now, and he has suffered a serious injury to his heart. If we don't bring him to the States for surgery, he could die."

"Then do it." He turned toward the window, the sunlight gleaming from his white hair and reflecting off the ornate buckle of his belt. "That's what that charity does, isn't it?"

"Children of the Day is working on the case, but it's

more complicated than most. The boy has no relatives left there to make decisions for him. But you are his grandfather, and if you got involved—"

"No!" He swung back toward Steve, his face such an alarming shade of red that Steve feared for his health. "Gregory made his decision, and I made mine. That child is no kin of mine."

"He's your flesh and blood, whether you want to claim him or not." Anger wasn't going to help. Steve pushed down the rising tide of indignation. "If you don't help him, the boy could die."

General Willis stood looking out the window for a few minutes, but Steve doubted that he was seeing the quiet gardens beyond the window.

Finally he turned back, his face rigid. "You say the child needs surgery. How bad is it?"

"He may need surgery," Steve corrected. "The blast that killed his mother tore a hole between the chambers of his heart. The doctors say there's a chance that it will heal naturally, but if it doesn't, he has to be where he can receive immediate open heart surgery. That's why we want to bring him here."

If his words touched the gruff old man, he didn't give any sign of it. "Very well." His voice grated on the words. "I'm not accepting any responsibility, but I suppose I should do something. You can count on me for whatever financial resources are needed."

"That's very generous." He said the words politely, when what he wanted to do was grab the man, shake him and force him to see that this was Greg's son they were talking about.

But he knew his limitations. He couldn't change the general's heart. Only God could do that.

"This is between us, understand? I don't want my name brought into it." The general pointed a finger at him. "No word of my help gets out to anyone."

Caitlyn's face formed in Steve's mind. "The caseworker from Children of the Day will have to be told."

"No!" His fist thudded the nearest lamp table for emphasis, and the brass lamp rocked dangerously. "No one knows I'm involved. Those are my conditions. Take it or leave it."

A thousand arguments flooded his mind, but he choked them back. Now wasn't the time to argue. Maybe, after the general had a chance to think about this, he'd be more amenable.

So he'd take the offer, because that was the only possibility at the moment, and at least it left an avenue open for further conversation about the child.

"All right. I'll do it the way you want it."

The general strode quickly to the door and threw it open. "I don't want to hear about this ever again, understand? Just let me know when money is needed, and I'll write a check. But I don't want to discuss this situation ever." He nodded toward the hallway. "Good day."

Steve walked out, his mind churning. Had he handled it in the right way? Impossible to know. The general's reaction could have been the same no matter how he was approached or by whom.

Lord, if I've messed this up, I'm sorry. I'm asking You to work on him, because it looks like he won't listen to anything else from me.

He headed for his car, his mind on the other problem this situation raised. How was he going to work with Caitlyn without betraying the general's secret? He didn't have an answer to that.

Chapter 5

"Amanda, slow down."

Josie clung to Caitlyn's hand as they walked down the long hallway in the church's educational wing, but Amanda had darted ahead, and she didn't respond to the sound of Caitlyn's voice.

"Amanda!"

This time Amanda did slow a bit, looking back over her shoulder at her aunt. For an instant Caitlyn felt as if she and Carolyn were on their way to a Sunday-school class again, with Carolyn running ahead as she always did, then darting that impish look at her sister, daring her to run, too.

She glanced into one of the rooms as she passed, trying to push the image of her sister out of her mind. It refused to go.

Carolyn had always been the daring one, and following her had inevitably led to mischief. Older by two years, Caitlyn should have known better, but too often, she'd been the one who'd had to get Carolyn out of trouble.

The Sunday-school rooms had been repainted and refurnished since their day, of course, but the rooms still seemed familiar, with their pictures of Jesus and their low tables and child-size chairs.

She and Carolyn had been in church school faithfully every Sunday morning. They'd sung in the children's choir and participated in the pageants. But that was a long time ago.

Amanda skipped back down the hall to them and grabbed Josie's hand, tugging at her. "Come on, slowpoke. Run with me, pokey slow, pokey slow."

Josie leaned against Caitlyn's leg. "Manda's teasing me, Auntie Caitlyn. Make her stop."

She wasn't sure which bothered her more—Amanda's naughtiness or Josie's whining. "Both of you stop fussing. Amanda, where is…" She paused, not sure she wanted to use the words *grief center* to a child. "Where is Mrs. Olga's room?"

"Around the corner." Amanda pointed, and then dashed off again. "I'll beat you," she shouted, her voice echoing from the block walls.

Caitlyn's nerves tightened. The situation with the girls seemed to slide further out of her control with every passing day.

Back in New York, when she'd first heard the news, she'd been grief-stricken. But she'd thought the task ahead of her would be fairly simple.

Now she wasn't so sure. She worried about her mother's well-being, worried about succeeding at her new job, and most of all worried about helping the twins deal with their grief. Perhaps Mrs. Terenkov, Anna's mother, would be able to give her some guidance.

She rounded the corner just in time to see Amanda crash straight into a woman emerging from one of the rooms.

"Amanda!" She hurried to them, but luckily the woman was laughing, bending to catch Amanda in a hug.

"Manda, Manda, always in a hurry." The woman spun toward them, catching Josie up in an equally enthusiastic hug. "And here's my Josie-bug. How are you today?"

"I bumped my elbow." Josie solemnly displayed a chubby elbow with not a mark on it, which the woman kissed with an extravagant smack.

"There you are, my darling." She ruffled Josie's bangs and then turned to Caitlyn. "And you are Caitlyn, of course. I've heard of you from my Anna." Caitlyn found herself also enveloped in a hug.

Before she could figure out how to respond to this display of affection from someone she'd never met, Mrs. Terenkov had turned back to the children, chattering away to them as easily as if she were another five-year-old.

Caitlyn gave herself a mental shake. She'd expected an older version of Anna, if she'd thought of it at all. True, the family resemblance was strong, with Olga having the same snapping blue eyes and blond hair, the same quick movements.

But there the similarity ended. Anna was businesslike, perhaps a little reserved, a bit formal and serious. Olga bubbled with life, laughing, gesturing, chattering away with her faint Russian accent decorated with Texasisms. She wore a long denim skirt, its belt sporting an oversize silver buckle embossed with a longhorn steer, and a colorful embroidered blouse.

"In you go." Olga shooed the twins through a door decorated with balloons, as if for a party.

This was a grief-counseling center? Caitlyn peered into a cheerful playroom, its walls adorned with murals of Bible scenes, all of them featuring children, except for one wall taken up by an overflowing bulletin board, labeled Wall of Hope.

Several children were already in the room, pulling puzzles and games from the shelves, and the twins ran to join them, with Amanda shouting, of course.

"So, Caitlyn, what do you think of my little haven?" Olga's expression was shrewd, as if she guessed at Caitlyn's doubts.

"It's very cheerful." Her gaze lingered on the children. "I didn't realize there would be so many kids needing grief counseling."

Olga's gaze softened as she looked at her little flock. "There will be more still to come, I'm afraid. We've had many losses."

"But—does the surviving spouse usually stay here in Prairie Springs?" She'd think they'd want to move close to family, rather than staying near the army post, with all its reminders.

"Gold Star families can stay on post for another six months after their loss. Many choose to do that." She smiled at Caitlyn's expression. "You are thinking that you would want to get away."

"I guess I am."

"But you see, here they have support. They have other army spouses who understand what they're going through. It can ease the adjustment for them."

That made a lot of sense. In spite of her slightly outrageous air, Olga seemed to have a solid core of warmth and common sense.

"So you usually have the children for about six months?"

She nodded. "The twins, of course, I hope will be around longer."

"How are they doing? Really?" She asked the question she'd been longing to ask.

Olga shrugged. "It's early yet. So far they are not talking much about their loss. I'm hoping our Adopt a Soldier program will help them open up."

"Adopt a Soldier?"

"Each child picks a deployed soldier to correspond with. They seem—"

"I don't think so." Everything in her recoiled at the thought. "The twins have just lost both of their parents over there. I don't think it's a good idea for them to get attached to someone else who's in danger."

"No?" Olga shrugged. "Well, I must start. We can talk about it when you pick them up." She stepped into the room and began to close the door.

"I thought I would stay—" she began.

"Sorry, no visitors." Olga closed the door firmly, leaving Caitlyn staring at it.

Steve stepped out of Pastor Franklin Fields's office and stopped dead in his tracks. He knew the twins came to the church for the grief support group, of course, but he'd forgotten it was today. Otherwise, he might have arranged his visit with Frank for another time.

Avoiding Caitlyn was not a solution to his problem. He knew that as well as anyone, but still, he dreaded talking to her with the memory of his visit to General Willis fresh in his mind.

Actually, Caitlyn looked a tad disconcerted at the sight of him, too. She hesitated for a second and then strode down the hall toward him as if she were hurrying down Fifth Avenue, or wherever she hung out in New York City.

"Hey, there, Caitlyn," he said, trying to sound casual. "Dropping the girls off, are you?"

She gave a quick nod, her face clouding for an instant, as if something about that bothered her. "I didn't expect to see you here."

"Pastor Fields and I had to talk about a few projects we have going on. Have you met yet?"

She shook her head, looking up as a tall figure emerged from the office behind him.

He stepped clear of the door in order to make the introductions. "Caitlyn, this is Reverend Franklin Fields. Frank, Caitlyn Villard, Betty's daughter."

"How nice it is to meet you." Frank's hand enveloped Caitlyn's. "Betty's a very valued part of our church family."

Caitlyn murmured something conventional in response. She probably found Frank a little intimidating at first glance, as most people did, given his height, his composure and his iron jaw. It'd be a shame if she didn't look beyond the stone wall of Frank's exterior to the warm, compassionate human being he really was.

"Well, I must be going." As usual, Frank was on his way to his next responsibility. Small talk wasn't his strong suit. "I look forward to seeing you at worship on Sunday, Caitlyn." He strode off down the hall.

Steve caught a faintly disconcerted look on Caitlyn's

face as she looked after him. "What's wrong? Weren't you planning to go to church this week?"

Now the look turned annoyed as she glanced at him. "I'm sure I will. My mother always attends."

Something about the way she phrased that made his eyebrow lift. "And you're not in the habit?"

"I didn't say that. I suppose since I've been away—" She stopped, as if deciding he didn't need to hear the rest of that sentence.

He thought he could fill it in, in any event. Caitlyn had drifted away from church as she'd drifted away from her family. What would it take to bring her back?

She turned, looking down the hallway toward the rooms that the church had devoted to the grief center. They included the children's playroom, an adult meeting room and Olga's small, overcrowded office.

"What do you know about Olga—Mrs. Terenkov?" Caitlyn asked abruptly.

"You may as well say Olga. She's on a first-name basis with everyone in town, to say nothing of half the state of Texas."

"Olga, then. She's a little…" Caitlyn paused, as if searching for the right word.

"Overwhelming? Enthusiastic? Outrageous?" he suggested.

Her face relaxed. "All three. But is she really qualified as a counselor?"

"Her credentials are hanging on her office wall, if you want to read them. Of course, some of them are in Russian, so that might make it difficult. I could translate, if you like."

"Very funny." She frowned slightly. "I'm just concerned about the twins. That's all. Olga mentioned something about her Adopt a Soldier program. I'm not sure it's a good idea for Amanda and Josie. Won't it just remind them of their own loss?"

It was the first time she'd seemed to defer to his opinion, and he felt a strong desire to take away the worried look from her face.

"I don't suppose there's anything that wouldn't remind them of that, do you?" he asked gently. "I understand Olga has found it a good way to get the children talking about their loss, and talking is the first step toward healing."

He believed what he was saying. Of course he did. So why was it he'd never found it possible to talk about his own loss?

He shoved that thought away. This was about Caitlyn and her nieces, not about him.

"You may be right. This is uncharted territory for me." But Caitlyn's hazel eyes were still clouded with worry.

Instinctively, he touched her hand in a moment of sympathy, and again felt the current of energy that flowed between them. She looked up, her eyes darkening a little.

He cleared his throat, trying to focus. "Why don't you talk to the twins about the program? Just see how they feel about it. I wouldn't push them to participate if they don't want to."

She nodded, taking a step back as if she'd decided they were standing a little too close. "That's a good idea. Thank you."

"Anytime."

She nodded again, and he could almost see her change mental gears. "By the way, I'd hoped to get in touch with you today or tomorrow. How is the search for Ali's relatives going?"

He pasted a smile on his face and trusted she wouldn't realize how phony it was. "I'm making some progress, but I don't have anything definite yet."

At least, he hoped it could be described as progress. He was on the trail of a friend of Gregory Willis's, who might be able to shed some light on the rift between the general and his son.

She frowned a little. "I'd hoped to be further along than this by now. I'm meeting with Jake Hopkins this afternoon after I drop the children at home. He's going to brief me on Texas law as it pertains to this situation."

"You can count on Jake. And just so you won't think I'm lying down on the job, I do have one bit of good news. I have an anonymous donor who's willing to put up whatever funds are needed for Ali's trip and his care."

"Really?" Her face lit with pleasure. "That's wonderful. Who is it?"

He grinned. "You do know what anonymous means, don't you?"

"Well, I can understand someone not wanting publicity about their generosity, but surely COTD can be trusted with his or her identity."

"Sorry." He could imagine the general's reaction to Steve's breaking his promise, to say nothing of his own guilt if he did such a thing. "You have your attorney-client confidentiality, and I have the bond of secrecy between a pastor and his flock."

"It's someone in the military, then?"

"Nice try, Counselor. I'm not talking."

She looked ready to pursue the subject, so he took a quick step away. "I have to head out. I'll check in with you as soon as I have something, all right?"

He didn't give her a chance to answer, just continued down the hall.

Keeping secrets was part of his job, but it had never bothered him as much as it did right now. And he guessed that was a measure of how much Caitlyn Villard affected him.

"Thanks so much for fitting me in today." Caitlyn followed Jake Hopkins from the outer reception area, empty now since his secretary must have gone home, and into his inner office.

"No problem." That slow Texas drawl told her Jake was a native. He was also tall, tanned and casual—his white shirt was rolled to the elbows, and if he'd started the day with a tie, it wasn't in evidence now.

He limped to the wide desk, seeming to lean heavily on the wooden walking stick he used, and settled into the leather chair behind it, waving to a pair of matched client's chairs that faced the desk.

One of the black leather chairs was already occupied by a bad-tempered-looking orange cat. Caitlyn chose the opposite one.

"Anna tells me you do a great deal of pro bono work for the foundation."

And hopefully he was about to do a bit more. If he'd found a simple process for getting Ali cleared to come to the States, she'd be eternally grateful.

He nodded. "Glad to help out any way I can. Those folks do a Texas-size job of dealing with the woes of the world."

"Yes, they do."

"It sure seems like you're a big asset to them, according to Anna. Lucky for them you came back to Prairie Springs, though I'm sorry for the reason."

"Thank you." She was resigned by this time to the fact that everyone in town seemed to know about her return and Carolyn's and Dean's deaths.

He quirked an eyebrow. "You thinkin' about getting licensed in Texas, now that you're here? Wouldn't be tough at all, you know."

Just thinking about applying to the bar in Texas set her nerves on end. That would be admitting she'd be here for the foreseeable future.

"I'm not planning on that at the moment." She managed a smile. "Have you come up with anything helpful about our little patient?"

Jake leaned forward, elbows on the desk, and linked his fingers together. "I had to do some searching, I confess. This situation hasn't come up in my practice before, but I think I've got it taped now."

"Great."

Well, it wasn't really great as far as she was concerned, because it meant admitting that she had to rely on someone else. Caitlyn flipped open her notebook. But at least the conversation was safely away from the subject of her future.

"First off, is there any question of the boy's legitimacy?"

"Apparently not, as far as we can tell. Dr. Montgomery found Ali's mother's marriage license among her belongings after her death." She drew out the copy Dr. Mike had sent and handed it to him. "We felt that the original should stay with the boy."

"Wise precaution." He looked over the form, nodding. "Now, I assume you also have the boy's birth certificate and a record of his registration as a U.S. citizen born in a foreign country."

"Registration?" She sounded blank. She hated that.

"The father should have registered his birth at an American consulate as soon as possible after the boy's birth. Do you know if that was done?"

"I've no idea." And how difficult might it be, tracking down the birth of one child in a war-torn country? "I'll get going on finding the documentation. It has to be somewhere."

"Once you have proof of that, the rest should fall into place," Jake said. "Now, the next thing we need is a relative of the father who's willing to petition the court for a managing conservatorship."

"Not a guardianship?"

He shook his head. "That would be much more complicated, and since time is of the essence, we'll get the boy here faster this way. The relative agrees to assume responsibility, I explain to the judge that this is a medical emergency, and we're off and running. Who is the relative?"

"We don't have one yet." They should have. Why hadn't Steve come up with anything? "I'm working on it with Chaplain Steve Windham."

"Steve knows his way around army red tape. He'll find someone in no time." Jake shoved his chair back. "Just you call me as soon as you have a willing relative, and we can have it done in no time at all."

"All right, I'll do that." Given how confident Jake was, it was a wonder that Steve hadn't found a relative already. "And thanks again for your help."

"My pleasure." Jake shook hands, leaning on the desk for support. "And when you decide to get yourself licensed in Texas, you just let me know and I'll walk you through the procedure."

"Thank you." She didn't expect to take him up on that, but it was nice of him to offer. She slipped her notebook into her bag and then paused. "One more thing, Jake. What if we can't find a willing relative?"

He shook his head. "I'm not saying we couldn't get things straightened out eventually. Trouble is, if his medical condition goes bad, it might not be in time."

His words set up an echo in her heart. She seemed to see again that thin face, those big dark eyes.

"We'll find someone."

I promise, she said silently to the wistful little boy. *I promise.*

So that meant she had to get Steve moving on this. Either that, or figure out a way to do it herself.

Chapter 6

Caitlyn grappled with the difficulties presented by Ali's case as she drove back to the house. The time factor was what she feared most.

It wasn't that she hadn't dealt with tough deadlines before, but those had been with business cases and liability suits. Now it was a child's life hanging in the balance.

That single fact was paralyzing her. Her normal working life was structured exactly the way she wanted it, with no personal emotions to risk.

She pulled into the driveway and moved through the heat to the house. It had been a stifling day, and Mama's flowers drooped dispiritedly against the porch. If only it would rain. She glanced up at the cloudless sky. That didn't seem likely.

She hurried into the house, already accustomed, in the few weeks she'd been home, to the welcoming aroma of dinner cooking. But today she didn't smell a thing.

Puzzled, she followed the sound of children's voices into the family room that adjoined the kitchen. The twins were watching a video that seemed to feature singing animated vegetables, and Mama lay back in her recliner, eyes closed.

Caitlyn's heart lurched. "Mama, what's wrong? Are you sick?"

The twins turned around at the sound of her voice, and her mother opened her eyes.

"Grammy has a headache," Amanda said. "So we're keeping quiet and being very good."

"That's nice of you." Caitlyn turned from the twins to her mother. "Mama, are you okay?"

"I'm fine, fine." Her mother glanced at the clock. "Goodness, look at the time. I'd best be getting supper on."

The exhaustion in her mother's face frightened Caitlyn. Her mom never admitted weakness, and if she was sick, no one heard about it.

"You'll do nothing of the kind. You sit right there and tell me what's wrong. Supper can wait."

Her mother put one hand to her forehead. "Just foolish, I guess, running around in this heat trying to get some errands done after my checkup. It gave me a headache."

"You look exhausted." Why hadn't she noticed that earlier?

Mama shrugged. "I didn't sleep very well last night. Josie was up with a nightmare, and afterward, I couldn't seem to doze off again."

And she had slept right through it. Guilt was a weight on her shoulders.

"Mama, you're doing too much, that's all." And she

was supposed to be helping. "From now on, the monitor goes in my room."

The twins insisted they were too big to have a baby monitor in their room at night, but her mother had put one in from the time they came to live with her anyway, just to ensure that she always heard them.

"You need your rest—" Mama began, but Caitlyn cut her off.

"No arguments. From now on, I'll be in charge of the middle-of-the-night events. Now, you go right on up to your bedroom and have a rest. I'll take care of supper and the girls."

To her astonishment, her mother didn't argue. Instead she nodded. "Maybe I will, at that. But you call me if you need me."

"I won't." Caitlyn pressed her cheek against her mother's. "Go on now."

Her mother headed up the steps, detouring to the freezer to take out an ice pack. The twins turned back to their video.

Caitlyn looked around the kitchen, hoping for inspiration. With the hours she usually worked, she rarely cooked. She could make a terrific crab omelet, her special brunch dish, but she didn't suppose the five-year-olds would go for that.

Just when she'd found a package of macaroni and cheese, the telephone rang.

"Hi, Caitlyn, how is small-town life treating you? Are you ready to come back to us yet?"

Longing swept through her at the sound of Julia Maitland's voice, her best friend since college. They still saw each other in New York at least once a week, despite the fact that their careers had gone in different directions, with her friend now a buyer for a department-store chain. Julia was always trying to get Caitlyn into something other than what she called her lawyer suits.

"I wish I were." She glanced at the twins and felt faintly guilty again. Did she really wish that? "What's going on with you?"

"Nothing too exciting. Everyone heads out of the city on the weekends in July, you know that. Or else takes off on a long vacation. Seriously, how are you? I'm sure it's been rough."

"Okay, I guess. There's still a lot to do here with the family. And I did take a part-time job, just to have some money coming in."

"I know how that is. But listen, I just might have a solution to that part of your problem. You remember my cousin Becky?"

Caitlyn scoured her memory. "The one who wants to be an actress?"

"That's her. Well, her parents are funding her for six months in the city to see if she can make it. Becky needs a place to stay, obviously, and I thought of you right away. Would you consider subletting your place?"

Instantly her mind began ticking off advantages and disadvantages. Subletting would solve her money problems for the moment, at least. But it would also mean admitting that she was losing the life that she loved. Everything in her rebelled at that thought.

"I don't know," she began, and then turned at the sound of battle in the family room. "I have to go, Jules. The twins have started World War Three in the next room. How soon do you have to have an answer?"

"I can't give you more than a week, I'm afraid." Julia's tone grew serious. "You know I'd much rather have you back here than my cousin any day, but it sounds as if you're needed there."

"At the moment, anyway. I'll call you soon with an answer."

She hung up and strode into the family room, forcibly separating the twins. "What is going on? Couldn't you see I was on the phone?"

"Manda called me a baby," Josie wailed. "I'm not a baby just 'cause I had a nightmare."

"No, of course you're not. Everyone has nightmares sometimes."

"Well, she hit me." Amanda sniffed, as if trying to produce tears. "And you're not s'posed to hit, no matter what."

"No, you're not," she agreed, wondering how her mother had dealt with this for six months.

"Listen, since Grammy doesn't feel good, why don't you come and help me with the supper? We'll make some macaroni and cheese and fruit salad."

"Yaaay," they chorused. Turning off their tears in an instant, the twins raced for the kitchen.

Caitlyn followed more slowly. Maybe she had to apply more of her legal-negotiating skills to dealing with the twins.

In a few minutes the girls were deeply engrossed in adding fruit to the salad. With the macaroni cooking, Caitlyn leaned on the counter, watching them.

Amanda's eyes sparkled. She waved a wooden spoon while Josie counted blueberries solemnly into a bowl.

"Hurry up, hurry up," she chanted, and Josie pouted.

Eager to avoid another battle, Caitlyn sought for a change of subject. "Did you have a good time with Mrs. Olga today?"

They nodded. "Mrs. Olga's nice. We do fun games," Amanda said.

"And we made pictures to send to some soldiers," Josie added.

That sounded like part of the Adopt a Soldier program, and she thought of Steve's advice. *Talk to them about it.*

Her stomach clenched. It would be the first time she'd brought up anything that might touch upon their parents' deaths, but she had to deal with it. She wouldn't pass it off to Mama.

"Mrs. Olga told me about how you might adopt a soldier from Fort Bonnell who's overseas," she said cautiously. "You could write to him or her and send pictures, and they'd write back. Do you think you'd like to do that? You don't have to if you don't want to."

"We want to," Amanda announced. "Lots of kids do that. It's fun. They get letters and pictures back, and even e-mails. Can we get e-mails on your computer, Auntie Caitlyn?"

"I suppose." She focused on her other niece. "What about you, Josie?"

Josie nodded slowly. "I told Mrs. Olga maybe we could have two soldiers who were married to each other." Her voice dropped to a whisper. "That would be sort of like Mommy and Daddy."

Her heart seemed to be shredding into tiny pieces. "Do you think that might make you feel sad?" Her voice sounded choked.

"Maybe a little bit," Amanda said. "But it would be nice, too."

Josie nodded, her face serious. "I think Mommy would like us to do it."

Caitlyn fought back tears as panic rippled through

her. She wanted to race back to New York, to pick up again a life where nothing tore her heart to shreds on a daily basis.

But she couldn't.

"Okay." She managed a smile. "I guess we'll ask Mrs. Olga to find us a couple of soldiers to adopt."

And pray this was the right decision. She paused, startled at her thought. Pray? When had she started thinking of that as the first course of action? Maybe she'd been around Chaplain Steve too much.

Steve sat at his desk, staring at the computer screen. But he wasn't working, he was praying.

Lord, please, show me the way out of this situation. I thought I was doing the right thing by approaching Willis alone. Or was I being proud, thinking I was the only one who could do it? That's just what I believe Caitlyn does, but I'm the guilty one this time.

And now he was stuck, unable to tell her about the general, unable to show Marlon Willis that his lack of forgiveness hurt both him and an innocent child.

He buried his face in his hands.

Please, Father, forgive me. Show me how to make this right without breaking faith with anyone, most of all with You.

A rap on the door jerked him back into the moment. *In Jesus' name, Amen.*

"Come in."

The words were barely out of his mouth when the door flew open. One look at Caitlyn's face told him something had happened. Almost without thinking, he got to his feet and held out his hand to her.

"Caitlyn, what is it? What's wrong?"

"Wrong? I don't know how you can ask me that."

She'd found out about the general. That had to be it. She'd found out, and she was furious with him. Justifiably so.

He uttered a silent, wordless prayer for guidance. "I take it you know about Greg Willis's family. How did you find out?"

Her eyes sparked fire. "I should have found out from you."

"Yes. You should have."

His words didn't seem to blunt her anger, but perhaps they deflected it a little.

Her jaw tightened, as if to hold back a hasty response. "I hadn't heard from you, so I used some of COTD's contacts to look into Gregory Willis. They found General Willis in a matter of hours, right here in town. If they could do it, you obviously did, too."

He nodded. "Yes. I did."

"Why didn't you tell me? Were you trying to make me fail?"

"No!" That was the last thing he'd have her believe. "Caitlyn, you can't believe that."

"Then tell me what to think. Why did you keep this a secret? You knew from the moment I told you at the pool, didn't you?"

"I didn't. Caitlyn, you have to trust me on that. I vaguely remembered General Willis as a friend of my father, that's all, and I knew he had a son. It wasn't until I looked into it further that I found out the son was the Gregory Willis we were looking for."

"And you didn't tell me."

How could he explain this so that she'd understand? "I knew Marlon Willis had a reputation as a crusty old guy who didn't like interference from anyone. I thought his friendship with my father might ease the way if I went to see him alone."

"And did it?" She didn't look as if she'd forgiven him, but at least she was listening.

"Not really." He sighed. "Caitlyn, I'm sorry. I can't divulge what he said to me. Just take my word for it—we're not going to get anywhere with the general."

"I gather he's your anonymous donor." She took a few steps across the office, as if she couldn't stand still any longer. "Never mind, you don't have to tell me."

"We'll have to go on without him. We'll find another way—"

"We can't," she said flatly. "I met with Jake Hopkins. He says we have to have a relative who will agree to take on legal responsibility for the boy before we can bring him to the States."

That hit him hard. "I'm sorry. I didn't know. If I talk with General Willis again—"

"No. You've done enough. This time I'll talk with him."

It was what he expected her to say, but he had to dissuade her. "You don't know what you're getting into. Please, let me."

She shook her head decisively. "No, thanks. I'll do it myself."

"That's your way of dealing with everything, isn't it?" The words were out without thought, and he instantly regretted them.

She stiffened. "Funny, this time you were the one who did that." Turning, she stormed out of the office, slamming the door.

* * *

Caitlyn exited General Willis's house into a pounding rainstorm. Appropriate, since she felt as if she'd just been put through a wringer.

She paused on the front step to put up her umbrella. It was pouring so hard she could barely see her car, parked at the bend of the circular driveway, but if she lingered any longer she was afraid the general would come out to chase her off his property, maybe with one of the guns he had mounted in his study. He certainly seemed capable of it.

Taking a breath as if she were about to plunge into a pool, she darted out into the rain. The wind drove the raindrops sideways, drenching her slacks so that they clung to her legs after only a few steps. By the time she neared the car, she was breathless.

Head down, she bolted toward the door and right into the man who waited there.

"Steve." Her breath caught.

He grasped her elbow, supporting her. "I have to talk to you. Please, Caitlyn."

Much as she wanted to hold on to her anger with him, she didn't want to appear childish. And now that she knew what the general was like, she could understand, to some extent, how Steve had gotten into the situation he had.

"Let's get in the car, for goodness' sake." She fumbled with her keys.

In a moment they were both in the front seat. She started the air conditioner to take the moisture out of the air and tried to catch her breath.

"I'm sorry," he said. "You look as if the general gave you a rough time."

She nodded, pushing damp hair out of her face. "I suppose not any worse than he gave you. He does roll over a person, doesn't he?"

"Yes." Steve shook his head, his eyes dark with concern. "I'm sorry I couldn't speak about it before, but now that you've talked to him, it doesn't matter. I told him about Ali's condition and his mother's death. I tried to persuade him to take responsibility for Greg's child, but he wouldn't even consider it. He had disowned Greg a few years ago."

The general's scathing words about his dead son still seemed to ring in her ears. "That's a terrible thing, to cut your own child out of your life."

Steve turned more fully toward her, close in the confines of the small car. "I'm sorry I handled the situation the way I did. If we'd gone together to see him initially, maybe it would have made a difference."

She almost responded sharply that he should have done just that, but she discovered that her anger had slipped away in the past hour.

"To be honest, I don't think it would have made any difference. General Willis has to be the most inflexible person I've ever met."

"The saddest thing is that he doesn't even see that he's hurting himself more than anyone." Steve's forehead creased. "I feel so helpless. I want to minister to him, but he won't let me."

"That really matters to you, doesn't it?" She looked at him, feeling as if she was seeing him in a way she never had before.

Steve cared, really cared deeply, behind that casual, easygoing manner of his. He wanted to love even that brusque, annoying man who was such a roadblock to them.

"Of course." He looked a little surprised, as if any other option hadn't occurred to him.

"You know, people are right about you. You really are a good guy."

He gave her that lopsided smile. "I try. The Lord knows I can't do it on my own."

Usually she would back away from so personal a statement, determined to keep things light and casual. But this was different. They were cut off from the rest of the world with the rain thundering on the car's roof, the fogged windows shutting out everyone and everything but the two of them.

"You depend on your faith."

"I rely on it," he said quietly. "I know that God is always there to help, and that when I try to go it alone, I'll mess up."

She almost envied him for a moment. It would be nice to feel that God cared that much about every detail of your life. "I guess that's where we're different. I've always done everything on my own."

His eyebrow raised. "Everything?"

She shrugged. "It seemed that way to me, anyway. Things weren't so easy for us after Daddy left us. I couldn't put my burdens on Mama—she had enough to deal with. So I learned how to handle things myself."

He reached out to brush a strand of damp hair from her face, his fingers stroking her cheek and setting up a wave of warmth in their wake.

"You were just a kid then," he murmured. "What—ten or eleven?"

"Twelve. Carolyn was only ten, so she needed Mama more than I did."

Concentrate, don't just react to how close he is.

She felt pride in what she'd accomplished, after all. Maybe she'd missed a few things in high school, but she'd done everything on her own, studying harder than anyone, determined that her grades would be the best, that she'd be the one to take home a scholarship, that she'd succeed.

"I don't regret it. It made me strong."

"You were a kid," he said softly. He was so close she could see the fine lines at the corners of his eyes, the white flecks deep in the blue. There was a fine sheen of moisture on his tanned skin.

He leaned closer. She couldn't breathe, couldn't think…

And then his lips found hers, and all she could think about was his embrace.

His lips were warm and firm, and his strong hand cradled her head gently, protectively. Warmth and tenderness flowed through her, and she relaxed into the kiss. The outside world was gone, and she never wanted this moment to end.

Too soon it did. Steve drew back and blinked, seeming to wake himself from the dream they'd momentarily shared.

"I'm not sure I should have done that."

"I'm not either," she said. "But I'm glad you did."

For a moment longer their gazes clung. Then Steve leaned back against the door, as if he needed to put some distance between them.

She cleared her throat.

"What—what are we going to do now?"

His smile flickered. "I did hear you say 'we,' didn't I?"

"We." She nodded slowly, wondering if she was doing the right thing. "Will you work with me on getting Ali here, Steve?"

"I will." His face was solemn, as if he was taking a vow.

Chapter 7

"Hi, kids." Steve waved to the children playing on the swings in the backyard as he headed into the offices of Children of the Day the morning after his encounter with Caitlyn.

At least the air was clear between them now about the general. He'd been thanking God for that ever since.

Unfortunately, a whole new set of complications had emerged when he'd given in to his longing to hold her in his arms.

Caitlyn had revealed more about herself than she'd probably realized. He'd seen the little girl in her eyes, struggling with making sense of the fact that her father could just walk away from her.

And in the emotion of that moment, he'd just wanted to comfort and hold her. He hadn't thought through the difficulties of getting involved with her.

Caitlyn's life was complicated enough already, dealing with being a mother to the twins, with her own unresolved grief and with the life decisions she had to make. Adding in a potential relationship, especially with someone here in Prairie Springs, was more trouble she didn't need.

As for him—well, he wasn't sure he was ready for a serious commitment yet. Maybe he never would be.

He should be careful. But he couldn't stay away from Caitlyn, not when a child's life was at stake. So they had no choice but to deal with this.

He tapped on the partially open door to Caitlyn's office, amused that she had adopted Anna's open-door policy already. In response to her voice, he went in, to find her alone and staring at her computer screen. She looked up at his entrance.

"Good morning." Her smile was cool and professional. She had her armor on again, and the vulnerable woman of yesterday was nowhere in sight.

Well, hadn't he just been telling himself that was for the best? He should be pleased.

"Hi." He crossed to the desk and pulled a chair up next to her. "What's happening? Have you found anything yet?"

She handed him a computer printout. "Only bad things, unfortunately. I've had no success with the embassy where Greg Willis would have registered his son's birth."

"They could have left the area for the baby's birth, I guess," he suggested.

Caitlyn leaned back in her chair, frowning. "They could have, but if they did, how are we supposed to find out where? Without some lead, I'm left checking every consulate in the Middle East."

"Not a good option, I agree."

Her frown deepened. "You don't suppose we're on the wrong track entirely, do you? I mean, we're assuming Ali is Greg's son because of the marriage license, but we don't have a birth certificate to back that up."

That hadn't occurred to him. He stared absently at the list she'd made of avenues they should explore. If Ali wasn't Greg's son—still, if that were the case, wouldn't the general have mentioned it? Of course, he might not know, given the way he'd cut his son off.

"I guess it's possible, but I think we have to go on the assumption that he's Greg's child unless something comes up to disprove it. I had an e-mail from Mike saying he was trying to get in touch with any friends of the mother. That may help."

"Good. What about friends of the father? They might know where the couple was living when Ali was born."

He'd already thought of that. "I've started trying to contact people who served with him. Many of them seem to have left the military since then, so finding them isn't as easy as I'd expected it to be, but I'm sure to catch up with them somehow."

"All right. And I'll keep working on embassies and consulates, as well." Caitlyn was looking at the paper, not at him. "I talked with General Willis's older sister in Austin, who appears to be his only close relative. She can see us this afternoon. Of course, if you're busy, I can go alone."

She almost sounded as if she'd prefer that, but they were in this together.

"No, that's fine with me."

Her eyebrows lifted. "As I've observed before, army chaplains seem to have a lot of freedom."

"We're accountable to a higher authority." He grinned. "On the other hand, you're accountable to Anna, and she expects results."

"Yes." Her eyes clouded, as if reminded of all that was at stake. "I'd like—"

She cut off abruptly as the door opened again. Jake Hopkins came in, a sheaf of papers in one hand, the other grasping an ebony cane with a silver handle. Jake seemed to enjoy displaying his collection of canes, though he'd immediately shoot down any hint of sympathy for his injury.

"Hey, there, Steve. How you doing, boy?" He nodded to Caitlyn. "When did you hook up with this good ole boy, Caitlyn?"

"Anna wished me on her. It's good to see you, too." He stood to offer a chair to Jake, but Jake shook his head.

"Can't stay long enough to sit."

"You're always in a rush these days—you're startin' to act like a Yankee. You have any good news for us?"

Jake shrugged. "I've told Caitlyn everything I know about the process. I can't do another thing until you come up with a relative and the paperwork we need, so get cracking."

"We are," he protested. "Believe it or not, this is work we're doin' here."

Jake raised an eyebrow in doubt. "Well, I'm on a different errand today." He handed the papers he held to Caitlyn. "These are the forms you need to apply to the Texas bar. I just reckoned I'd drop them off for you."

Caitlyn looked taken aback. "Thanks, but I don't think—"

"Hey, who wouldn't want to practice Texas law?" He turned even as he spoke. "Sorry, I have to go. I'm due in court."

"I thought you were awfully well dressed today." Steve walked to the door with him. "We'll be in touch as soon as we have anything."

"Do that." Jake thumped his way out.

Steve turned back to Caitlyn, eyeing the forms. "So you're thinking of getting licensed in Texas?"

"No." She shoved the forms into a drawer and shut it firmly. "I'm not."

He leaned one hip against the corner of the desk, looking down at her. Didn't she realize yet how much she was needed here?

"Why not? Jake would tell you that Prairie Springs is a pretty nice place to practice law."

Her face seemed to tighten. "I left Prairie Springs to make something of myself. Coming back would be—regressing. I'm not interested in arguing local dog law violations and representing Saturday-night drunks."

"A real type-A high achiever, aren't you? I thought maybe now that you've proved yourself in the big city, you could be happy here. For the sake of your mother and the twins, if not for yourself."

Her hands clenched into fists in her lap. "Maybe they'd all be better off away from constant reminders of their grief."

He wanted to take those strained hands in his, but he didn't dare. "Your grief, too," he said softly. "You never speak of that."

"I'm fine."

"If you keep it locked up inside—"

"Just leave it alone." She glared at him. "You don't

have any idea what I'm feeling. Let's get back to business, shall we?"

I do know exactly what you're feeling, Caitlyn. But you wouldn't believe that unless I told you things I have no intention of saying.

"All right," he said. "Sorry. What time shall I pick you up to drive to Austin?"

"Has it occurred to you that a woman who's living in a retirement home might not be eager to take on the responsibility of a five-year-old?"

Caitlyn fretted over Steve's question as he drove his red pickup truck through the scrolled wrought-iron gates of Crestview Estates in Austin that afternoon.

"We don't have too many options." She had to admit, that question had been plaguing her, too. "Maybe she can at least point us in the direction of some more likely relative."

"If there is one." Steve seemed a bit pessimistic for him today.

"Or Miss Willis might be eager to help out. We have to try. At least money probably isn't a deterrent."

"You have a point." Steve leaned forward to peer at a street sign, and she glanced around.

Crestview Estates, with its rolling, manicured lawns, carefully tended flower beds and winding residential streets, was a typical upscale gated community. Whatever facilities there were to extend geriatric care to the residents were well disguised.

"There's the street." She pointed to the sign, half hidden by the arching branches of a cottonwood tree.

During the half-hour drive from Prairie Springs to Austin, they'd kept the conversation strictly on business.

She had a sneaking feeling that she needed to apologize for her rudeness that morning, but she didn't want to bring it up.

The truth was that she was afraid of going too deep, of showing too much.

She usually didn't have any trouble keeping things superficial with people. Only Steve seemed to have the ability to force her deeper. With him, she had to have her guard up at all times.

Steve drove down a quiet street lined with elegant homes and pulled into the driveway of a gracious one-story house whose gray shingles blended into the foliage that surrounded it. Everything about the property was immaculate, and it was no doubt cared for by an army of gardeners.

He was already coming around to her door, so Caitlyn opened it quickly and slid out. She preceded him up the three steps to the wide front porch, noting the wheelchair ramp that curved to ground level.

She saw Steve looking at it.

"Maybe all the houses have them."

"Maybe." He was noncommittal.

She rang the bell, and the door was opened immediately by a maid in a neat black uniform. Caitlyn blinked, feeling as if she'd dropped back in time. Who had uniformed maids anymore?

"Ms. Villard and Chaplain Windham to see Miss Willis." She almost felt as if she should have a visiting card to hand over.

"*Sí,* yes, ma'am, she is waiting for you." The smiling young woman closed the door and then led them quickly through an archway into a living room. "They are here, ma'am."

The woman at the window lowered a small pair of binoculars and turned her wheelchair toward them.

"Welcome, both of you. It's nice of you to come all this way." She gestured with the glasses. "I was just watching the birds at the feeder."

Miss Lydia Willis was birdlike herself, tiny and so delicate that it seemed a breeze might blow her off course. She moved the chair closer. Bright blue eyes peered up at them curiously. "You are Ms. Villard?"

"I'm Caitlyn Villard, Miss Willis." She shook hands carefully, half-afraid the woman would bruise. "I'm the care coordinator at Children of the Day in Prairie Springs. And this is Chaplain Steve Windham."

Steve bent over the woman's hand with so courtly an air that it was almost a bow. "A pleasure to meet you, ma'am."

"Please, sit down and tell me how I can help you. You said it had something to do with my late nephew?" Her eyes filled with tears, but she blinked them away.

Caitlyn exchanged glances with Steve. Obviously this fragile elderly lady wasn't going to take charge of a five-year-old. Still, they couldn't know how she might help them unless they tried.

"We've recently learned that Gregory Willis was married while he was deployed in the Middle East," she began. Was this news to the woman? If so, maybe she should have led up to it more gently.

But Miss Willis was already nodding. "Yes, I know about that. Goodness, what a terrible time that was. Marlon, my brother, you know, was absolutely livid about it."

"We know," Steve said, with great understatement.

"You mustn't think Marlon was prejudiced against that poor young woman because of her background," she said quickly. "I don't believe that was it at all. But Marlon had always envisioned a quick rise to the top in the military for Gregory, and he knew that having married a local person while on deployment would be a terrible obstacle for him."

Steve nodded. "I'm afraid that's true. Like it or not, the army wouldn't consider such a marriage a career asset."

"And I'm sure Marlon thought Gregory was making a mistake, acting out of the emotion of the moment instead of thinking it through properly."

"People in love seldom stop to think things through," Caitlyn said.

Not that she had any personal experience of that. Her romances had always been both brief and rational. She wasn't the type of person to fall head over heels.

"I suppose that's true." Miss Willis wiped her eyes with a lace-edged handkerchief that seemed like a relic of a bygone age. "It was so sad, all of it. Marlon was hasty, acting on impulse himself, saying if Gregory did this he was no son of his. Of course he didn't mean it, but once Marlon said that, he found it impossible to go back on it." She shook her head sadly. "Gregory died, and they'd never made up. Tragic, but at least it's over now."

"Well, not quite." She hated to distress the woman further, but she didn't have a choice. Ali's life hung in the balance. "It's recently come to light that Gregory and his wife had a son. The boy's mother was killed in a bombing, but the little boy, Ali, is safe at an army hospital."

The handkerchief dropped in her lap. "You're sure? Oh my, I can hardly take it in. A little boy. Gregory's son. Does Marlon know?"

"Yes. I talked with him about it," Steve said.

Something in his voice must have alerted her. Her

gaze seemed to search Steve's face. "Marlon's being adamant, isn't he? I always said he was the most stubborn man I ever met."

"Yes, ma'am, I'm afraid so. The thing is that it's possible the child may need heart surgery, and we'd like to bring him to the States as soon as possible. But we can only do that if a relative takes legal responsibility for him."

Tears glistened in her eyes again. "Young man, I would do it in an instant. But I don't suppose—" She broke off, gesturing to the wheelchair.

"No, ma'am, I'm afraid the court might not find you well enough to take charge of a young child."

"There must be something I can do." She tapped her fingers on the arm of the chair. "Do you need money?"

"No, we're all right in that respect," Steve said.

"From Marlon, I suppose," she said shrewdly. "He won't bend on his word, but he's not heartless. He wouldn't leave a child in distress."

"Much as we're grateful for the funds," Caitlyn said, "the need for a relative to act as conservator with the court is more pressing. Can you think of anyone, no matter how distant, we might approach?"

The woman shook her head, and Caitlyn's heart clenched. She hadn't realized until this moment how much she'd counted on Miss Willis to come up with something helpful.

"I'm afraid the Willis clan has dwindled to just Marlon and me, without a soul to come after us." She gave a small, ladylike sigh. "To think that Marlon has a grandson, if only he'd get off his high horse and acknowledge the boy."

"He wouldn't listen to us," Steve said. "Do you think you might try to reason with him?"

"I'll try, of course." She sat very erect in the chair. "I can't guarantee he'll listen."

"Anything you could do would help."

Miss Willis nodded. "When I think of how he doted on Gregory, talking about him all the time, showing me endless photos and movies, proud as could be of every accomplishment. It's just not right that he'd turn his back on Gregory's son."

The tears sparkled in her eyes again, and Steve leaned across to put his strong, tanned hand over hers. "Don't distress yourself, Miss Willis. God has a way of working things out, and I have to believe that His eye is on little Ali."

She clasped his hand. "Will you just say a prayer for him with me, Chaplain? I'd like that."

"Of course." Steve reached out to Caitlyn and took her hand, too, holding it in a warm, firm clasp. He bowed his head.

"Father, we know that You care for all Your creations, that not the smallest sparrow falls without Your knowledge. We hold little Ali up to You, asking Your blessing on him. Keep him safe, Father, and show us the way to help him. In Jesus' name, Amen."

"Amen," Miss Willis whispered.

Caitlyn's hand tingled when she drew it away from Steve's clasp. She hadn't seen him in chaplain mode before, and she found her respect for him growing. He did know how to comfort and care, and when he'd prayed, she'd actually prayed with him.

She tried to settle the emotion that seemed to well

up inside her. No matter how much of a good guy Steve Windham was, he wasn't the guy for her, and she'd better remember that.

The chorus of women's voices was so loud when Caitlyn walked into the Fort Bonnell gym on Saturday that she nearly turned around and walked back out again.

How ridiculous was that? If she could walk into a New York courtroom with perfect composure, she could certainly handle a roomful of women packing boxes to send to soldiers.

It was being back in Prairie Springs, she knew that. Here, she felt again like the studious teenage wallflower she'd once been.

Well, she wasn't that person any longer. And she was certainly smart enough to know that most teenagers had feelings of insecurity, even if she hadn't been able to see that then.

She walked along the end of the long rows of tables, searching for someone to tell her what she was supposed to do. Mama had talked her into coming in her place, and since the twins were off on a play date, it had seemed the perfect time to give her mother a break.

The tables were lined primarily with women, although there was a sprinkling of teenagers and a few older men, as well as some men and women in uniform. Everyone seemed to know what to do as they wrapped an assortment of objects to put into the boxes that were headed overseas.

Finally she saw a familiar face. Sarah, the twins' kindergarten teacher, worked at the end of a row. Spotting Caitlyn, she gave her a welcoming smile and gestured her over.

"Your first time?" she asked.

Caitlyn nodded. "I'm taking my mother's place today. I need someone to put me to work."

"Just grab some paper and start wrapping," Sarah said. "And you'd better get used to it. I sometimes find myself wrapping in my sleep. We do this on post once a month, and at Children of the Day once a month, also."

"That's a lot of packages." She pulled out some bubble wrap.

"Nowhere near enough." Sarah's blue eyes darkened with concern. "I'd like to be sure every single soldier got a package from home once a month, but we can't do that. We focus on the units from Fort Bonnell."

Caitlyn, all thumbs at first, got into the swing of things quickly. Items—everything from soap to paperback books to CDs—appeared in front of her, dropped by runners, most of them teenagers who seemed to make a game of it. She and Sarah wrapped and packed until the box was full. Finished boxes were slid under the table to be picked up by another team.

"How are the twins doing?" Sarah seemed to have the routine down pat enough that she could chat without diminishing her speed.

Caitlyn felt her forehead wrinkle and deliberately smoothed it out. "I wish I knew. I guess worrying comes with the territory. Some days I think they're doing well, but then Josie will start having nightmares, or Amanda will get defiant and aggressive, and I wonder if they're making any progress at all."

Sarah's busy hands stilled. "I know how worrisome taking care of kids can be. But it's bound to be up and down. Nothing about children's development goes in a straight line, and that's especially true when they're dealing with grief. This is a huge hurdle for them to overcome."

"Yes." Her throat tightened. "It is."

"It must be so hard for you. You have your own grief to deal with, as well." Sarah's warmth seemed to surround her.

Oddly enough, it was easier to hear that from Sarah than Steve.

"Thanks for your concern." She wrapped a CD with concentrated care. "To tell you the truth, sometimes I just feel so angry with Carolyn. I know that's stupid."

"It's not stupid at all," Sarah said quickly. "Anger is a part of the grieving process." She tilted her head to the side, studying Caitlyn's face. "Have you considered talking to Steve Windham about it? He's very good at counseling the bereaved."

"I—no, I haven't. I mean, we're working together, and maybe it's better not to mix the roles."

"Speaking of Steve, there he is." Sarah nudged her, nodding toward the far end of the room. "He always helps out at these things."

She glanced across the room. Steve, in uniform, bent over a table, talking with one of the volunteers. "He seems to be everywhere."

Sarah chuckled. "I guess he is involved in just about everything that goes on in Prairie Springs. Part of it is his job, I guess, but I think mostly he just has a heart for helping others, especially those who've lost someone. Of course, he really knows how that feels."

Caitlyn blinked, and then turned to look at Sarah. "What do you mean?"

It was Sarah's turn to look surprised. "You didn't know? Well, no, I guess you wouldn't."

"Know what?"

Something bad, obviously. She seemed to feel it looming over her, like a storm about to break.

"Steve was a chaplain with the first wave of invasion troops that went into Iraq. He was engaged then, to another officer. They were going to be married when their deployment was up." Sarah paused. "She was killed in fighting the first month they were there."

It hit her like a blow, and she pressed her palms against the tabletop to steady herself. "I didn't know." Her mouth was so dry she could barely get the words out. "He's never mentioned it."

"He wouldn't." Sarah's voice was weighted with sorrow. "He doesn't talk about it at all."

And she'd rejected his attempts to comfort her, saying he didn't know how she felt. How hurtful that must have been. And how would she face him, knowing it?

Chapter 8

Caitlyn stood next to her mother as Pastor Fields stretched his arms out in the benediction at the end of the Sunday-morning worship service. His deep voice resounded through the crowded sanctuary.

"Go now in peace, and may the peace of God go with you."

"Amen," the congregation responded in unison, and the organ swelled, filling the high-ceilinged sanctuary with its own Amen.

She wasn't quite sure how she felt about the service this morning. She'd come, as she had since she'd been back in Prairie Springs, because her mother and the twins assumed that she would.

And maybe, if she were truthful with herself, she'd begun to feel the need for spiritual support in the increasingly worrisome effort to save Ali, to say nothing of coping with the twins and helping her mother with her grief.

Pastor Fields had actually been less comforting than challenging this morning, but he certainly had made her think. Caitlyn lingered in the pew as her mother began greeting friends, listening to the organ postlude, her gaze fixed on the stained-glass window of Jesus and his disciples.

Her mind was still caught up in the sermon. Franklin Fields obviously didn't think people were put here to fulfill their own potential, but to do the work God had already prepared for them to do.

Something in her rebelled at that. Wasn't it right to use the talents God had given her? Surely, if she were intended to be doing something else, He wouldn't have given her the drive to succeed as an attorney, would He?

Her internal argument was ended by her mother waving to her from the end of the pew.

"We'd best be getting over to Fellowship Hall, so I can see to my casserole dish."

She nodded, sliding along the pew. There was a potluck lunch after worship today, which apparently happened at least once a month, and her mother had brought what looked like enough food to feed an army.

"Should I go down to fetch the twins?" Amanda and Josie had gone out of the sanctuary after the children's talk, headed for junior church with other children.

Mama shook her head. "Their teacher will bring them up to Fellowship Hall to meet us."

Her mother plowed purposefully through the crowd, intent on her casserole, and Caitlyn followed in her wake, thinking wistfully of Sunday mornings spent with coffee, a bagel, the *Times* crossword and no uncomfortable spiritual challenges.

The vast room that was the center of the church's

fellowship was already filling up with people. Several women hustled back and forth between the kitchen and serving tables. Her mother rushed off to join them, and Caitlyn looked around for the twins.

A line of children came through the double doors, breaking apart as kids spotted their families and rushed to join them. Amanda raced across the beige carpeting at full speed and flung herself at Caitlyn's knees, nearly knocking her over.

"I made a boat," she exclaimed, waving her paper craft.

"I did, too," Josie added, coming up behind her a little more slowly. "We had a story about Paul."

"Did you know he was in a wrecked ship?" Amanda said. "That means it had an accident," she added.

"Yes, I think maybe I've heard that story."

Caitlyn knelt to admire the paper boats, complete with a tiny figure meant to be Paul. Josie's was neatly colored, while Amanda had filled in part of a sail and then had apparently become bored and started practicing writing her letters along the hull.

"Here comes Grammy. Maybe we should find seats, and then you can show her your boats."

"Don't worry about sitting down just yet." Her mother came up in time to hear her. "Everyone will visit for a few minutes until Pastor asks the blessing. Now, do be sure you greet all our military guests."

There were quite a few uniforms in the hall, she realized. That must explain why her mother brought so much food.

"Do they all attend worship here?" She'd seen a few uniforms in the sanctuary, but surely not this many.

Mama shook her head. "Most of them worship at

Steve's chapel, or one of the other chapels on post. They have a standing invitation to come here for our potlucks, though, and Steve usually rounds up quite a few of them. He's good about that."

Her mother never had anything but praise for Steve. Caitlyn could feel the tension mounting inside her. She'd expected that today, at least, she wouldn't be running into Steve. How on earth would she face him, knowing what she knew now about his loss?

You can never call back a word once it's spoken.

One of the maxims her mother had drilled into her and Carolyn as children surfaced from the recesses of her memory. She should have thought of that before she'd snapped at Steve, rejecting the sympathy he offered.

Steve couldn't know that Sarah had told her about the death of his fiancée. And there was certainly no reason for her to feel disappointment that he hadn't told her himself. They barely knew each other.

And besides, there was that kiss. She might have begun to believe that they were growing closer. But Steve hadn't meant anything by it, obviously. And she shouldn't read anything into it.

"Auntie Caitlyn!" Amanda tugged at her arm, and it sounded as if she'd repeated the name several times. "Guess what?"

"Guess what" was the way Amanda always prefaced something she wanted to be sure you heard and paid proper attention to. "What, Amanda?"

"Some of the kids in Sunday school made cookies and candy and sended it to their soldiers."

"Sent it," she corrected automatically.

"Sent it," Amanda repeated. "Me and Josie want to do that, too."

"We do." Josie grabbed her other arm.

That sounded messy. "But you don't have the names of your soldiers yet."

"Yes, we do," Amanda said. "Mrs. Olga called Grammy and told her—told her—their names. They're…" She paused, obviously trying to remember.

"Whitney." Josie said the name carefully. "That's the lady. And John. They're married to each other."

"Like Mommy and Daddy," Amanda added.

Her heart squeezed, but she managed a smile. "We'll have to ask Grammy about baking the cookies. It's her kitchen."

Her mother was already nodding. "We'll do it tonight, okay?"

"Aunt Caitlyn, too," Amanda insisted. "She has to help us."

She nodded. "Me, too."

"You too what?" That deep voice from behind her set her heart thudding loudly enough that it resounded in her ears.

"Making cookies, Chaplain Steve." Amanda made a dive for him, grabbing his leg and probably wrinkling his uniform pants. "We're making cookies to send to our soldiers."

"Well, that sounds like a great idea. But are you sure Aunt Caitlyn knows how to make cookies? You might have to teach her." He looked at her, eyes crinkling.

It really wasn't fair for a man to be that attractive. Or to make her heart turn soft at a smile.

Amanda had erupted in giggles. "'Course she does. Everybody knows how to make cookies."

"Not me," he said. "I've never learned. I should have someone like you to teach me."

"Come tonight," Amanda shouted, heedless of her grandmother's shushing sounds. "Come tonight and help us make cookies."

"Please," Josie added softly, clinging to his hand, her small one lost in his.

His face softened as he looked at Josie.

"If Aunt Caitlyn says it's all right." He looked at Caitlyn, and her heart seemed to melt.

She cleared her throat. "It's fine, if you're sure it's not too much trouble for you to get away from your other duties."

What was she saying? If he came, she'd have to go through several hours with him, trying not to betray the fact that she knew something about him that he'd obviously prefer she didn't.

He smiled, his deep blue eyes taking her breath away. "I wouldn't miss it for anything."

Steve moved Amanda bodily out of reach of the hot oven door as Caitlyn slid a cookie sheet in. Caitlyn closed the door and set the timer.

"Trying to keep from singeing this batch?" he asked, just to tease her. She looked so serious about this whole operation, as if even the cookies she made had to be perfect.

"These aren't burned." She snatched up one of the offending chocolate-chip cookies and took a bite. "Delicious. Just a little bit crispy."

"They're not s'posed to be crispy," Amanda volunteered. "The krispy treats are s'posed to be crispy. Can I have one?"

Caitlyn grabbed her in a big hug and tickled her.

"You're going to turn into a cookie if you don't watch out."

Amanda giggled, trying to tickle her back, and the two of them tussled for a moment.

Caitlyn had come a long way from the woman she'd been a few weeks ago. He watched her, smiling a little, as she withstood a tackle from both of her nieces at once.

Then, she'd been so uncomfortable with children that she hadn't even known how to get the twins from the school to the car without a struggle. Now she laughed and hugged easily, showing a warm, loving side that he found very appealing.

And not just with her nieces. He picked up a fork and began flattening the peanut-butter cookies in the criss-cross pattern that Amanda had demonstrated. Caitlyn had softened in other ways.

Her determination to solve Ali's problem now seemed motivated as much by her concern for the child as by her need to succeed at every task she undertook. And he'd seen the caring she put into trying to ease Betty's burdens. He could only hope that meant she'd given up any thought of rushing back to the city.

"I want to put more cookies in the tins." Josie climbed on a chair and leaned over the table. "Are these ready, Chaplain Steve?"

He touched the ones she indicated. "They're cool, all right. Pick them up gently, remember."

Josie nodded, bending over the cooling racks, the tip of her tongue sticking out as she concentrated on moving Betty's peanut-butter chocolate-chip oatmeal cookies to the tin.

As usual, Betty had overdone things, insisting on making several different types of cookies as well as the pan of brownies she was frosting at the moment. Still, that batch of oatmeal cookies was probably his fault, since he'd mentioned that they were his favorite.

Amanda went over to her grandmother. "I want to do the frosting," she declared, tugging at Betty's apron. "Please, please, please." Her voice became louder with every word.

He exchanged glances with Caitlyn. *Too much sugar,* she mouthed.

"I love the way you're packing those cookies," he said loudly enough to be heard over Amanda's repeated insistence. "When I was in Iraq a couple of years ago, all the soldiers thought it was the best thing in the world to get a box packed like that."

"It was?" Amanda stopped pestering her grandmother and came to the table. "Why?"

"Why?" He tugged at her ponytail. "Because most of the time we were eating little packages of freeze-dried food." He made a face. "Nowhere near as good as a homemade cookie, believe me. They're the best."

"Who sent you cookies when you were far, far away?" Josie asked.

"My mama did. She sent me all my favorites. And sometimes people from the church would send me a big package. I shared them with all the people who didn't get a package."

"They didn't get any for their very own selves?" Josie's eyes filled with quick tears. "Everyone should get some."

"You're right, sugar." He bent and kissed the top of her head, touched by her compassion. "It can be pretty lonesome when you're deployed. A package makes you feel as if someone loves you."

He remembered, too vividly, what that had been like.

For a little while he'd had Elaine, even when they weren't together all the time. But then—

His throat tightened so much that he thought he couldn't speak. Why was it that his grief seemed so near the surface now? Something about what he felt for Caitlyn seemed to have reactivated it, making it harder to keep under control.

He thought, as he often did when he needed guidance, of his father. Daddy had been the exemplar of what a chaplain should be. He'd never have let his own feelings get in the way of what he should do.

"All right, now." Betty turned from the pan of brownies. "That's enough helping for two little girls. It's time to get ready for bed."

That was greeted with groans, of course, but in a few minutes she was ushering them toward the stairs.

"I'll come back and help with the cleanup after I get them to bed," she said.

"No, you will not." Caitlyn put down the spatula she was holding. "You'll go to bed yourself—read, watch TV, knit, if you want to, but do it in bed. You need some rest."

He expected an argument from Betty, but instead she nodded. "I guess I will. Thank you."

Caitlyn watched her mother take the children upstairs, a worried look on her face. "I'm afraid she's still doing too much. I wish—"

"I know." He carried a handful of bowls and spoons to the sink. "But Betty Villard is a hard person to get to slow down. It seems to me you're doing a pretty good job of it."

"I hope so." She carried the rest of the dirty dishes over to the sink. "You don't need to do this. I can take care of it."

Somehow he wasn't ready to leave just yet. "I'll wash.

You dry." He put the stopper in the sink and began running hot water.

She didn't argue either, just grabbed a tea towel from the rack. "I don't think she's sick." She was obviously still talking about her mother. "Just grieving and very tired."

He nodded, realizing that what she needed most now was a listening ear. "You're doing all you can."

"I'm trying." She stared at the bowl she was drying, moving the striped towel around it in slow circles. "I realize there's no chance I'll be able to leave soon. I called a friend of mine, and she's arranging a sublet of my apartment for the next six months."

He was relieved. Surprised, but still relieved. That was what he'd hoped for personally, but this was about her feelings, not his.

"I'm glad you'll have some money coming in from that. What about your job?"

He could feel the tension that gripped her at the question. She was worried about her career—that much was obvious.

"I don't know. At the moment they're holding a place for me. How long they'll be willing to do that, I have no idea." She set the bowl down with a clunk. "I can't lose that position after everything I've sacrificed to get this far. I can't."

She was obviously near tears, and he wasn't sure how to comfort her.

"Talk to me about it, Caitlyn. Why is this particular job so important to you? No one can take your credentials away. There are plenty of other things you can do. You could even go into practice for yourself."

And stay right here for good.

But he couldn't ask her to do anything that implied a

future between them. He had to keep this focused on what was best for her, for the twins, for her mother.

She darted him a suspicious look. "You weren't by any chance listening in on Pastor Fields's sermon today, were you?"

"I was too busy giving my own. Why?"

She twisted the tea towel between her hands. "He said that most of the self-improvement models out there get it wrong. He feels that many people put too much emphasis on fulfilling their own potential and not enough on finding the place God prepared for them."

"Sounds like a good sermon."

"Do you agree with that idea?" She impaled him with a look that demanded an honest answer.

"I think that when you're in the place where God wants you, you'll be happy. You'll feel as if you fit." He'd certainly found that to be true in his own life. "Were you happy in your job, or did you do it because—"

He stopped, not sure he should say what he was thinking.

"What? Go on."

He leaned against the sink, watching her. Their faces were very close, and the room very still. "I thought maybe your drive to succeed had something to do with wanting to please your father."

He expected her to flare back at that, but she didn't. She looked up at him, her eyes suddenly wide and lost, all her defiant energy gone.

"It was tough to do that. Carolyn was always his favorite, you know. He laughed and played with her, not with me."

"I'm sure he loved you—" But how could he be sure?

He only knew that the man had walked away from his family and never even bothered to support them after that.

She shook her head. "The only time he was pleased with me was when I accomplished something. So I did."

"He was wrong." Criminally wrong, to do that to a child.

"I'm not complaining." She tried to rally. "It gave me the drive to get where I am."

But a tear hung on her lashes, denying the words. He might have been able to hold back, if it weren't for that tear. It cut him right to the heart.

He took her shoulders and drew her into his arms, pressing his cheek against the silk of her hair.

"It's okay," he murmured. "It is, really. He didn't deserve to have a daughter like you." He tilted her face up so that he could see it. "I mean it. You're bright and beautiful and loving and caring—"

His mind stopped working. He bent his head and kissed her.

Her lips softened under his, and she slid her arms around him. It shook him as thoroughly as the kiss they'd shared in the car, but this was better. Her arms were around him and he was holding her close.

What was he doing? He'd already convinced himself that she was off limits. He couldn't be counseling her one minute and kissing her the next, even if he was ready for a relationship. He pulled back. Reluctantly.

"I'm sorry," he whispered. "I shouldn't have."

Her gaze bored into him, as if she'd see to his very soul. "Why not?" Her lips trembled just a little. "That's what you said before. Is it because of your fiancée?"

* * *

Caitlyn froze, appalled at the words that had come out of her mouth.

"I'm sorry—" she began.

Steve shook his head, his face so tight she couldn't read his emotions. He glanced around.

"Let's go outside and get some air."

Not sure she wanted to hear whatever was going to come next, she nodded. He held the door, and they walked out onto the porch that wrapped around the Victorian house.

Dusk had drawn in while they'd been working. The air was still sultry, but a gentle breeze teased at her hair. She crossed to the creaky old porch swing, shifted a patchwork pillow and sat down.

Steve moved as if to sit next to her, then seemed to change his mind and went to lean against the porch railing. "How did you know about her?"

His voice was even, and in the semidark, she couldn't see his expression clearly. Maybe that had been in his mind when he'd suggested they come outside.

"Sarah mentioned it. When we were on post, packing boxes."

He didn't move, didn't speak. And she realized she wanted him to. Despite all her firm assertions that she didn't want to be involved with him, she longed to feel they were close enough that he'd tell her.

"I'm sorry," she said when the silence had stretched on too long. "We weren't gossiping about you. Sarah had forgotten that I wouldn't know, and she made some reference to it. Then she had to tell me."

"It's okay." He sounded more himself now, and the

tension inside her eased. "It's no big secret. Everyone here knows."

They know, but they don't talk about it, she realized, remembering Sarah's words.

"What was her name?" She couldn't help but venture the question.

"Elaine." Even in the near dark, she could see how tense his body was. His taut hands pressed against the porch railing. "She was a captain in the unit I accompanied to Iraq."

"I take it you didn't have long together?" she asked gently.

The negative movement of his head was a silhouette. Silence again, and this time she felt she couldn't be the one to break it.

Finally he cleared his throat. "She was killed in action." His tone had a note of finality.

"I'm sorry for your loss." The conventional words had never held so much meaning for her. "And I'm sorry for saying that you didn't understand."

He shrugged. "It's all right." He cleared his throat again. "Even if I hadn't lost someone myself in that way, understanding would still be part of my job."

I don't want to be part of your job, Steve. Don't you get that?

She tried to tell herself that it didn't matter, that she wasn't disappointed.

But that would be a lie. She couldn't kid herself about this any longer.

She'd tried not to care, but it had slipped up on her when she wasn't looking. Ironic, wasn't it? She was finally ready to open her heart, and she'd picked a man whose own heart was securely shut.

Chapter 9

Steve slid a hymnal into the rack and glanced around the small sanctuary of the Fort Bonnell Christian Chapel. Everything was ready for the next service. He had a couple of volunteers to do the actual cleaning up, but still, he always wanted to check things out for himself.

There were times, even after two years here, that he still felt like an impostor when he stood in front of the congregation. His father had been such a commanding presence when he spoke from that same pulpit.

In spite of the personnel turnover that was natural on any army post, people still mentioned his daddy and asked how he and Mama were doing. It was good to think he'd had such an influence on people.

Maybe he should talk with his father about this situation with General Willis. Ask for his advice. But he was somehow reluctant to do that. He ought to be able to minister to the general himself, if that was what God willed.

He sank down on the front pew, his gaze fixed on the simple gold cross placed on the plain cream wall in front of him. Everything about the chapel was simple, and that was fine with him. That was what a military chapel should be.

After spending time in a war zone giving sermons perched on the back of a tank, he found he didn't need stained glass or padded pews to keep his attention focused on worship. Brushing that close to death every day had been great training in mental discipline.

Now he'd sought out the quiet of the chapel because he was troubled, and not just about Ali and General Willis.

He bowed his head. *Lord, I don't know what to do with these feelings for Caitlyn. Each time I'm with her I seem to care a little more, but those very feelings seem to make me think about Elaine. Please, guide me to do the right thing.*

He leaned back, rubbing the nape of his neck as he stared at the cross. He'd been avoiding the obvious answer, and maybe he'd better face it.

Possibly the only reason God had brought Caitlyn into his life was so that he could help her become a mother to those two little girls. Their time together might have nothing to do with him, and everything to do with those precious children.

If so, that should be enough for him.

Guide me, he murmured again, and rose. He should check with his secretary and see if the call he was expecting had come through.

As he approached it, the door leading to the hallway and his office swung open. Caitlyn came in, blinking for a moment at the sunlight that poured through the plain glass of the windows.

"Caitlyn." It startled him, having her so close. "What brings you here?"

Your relationship is nothing more than platonic. He reminded himself. *So stop noticing how the breeze had teased tendrils of her golden-brown hair in her face, and how the green of her shirt brought out the greenish tones of her hazel eyes.*

She looked a little surprised. "You called me, remember? Anna left your message on my desk."

"You didn't need to make a special trip." He gestured to the pew, and when she sat down, he sat next to her. But not too close.

"I had to come on post anyway, to pick up some things that are being donated for the Children of the Day fundraiser. Have you learned anything new about Greg Willis?"

"Not yet, but it's looking hopeful. I finally found someone who served with Greg at about the right time."

"What did he say?" Caitlyn's face lit with hope.

"I haven't spoken with him yet, but I talked with his wife. She said she'd have him call me as soon as he came in." He glanced at his watch. "Which should be soon."

"Thank goodness." Caitlyn's words were heartfelt. "I was beginning to feel as if every effort we made was doomed to failure. If this man knew Greg at the right time, surely he'll know where Ali was born."

"Paul Peterson. They were in the same outfit, and my sources said they were close friends. He's retired from the service, so it took a little time to track him down."

He looked at his watch again, willing the man to call. *Lord, we need a break if we're going to succeed. Please, let this man lead us to some answers.*

Caitlyn glanced around the sanctuary, with its rows

of blond wood benches and its simple windows. "So this is your chapel."

"Not really mine." He smiled. "Before you came in, I was thinking that sometimes I feel as if my daddy's still in charge here."

To his surprise, she didn't smile in return. "I'd think that might make your job a little difficult. Feeling as if you're following in his footsteps, I mean."

He considered. "He *is* a tough act to follow, in a way. He was absolutely dedicated to his calling. That was one thing my brother and I learned early as kids—that Daddy's chaplaincy wasn't just a job, and that it had to come first."

She tilted her head to the side, that silky hair caressing her shoulder. "That seems a little hard on his family."

"Don't get me wrong," he said quickly. "He's the greatest. If I can be half the chaplain he was, I'll be happy."

"It must be nice to feel that way about your father." Now it was Caitlyn whose gaze was fixed on the cross, as if she looked for answers there.

He leaned his elbow on the back of the pew, so that he could face her more fully. He wanted to see her face. "Do you ever hear from him?"

"I get a Christmas card from time to time. And sometimes a check for my birthday, although often as not, it would arrive on Carolyn's birthday instead of mine."

"That's rough."

Her face clouded a little. "Carolyn's birthday is next week, did you know that? I'm not sure how to deal with that with the girls."

"Have they mentioned it to you?"

"Not yet. Dates don't mean much at their age. I don't

know whether I should just ignore it and hope they don't remember, or bring it up and see how they feel."

He didn't have an answer for this one. "Maybe you should talk to Olga about it. She's the expert, especially with children, and they may have mentioned it to her."

"That's true." She shook her head. "It's silly, I suppose, but I keep thinking I should know these things by instinct."

That one he did know that answer to. "Even birth parents struggle with issues like that. You're not alone in needing help."

Her lips curved slightly. "You're really good at making people feel better, you know that?"

That smile had his gaze riveted to her face. So maybe it was a good thing that the door swung open again. Joannie Parker, his secretary, came in holding the cordless phone aloft.

"It's that call you were expecting." She glanced from him to Caitlyn, her eyes bright with curiosity as she handed him the phone.

"Thanks, Joannie." His heart thudded. *Please, let this be the lead we've been looking for.*

"I'll leave you alone," she said, and went back through the door toward the office.

He pressed the phone to his ear, very aware of Caitlyn's gaze on his face. She was depending on this so much. He just hoped she wasn't going to be disappointed.

"Thanks so much for calling back, Mr. Peterson. I wanted to talk with you about an army buddy of yours, Gregory Willis."

A few minutes later, he knew neither one of them would be disappointed this time. He had to struggle to control his grin as he expressed his thanks and hung up.

Then he looked at Caitlyn, the smile splitting his face.

"He knew! Greg took his wife to Athens for the baby's birth. It seems she had a friend who was a doctor there. So if Greg followed the rules, that's where he'd have registered the baby's birth—at the American embassy in Athens."

"What a relief!" She grabbed his arm, holding it tight in her excitement. "That's the first break to come our way. Steve, we may actually be able to do this!"

Her face was lit with happiness, and her eyes danced as she looked up at him. It took everything he had to keep his emotions in control.

He had to. Because otherwise he might have been tempted to kiss her again, and that was exactly the wrong thing to do.

No reply yet from the embassy in Athens.

Caitlyn swung away from the computer in the family room that evening. She hadn't quite figured out the time difference between Texas and Greece, but people did e-mail at any time of the day or night. The answer could come through at any moment.

She stood, stretching. By the time she had gotten the twins to bed, all she wanted to do was collapse in a chair. How her mother had managed to take care of them all these months, she couldn't imagine.

"All finished?" Mama, sitting at the kitchen table with a glass of sweet iced tea, smiled at her.

Caitlyn nodded, crossing the family room to join her. She stepped on something, discovered a marker one of the twins had missed during cleanup and put it on the breakfast bar that separated the two rooms.

"The message I hoped for hasn't come through yet, but I guess it's still early for an answer."

Mama, who'd heard about little Ali and his problems, nodded understandingly. "Surely you'll hear something soon. I'll keep praying."

"Thanks, Mama."

She poured a glass of tea from the pitcher on the counter, added ice and sat down across from her mother, wondering how to bring up the subject that had been needling her for the past few days.

"There was an e-mail from Whitney for the girls," she said. That was the first thing her eyes had been drawn to when her e-mail appeared, even before work. "They'll want to hear it first thing in the morning."

"That's so nice. She really seems to be enjoying writing to the children as much as they like writing to her." Her mother turned the cold glass on the tabletop, making a small ring of condensation. "I confess, I had my doubts about this at first, but it seems to be working out all right."

Caitlyn nodded. "It's so strange, reading about Whitney's life there. I'd be terrified, but she just seems so upbeat."

"That's how Carolyn was." Her mother's voice was soft. "I'm sure she must have been worried and missing the children terribly, but she always sounded positive when she wrote and called."

Caitlyn wanted to say that Carolyn should never have gone, but she bit back the words. It would only upset Mama, and no words could change things now.

Maybe the only way to ask the one question gnawing at her was to blurt it out. She took a breath. "Do you know why Carolyn and Dean picked me to be the twins' guardian?"

Her mother looked startled. "Well, who else would they choose?"

"You. One of their married friends. I know Dean didn't have any family, but surely—"

Her mother's face clouded. "Are you saying you don't want to be the children's guardian?"

"No, no, that's not it at all." She clasped her mother's hand warmly. That was why she'd hesitated to ask the question. She'd been afraid Mama would misunderstand. "It's just that Carolyn and I weren't, well, very close." That was the understatement of the year, wasn't it? "And she never even talked to me about it."

"She should have." Mama's hand clasped hers. "I told her that, but she kept putting it off."

That was Carolyn's nature, of course. She'd always put off the things she didn't want to do, leading to countless Sunday nights staying up late, trying to get her homework finished before school on Monday. But this was considerably more serious.

"The letters from Whitney have made me think more about Carolyn," she said. "About the decisions she had to make when she knew she was going to be deployed."

Mama nodded. "It was a difficult time."

"I guess I just wanted to know what was in her mind when she made the decision. Did she pick me because I was the only person available?"

"Oh, darlin', no!" Her mother's eyes darkened with emotion. "Goodness, that wasn't her thinking at all. We did talk about it a bit. She and Dean both realized that at my age, raising those two girls wasn't a good idea."

She wasn't sure the short term had been a good idea, either, but she knew better than to bring that up.

"Carolyn named you as guardian because she admired you," Mama said. "I suppose she never told you that, but she always bragged about her big sister—how smart and efficient and successful you are. When it came right down to it, she knew she could count on you to do the very best for her children."

There was a lump in her throat that threatened to choke her. "I never knew. We were always so different. It seemed we had nothing in common."

"When you were children—" Her mother stopped, as if she had difficulty speaking, as well. "I think that your father may have contributed to the differences between you two." She shook her head. "Well, that's past history, isn't it?"

Was it? Was it really in the past if it affected what she did and how she felt today?

Mama patted her hand. "I just wish you two could have spent more time together as adults. I think you would have learned to be friends."

Friends. She felt her heart twisting at her mother's words.

"I wish that, too," she whispered. "I do."

She'd do her best, Caitlyn thought as she watched the twins in the swimming pool the next afternoon. In the light of day, she wasn't positive her mother had been right about Carolyn's motivation, and she wasn't sure she'd entirely forgiven her sister for the choices she'd made, but that didn't seem to matter so much.

The children were what was important. Carolyn had entrusted them to her.

The swimming lesson was over, and the twins were playing with their friends in the shallow end of the pool. Smiling, she watched Amanda make a valiant effort to swim on her back and go bubbling under, to come up spitting water.

The truth was, she loved those children, and she'd find a way to do her best for them.

Someone stopped next to her, and she looked up to see Steve, in swim trunks, with a towel slung over his shoulder.

"Aren't you going in today?" He lifted one eyebrow in a question.

"I'm not much of a swimmer." While Carolyn had spent summers at the pool, she'd been working, saving money for college. "You enjoy it."

"Will do."

His smile was as friendly as always, but somehow she felt that he was keeping his distance. Having regrets about how close they'd gotten? Probably so.

She watched as he dived into the deep end, his movements sure and confident. He swam underwater for the width of the pool and backstroked across, his strokes even, eating up the distance easily. He held on to the side for a moment, seeming to watch the children playing, and then swam toward the shallow end, submerging when he reached the rope.

He surfaced next to Amanda, making her squeal, and in another moment all the children had joined her in an effort to dunk him.

Steve had a nice way with children, always seeming to know who needed to be drawn into things, who needed a firm hand. Even as she thought that, he shook his head at Amanda, who was splashing her sister. The little girl desisted, far faster than she would have for Caitlyn.

She was drifting, Caitlyn realized. Not just at the moment, sitting in the sun half-asleep, but in making decisions about her future.

Why does it have to be so hard? It no longer seemed so unfamiliar to pray. In fact, it was becoming a larger and larger part of her internal conversations.

Lord, I just don't understand. I'm trying to do my best for the children, but does that mean I have to give up the career that means so much to me? I do good work there, don't I?

She could practice law in Texas, of course, but that wasn't her dream. It wasn't what she'd worked so hard for all these years. Did she have to surrender that?

If she asked Steve that question, he'd have an answer. He thought he knew what she ought to do, and he never seemed hesitate to tell her. Which was an awfully good reason not to ask him.

Some of the mothers were gathering up beach towels and calling their children out of the pool. She glanced at her watch. It was about time to head home. Steve came toward her, wading through the water, the twins hanging on to his hands.

"Get wet, Auntie Caitlyn." Holding the edge of the pool, Amanda splashed her, and the water felt beautifully cool on her legs.

"No, thanks." She drew her legs back. "You were doing a great job in your lesson. You, too, Josie. I liked the way you floated on your back."

"I'm going to swim well enough to go in the deep end pretty soon," Amanda said, pulling herself out of the pool and standing dripping until Caitlyn wrapped a towel around her. "And when I can swim in the deep end, I'll go off the high dive, just like Mommy used to."

She was mentioning her mother more easily in conversation these days, and that had to be good, didn't it?

"Your mommy was a good swimmer."

"And diver," Josie said. "I 'memer when she went off the high dive. I want to do it, too."

"You're a scaredy-cat," Amanda said. "You won't do it."

"Will too," Josie said predictably, her lower lip trembling.

"Neither of you will do it until you can swim much, much better than you can right now," Caitlyn said firmly. "And I won't do it at all."

"You won't?" Amanda stared at her, surprised, maybe even a little disappointed. "Why not?"

It hadn't occurred to her that it would be hard to admit she couldn't do something to a child, but it was.

"I'm not a very good swimmer," she said. "And I was always afraid of the high dive."

Carolyn had teased her to go up one day, she remembered. Her annoyance with Carolyn for embarrassing her in front of their friends had been enough to get her partway up the ladder. And then she'd panicked and scrambled back down again.

"You're afraid." Amanda looked at her as accusingly as if she'd committed a sin.

Before she could think of an answer to that, Steve spoke.

"Everyone's afraid of something," he said. "It's unkind to tease them about it. You wouldn't want them to tease you about the things you're afraid of."

"They couldn't," Amanda declared. "'Cause I'm not afraid of anything."

"Not anything?" Steve asked gently. "Not loud thunderstorms or the dark?"

Amanda blinked. "Well, maybe the dark. Just a little bit."

"Me, too." Josie came to Caitlyn for her towel. "And I don't like loud thunder or big dogs."

Caitlyn wrapped the towel around her, holding Josie close when she shivered.

"What are you scared of, Chaplain Steve?" Amanda sounded determined to get an admission out of him.

He bent over her. "You really want to know?" he asked.

She nodded.

"Nosy little girls," he declared, and tickled her.

What are you afraid of, Chaplain Steve? She wouldn't ask, but she wanted to know. *Does it have anything to do with your lost love?*

Chapter 10

"Chaplain Steve, Chaplain Steve!"

Steve lifted the stack of boxes he carried just as Amanda and Josie barreled into his legs. That seemed to be the twins' standard form of greeting, but he hadn't expected to run into them at the elementary-school gym this afternoon.

"Hi, gang. Take it easy, okay? I'll get into trouble if I drop these boxes."

He juggled the boxes into one arm so he could ruffle the twins' chestnut hair. They wore identical denim shorts and striped blue-and-white shirts today, but he could always tell them apart.

"What's in them?" Amanda scrutinized the cardboard cartons, as if assessing the likelihood that they contained toys.

"Prizes for the games at the carnival. Do you think you'll win one?"

"I will, I will." Amanda bounced up and down. "Grammy says I can play the fish game and the throwing-the-ball game, and maybe even get some cotton candy, 'cause all the money is for poor children."

"That's right." He hefted the boxes. "That's why lots of people are donating prizes, too. Because all the money we raise at the carnival will help children."

Betty hurried up to him, looking distracted. "Are those prizes? They go right on that table." She gave Amanda a gentle push. "Stay out of Chaplain Steve's way, please, girls. Everyone has work to do."

"They're fine," Steve said quickly. "In fact, maybe between them, they could carry one of these boxes for me. Do you two think you're strong enough?"

"I can do it," Amanda exclaimed, and Josie nodded solemnly.

Steve bent to let them take the lightest carton off the top of the stack. They balanced it between them, hanging on with both hands, and followed as their grandmother led the way to the table where the boxes of prizes were stacked.

Steve smiled at the identical expressions on their intent little faces. He ministered to every bereaved person in the Fort Bonnell family, but he'd have to admit that the twins had a special place in his heart.

The table was filling up with cartons containing all sorts of prizes, and he was sure there'd be more coming in. Everyone rallied around when it came to raising money for Children of the Day, Prairie Springs's favorite charity.

Funny, how even people who'd been doubtful at first about Anna's grand idea, now bragged that the foundation was known around the world for its good work.

"Caitlyn's not around today?" He posed the question casually once the boxes were put away.

"She'll probably pop in soon. She said she had some work to do at the office before she came." Betty pushed up her glasses, put her hands on her hips and looked around the gym. "Goodness, do you think we'll ever be ready in time?"

All around them, half-finished booths fought for space with half-erected games. Two volunteers were attempting to hang a banner that read, Children of the Day Charity Carnival across the width of the gym, and a makeshift stage at one end of the long gymnasium was still just a pile of lumber.

"It'll be fine," he said. "It looked terrible at this point last year, but we managed to have everything ready on time, remember?"

Behind her glasses, Betty's eyes glistened, and he realized that last year, Carolyn had been one of their most faithful volunteers.

She cleared her throat. "Yes, I guess you're right about that."

"Steve, how about getting us some more volunteers?" Anna said, pausing as she passed, like a hummingbird in flight. "We need more muscle to get these booths finished. Can you bring us some military?"

"Yes, ma'am." He saluted. "I'll get on that right away."

Anna grinned. "Sorry. I didn't mean to be bossy. I'm a little distracted. Oh, there's Sarah. I have to talk to her about the balloons." She rushed off.

"Look. There's your teacher, Ms. Sarah." He pointed her out to the twins. "Why don't you go say hi."

Betty looked as if she could stand a moment's break to regain her composure.

"We'll tell her we're going to be in her class, just in case she forgot," Amanda said. Grabbing Josie's hand, she scurried off.

"Are you okay?" He bent over Betty, wishing he could take back his casual words.

"I'm fine." She patted his arm. "It's nothing you said, dear. Really. You get on with your work."

He nodded. "Well, I'd better bring another load in from the truck before Anna comes back and catches me loafing." But when he turned toward the door, Caitlyn was entering.

She glanced around the room, spotted him with her mother and came rushing over. Her eyes danced with excitement. Something must have happened.

"Hi, Mama. Steve, you're just the person I wanted to see. Guess what?"

"You sound like Amanda," he teased. "I'm guessing it's something good."

Distracted, she glanced around. "Where are the children?"

"Over there with Sarah," her mother said. "I'm just going to run to the kitchen and check the coffee while they're occupied." Betty hurried off on her self-appointed rounds.

He caught Caitlyn's hand and just as quickly dropped it. The power of her touch was just too strong.

"Come on, tell me," he said.

She blinked, as if recalling her attention. "I have it! The embassy sent us confirmation of Ali's birth registration and a copy of the birth certificate. We've done it, Steve."

"Praise God. That's terrific." He didn't need to be

touching her, he realized, to feel that pull. "We're getting there."

"We are." But she sobered. "I have Jake working on a plan of action if we can't get the general on board. It won't be easy. Have you heard anything at all from Miss Willis?"

"I talked with her about it this morning. She said not to count on his support yet, but that she's been working on him. I guess all we can do is pray she succeeds."

"I have been," Caitlyn said softly.

"So have—"

He cut off what he was saying at the sound of a cry, but he wasn't as fast as Caitlyn, who had already left his side.

He swung around, a wordless prayer forming in his mind, and spotted the source immediately.

Amanda clung to a board, halfway up the unfinished stage. She stared down, openmouthed, at Josie, lying crumpled underneath.

"How much farther?"

Caitlyn sat in the backseat of her car, holding a compress against the cut on Josie's forehead, while Steve drove them to the emergency room. Josie leaned close against her, whimpering a little.

"We're almost there. Hold on, sweetheart." His gaze met Caitlyn's in the rearview mirror. "You hold on, too," he said. "I know the injury looks scary, but I don't think it's too bad."

She tried to manage a smile, without much success. "Sarah said she didn't think it would even need stitches. And I'm sure she's seen plenty of children's bumps and cuts."

She was repeating the kindergarten teacher's words to reassure herself as much as anything.

In that instant when she'd heard the cry, she'd known it was Josie without even looking. Maybe she was actually developing some maternal instincts.

"I should never have taken my eyes off them."

"Don't start blaming yourself." Steve's tone was brisk. "Every parent feels that way when a child is hurt, but you can't wrap them in cotton at this stage. Five is old enough to trust with a bit of independence."

"I'm sorry," Josie wailed suddenly. "I'm sorry. I didn't mean to be naughty."

"Sweetheart, I know that. It's all right. I'm not mad at you." She kissed Josie's cheek gently.

She and Steve both knew who had instigated climbing on the makeshift stage. Amanda had led, and Josie had followed, of course.

"The doctor is going to fix your forehead up as good as new, I promise."

"I don't want a doctor. I want to go home."

"Hush now. You have to let the doctor take a look at it, so we'll know how to take care of you. Then we'll go home, and you can tell Grammy and Amanda all about the hospital."

They'd convinced her mother that it would be best if she took Amanda home while Caitlyn and Steve went to the hospital. Mama had been so upset—blaming herself, of course.

Still, Steve was right. Both of the girls had known they were doing something they shouldn't.

At some point it would be appropriate to point out to Josie that she didn't have to do everything Amanda did. But that time wasn't now.

"Here we are." Steve pulled up to the E.R. entrance, stopped and turned the blinkers on. He slid out and hurried around, coming to the backdoor and opening it.

"I can take her," she said, but Steve was already lifting Josie out.

"I'll carry her in and then come back to move the car."

Caitlyn nodded and followed him inside, her prayers flowing quickly.

Despite her fears, the emergency room ran smoothly and efficiently. By the time Caitlyn had filled out the paperwork, the nurses were ready to take Josie back to an exam room.

There things slowed down, however. Josie looked forlorn and tearful, lying on the high white table, and nothing Caitlyn could think of to say seemed to cheer her up. The door swung open finally, but it was Steve, not the promised doctor.

"How are we doing?" He sent an inquiring glance toward her while he bent over to give Josie a quick kiss, and she was suddenly, irrationally, glad that he was there to help.

"We're waiting for the doctor."

"I don't want a doctor," Josie wailed. "Manda said he'll sew me up with a big needle."

"Amanda doesn't know anything about it. She's never even been to an emergency room." Caitlyn smoothed the bangs back from the little girl's forehead. "Remember, you're going to tell her all about it when we get home."

"You'll be the one who knows about it," Steve pointed out. "Not Amanda."

"Oh." Josie seemed to absorb that. "I still don't want to get sewed."

"Well, let's have a look and see what's what," the doctor said, coming in. She was a brisk young woman with a warm smile. "What have you been doing with your- self, young lady?"

"I climbed up 'cause Manda said to." Josie pouted. "I'm not going to do that anymore."

"Manda is her twin," Caitlyn explained.

"You have a twin sister?" The doctor checked her over with gentle, efficient movements while she talked. "That must be fun. Can people tell you apart?"

"Mostly," Josie said. She seemed to be losing her fear under the doctor's friendly manner. "Sometimes some- body might call me Manda if they don't know us very much, but I just tell them I'm Josie."

"Good for you." The doctor looked up at Caitlyn. "I don't think we need stitches. We'll just clean up the cut and put a butterfly on it."

"A butterfly?" Josie's eyes went wide.

"Not a real one, sugar." Steve leaned over, holding her hand. "That's a kind of bandage."

"A special one," the doctor said, nodding to the nurse who'd followed her in with a tray. "Now, if Mommy will just hold her head still on this side, we'll get that all cleaned up."

Caitlyn took Josie's head in her hands where the doc- tor indicated, not bothering to correct the assumption. She was grateful there would be no stitches. She didn't think she could watch that.

Surprisingly, Josie didn't cry during the cleaning. Her eyes filled up at one point, but she clutched Steve's hand tightly and kept her gaze fixed firmly on Caitlyn's face.

Caitlyn murmured softly to her, the kind of soothing nonsense she remembered Mama saying when she'd hurt herself as a child. It seemed to work.

Finally the bandage was on. The doctor smiled at them.

"All finished. Trust me, it's always harder on the parents than on the child. The nurse will give you an instruction sheet, and you can check with her pediatrician in a day or two if you want."

"Thank you."

They weren't the parents, she and Steve. But for a moment, she felt as if they were.

Caitlyn had to force her feet to keep moving after she'd tucked in both the girls and her mother. Mama had been wiped out by the emergency, and she hadn't objected to having an early night. And Amanda had been too intimidated by the havoc she'd caused to put up any bedtime arguments.

Caitlyn felt ready to collapse, herself, but Steve had insisted on coming back to see if they needed anything, and he was still in the family room.

She'd been so thankful for his help. Just having another person Josie loved and trusted there had made all the difference.

But she shouldn't lean on him. It wasn't fair to either of them.

She found Steve on the sofa in the family room, paging through a photo album. She caught a glimpse of the pictures and tensed up.

"Where did you get that?"

He looked up, obviously surprised at her tone. "It was right here, on the coffee table. Is something wrong?"

"Sorry." She sank onto the sofa, pushing her hair back from her face with a sigh. "I didn't mean to snap. I guess Mama was looking at it."

"Problem?" He waited for more.

"It's just that she gets out the photo albums and looks at Carolyn's pictures when she's feeling low. I think the approach of Carolyn's birthday is hurting her more than she wants to let on."

"The first year is always hard." Steve's eyes seemed to turn a deeper shade of blue with empathy. "There are all those holidays to get through for the first time without the person you love."

"I guess so." Steve certainly had more experience in dealing with this sort of thing than she did. "But getting out the albums, crying over the pictures—wouldn't it be better if she didn't dwell on her loss so much?"

"She's always thinking about Carolyn, you know, even when she doesn't talk about her. Maybe she's taking comfort from looking at the photos of happier times, even if it makes her cry."

She leaned back against the cushions, her gaze on his strong face. "Does that work for you?"

His hand clenched on the album. "This isn't about me. I'm here to help you."

Frustration rose in her, and she shook her head. He was so good at evading anything personal. "I wanted to talk with you as a friend, not as a pastor."

For a moment he didn't speak, and she wondered what he was thinking. "I guess I can't really separate them," he said finally. "Maybe it would be better if I could, but I can't."

"Is that something they teach you in seminary?"

"Not exactly. I probably absorbed it a long time ago, from my father. He believed a pastor always had to be strong for the people who depended on him."

She considered that. "Don't you think people might

be helped by seeing that you have problems, too? Seeing how you deal with personal hurts?"

He didn't answer, but a muscle twitched in his jaw.

"Sorry." Obviously she couldn't change him. "I didn't mean to bug you about it. Let me see what you were looking at."

"Early high-school years, I think." He seemed relieved at the change of subject. He handed over the album. "Carolyn with a bunch of giggling girls, all hanging on the fence at a football game."

"Carolyn's posse, we called them." She stared at the young faces, wondering where they all were now. "You know, I used to envy Carolyn in a way. She made friends so easily. She just had to laugh, and people were drawn to her."

"And you?" He propped his arm on the back of the couch, facing her.

She shrugged. "You know who I was in the high-school pecking order. The brain, the geek, the wall-flower—whatever you want to call it."

"I wouldn't have described you that way. You just always seemed too preoccupied with making all A's to be bothered with the kind of petty things that interested most of us."

She flipped a page. Carolyn, again surrounded by friends, on the pep squad, waving pompoms in the air. Did Steve really think she hadn't minded being the one who was always on the outside?

"I told myself that I wasn't interested in the frivolous stuff that Carolyn was into. I was too busy getting ready to take the world by storm. But maybe at some level, I wanted to be like her."

She touched the image of Carolyn's smiling face, and

her throat clogged with tears. "She was so young." The tears spilled over, and she wiped them away quickly. "Sorry," she muttered. "I don't know what's wrong with me. I never cry."

"It's been an emotional day," he said, his voice low and soft. "You're allowed."

Her control, always so solid, seemed to shimmer. To shatter. "I let Carolyn down." She put her hands to her face. "I let Josie get hurt."

"Oh, Caitlyn, don't." His voice sounded affected by tears as well. "Don't, sugar. It wasn't your fault. It wasn't."

His arm slid around her, and she buried her face in his shoulder, letting herself absorb his warmth and comfort.

She shouldn't. She shouldn't depend on him. But right now, she couldn't seem to help it.

Chapter 11

Steve had been right about one thing, Caitlyn decided the next day as she turned onto a quiet residential street in Prairie Springs. She was affected more than she'd realized by her memories of Carolyn.

She'd known, intellectually, that grieving took time, but she hadn't understood at the deepest level just how difficult it would be. The longer she was here, around her mother and the twins, the more acute her grief seemed to become.

The answer was, as it always had been for her, to keep busy. That had gotten her through every other crisis in her life, including her father's desertion, and it would get her through this.

She'd been invited to lunch with Sarah Alpert today, and later she'd be totally preoccupied with the charity carnival. That would keep her too busy to think. In a few more days Carolyn's birthday would be in the past, and they would all start to feel better.

She drew up at the number Sarah had given her, only to realize that Sarah Alpert's small yellow craftsman bungalow was directly across the street from General Willis's imposing residence. She should have noticed the similarity of the addresses, but she hadn't been thinking about that.

She eyed the general's place cautiously, but no one was visible out on the lawn or at the windows. She slid out of the car, forced herself not to look over her shoulder at the house and hurried to Sarah's door, feeling as if the general might emerge at any moment and order her off his street.

"Caitlyn, welcome." Sarah opened the door before she could knock, her smile warm.

Everything about Sarah was warm, she decided, from the firelight glow of her red hair to the caring expression in her eyes. The only surprising thing was that she poured all that warmth and caring onto other people's children, instead of onto a family of her own.

"I didn't know you lived across from—" She stopped, realizing too late that she couldn't explain how she knew the general.

Sarah glanced at the place across the street before ushering Caitlyn in and closing the door.

"Don't worry about it," she said. "You didn't give anything away. I already know that General Willis is Ali's grandfather."

Caitlyn blinked. "You know? But how did you find out? I haven't said anything to anyone but Anna and Steve. General Willis doesn't want it known, I'm afraid, which is making everything so difficult."

"I realize that." Sarah brushed a strand of long red hair back over the shoulder of the simple white T-shirt she wore with cutoffs. "But I was helping Anna with some of the medical paperwork on Ali, and she let it slip. I won't say anything about it to anyone."

"Thanks." Caitlyn smiled ruefully. "The man scares me to death, to be honest. I don't want him thinking I told his secret."

"Marlon Willis isn't a bad guy, although he can seem pretty crusty. He's just unforgiving about his son, I'm afraid."

Sarah led the way through a living room filled with chintzes and plants and into a dining nook that overlooked a tiny back garden that was as charming as the house.

"Yes, he is." Caitlyn thought of his harsh words. "I have trouble understanding how he can still carry a grudge against Gregory years after his death. Or how he can refuse to recognize his only grandchild."

"Please, sit down." Sarah nodded to one of the two chairs that were drawn up to the drop-leaf table. "Would you rather have iced tea or soda?"

"Tea, please, Sarah. This is lovely. You have a charming house."

She went into the adjoining kitchen. "Thanks. I was lucky to find something I could afford in the historic district. I love living here."

Caitlyn heard the clinking of ice cubes in the kitchen. In a moment Sarah returned with a pitcher and two frosted glasses.

"You know, as far as General Willis is concerned, I don't see how he imagines he can keep this a secret." Sarah poured tea into one of the glasses and topped it with a sprig of mint. "Once Ali gets here, whether he claims the boy or not, word is going to get out. He's naive to think anything else."

Caitlyn stared at her for a moment. "You know, that's true. Steve and I have been looking at his refusal to accept the boy from such a narrow angle that we never thought of that."

"Maybe the general didn't, either." Sarah frowned. "I'd hate to think of him taking Ali just because of public opinion, though. That poor child needs to have someone who will love him."

Sarah said the words with such passion that Caitlyn's throat tightened. Here was someone who really cared. "You sound as if you'd like to mother him."

"I'd like to mother all of them. There are way too many lonely, hurting children in the world." Sarah shook her head, as if reminding herself that was impossible. "Goodness, I'm forgetting myself. Let me get the salads. I hope the tea isn't too strong."

"Wonderful." She took a sip of the sweet tea that was fragrant with mint. "This is so nice of you."

"I've wanted a chance to get to know you a little better." Sarah came back with plates bearing flaky croissants piled high with chicken salad. She slid into her seat. "Do you mind if I ask a blessing?"

"Please do." Caitlyn clasped her hands on the napkin in her lap.

Sarah bowed her head. "Father, we ask You to remember Ali today, and all the other children who need Your love. Guide us to help him. Bless this food, and use us to further Your will. Amen."

"Amen," Caitlyn echoed softly, touched.

"Have you heard any more about how Ali is doing?" Sarah asked as she passed salt and pepper.

"We had a report yesterday from Dr. Mike saying he's stable and gaining strength." She realized Sarah might not know who Dr. Mike was. "That's Major Mike Montgomery, the army doctor who's been looking after him."

Sarah nodded, her expression clouding. "Yes. I know Dr. Mike."

"That's right, I'd forgotten that Steve said he was stationed here at Fort Bonnell before he went overseas. Were you friends then?"

Sarah put down her fork, the food on it untasted. "You could say that. We were engaged."

"Sarah, I'm sorry. I didn't know." She wasn't sure what to say. This was obviously a delicate subject, and she had stumbled onto it, oblivious.

Sarah forced a smile. "It just didn't work out. That happens. It's best just to part as friends and go on with your lives."

"I guess you're right."

But there was something in Sarah's eyes that said she wasn't over Mike as completely as she proclaimed. Maybe that explained why she was still single.

At least Sarah had loved someone, even if it hadn't worked out. She couldn't say the same for herself.

She'd been so busy with her career that she'd never taken the time for a relationship, even one that ended badly. What did that say about her?

"Catch a fish, win a prize!" Steve shouted, working the fishing game designed for the youngest participants in the charity carnival. Naturally, everyone who tried the game won a prize. Thanks to the generosity of local merchants, he had a huge carton filled with small toys to hand out.

He'd been constantly busy since the carnival opened, and the intensity didn't show any signs of lessening. The cement-block walls of the gym were decorated with bright, colorful posters of the work Children of the Day did around the world.

A steady stream of people still came through the gym doors, and the roar of talk and laughter seemed to shake the rafters. Prairie Springs was turning out in force to support its favorite charity.

There were a good number of folks from Fort Bonnell, as well. That turnout pleased him. A bit of friction naturally existed between the small town and the giant army post that dwarfed it, with the usual stress of soldiers getting into trouble when they were off post. Having soldiers support local events brought a positive balance.

"Hey, Chaplain, how are you?"

The man who halted in front of the fishing booth looked like a typical rancher in jeans, western boots and a plaid shirt, but Steve had known Evan Patterson since even before he wore army green.

"Hey, Evan." He grabbed Evan's hand. "This can't be your little Paige! How did she get so big since the last time I saw her?"

The little girl with Evan smiled proudly, clasping both hands on the edge of the fishing trough. "I'm five," she announced proudly. "I'm going to go to kindergarten pretty soon."

"I guess you will, sugar."

The child's smile touched his heart. Big hazel eyes, tousled blondish-brown hair—Paige looked a lot like her daddy, and judging by the way she looked at him, she adored him.

Evan hadn't had an easy time of it since his wife left them, but he sure was doing a good job of loving that little girl.

"Reckon she better have a few tries with that fishing net of yours."

Evan handed over a bill. Steve gave him the net, and Evan put it in his daughter's hands. "Pick out a good one, now, honey."

Paige watched the plastic fish bob past with big eyes. It looked as if she'd be awhile deciding which to catch.

Steve leaned against the counter, glad to catch up with a man who'd stood beside him during some of the roughest days of his life. They ought to get together more often, and he felt a bit guilty about that. Just because Evan lived out of town on his ranch was no reason to fall out of touch.

"How's your sister doing since she was deployed?"

"Whitney sounds fine, but then, she would." Evan's expression said that they both knew what it was like in a war zone. They'd spent a lot of time there together. "I hear she's been getting letters from Betty Villard's granddaughters."

Steve nodded. "They're in Olga's grief program at the church, and I understand she set it up."

"Rough, what happened to those little girls." Evan glanced protectively at his daughter. "I guess it's really the aunt who's doing the writing for them. They must be about my daughter's age, since they're in her Sunday-school class."

Paige looked up from her preoccupation with the fish. "Who, Daddy? Who's in my Sunday-school class?"

"Amanda and Josie," Steve supplied the names. "Do you know them?"

"Sure. They're twins. I wish I had a twin."

That was one thing her doting father couldn't possibly supply. Steve pointed to a pair of yellow fish. "Those two look like twins. Why not see if you can catch both of them."

With a fair amount of splashing, she managed to get both fish into the net. "I did it, Daddy!"

"You sure did, sweetheart."

"That means you get a prize. Two prizes, as a matter of fact." Steve took the dripping fish and reached into his box. "How about a doll and a crown?"

"Wow!" She plopped the plastic tiara on her head and clutched the small plastic doll. "Thank you."

"You're welcome." He looked up, and his heart gave a little lurch. "Hey, Evan, here's Caitlyn Villard and the twins now. You folks ought to meet each other."

He waved. The twins, spotting him, came running.

Evan's eyes widened appreciatively as Caitlyn came up to the booth. Well, no wonder. She looked great in a pair of white slacks and a shirt the color of strawberry ice cream.

The twins were distracted from him by the sight of Evan's daughter and her prizes, giving him a moment to perform introductions.

"Caitlyn, this is Evan Patterson. He owns a ranch just outside of town, and his daughter, Paige, is in the twins' Sunday-school class. His kid sister, Whitney, is one of the soldiers the twins are writing to."

"How nice to meet you. I didn't realize Whitney had

family locally." Caitlyn shook hands, looking up at Evan with a warm smile. "Her e-mails to the twins have been so interesting."

Evan propped his hand on the counter and smiled down at her. "You folks are probably hearing from her more often than I am. I haven't had an e-mail in a couple of days. What's she been telling you?"

It wouldn't be fair to say that Evan was putting on the charm. He was just a naturally friendly, laid-back guy— or at least he had been before his wife broke his heart. It was a good sign that he was ready to smile at a pretty girl, wasn't it?

"She writes about camp life, what they have to eat, the children that she sees in the village. Anything she thinks will interest a couple of five-year-olds, I suppose."

Evan looked at the girls, who were chattering away excitedly. "Will you listen to that? How about if we walk these three around together for a bit? You can tell me how you're enjoying Prairie Springs."

Caitlyn shot a look toward Steve, as if wanting his advice.

"Sure, why don't you do that," he said. Well, what else could he say? Evan was a good ole boy, and he sure didn't have any claim on Caitlyn. "Go ahead."

"Fine. Thanks." She smiled at Evan. "We'll see you later, Steve."

"See you," he echoed, and watched the five of them walk off together.

That was good, he told himself. He wasn't emotionally free to love anybody, and Caitlyn deserved a little happiness.

So why did he feel like giving his fish pond a good hearty kick?

* * *

The carnival was finally winding down, and as much fun as it had been, Caitlyn was just as glad to see it come to an end. Mama had taken charge of the twins so she could work the cotton-candy stand. After all this excitement, the twins were probably overtired and long past ready to go home.

She was, too. At the moment, all she could think of was that she wanted to stand in a hot shower for about an hour or two. There was cotton candy in her hair, and she'd begun to think she'd never get the smell of sugar out of her system.

All around her, people were closing down their stands. Tired adults lugged even more exhausted children toward the exit, more than a few of the little ones crying out of sheer fatigue and overexcitement. They'd be lucky to get the twins home without a bout of tears.

Still, the children had enjoyed themselves. The twins had spent over an hour with Evan's little girl, making her realize how good it was for them to have someone else to play with besides each other.

It would probably help both of them if she made more of an effort to have that happen. She'd have to check with Mama about the possibility of setting up a play date, maybe with Evan's daughter and a few other children from Sunday school. It could help Josie get out from under Amanda's shadow, and probably other kids wouldn't let Amanda boss them around the way she did her sister.

Evan had certainly been easy to talk to, with none of the undercurrents she felt so strongly when she was with Steve. And he'd been a font of information.

Evan obviously thought highly of Steve. *He was al-*

ways there, always calm. It seemed like you could just look at him and feel better when everything was going crazy around us.

She took out her cash box and started to count the money, fairly sure no one would want cotton candy for the trip home.

Steve was a calming influence, all right. But what did he mean by shoving her off on Evan? Was that a not-so-gentle hint that she'd gotten too close to him? The more she thought of it, the more annoyed she became.

And it was Steve's misfortune that he came wandering over to her booth just when she had a good head of steam building.

"Went pretty well, didn't it?" Steve shifted from one foot to the other. "We had even more people than last year. And a news crew interviewed Anna for one of the Austin television stations. That'll be great publicity for COTD."

"Yes, it will." She began shutting down, not looking at him.

"I just wish she could have told those reporters that Ali was on his way." Steve leaned on the counter, apparently not intending to go anywhere very soon.

Still, his comment distracted her from her irritation with him.

"I'm concerned that we're wasting too much time waiting for the general to come to his senses. I'm going to meet with Jake tomorrow to go over alternate plans."

"I guess we have to come up with something." He paused. "You know, Jake's a good ole boy." He wasn't looking at her. "You two should have a lot in common, I'd think, both of you attorneys."

She slammed the door of the cotton-candy machine closed, making him look at her, startled.

"First Evan, now Jake. Will you please stop trying to fix me up with someone?"

"I didn't mean—"

"Oh, yes, you did." She planted her hands on the counter, determined to get this said. "Look, I don't know what's going on with you, but if I want a romance, I'll find my own candidate. Okay?"

He raised his hands in a gesture of surrender. "Sorry. Maybe I was being a tad pushy. Forget it."

"Fine." She snapped the word. She could forget his clumsy matchmaking efforts.

But she couldn't forget that he obviously felt she was leaning on him too much. He was clearly trying to let her know that he was off limits.

Well, fine. He was the one who'd kissed her, after all. But she'd gotten the message now. She wouldn't be weeping on his shoulder again any time soon.

Mama approached through the thinning crowd, pulling two tired girls along by the hand. "I'm going to head for home with these two. Now, don't feel you have to rush home, if you and Steve are talking."

Was her mother attempting a little matchmaking, too? "I'll be home as soon as I can. Believe me, all I want is to take a shower and get to bed."

Amanda tugged on Steve's pant leg. "We're going swimming tomorrow, Chaplain Steve. Why don't you come, too?"

"I'm sure Chaplain Steve has work to do," Caitlyn said quickly. Maybe it was time all of them stopped relying on Steve.

"Tell you what." He squatted down to Amanda's level.

"I do have a lot of errands to run tomorrow. But if I can, I'll come by the pool. Okay?"

"Okay." Amanda leaned against her grandmother, obviously too tired even to pester him.

"We're off now." Her mother turned the twins toward the door. "We'll see you later."

"Bye. I'll be home soon." When they were gone, she turned to Steve. "You don't have to do that. I'm sure you have things to do tomorrow."

"I said I'd try, and I will." He gave her a distant look. "Tomorrow is Carolyn's birthday, isn't it? Did you talk to the girls about that?"

"No. I decided not to bring it up." It was her decision, after all.

"I see."

He sounded annoyed. Well, fine. She was annoyed, too. She'd never felt so out of patience with him before, and right at the moment, she didn't care what he thought of her.

Chapter 12

He hadn't been making it up when he'd told the twins that he had a lot of errands to run. Steve trotted across the lawn toward the office wing of Prairie Springs Christian Church, intent on crossing a few more things off his list before the day grew any older.

He and Pastor Frank were cosponsoring a visiting missionary in September, and plans were already well under way. He just needed to check a few details on the arrangements with Frank so that he could send out a letter to the speaker.

As he reached the door, he spotted Olga Terenkov rounding the corner from the rear parking lot. She juggled what seemed to be a hot casserole dish, in addition to the oversize embroidered tote bag she always carried. She looked as if she could use a hand.

He smiled as she drew closer. Olga's denim skirt, cow-girl boots and the Stetson topping her blond hair announced the enormous pride she took in being a Texan. With a Russian accent.

"You've got your hands full." He swung the door open. "Any chance you want me to carry that?"

"I can manage, Steve, but thank you. How nice it is to see you today. I didn't have a chance to talk to you last night because I was so busy in the kitchen."

"And I was so busy with the fish pond, I never had a chance to eat." He followed her into the hallway. "We did pretty well, I hear."

Olga beamed. "The most we've ever made from the carnival. A Texas-size turnout, wasn't it? People are so kind."

"They sure are." He sniffed. "That smells like your special perogies. How about inviting me to share lunch with you?"

Olga's gaze slid away from his. "They are not for my lunch. But I promise, I'll make some for you another day." She paused in front of her office door, fumbling for keys in that oversize bag.

He took the casserole dish so she could find them. "You brought this to take to someone in need?" He did a quick mental inventory of folks on the prayer list he and Frank shared.

"No, not exactly." To his astonishment, Olga's fair skin flushed bright pink. "I brought them as a treat for Franklin."

"Franklin," he repeated. "It's not his birthday, is it?"

"No." The blush deepened. She turned away, hustling into her tiny office.

He followed her, setting the casserole dish on top of the bookcase where she indicated. Olga was a generous soul, always giving to people. What was there about bringing food to Frank to merit that blush? The answer that occurred to him had him staring at her, dumbfounded.

"Olga, is there something I should know about going on between you and Frank?"

"No. Yes." Suddenly Olga looked like the girl she must have been, caught between laughter and tears. "It is so foolish at my age, but I cannot help it. I have feelings for him."

He stared at her in consternation. Feelings for Frank Fields? That was a shocker.

"I know, I know what you are going to say. That I am too old for such things." Olga's Russian accent was becoming more pronounced as she spoke, a sure sign of emotion.

"That's not what I was going to say at all." He spoke slowly, feeling his way, anxious not to hurt her by his reaction. "But Franklin Fields—does he return your feelings?"

She shrugged extravagantly. "Who can tell with him, he hides his feelings so well. We have been friends and colleagues for such a long time. He probably doesn't think of me any other way."

"But you think of him that way." This didn't seem like a situation that would end well.

Olga fidgeted with the set of Russian nesting dolls on the table. "I didn't expect to. After Anna's father died in Afghanistan, I never expected to love anyone again. But sometimes love can surprise you."

The words seemed to resonate inside him, and he tried to shake them off.

"All this time I work with Frank."

Olga's usually firm grasp of English grammar was deserting her in her excitement, and Steve realized he was probably the only person she'd confided this in, which put an even bigger burden on him to handle it delicately.

"I admire and respect him, nothing more. But one day he turns and looks at me and *poof!* Just like that, I knew I loved him."

He had to speak. He couldn't let Olga walk right into disaster without trying to head her off.

"Olga, you know I love you."

She swung toward him, patting his cheek. "And I you. You are a dear boy."

"I just think—well, I'm afraid that Frank isn't looking for romance."

He shook his head, feeling as if he heard an echo. Wasn't that what Caitlyn had said to him last night?

"Well, of course not." She smiled fondly. "I know he is not looking for a new love. But if only I can break through that reserve of his, I am sure that he will see he cares for me, too."

"Olga, darlin'—" He took her hands in his. He'd have to tell her what he knew to be true. "Listen to me. Franklin doesn't want it generally known, but before he came here to Prairie Springs, he suffered a terrible personal loss. I don't want you to get hurt, but I'm afraid he's just not open to love."

Olga just looked at him for a long moment, her wide blue eyes slowly filling with tears.

"I'm sorry." He felt like a heel for telling her, but what else could he do?

"I am sorry, too." Making an obvious effort to control herself, she patted his hands. "Because I think, you know, that you are not just talking about Frank. You are talking about yourself, too."

* * *

Even sitting in the hot sunshine at the pool watching the twins take their swimming lesson, Caitlyn felt as if she were stuck under a dark cloud that pressed down on her, filling her with dread.

She leaned back in the lounge chair and tried to think about something—anything—other than the fact that today was Carolyn's birthday. And Carolyn was gone.

Dead. She used the word deliberately in her mind. No more euphemisms about it. Carolyn was dead, and anything that had been left unsaid between them would go forever unspoken.

She tried to focus on Amanda's efforts to conquer swimming on her back, but her mother's wistful words kept intruding. If only she and Carolyn had had the time to get to know one another as adults. They might have learned to be friends.

But they hadn't, and there was no going back.

There was no going back to the events of the previous night, either. Each time she thought of Steve's attitude toward her at the carnival, she became more upset.

What did he mean by trying to fix her up with someone, as if they were back in high school? She certainly wasn't interested in either Evan or Jake, as nice as they were, because she—

Well, she'd better not go there, either. Admitting that she had feelings, deep feelings, for Steve would only lead to heartbreak.

Maybe she should accept the fact that this was going to be a difficult day on all fronts, and let it go at that.

Mama would no doubt spend the afternoon crying. When they got home, she'd pretend nothing was wrong, but they'd all know there was. She'd try to ignore Mama's red eyes and keep the girls from making some comment.

Her throat tightened at the thought. Would it have been better to discuss Carolyn's birthday out in the open? She just didn't know.

Amanda, giving up on the backstroke, had decided to splash a little boy who was doing better at it than she had. Caitlyn started to get up, but the swim teacher had already intervened.

That was a relief. Amanda had to be corrected, obviously, but she didn't want to have to punish her today, of all days. She leaned back just as a tall shadow loomed across the hot white concrete.

She knew without turning to see who it was. She must be pretty far gone, if she recognized him without even looking.

Steve paused for a moment, not speaking, the shadow perfectly still. Then he dragged a chair over next to her, the metal base shrieking on the concrete, and sat down.

She turned to study his face, grateful that she could hide behind the cover of her dark sunglasses.

Today he looked distracted. Sober, with the usual easy smile gone from his eyes.

"I'm sorry," he said abruptly. "I owe you an apology for last night. I was out of line."

She waited for more, but apparently that was all he had to say on the subject.

"It's all right," she said, when the silence had stretched on too long. "Don't worry about it."

But it wasn't all right, not really. Steve had had some reason for his sudden attempt to interest her in other men. Either he didn't know himself what that was, or he wasn't willing to say it to her. He couldn't be honest with her about his feelings. There was nothing she could do about that.

He leaned his elbows on his knees, hands linked loosely. Instead of swim trunks he wore his usual uniform, so he evidently didn't intend to stay. The afternoon sunlight brought out golden highlights in his hair.

She wanted to brush that hair back away from his eyes, soothe away the worry lines that crinkled his forehead. But she couldn't.

Maybe a change of subject would restore a measure of peace between them. Steve obviously only wanted to be friends with her, so she'd talk to him casually, as a friend.

"Did you get all your errands accomplished?"

"What?" For a moment he didn't seem to know what she was talking about. "Oh, that. Yes, I did."

But the mention seemed to make him more distracted instead of less.

She sighed, turning her attention to the twins. The lesson was over, so the children were enjoying some free play in the pool. At least, she supposed *enjoy* was the right word. There was a lot of shouting and splashing going on, their high voices echoing shrilly as the kids played. Some of the waiting mothers were already pulling out beach bags and gathering scattered belongings, getting ready to leave.

Amanda pulled herself out of the pool and stood on the edge for a moment. "Look at me, look at me, everybody!" She jumped in, splashing everyone within reach.

Caitlyn bit her lip. Should she go and correct her now, or hope that was a onetime outburst that could be ignored?

Amanda jumped up and down in waist-deep water,

splashing Josie unmercifully. Josie backed away, holding out her hands in a futile effort to stem the tide.

"Scaredy-cat, scaredy-cat. You're too scared to jump in the water."

Josie began to cry. Caitlyn swung her legs off the lounge chair and reached the edge of the pool a step ahead of Steve.

"Amanda Susan Mayhew. You come out of the pool this instant."

Amanda looked so startled at Caitlyn's tone that she froze for a moment. Then, pouting, she trudged through the water to the steps. She climbed out, her lower lip jutting.

She stopped a few feet in front of Caitlyn, planting her hands on her hips. "I didn't do anything."

"You teased your sister." She tried to keep her voice calm and matter-of-fact. "You jumped off the edge of the pool, which you know isn't allowed. Now sit down on that chair until I tell you to get up."

"I don't want a time-out!" Amanda stamped a bare, wet foot on the concrete. "I don't."

"Too bad. You earned it. Now sit."

Amanda blinked. Then, lower lip protruding, she stamped across to the chair and sat, folding her arms in mute protest.

The overacting was so blatant that Caitlyn had to fight to suppress a grin. She caught Steve's gaze and saw that he had the same reaction. She bit her lip, averting her face so that Amanda wouldn't see her.

But Amanda was staring at something in the distance, her mouth open.

"Auntie Caitlyn, look! Josie!"

She turned in the direction Amanda pointed. Her heart stopped as a wave of sheer terror washed over her.

Josie was three-quarters of the way up the ladder that led to the high dive, climbing steadily.

Caitlyn wasn't sure how she got to the base of the high dive. She just knew she was there, gripping the ladder, with Steve right beside her.

"Josie," she called the name, trying to keep panic out of her voice.

Josie turned just enough to look at her, clinging to the railings. Her small face was set.

"Please, sweetheart, come down."

Josie shook her head.

"Josie, come down now."

But Josie reached upward. Her hand missed the railing. Her little body wobbled, swinging out from the stairs.

Someone gasped. Caitlyn kept her eyes on Josie, as if she could pin the child to the ladder by the force of her gaze.

After a seemingly endless moment Josie grasped the railing.

She could breathe again. Somehow, she had to stay calm. Upsetting Josie would only make matters worse.

"Josie, that's enough. You almost fell. Come back down here."

Josie climbed up another step. Then she paused and looked down again. "I can't. I'm going to jump off the high dive like Mommy did."

"No, Josie. No."

No answer. In that moment, as she listened for a response, she realized that the whole area had gone perfectly silent. The lifeguards had cleared the pool already. Even now they moved into place around the edge of the deep end, ready to dive into the pool the instant Josie hit the water.

Terror gripped her like a physical thing, a vise tightening on the back of her neck. Hitting the water from that height would be bad enough. What if Josie lost her grip before she reached the platform? For an instant she seemed to see her falling, falling...

"I have to go up after her."

Steve caught her hand, trying to pull it off the railing. "No, Caitlyn. Let me. I know you hate heights. Let me do it."

She stared at him. Steve meant well, but he didn't understand.

"I have to. The twins are my responsibility. I have to go."

She turned back to the ladder, grabbed the railing and started climbing.

The metal railings scorched her hands, but she held on tight. *Don't look up, don't look down, just keep going.* If she let herself think, she might panic.

Please, Lord, please, Lord. Let me be in time. Let me say the right thing.

Other people were praying, too. She could almost feel their prayers, helping to lift her up the ladder.

Steve, too. He would be praying.

Hear us, Father. Protect Your child.

Her sandal caught, and her foot nearly slid out of it. She stumbled, caught herself, her heart pounding erratically. She stood still for a moment.

Breathe. Don't look down. Breathe.

She had to get rid of the sandals before they tripped her up entirely. Holding onto the railing, she shook off the right one. Down, down…she finally heard it hit. She wouldn't think about how far it was. Then the left one.

Her toes clung to the rubber matting on the steps. That was better. She could move faster.

Climb, don't look down. What was the song she and Carolyn had sung at church camp so many times?

We are climbing Jacob's ladder…

Please, Father…

And she was at the top. Her breath caught. Josie stood at the edge of the platform, looking down at the water far below. Air, nothing but thin air surrounded her little body, and the slightest waver could send her over.

Carefully. Don't scare her.

Caitlyn sat down on the platform, swinging her legs around until she had the railing's post at her back. It gave her the faint illusion of stability.

"Josie," she said softly. "Come here, sweetie."

Nothing. Not even a shake of the head.

Keep your voice calm and conversational. Don't give way to the panic, or she might panic, too.

"It makes me dizzy to watch you standing there. Take a step back toward me, okay?"

A moment passed, then another.

Finally Josie took a cautious step backward. Her small figure in her pink-and-white polka-dot swimsuit was very straight.

I want you in my arms, baby. Don't you understand that?

"What are you doing up here?" She forced herself to sound relaxed.

"It's Mommy's birthday today." Josie's voice was matter-of-fact. "I'm going to jump off the high dive like she did."

Her throat clutched, and she had to clear it before she could speak. "You know, I remember the first time your mommy went off the high dive," she said. "I was here that day, watching her. She was eleven. That's six whole years older than you are."

Josie's head turned slightly, as if to say she was listening.

"You know, I don't think Mommy would want you to jump off when you're five. I think she'd want you to wait until you're older, like she did."

No response, and her mind raced, trying to find another argument that the child would heed.

"Mommy was a soldier, and she always followed the rules, remember?"

A nod this time.

"Well, the rules are that no one's allowed to climb the high dive without the lifeguard's permission. And you don't have that, do you?"

Josie shook her head. Slowly, slowly she turned around. Her face was white, her eyes huge and dark. "Manda said I was a scaredy-cat."

Her heart twisted. "Manda didn't mean it, sugar. Sometimes sisters tease each other or say things that hurt each other's feelings, but they don't really mean it. Your mommy and I did that when we were little, you know. Just like you and Amanda."

Josie took a step toward her, her face lightening a bit. "You did?"

"Yes, we did." She could almost breathe, now that Josie had moved toward her. "You and Amanda are a lot like your mommy and I were when we were little."

"I didn't know that."

Her heart hurt. Josie didn't know that because she never talked about Carolyn with her.

"I'm sorry, Josie. I think you wanted to talk about Mommy's birthday, and I didn't let you because it made me sad. And Amanda's being mean because she's sad. And you climbed up here because you're sad."

She took a breath, sent up another silent, fervent prayer.

"Wouldn't it be better if we could just be sad together, instead? I really need you to give me a hug right now."

She held out her arms. With a choked sob, Josie ran into them.

Caitlyn held her close, her tears spilling over. *Thank You, Father. Thank You.*

Chapter 13

Steve couldn't help himself. He had to run over to Caitlyn's that evening, just to be sure everything was all right with her and the children.

Every time he thought about how dangerous Josie's adventure had been, chills gripped his spine, and he sensed again the helplessness he'd felt as he'd watched Caitlyn climb that ladder after her.

Thank You, Father. You surely were with us in our trial today.

He'd been murmuring that prayer for hours, but it still seemed he hadn't said it enough.

Us. He couldn't help putting himself with Caitlyn and the children, either. Somehow, that fact made it seem that a relationship between him and Caitlyn wasn't so impossible after all. Maybe he was finally going to put the past behind him.

If he could.

He'd insisted on driving Caitlyn and the twins home after the incident, while the shaken swim teacher followed in his car. Caitlyn had seemed...

He paused, thinking about her reactions.

Okay, he supposed, all things considered. She'd climbed back down the ladder with Josie as if she'd never even thought of being afraid of the height. Her attention and concern was all for the children, without a thought left for him.

Well, that was what he'd wanted, wasn't it? He'd asked God to use him to bring her and the twins together. He hadn't expected it to happen quite so dramatically, but it seemed to him she was on her way now.

If that was all that came out of his relationship with her, if there wasn't going to be anything else, then he had to be content with that.

He parked at the curb and crossed to the wide front porch of Betty's house. He'd never felt quite so indecisive in his life, and he didn't like it.

He knocked on the door, glancing at his watch. It was later than he'd thought. The twins were probably already in bed.

Caitlyn opened the door. Her face was drawn with exhaustion. Maybe he should have just called.

"I probably shouldn't have come. I wanted to be sure y'all are okay."

Caitlyn glanced behind her. "I just got the girls settled. If they hear your voice, they'll be up again. Do you mind if we sit out here?"

"Not at all, but you don't have to take the time for me if you'd rather just relax."

She shook her head. "It's okay."

He held the screen door as she came out and followed her to the porch swing. This time he sat down next to her instead of shying away, as he had the last time they'd sat out here.

"They're okay," she said, her breath coming out in a sigh. She collapsed back against the cushions, as if the effort to stay upright was just too much.

"Difficult time?"

She managed a faint smile. "You know, I honestly think Amanda was more upset about what happened than Josie was. Mama and I took turns reassuring first one, then the other. Then just when we thought we'd gotten them both calmed down, someone would start to cry, and we'd have to do it all over again."

"I hope your mother wasn't too upset." Betty had been through too much in recent months to have to deal with more anxiety.

"Less so than I'd have thought. She says that after raising the two of us, she's used to kids trying to damage themselves." A shiver went through her. "I'm just glad she wasn't there to see it. That would have been far worse."

He touched her hand lightly. "What about you? How are you?"

Her forehead wrinkled. "How am I? I feel as if God picked me up, turned me around and put me back down again."

He hesitated, wondering how much to say. "Seems to me after an experience like that, a person might see things a bit different."

"Yes." For a moment he thought she wouldn't go on, but then her eyes met his candidly. "I get it now. What you were trying to help me understand. I love them. They're my responsibility for life."

Something that had been taut inside him seemed to ease. "Congratulations. You're a parent."

"Not a very good one."

"Don't say that. It's natural to worry about it, but you shouldn't. You'll do fine."

"I didn't do so fine dealing with Carolyn's birthday, did I?" She pressed her hand against the base of her neck, as if tension had tightened the muscles.

"You handled it the way you thought was best for the girls."

Maybe, if she'd taken his advice, Josie wouldn't have been up on that high dive today. But if so, maybe Caitlyn wouldn't have come to this realization about the children. God had a plan that he wasn't privy to, obviously, and sometimes the things that looked the worst turned out to be for the best.

"But I was wrong." The words seemed to burst out of her. "I was wrong. I should have talked to them about Carolyn's birthday, and I took the coward's way out. Is it always going to be this hard?"

He could hear the pain that lay beneath the words, and he wanted to do something to ease the hurt, but he knew he couldn't, not really. "You're still learning, so give yourself a pass on a few mistakes. Anyway, I guess kids can always come up with new ways to try their parents, even very experienced ones."

"With me the twins get inexperience." She managed a smile. "But I guess we can learn together."

He hesitated. He didn't want to bring up something else painful, but if not now, when would he ever do it? "I've been thinking that it might help your relationship with the girls if you dealt with your own unresolved feelings about your sister."

Her face tightened. "There's nothing to resolve. Carolyn's gone."

"Carolyn's gone, and you're angry with her for dying."

She shook her head. "You may be right, but I'm just too tired to analyze my own grief right now."

He couldn't seem to leave it alone. "If you could just deal with your own grief—"

She shot off the swing so abruptly that it shook. "Don't, Steve."

He stood, too, his heart wrenching with pity for her. "I'm sorry. I'm just trying to help."

"Help?" She echoed the word. "How can you help me deal with my grief? You know, I had it right the first time when I said you didn't understand. You try to help everyone else, when the truth is that you haven't even dealt with your own grief yet."

He stood there for a moment, feeling as if she'd slapped him. Then he turned and walked away, leaving her all alone.

Caitlyn hung up the phone in her office and pushed back from her desk, feeling as if she'd been hit with a sledgehammer. This Monday had been difficult enough without a pressure-filled call from her boss back in New York about her continued absence.

She ran her fingers through her hair. Coffee, she needed coffee. It would clear her mind. Too bad it wouldn't work that well on her heart.

She'd been busy kicking herself since snapping at Steve. She'd spoken out of her own hurt and exhaustion, but that didn't excuse it.

She'd started to call him a dozen times on Sunday, but each time she'd backed away. Maybe she shouldn't have said the words, but she knew in her heart they were true. Steve was counseling other people with their grief, but he had yet to deal with his own. The proof of that was in the way he'd walked away without a word.

She crossed the office and headed down the hall toward the kitchen, where surely there would be some coffee brewing. Maybe she ought to concentrate on her job problems, although they seemed almost as intractable as Steve.

Olga was already standing at the coffeemaker, pouring a mug. After one look at Caitlyn's face, she handed it to her.

"You are in need of this much more than I am," she said.

"Thanks." She put a spoonful of sugar into the mug while Olga fixed another for herself. "I guess I need something to wake me up this morning."

Olga took her arm and led her to a seat at the table, sitting down next to her. "It is more than waking up that's the problem, I think."

She stared down at her coffee, unwilling to open her mouth about any of her problems for fear too much would come spilling out.

Olga patted her hand. "I won't say anything to anyone. That's part of being a counselor, whether we're in my office or at the kitchen table."

She thought of Steve, unable to tell her about General Willis no matter how much he'd wanted to. Olga, too, had her code.

"Life just seems so difficult right now." The temptation to pour it out to a sympathetic ear was too strong. "My firm back in New York is putting pressure on me to go back."

"That bothers you." Olga's voice was warm and caring.

"I thought I'd have more time. The twins—there's so much still to be done here. And besides, there's Ali. I have a responsibility to him, too."

"Responsibilities in many directions, it seems. That makes it hard to decide which is most important."

Something in her bristled at that. Would she really say that her career was more important than the twins? Of course she wouldn't.

"The girls come first. They have to."

Olga nodded. "It makes decisions easier when you know what comes first."

"It's not as simple as that." If it were, she wouldn't be struggling. "Frankly, I can make a lot more money back in New York."

"And the twins need money."

"Well, no, but—" She shook her head. "All right, I get it. When I talk about going back, it's for my sake, not theirs."

Olga smiled. "I wouldn't put it so harshly, but yes, I think that's so."

"Fair enough, but I can't spend the rest of my life in Prairie Springs."

Olga's eyebrows shot up. "What is wrong with Prairie Springs?"

Caitlyn couldn't help but smile at the expression on her face. "Nothing. Everything. I spent eighteen years of my life preparing to leave this place."

"And I spent many more years of my life preparing to be here!" Olga threw up her hands in an extravagant gesture.

"You're an adopted Texan," she said. "You chose this life."

"Of course! I love it here. I love all things Texas—the size, the people, the friendliness that just wraps around you." She smiled slyly. "And the wonderful men. Like Steve."

The name pricked her heart. "Now, Olga, don't tell me you have a crush on him."

"He is a sweet boy, but no, I do not. I think perhaps he is interested in you."

Not anymore. She shook her head. "Don't try to matchmake for me. I'm not in the market."

"Why not? He would be a wonderful father for the twins, besides being perfect for you."

"I'm not interested." Did Olga know what a fib that was? She sought for a way to divert Olga's attention from her love life. "Anyway, you should be looking for a romance of your own. You're still youthful, beautiful and so full of life. Isn't there some cowboy we can lasso for you?"

To her surprise, Olga's blue eye grew serious at the question. "I am, as the saying goes, into someone who's just not into me."

"Olga, I'm sorry." She clasped Olga's hand, wondering who on earth her mystery man could be. "I shouldn't have said anything."

"It's all right." She seemed to look off into space for a moment, perhaps envisioning the man of her dreams. Then she shook her head. "It is probably for the best. Anna wouldn't like me to date, anyway."

"I'm sure—" she began, and then censored herself. How did she know how Anna would react at the thought of her mother dating?

"Yes, it is best." But the sorrow in Olga's voice made

Caitlyn long to do something to make the situation better for her.

"You know, mothers and daughters, no matter how much they love each other, can struggle sometimes." Her own relationship with her mother had certainly changed and deepened since she'd come home. "Anna might be bothered at first, but maybe she just needs help seeing you in a new light."

"Maybe," Olga said, her tone doubtful. She patted Caitlyn's hand. "I'll tell you what, little Caitlyn. I will pray for you, and you will pray for me. And maybe our Father will show us the answers for both of us."

"I hope so." She really did, although she suspected that her faith wasn't nearly as strong as Olga's.

"Caitlyn, come in," Anna's voice called as Caitlyn tapped at the French door in response to a message that Anna wanted to see her.

She pushed open the door and came face-to-face with Steve. For a moment she couldn't speak—couldn't even breathe.

Finally she managed a nod. "Hi, Steve." Her voice sounded strained, even to her.

Steve's smile was more of a grimace. Well, what could she expect? She responded to his concern for her family by slapping him in the face with his own grief.

"Come over here, you two." Anna didn't seem to notice anything wrong. "Dr. Mike is calling any minute now, and he wants to talk to all of us."

"Is something wrong?" She turned toward the desk, glad to have something to distract her from Steve's presence. He took a step back, gesturing for her to go first.

Anna shrugged, spreading her hands in a movement

that reminded Caitlyn of Olga. "I guess we'll find out as soon as his call comes through."

Steve followed her to the desk. "I wish we had more progress to report on Ali's situation."

He sounded more natural now, and Caitlyn felt as if she could breathe again.

"Here he comes." Anna came to attention behind her computer, and they hurried around the desk.

Steve pulled a chair over for her and then stood behind it. She was very aware of his hands braced on its back, inches from her shoulders.

Dr. Mike's face came into focus on the screen against a background of what looked like a mud wall.

Anna adjusted the microphone. "It's good to see you, Mike. How are things there?"

There was a pause before his voice came through. "A little quieter, thank the good Lord for that. What's going on with you folks? You make any progress with General Willis yet?"

"I wish we had." Steve leaned forward between the chairs, speaking quickly as if to take the brunt of their failure upon himself. "We've tried everything we can think of, but he's refusing even to see us."

Dr. Mike shook his head, and Caitlyn's heart sank at the seriousness of his expression. They were going to hear something bad—she knew it.

"How is Ali?" Anna said urgently, as if she'd gotten the same message. "Is something wrong?"

"The situation isn't critical," he said. "Yet. But Ali is not improving the way we'd hoped he would. It's beginning to look as if his condition isn't going to resolve itself."

"You're saying he doesn't have much time left." Anna's tone was clear.

"I wouldn't put it quite that bluntly." Mike gave them a tired smile. "But the sooner we get him someplace that's prepared to do pediatric cardiac surgery, the better off he's going to be. If he should have a crisis here, we're just not equipped to handle it."

"It's so frustrating." Caitlyn's hands clenched. "The child is an American citizen. There has to be a way we can get him here."

"Has Jake Hopkins been able to come up with anything?" Steve put the question so cautiously that she knew he was remembering her anger at his attempt to push her toward the attorney.

"He's not very hopeful," she admitted. "If we can't get the cooperation of a relative, and that means the general, our next best bet is a diplomatic intervention. He spoke to you about it, didn't he, Anna?"

She nodded. "I've been contacting everyone I can think of. We've had some encouragement, but nothing solid yet."

Mike frowned. "There's no way to have the foundation take responsibility for Ali?"

"Jake says not." Caitlyn hated admitting that, and she could feel Anna's frustration in the way her hands gripped the edge of the desk. "Children of the Day simply doesn't have any standing in the case, not legally, anyway. State law says we need a relative."

She glanced at Steve. He'd fallen silent just when she'd expected his comments. He seemed to be staring at the computer screen without seeing it, as three vertical lines appeared between his brows.

She nudged him. "Any suggestions?"

He looked at her as if she were a stranger, and blinked, turning back to the screen. "Mike, do you think you can get us some video clips of Ali?"

Mike's eyebrows lifted in surprise. "Yes, I guess so. One of the nurses who is stationed here has been showing off a new camera. In fact, she might have already taken some footage of Ali."

"Can you get it to us as soon as possible? It doesn't have to be anything lengthy or elaborate. Just something that shows what he looks like—maybe have him say a few words in English if possible."

"You're thinking about what Miss Willis said," Caitlyn observed. She glanced from Anna to Mike's image. "She talked to us about how proud the general was of Greg, and she said that the general was always showing her pictures and movies of him." She felt a tentative excitement beginning to build.

Steve nodded, a smile touching his face, and she realized they were looking at each other as friends again. "He doesn't want to see us. I wonder how he'd react to seeing his grandson?"

"I hate to put a damper on the idea, but how are we going to get him to watch it?"

He gave her that easy, lopsided grin that never failed to touch her heart. "That part is still to be worked out," he admitted. "But I think we might be able to get some help from Miss Willis."

"I know she'd do anything she could." Her excitement rose to match his. For a moment, as their eyes met, it was as if they were the only ones there.

Her breath caught as her heart seemed to go into a spasm. How long was this going to hurt so much?

Chapter 14

"He's coming. I can see his car pulling into the driveway. Are you ready?" Miss Willis, her wheelchair pulled up to the side window of her brother's study, swung around toward them, her face bright with anticipation.

Steve nodded, though what he was feeling was closer to dread. They were about to confront the general for what would undoubtedly be their last chance.

He glanced at Caitlyn, who stood next to the table on which they'd placed the laptop computer he'd brought. Her hands twisted together.

"We're as ready as we'll ever be, I guess," he said, trying to smile.

Miss Willis gave a nod and wheeled herself out into the middle of the room. She obviously intended that she be the first person General Willis saw when he entered the room.

That was for the best, although they hadn't really considered that when they made their plans. At least that would buy them a couple of brief moments while the general reacted to his sister's presence. When he saw them, the fireworks were bound to start.

He could only hope and pray that he wasn't creating an irreparable breach between Miss Willis and her brother by accepting her help in this.

Still, Lydia Willis was as determined, in her own way, as her brother was in his. If anything, that should play to their advantage. They wouldn't even have gotten into the house without her.

Miss Willis had planned their attack, as organized as a general herself. They would arrive at a time when she knew her brother was out on his usual round of activities. He was as regular about his routine as if he were still in the army, she'd declared.

She would tell the housekeeper she'd wait in the study for him. They'd be all ready when he entered the room.

An ambush, Miss Willis had insisted, her eyes sparkling.

He could hear the sound of the front door closing. Then came the faint murmur of voices—obviously the general and his housekeeper. She'd be telling him about his unexpected guests.

Next came footsteps approaching the room, sounding on the tile floor of the hallway in a crisp, military fashion.

There was barely time for one last prayer.

Our Father, we pray for Your guidance now. Open Marlon Willis's heart to hear our words. Open it to love You and to love this child of Yours who needs so much. Amen.

The door opened.

Marlon Willis strode into the room, erect and military. He saw his sister first, and his expression softened in pleasure.

"Lyddie, I didn't expect—" His words cut off abruptly when he saw who else had invaded his study. "What are you doing here?" he barked.

Before Steve could respond, Miss Willis spoke.

"I invited them, Marlon."

Color mounted in his face. "Well, you can uninvite them. I don't want the two of them in my house."

"You have to listen to them." Miss Willis sounded perfectly calm and composed. "They have something to say to you."

"I already know what they have to say, and I don't want to hear it again. I thought I'd already made that perfectly clear." He divided a glare between Caitlyn and Steve.

It was a look that had probably made many a young lieutenant quake in his boots, but Steve didn't feel even a tremor. He answered to a higher authority than a three-star general.

He should draw the general's fire from his sister. "We have some important information for you, sir."

General Willis's face darkened. "I told you I don't want to hear it. Now get out of my house, both of you, before I call the police."

"I'm sorry, sir, but we can't do that. Not until you've heard what we have to say."

General Willis stared at him for another second. Then he wheeled around. "Then I'll leave. You can find your own way out of my house."

Steve exchanged a startled glance with Caitlyn. That was the one thing they hadn't counted on—that General Willis would walk out on them before they could say anything.

Willis headed for the door, but before he could reach it, his sister wheeled her chair in front of it. Her cheeks bore a pink flush, and her face was set.

"Marlon Willis, I've heard enough of this foolishness. You will listen to what these young people have to say, and you will behave like the gentleman you were raised to be. I declare, Mama would spin in her grave if she could hear you today."

It was classic big sister scolding little brother, and the fact that they were both white-haired didn't alter the character of the exchange one bit.

"I'm sorry you had to hear this, Lyddie." The general had the grace to look abashed at his sister's lecture, but his face was still scarlet and his breath came in short, explosive gasps. "I don't know what story these two spun to involve you in their shenanigans, but—"

"They told me about Gregory's son."

Silence for a moment. Then he shook his head, for all the world like a bull shaking off flies that were tormenting him. "I don't want to talk about it."

"That doesn't change the truth," Miss Willis declared crisply. "Gregory had a child. That boy is now alone and helpless. You must love him for the sake of Gregory, if not for his own."

He flared up at that. "Gregory made his choice against my wishes. I told him I wouldn't be responsible for the consequences if he didn't listen to me."

"Gregory is dead." She paled a little on the word, but her gaze held his steadily. "This boy is all that is left of him. How can you turn your back on his only child?"

He was still shaking his head, but not with the decision he'd shown before. Steve's fists clenched.

Let it be Your voice he hears, Lord. Help him to listen to You.

"He threw it all away." When he spoke, the general's words were almost a lament. "All of the plans we made, all of his accomplishments."

"He was a fine boy," Miss Willis said gently. "One of the best."

"I told him a hasty marriage was a mistake. He always listened to me before." His gaze was tormented. "Why wouldn't he listen to me then?"

"Marlon, dear." Her voice was very gentle. "He was a man in love."

"I just wanted him to wait for a few more months. Until his tour was up. To make sure the relationship was genuine. Why couldn't he wait?"

"I know how he felt." Steve was astonished at the sound of his own voice. "Don't you remember what it was like?"

Please, Father, let this be the right thing to say.

The general turned slowly to focus on him. "What do you mean?"

"The first time you're deployed in a battle zone. Don't you remember what that was like?"

"It was a long time ago."

"You don't forget. I was there in the first wave into Iraq. I'll never forget."

The general nodded. "I suppose you're right. You never do forget that."

"It's as clear to me as if it happened yesterday." His throat tightened, and he had to force himself to go on. "The pressure, the uncertainty. The tension of all the soldiers around you. The sense that your life could end at any minute when you see your friends die."

A spasm of some emotion crossed General Willis's face. "That's what it is to be a soldier. Gregory chose that life."

"He followed his father's example," Steve said, "just as I did mine when I became a chaplain. And I know that if you have a chance at happiness when you're in a situation like that, you can't turn away."

He was betraying too much of himself, and Caitlyn was there, listening. But he had no choice. Ali's life depended on what was said in this room today.

The general's face was rigid. Were they getting through to him at all? Only the faintest hum from the computer broke the silence.

"I think I know what Gregory was feeling," Steve said quietly. "I've felt the same thing, too. When you find love in the middle of destruction, it's so rare and beautiful that you can't ignore it."

"You can wait." His voice was harsh.

"No. You can't wait, either, because if you wait, you might lose it." He thought of Elaine and felt as if his heart would break all over again. "Please—" his voice choked, "don't turn your back on your son."

"It's too late." Willis shook his head, and Steve thought there were tears in his eyes. "It's too late. If Gregory had lived—but now it's too late."

"It's not too late."

Steve blinked. He turned to stare at Caitlyn. She was looking at General Willis, not at him.

"It's never too late," she said. "It's never too late to make peace with those we love."

* * *

Caitlyn stiffened to bear the weight of the general's stare as he turned toward her. Was she doing the right thing by intervening now? She wasn't sure, but somehow she felt compelled to speak.

"What do you know about it?" His voice was gruff, his gaze frosty.

She swallowed the lump in her throat. "My sister and I weren't as close as sisters should be. I never had the chance to make peace with her."

"It's not the same," he began.

"My sister was a soldier." Caitlyn realized that for the first time, she was saying the words proudly. "Don't you tell me it's not the same. She died in action, along with her husband."

She stared at the general, daring him to make light of her loss in comparison with his.

He didn't move, but it almost seemed that he winced in pain. "I'm sorry for your sacrifice," he said finally.

"I think it's earned me the right to be heard." She held herself upright, her hand pressing against the table.

He jerked a nod of acceptance.

"My sister left five-year-old twin girls," she said. "They're the same age as Ali. I'm responsible for them now."

She thought he was about to speak, so she swept on. She had to get this said while she could, because it had been burning in her the whole time she'd been standing in the general's study, listening to his grief.

"I thought I could ignore my feelings and just go on. But I can't." Her voice shook. "I'm angry with Carolyn, you know that? I'm angry with her for dying and for leaving her children. I'm angry that we never got the chance to be friends as adults. Angry that Carolyn left me to be a parent to those girls when I don't know how."

She took a breath, realizing she felt freer for having said it.

"I don't have the answers yet, but I know now I have to deal with my anger and grief so I can love those children." She took a step toward him, holding out her hand. "Please. Don't let your anger and disappointment get in the way of loving that child."

He didn't respond.

She sagged, reaching behind her to grasp the table. She'd failed, and she didn't have anything left.

"Listen to them," Miss Willis said softly. "This little boy is all that we have left of Gregory."

Still he didn't react. And then Caitlyn realized that there were tears in his eyes. His lips were pressed so tightly together because he had to keep them from trembling.

Now was the time. She glanced at Steve, and he nodded. She switched on the video clip they had set up on the computer.

For a second nothing happened, and she had a moment's fear that she'd messed it up. Then the flap of an army tent appeared on the computer screen.

A hand pushed the tent flap away, and the camera moved inside, to focus on a small figure sitting crosslegged on a cot. The camera zoomed in.

The boy was playing with a toy soldier—one of those little action figures so beloved by little boys. He looked up suddenly, smiling at the camera, and she heard General Willis gasp.

"Hi, Dr. Mike." Ali gave an engaging smile. "See my soldier?"

"That's pretty cool." The voice of the cameraman was Dr. Mike's. "Where did you get him, Ali?"

"One of the nurses, she gave it to me. She say he is like my father."

"He sure is. That was a nice present. Do you remember your daddy?"

Ali's eyes were huge in his thin face. "I remember. He used to sing to me—a funny song about having Texas in his heart."

"I know that one." Mike sounded as if he was having trouble controlling his voice. "Listen, how about saying hello to our friends in Texas? Remember how we practiced it?"

Ali sat up very straight. "I remember." He grinned at the camera. "Howdy, y'all."

The screen went blank.

Caitlyn held her breath. That was it. They'd given everything they had. Would it be enough?

Please, Lord. Please, Lord.

She turned slowly to look at the general.

Tears streamed down his face. "Gregory," he murmured. "He's just like my Gregory."

Steve watched the general. The man had been staring out the window for the past five minutes, struggling to regain his control. He might never forgive them for having seen him weep. Steve could only pray that wouldn't make a difference to his decision.

Miss Willis had pulled her wheelchair up to the coffee table. She placidly drank a glass of sweet tea that she'd told the housekeeper to bring for them, taking control as if this afternoon visit were the most common thing in the world.

Caitlyn had a glass of tea in front of her, too. She'd taken a long drink of it when it was first handed to her. Since then she'd sat in the corner of the leather sofa, looking about as dazed as he felt.

They'd both said things in the past hour that they'd never intended to say. He'd given away too much about his feelings for Elaine—things he wasn't sure he understood himself yet.

The truth was that each time he'd taken a step toward Caitlyn, his memories of Elaine had stopped him. Unless and until he could come to her with a whole heart, he had to stay away.

As for what Caitlyn had said—well, that was what he'd been praying for. If Caitlyn was finally coming to terms with her feelings about her sister, maybe it had all been worth it, whatever the outcome.

Had they succeeded? Surely General Willis would cooperate after his emotional response to the sight of Ali, but still...

Please, Father. I know You've been with us today. Marlon Willis is so close. Please bring him the rest of the way he has to come.

Willis turned from the window, clearing his throat as he stared at them. "Well, why are you all sitting around drinking sweet tea?" he said abruptly. "We should be making plans."

"We're waiting for you, Marlon," Miss Willis said serenely.

"Let's talk strategy." He came toward them, rubbing his hands together, very much the general in control again. "What's our first step to getting my grandson here where he belongs?"

Thank You, Lord. Praise You for this answer to our prayers.

Steve nodded to Caitlyn, trying to emulate the general in controlling his emotion, although he felt like shouting with thanksgiving.

"Caitlyn is the one who has been working with the attorney on the legalities of the situation. She can fill you in."

Caitlyn straightened. "I'm an attorney myself, but since I'm not licensed in Texas, I've been consulting with Jake Hopkins, a local attorney."

That was a wise move, establishing her bona fides. Willis was someone who would respond to that.

"Hopkins is a good man," Willis said. "I've heard him mentioned favorably." He sat down in a leather armchair across from her, apparently ready to listen.

"The process shouldn't be difficult at all," she said, seeming to gain confidence as she went. "Jake will be happy to talk with you about it, but basically, you apply to the court to be Ali's conservator. In that role, you have the right to make decisions about his future. Including, obviously, where he lives and his medical care."

"I'm the boy's grandfather. I should be his guardian, not a conservator, whatever that means."

Obviously now that the general was in, he was in completely.

"You will be, in every way. It's just that applying for conservatorship is the simplest and fastest method of getting Ali to the States, in case he has to have surgery." Caitlyn was quick and incisive now that she was on familiar turf. "Jake will get an emergency hearing with a judge, and under the circumstances, it will be approved very quickly, possibly in a matter of hours. Then you'll have the authority to bring Ali here for good."

He nodded. "Sounds straightforward enough. What about Children of the Day? How do they fit in?"

"We'll be glad to arrange for transport and do anything we can to make things smooth and easy for you and Ali. We already have a pediatric cardiologist on standby in Austin, but if you prefer to make your own arrangements, of course you're free to do that."

"No, no." He waved that suggestion away. "This is your area of expertise."

"Very well." Caitlyn hesitated, and Steve wondered if she was about to express her relief. But she didn't. Maybe she guessed, as he did, that the general would prefer to keep things businesslike. "Jake will get in touch with you sometime today, Chaplain Steve will organize the transportation and I'll alert the medical team."

She rose, and he stood with her.

"Good," the general said gruffly. He hesitated, and then stuck out his hand. "Thank you. All three of you."

Steve didn't know about Caitlyn, but he was about ready to burst with pleasure. He shook hands with the general. Then he bent over Miss Willis, kissing her soft, wrinkled cheek.

"Thank you," he whispered. "We couldn't have done it without you."

She patted his cheek, her eyes sparkling. "We've done a good thing today, all of us."

A few more goodbyes, and then he was following Caitlyn out the front door. She seemed to be hurrying a little. Eager to get on with contacting Jake, he supposed.

She started down the few steps from the porch to the

sidewalk. At the bottom she stopped abruptly, clinging to the railing, her face averted.

"Caitlyn, what is it?" Alarmed, he put his arm around her for support. "Are you ill?"

"No." She looked up at him. Tears spilled over onto her cheeks, but she was smiling. "We've done it, Steve. We've really done it."

His heart seemed to be caught in a vise. "Yes." It was all he could say. "We've done it."

Chapter 15

Caitlyn hurried down the church hallway toward the grief center, on her way to pick up the twins from their session with Olga. Twenty-four busy hours had passed since their confrontation with General Willis. So much had been accomplished that it seemed impossible it had only been a day.

She'd been too busy to think about anything personal, and perhaps that was just as well. She hadn't quite assimilated the things she'd revealed about herself in that emotional exchange.

As for what Steve had revealed—no, she didn't want to consider what that meant for him. Or for them, if there was a *them*.

Olga came out of the children's center as Caitlyn reached it, her face breaking into a huge smile. "Caitlyn. I have been hoping to see you today so that I could say how happy I am at your accomplishment. It is an answer to our prayers."

"Not just my accomplishment," she said quickly. "Many people worked to make this happen. To tell you the truth, I'm still amazed that we succeeded."

She paused, considering the words. When had she become so pleased to share the credit for a success in which she'd participated?

Olga surveyed her. "The children are playing a game with the volunteers. Do you have time to wait until they have finished?"

She glanced at her watch. "Yes, of course."

"Come into my office, then." Olga opened the door. "We will have a little cup of tea."

She wasn't sure she wanted tea, but she let herself be led into Olga's small, cozy office, eclectic in its mixture of things Russian and Texan. Olga busied herself with an electric kettle, chattering away about the children's activities while she did.

The cozy room and Olga's voice were oddly soothing. Caitlyn leaned back in the rocking chair that was the visitor's chair. She hadn't slowed down in what felt like days.

Olga set a delicate china cup and saucer on the small table, and Caitlyn was reminded of Miss Willis. It looked like something she would use.

"You have been working hard for weeks on this project." Olga settled in the chair opposite her, balancing her own cup and saucer. "Now, when it is finished, will come the letdown."

"I guess that's true." Caitlyn took a sip of the pale brew, inhaling its mint fragrance. "The euphoria of succeeding has worn off." She'd often felt that way after a big case, so why should she be surprised at the feeling now?

"And with the end of your part in all this, Ali's future is in other people's hands," Olga said. "So you are at loose ends."

Caitlyn nodded. "I suppose that's true." She hadn't really paused to consider that.

"I understand, because it is the same for me. I work with a child or a family for weeks or months, and I become very attached to them. But then they move on. And I must be content that I did my best."

"I hadn't thought of it that way." She took another sip of the tea, feeling its relaxing warmth moving through her. "What we've accomplished for Ali and his grandfather is very satisfying."

Olga nodded. "It is. Still, I suppose you often experience that kind of satisfaction in your law practice, too."

Did she? She found herself looking at that question with a skeptical eye. Did she feel the personal involvement in her ordinary cases? The answer was no.

Well, that was natural enough. At the firm, she usually dealt with business issues, not with a little boy who needed a family. She might have an intellectual sense of triumph, but not an emotional one.

Was she really comparing the two? There was no comparison between a part-time job with a nonprofit and a career with a prestigious law firm.

Olga, bless her heart, had a way of leading you into thinking of things you really hadn't considered before, and maybe didn't want to consider now. Maybe a change of subject was a good idea.

"I've been meaning to mention to you that the twins haven't heard anything from Whitney and John in several days."

"They haven't?" Olga made a note on the pad at her

elbow. "Their unit may simply be out on a mission or in an area where there is fighting, so that they don't have time to communicate. I'll see if I can find out anything." She raised an eyebrow as she looked at Caitlyn. "Things are a little better with you and the twins, yes?"

"Yes, I guess they are." She hesitated, but Olga should know what was happening with the twins in order to counsel them appropriately. "They had a rough time of it on their mother's birthday. We all did, as a matter of fact, but I think we crossed a bridge or two in getting through it together."

Olga nodded. "Sometimes it's in the most difficult times that the most progress is made. You're finding that, I think."

"I suppose I am." She looked down at the liquid in her cup. "I've finally had to admit that I've been angry at Carolyn."

"Naturally," Olga said placidly.

"It doesn't seem natural to me," she protested. "My sister is dead. I should be sad, but not angry."

"The anger is a part of grief for everyone. It takes different forms for different people, but it has to be dealt with."

She thought about what Steve had said about confronting her emotions where Carolyn was concerned. "I guess I need to come to terms with those feelings, but I don't know how."

"You're talking about it instead of hiding from it," Olga pointed out. "That's a good first step."

She had felt a sense of relief since she'd come out with her feelings in that painful interview with the general. She hadn't wanted to, certainly hadn't planned it, but when she saw her own emotions mirrored in the general's, she'd had to speak.

"What comes next?" She managed a smile. "I know it might not be that cut-and-dried, but for the twins' sake, I have to work on this."

"I understand. You're a lawyer, and you are used to identifying a problem and then working on a solution. This is not that complicated, although it can be hard to do. Forgiving. And being forgiven." Olga smiled, perhaps a little sadly. "We all need that at times."

Her throat tightened with a familiar ache. "Carolyn's not here to forgive. Or to forgive me."

Olga leaned forward, patting Caitlyn's hand. "Carolyn is in God's hands now, and God knows her heart. And yours. Talk to Him about it. Talk to her, even, as if she could hear you. Let God show you what is needed, my dear."

"That's it?" She looked at Olga, finding comfort in the warmth of her expression.

"Yes." Olga rose. "I will check on the children. Just sit and finish your tea."

She should get up. Go on to the next thing—take the children home, help Mama with supper. Instead she leaned back in the rocker.

Is that what I need, Father? Tears stung her eyes. *I want so much to be a good mother to those children. I wish I had been a better sister to Carolyn.*

Forgive, Olga had said. And be forgiven.

I forgive you, Carolyn. I forgive you for dying, for leaving us, for forcing me into a new life. Please forgive me. Forgive me for being judgmental, for thinking my choices were so much better than yours. Forgive me for not being a better sister.

All was still in the small room. Peace seemed to settle into Caitlyn's heart.

Thank You, Father.

The sound of the door opening made her turn around. Amanda and Josie rushed in, and she held out her arms to them, her love overflowing.

Steve sat at his desk, a half-written letter of condolence in front of him for the family of a casualty. He couldn't seem to concentrate, and he wouldn't let the writing of those letters become rote.

He put down his pen and folded his hands, staring at the paper in front of him as he tried to form a prayer. The problem was that he honestly didn't know how to pray in this situation.

He did know what he'd advise anyone else to do, didn't he? Pray anyway, and tell God exactly that. Maybe it was time to take his own advice.

Father, I'm coming to You in need of guidance. I have feelings for Caitlyn. I can't deny that any longer. But I can't—

What? What couldn't he do? He couldn't even articulate his emotions in his prayers. So he couldn't possibly hope to spell them out to Caitlyn.

She has her own grief to deal with now, Lord. I know that. I shouldn't do or say anything that would complicate things for her. Shouldn't I just try to be a friend? Isn't that enough right now for both of us?

He hesitated. Was he really asking for God's guidance? Or was he superimposing his own answers instead of listening for God's word?

He clenched his hands tighter together. *Please, Father...*

The telephone rang. He reached out, clearing his throat as he picked up the receiver. "Hello. Chaplain Steve here."

"Chaplain Steve, you have to come right away." A child's voice, and it took a moment to recognize it as Amanda's.

"Amanda, calm down. Does your grammy know you're on the phone? What's wrong?"

"It's Auntie Caitlyn."

His heart seemed to stop. "What is it? Is she hurt? Is anyone else there?" He fumbled for the cell phone in his pocket, trying to think what to do. Keep Amanda on the line, call 911—

"No." Amanda's words were interrupted by a sob. "She's not hurt. She wants to take us away."

"Take you away," he echoed, trying to make sense of the child's words. "Take you away where? What makes you think that?"

"Me and Josie heard her. She told Grammy about a job in the city, and how we'd all have to go and live there." She choked a little. "Please come, Chaplain Steve. I don't want to go away."

"I'll be right there." He was standing even as he spoke. "Don't worry, sweetheart. Everything is going to be all right."

He hung up and hurried for the door. He had to get there. Had to talk some sense into Caitlyn before it was too late.

What on earth was she thinking of? She'd said she knew she had to put the children first. She'd said she loved them and wanted to be a good parent to them. How could she possibly even consider taking them away from everything they knew and loved?

The questions kept bouncing around in his mind as he

drove off post and crossed the bridge that led to Prairie Springs. He fumed at every stoplight, wanting to hurry. Needing to hurry, to tell Caitlyn that she couldn't possibly do this to them. To him.

No. He backed away from that thought in a hurry. This was about what was best for the children.

The drive seemed to take twice as long as usual. Everyone in Prairie Springs had apparently decided to be out and about just when he had to get there.

Finally he pulled up at the house. Maybe he should have called first to be sure Caitlyn was home. She could be at the office. He'd been so upset by Amanda's call that he hadn't even thought to ask her when this happened or where her aunt was now.

He crossed the lawn quickly to the porch, jogged up the steps and rang the bell, trying to form some coherent argument in his mind. But he couldn't. All he could think was that she couldn't possibly go.

Caitlyn opened the door. "Steve, hi. I wasn't expecting you."

"I know." He glanced past her to the hallway. Everything seemed quiet. "Are Betty and the children at home?"

She stepped back, gesturing for him to come in. "Mama took the girls to the park, since it's a little cooler today. If you want to see them, they should be back in about an hour."

"I've come to talk with you." He studied her face, trying to discern something different there, but she looked the same as always. Beautiful.

"Come on back to the family room." She walked ahead of him toward the rear of the hallway. "Is it something new about Ali? Do you have an arrival date yet?"

"Not yet." He hadn't even thought about Ali since Amanda's call. "They'll let me know as soon as there's space on a flight for him, but it could be fairly short notice."

"Well, everything's set as far as the medical team is concerned. And I understand from Miss Willis that the general has a crew working overtime to turn a guest bedroom into a perfect haven for a little boy."

They reached the family room. The rug was cluttered with a dollhouse and an array of tiny furniture. Caitlyn stepped over it and gestured toward the chintz-covered sofa.

"Have a seat. Sorry about the mess, but they'd just haul it all out again when they get back from the playground, so it was hardly worth clearing up." She smiled. "Besides, singing the 'time to clean up' song once a day is enough."

He stood where he was. "I don't need a seat. Just an answer. How can you possibly move the girls and Betty to New York just because of your job?"

She just stared at him. "What—how do you know about that?"

So it was true. Anger boiled up in him, mixed with pain. "How could you do that? Those children are already dealing with enough grief and heartache in their lives. How can you even consider taking them away from their home, their friends, everything they know and love, just so you can run back to your job?"

Caitlyn was staring at him with an expression he couldn't read. Finally she spoke. "Actually it wasn't the same job. I've been offered a junior partnership if I return to New York immediately to handle a case that's come up."

"And that's more important than the children?" He

wanted to grab her, hang on to her, force her to understand. "You can't uproot them. You can't leave."

You can't leave me. That was what he wanted to say, but he couldn't.

"I don't understand you, Caitlyn. I thought I knew you. I thought you were proud of what you'd accomplished here, that you—"

"I turned it down."

He could only stare at her. "What?"

"I turned the offer down."

Caitlyn was quaking inside, but she kept her back straight and her head high. If she could face down an opposing attorney in a courtroom, she could handle confronting Steve.

Except that in a courtroom, her heart wouldn't be torn by the accusation in Steve's voice.

"But I thought..." He let that trail off, looking as if he'd just been hit by a two-by-four.

"It's pretty obvious what you thought." She struggled to control the pain and anger. *How could you think that of me, Steve? Don't you know me any better than that?* "How did you know anything about the offer to begin with?"

"Amanda called me."

"Amanda," she echoed. "But how did she know? Mama and I certainly didn't discuss it in front of the children."

"I guess she was listening."

"I guess she was." Anger made her words staccato. "So you took the word of an eavesdropping five-year-old and jumped to the conclusion that I was going to pack up the girls and my mother and jaunt off to New York with them."

"I didn't—"

"Yes. You did." Her hands clenched. "That's exactly what you did. I thought we were beginning to know each other. I guess I was wrong."

He shook his head. "Look, I'm sorry. I guess I over-reacted. Amanda was so upset that all I could think of to do was get over here and try to stop you. If I'd thought it through, I'd have realized she might have misunderstood."

His obvious emotion seemed to take away some of her anger. It was satisfying to know that he cared enough to act without thinking when he thought she was going to leave.

He put out a hand, as if to placate her. "I apologize. As a friend, I shouldn't have jumped to conclusions about you."

As a friend.

She wanted to be his friend. Of course she did. But even as she thought it, she knew she wanted something more. And it was something she could never have unless Steve was able to open up to her.

"No. You shouldn't have." She took a deep breath, trying to sort out her words. "You know, as much as anyone, how much I've changed since I came back to Prairie Springs."

He nodded. He seemed to be relaxing a little, apparently convinced the crisis was over.

But she couldn't let it go at that.

"I know now what's important in my life. And it isn't just about doing the right thing for the twins and my mother. It's not just about sacrificing what I want for them."

She struggled her way through the maze of emotions, sensing that she had to articulate this as much for her own sake as his.

"I've found out that God has put me here for a purpose, and that here, with my mother and the children, is where my true happiness lies. I can't uproot them. I'll make a new life here."

"I'm glad for you." Steve's voice had become husky, and his eyes shone as if with unshed tears.

She focused on his face, praying for the courage to say what she felt had to be said. "I've opened my heart to you about why I'm staying. Now it's your turn. Why do you want me to stay?"

His expression became guarded. "Why, I… I told you. For the children, for Betty. I… I know you're going to be happier here…"

His stumbling over his answer told her everything she needed to know, even if it wasn't the answer she'd hoped for, and her heart seemed to turn to stone in her chest.

"It's all right, Steve." She longed to turn away and evade his gaze, but she wouldn't do that. She'd face this through.

"It's all right," she said again. "You don't need to say anything else. I understand. I know you can't say what you don't feel."

He stared at her for a long moment, and it seemed that he was trying to articulate some new argument. Then, quite suddenly, he shook his head. In a moment, he was gone.

Chapter 16

By the time Steve's mind actually started registering, he realized he'd driven back onto the post, as if on automatic pilot. But not to his office or the chapel. Instead his heart had brought him to the Monument for the Fallen.

He didn't want to be here. Hadn't been here, in fact, since Elaine's death.

But something stronger than his own desires seemed to be pushing him. He parked at the curb, got out, and walked slowly across the grass toward the monument.

The designer had created a parklike space with grass and trees surrounding the central monument. Benches faced the center, and around the perimeter stood marble columns bearing the names of the fallen who had passed through Fort Bonnell.

He sat down on the closest bench, trying not to look at the columns. He didn't want to wonder which of them carried Elaine's name.

Why do you want me to stay?

Caitlyn's question had been simple enough. It was the answer that was difficult.

Or maybe it hadn't been simple at all, because of what he knew lay beneath it. They both understood that she was really asking whether there was a possibility of a future for them.

It had taken courage for Caitlyn to bare her soul to him, telling him what lay in her heart. Once she'd have said that relying on someone else for her happiness was the one thing she couldn't do. Now she was willing to risk heartbreak to let him know how she felt.

He cared about her. So why couldn't he say that?

Maybe he just didn't have enough courage. Or maybe he had some unfinished business to take care of first.

I can't.

That was the coward's answer, wasn't it? In the years he'd been here, he'd tried to comfort other people in their grief. Maybe he'd even succeeded, with God's help.

But he hadn't ever faced his own.

I can't.

Struggling to focus on anything else, he watched as a small group of people crossed the strip of green. A middle-aged man and woman, holding hands as if for support. A younger woman, pushing a toddler in a stroller, her head held defiantly high.

They paused at the center monument for a moment, reading its inscription. He didn't have to go closer to know what it said.

Dedicated to our fallen comrades. We will never forget.

The younger woman bent, taking something from the basket of the stroller. It was a single red rose. She laid it reverently on the plinth of the monument.

The group stood for a moment longer, heads bowed.

He shouldn't watch them. He should get up, go to them, try to offer solace. That was his role in life. But he couldn't.

They crossed the grass again, obviously knowing which column to approach. There they stopped. The older woman's shoulders shook with sobs, and the man put his arm around her. For a moment none of them moved.

Then the young woman bent to lift the child from the stroller. She took the child's small hand, using it to trace the letters on the column. A name. Just a name, but it was all the world to them.

Steve buried his face in his hands. *I can't.* But he couldn't stop it, not now. The images flooded back. The sights, the sounds, the smells.

Chaos. It had been chaos when the roadside bomb went off.

He'd started to run, shaking off the soldier who tried to pull him to shelter, knowing that the blast had been close to Elaine's vehicle. Too close.

She had been gone when he reached her. He hadn't been able to offer the simplest of comfort to her in her dying moments. All he could do was hold her and weep for what might have been.

It should have been me.

The words shocked him. He knew all about survivor guilt. He'd dealt with it often enough. He'd thought he knew it so well that he couldn't possibly feel it himself, and yet there it was.

Father. His heart reached out in prayer before he formed the conscious thought. *I feel guilty because I am alive and Elaine is gone. How can I forgive myself for that?*

The moment he asked the question he knew how it sounded. He knew what he would say to anyone else in that situation.

You are still here because God has plans for your life. That was what he would say, and it was as true for him as for anyone else he might counsel.

God had plans for his life, and surely those plans didn't involve shutting his heart away from the pain of loving. If they did, God wouldn't have brought Caitlyn into his life, challenging him to feel again.

He tilted his head back, eyes closed, feeling the tears on his cheeks.

He felt a touch on his hand and opened his eyes. It was the young mother, her expression hesitant. She glanced at the older couple, as if for encouragement, and they nodded, their faces tearstained.

"Do you have someone here, too?"

He nodded, understanding what she meant.

"We thought you might want this. To leave." She held out another rose. "Take it. We brought plenty."

His throat was tight. Now it was his turn to be ministered to. He couldn't speak, but he had to.

"Thank you." His voice choked. "I'd like that."

He stood, taking the flower. He should say something more to them, but they obviously didn't expect that. They walked away together, moving more freely now, as if they'd left some of their burden behind.

For a moment he didn't move. Then, holding the rose, he went to find Elaine's name.

* * *

Caitlyn forked Mama's oven-baked chicken tenders onto Amanda's plate and smiled at her. "Okay now?"

Amanda grinned. "I'm okay. We get to stay here in Grammy's house forever and ever."

"And Grammy and Auntie Caitlyn will take care of us," Josie added.

Mama set a casserole of scalloped potatoes on the table and bent over to hug each of them. "And no more listening in on grown-up people's conversations. Misunderstandings can only lead to trouble."

Amanda's face clouded. "Chaplain Steve's not mad at us, is he?"

"No, I'm sure he's not." Caitlyn managed to keep a smile on her face, regardless of the pain in her heart caused by just hearing his name. She sat down. "Whose turn is it to ask the blessing?"

"Mine," Josie said. She folded her hands and squinted up her eyes. "God is great, God is good, and we thank Him for our food. By His hands we all are fed, give us, Lord, our daily bread. Amen."

"Amen," Caitlyn echoed. *And let me be content with what You give me, Father, even though Steve is not part of my future. Amen.*

It was going to hurt for a while. There was no doubt about that. But she'd be all right. They'd all be all right.

The doorbell rang.

"I declare, if it's not the telephone, it's the doorbell interrupting dinner." Her mother started to rise, but Caitlyn got up quickly.

"I'll get it, Mama. You sit still."

Before she reached the door, she could see Steve's

tall figure through the glass panels. Her heart began to pound.

She opened the door. His face was drawn, and she couldn't read his expression.

"Can we talk? Please?"

She nodded. "My mother and the twins are in the kitchen—" And they'll hear everything we have to say to each other. But he surely realized that.

Steve glanced around, as if looking for inspiration. Behind her, she could hear Josie asking who was there, while Amanda clamored to be excused from the table to find out. On the lawn next door, a clutch of teenage boys were playing a noisy game of touch football.

"Come on." He grabbed her hand. "We can sit in the truck. At least it'll be cool."

She wanted to protest, but he tugged her through the door. Giving in, she let herself be led to the pickup. She climbed into the passenger seat.

Steve hurried around the vehicle, got in and started the engine. A welcome blast of cool air came from the airconditioning vents.

"I guess I didn't plan this very well for a serious talk," he said.

Her heart began to thud again. "Is that what this is?"

He nodded. "I'm sorry. About before."

"It doesn't matter." She didn't want to rehash it, because if they did, she was bound to end up in tears. "If that's all—" She reached for the door handle.

He caught her hand before she could open the door. "No, that's not all."

He was very close in the narrow quarters of the front seat. She could see the fine lines around his eyes, the curve of his ear, the faint stubble on his chin that said he hadn't shaved since this morning. Her breath was doing something very strange, and she had to force herself to inhale.

He leaned back a little, looking at her. "Do you know where I went when I left here earlier?"

She shook her head.

"I went to the Monument for the Fallen." His jaw tightened. "Elaine's name is on it. I'd never even gone to see it before."

She really couldn't breathe, which seemed odd to think about at a time like this. "Why did you go now?"

He was silent for a moment. "I think God sent me there because I needed to say goodbye. And I needed to say goodbye because He brought you into my life."

"I don't want you to forget her."

"I know." His fingers closed over hers. "I know that. But there's a difference between not forgetting someone and using that person's death as a reason not to let anyone else in."

"Steve—" She said his name, troubled.

He took a breath, closing his eyes for a second. "I realized today that I've been feeling guilty for being alive when she was gone. I couldn't face it, but that feeling isn't right. That's not what she'd want for me, and it's certainly not what God wants for me."

Tears filled her eyes, and she tried to blink them back. "Are you all right now?"

He nodded. "Caitlyn, I want—"

"Wait." She put her fingers over his lips. "Let me say something first." She struggled to organize her thoughts. "The twins have to be my first concern now. I'm a mother. If I get involved with anyone, it has to be serious, for their sake. And I can't rush to change anything—"

He kissed her fingers, derailing her train of thought entirely. "Can I say something now?"

She nodded.

"When I walked away from the monument today, I knew I was free to love. We can take as much time as you and the twins need, but know this. I'm ready to be serious—I want to love you and those girls forever."

There weren't any words to respond to that. Caitlyn drew his face toward hers and kissed him—a kiss filled with the promise of a new tomorrow for all of them, with God's help.

Epilogue

With Steve holding her hand, Caitlyn hurried into the kitchen at Children of the Day, eager to share the good news he'd brought. Anna, Olga and Sarah sat at the table, coffee cups in front of them. Anna looked up instantly at their entrance, her eyes questioning.

"We have an announcement to make." Caitlyn glanced at Steve. "You tell them."

He grinned at her and then turned to the others. "I just got the word. The flight is all set up. Ali will be arriving in Texas next week."

"That's wonderful!" Anna grabbed first Caitlyn and then Steve in a huge hug. "I can't wait to greet that little boy. Does he have a medical attendant for the long flight here?"

"A nurse is coming with him. And David Ryland, a chopper pilot who's been seeing a lot of him and who is being rotated home, has arranged to come on the same plane. So he'll have plenty of company."

"You did a good job. Both of you," Olga said. Something in her bright eyes suggested that she knew what they weren't telling yet.

Caitlyn glanced at Steve, suspecting that her love was shining in every look, every touch, giving her away.

"Not just us. So many people have worked to make this happen. I have a feeling that the general pulled strings that went all the way to the Pentagon."

"One little life, saved from destruction," Anna said, and for a moment her expression was touched by sorrow, and Caitlyn knew that she was thinking of those who were lost.

"One at a time," she said softly, taking Anna's hand. "God's leading us to save one at a time."

Anna nodded, her face brightening. "We do His work in the world."

"Amen," Steve said, and each of them echoed the word.

* * * * *

Jill Lynn pens stories filled with humor, faith and happily-ever-afters. She's an ACFW Carol Award–winning author and has a bachelor's degree in communications from Bethel University. An avid fan of thrift stores, summer and coffee, she lives in Colorado with her husband and two children, who make her laugh on a daily basis. Connect with her at jill-lynn.com.

Books by Jill Lynn

Love Inspired

Colorado Grooms

The Rancher's Surprise Daughter
The Rancher's Unexpected Baby
The Bull Rider's Secret
Her Hidden Hope
Raising Honor
Choosing His Family

Falling for Texas
Her Texas Family
Her Texas Cowboy

Visit the Author Profile page at Harlequin.com for more titles.

THE BULL RIDER'S SECRET

Jill Lynn

My little children, let us not love in word,
neither in tongue; but in deed and in truth.

—1 *John* 3:18

To my siblings—I'm thankful for your
support and encouragement.

To Lost Valley Guest Ranch—A huge
thank-you for your contributions to this series.

To Shana Asaro—Thank you for being
a consistently fabulous editor.
You make every book so much better.

And to everyone at Love Inspired—
You're the best team, and I'm so
glad to work with you.

Chapter 1

Mackenzie Wilder didn't want to kill her brother in the true sense, just in the what-were-you-thinking, cartoon-wringing-of-the-neck sense. He'd gone and hired someone to help run the guest ranch for the summer—which meant the person would be completely involved in every aspect of her professional life—without asking for her input.

Had Luc talked to Emma before hiring this person? Not that it mattered. Their sister's head was so in-the-clouds in love right now that she'd say yes to anything and not even know what she was responding to.

Mackenzie bounded down the lodge steps, the screen door giving a loud whine and *snap* behind her. One of the new college-aged girls on staff for the summer was heading inside.

"Hey, Bea, have you seen Luc?"

"Earlier this morning he was in his office." Her face went dreamy, eyebrows bobbing. "He had some man candy with him, too." *Great.* Her brother had hired some young buckaroo who would have all of the female staff members sighing, swooning and requiring fainting couches all summer.

Maybe a what-were-you-thinking slug *was* in order.

"I just checked there, so now I'm headed to the barn. If you run into him, would you let him know I'm looking for him?"

If the man would just pick up his phone or respond to the texts she'd sent, Mackenzie wouldn't be on this scavenger hunt.

"Sure." Bea's short raven hair shifted with her perky nod.

"Thanks." Mackenzie's boots crunched across the parched asparagus-colored grass, the short walk doing nothing to calm her frustration. When she stepped inside the barn, it took her a minute to adjust to the lack of light. She heard her brother before she saw him and followed his voice. He was talking to Boone, one of the new staff members—almost all of them could be labeled that this summer. And the timing for the turnover couldn't be worse.

Usually they had at least a few veteran staff return for the summer. Ones who could lead and train the more transitional summer help. But this year, everyone seasoned had moved on to greener pastures. Which was why she and Luc had hoped to hire someone to work with them—or at least closely under their direction. Especially with Luc and his wife, Cate, expecting twin girls in July.

Luc finished his conversation, and Boone headed outside. Mackenzie waited for him to be out of hearing range before she laid into Luc.

"Tell me your hey-I-hired-someone text that I missed earlier this morning was a joke."

Luc scrubbed a hand through his short light brown hair, a grimace taking over his face. She was two inches taller than him, but he had her in brawn. Tall and straight, with muscles and barely existent curves, Mackenzie had accepted her body—or lack thereof—long ago.

"Nope. Not a joke. You know how much we need someone. And when I came across the right person yesterday, I snagged him." His hands went up like he was placating a skittish horse. "I know you're mad. Or I assume you are, but please trust me on this. Summer is completely stressing me out with the twins coming. We have no idea what that will look like, and I need to be available for them, for Cate."

"I get all of that." Mackenzie's rigid body kicked down a notch. "And of course we planned to hire someone, but I didn't think you'd go and do it without me."

"It just…happened." Luc leaned back against the workbench. "You know how hard it's been to find someone who's the right fit. And now summer season is here. We should have hired this person weeks ago. So, when I found a match, I jumped on it. I wasn't trying to overstep. I just—" his arms shot up in a helpless gesture "—feel better knowing we've got extra enforcements. Another lead. Someone who can handle the shooting range and staff and guests."

And how do you know this person can do all of those things? Do they have any experience?

But Mackenzie knew experience itself was over-rated. What mattered was leadership and customer-service skills. If someone could handle a horse and interact well with staff and guests, they could be trained.

She slid her tongue between her teeth to trap it. To keep from continuing her tirade. Luc normally didn't pull stunts like this. But the babies had him all twitterpated. She could probably extend some grace. This time. And if Luc liked this new guy, she probably would, too. They thought alike. Had that twin connection that tethered her to him.

"Okay." She tried to get okay with her *okay.* "So, who is it?"

"Me." That voice.

It came from behind her, and she whirled to face it. *Him.* Jace Hawke. He stood just inside the open barn door, holding a saddle, sunshine outlining his silhouette like he was some sort of gift from above.

What? Impossible. Luc would never have hired her high school boyfriend. The ex who had turned her heart from mushy soft to solid boulder.

With his cowboy hat on, Mackenzie couldn't tell if she was still taller than Jace by a quarter of an inch. Yes— they'd measured back when they'd been young and in love. Before he'd trampled her to smithereens.

She straightened her shoulders, wanting to use every advantage when it came to him. Wishing she were a giant and she could squash him like a bug, then flick him out of the barn.

"Kenzie Rae." He nodded in greeting. As if they were old friends, without a mountain range of hurt between them.

He'd always called her that. Like he'd trademarked it. Owned it. Owned her, really.

And he'd always had an irritating drawl.

Well, in high school it hadn't been irritating. Back then it had curled into her, deep and warm and mesmerizing. She'd been starry-eyed over him. For two and a half years they'd dated. And he'd taken off, leaving her a note? A stupid, worthless note.

Emma's fiancé was always surprising her with notes, and she thought it was romantic. The girl went all swoony over the gesture. But not Mackenzie. Notes were cop-outs. Used when someone didn't have the guts to say something to your face.

Jace's jeans and boots and blue button-up shirt fit him like a softened ball glove, outlining all of those I-left-you-to-go-ride-bulls muscles he'd accumulated over the years. And the same quiet confidence oozed from him.

The kind that destroyed everything in its wake. That told lies and then turned tail and ran.

"I'll store my saddle. Give you two a minute." He spoke to Luc, eyes toggling back to her before he strode toward the saddle room.

To store his saddle.

Because he was planning to stick around. Because Luc had hired him.

Seriously? Was she smack dab in the middle of a nightmare? Mackenzie slammed her eyelids closed. *He's not here. He's not here. I'm having a bad dream. I just need to wake up and then...* She peeked just as Jace disappeared through the saddle-room door. *He'll still be here.*

"You're playing me, right?" She held her brother's gaze. Glued herself there until he gave an answer as to why he'd do this to her.

His mouth was slightly ajar, as if he'd just been declared at fault in a deadly accident. "I didn't know it was like that. I didn't realize... I thought the two of you ended on good terms."

Because that was the story she'd spun the summer after graduation. Jace had left town to chase his dream and ride bulls...and she'd been all for it.

That had been so much easier to say than the truth: *he left me a note and took off. He never said goodbye. He destroyed me.*

Those weren't phrases Mackenzie let into her vocabulary. Ever. And she'd worked incredibly hard to not let anyone—especially her twin—know how much Jace's leaving had hurt her.

Turns out her efforts had worked.

"I ran into Jace in town last night, and we got to talking. He's good with animals and people. He knows cattle roping, team penning, steer wrestling. He can teach the other wranglers some new competitions. The guests would love it. I thought he'd be a perfect fit." Luc's shoulder lift said, *I'm sorry* and *I didn't know,* all rolled into one pathetic package that tugged on her sympathies.

Oh, Luc.

She understood why he'd hired Jace without talking to her first: the desperation he felt with twins on the way during their busiest time of year. But what was Jace even doing in town?

Why wasn't he off riding bulls? He couldn't need money, could he? Rodeoing would pay him far more than they ever could. And she'd followed enough of his career to know he'd been successful. Up until about three years ago, when she'd decided she couldn't handle it anymore and had to cut him loose. To not know what was going on with him. How he was faring. Not that Mackenzie ever planned to admit any of that.

Luc groaned. "I practically begged him to help us out for the summer."

Which translated in Luc-speak to "How can I go back on that? I can't unhire him."

Ugh. Her brother was her soft spot. Her best friend. And he was destroying her right now.

"When were you planning to share all of this with me? After he'd been working here for two weeks?" Mackenzie detested the tremor lacing her questions, even if it was so slight, Luc probably didn't catch it. She didn't do shaky. Or nervous.

She did strong and unbreakable.

Except when it came to Jace Hawke.

"I called you twice last night and you didn't answer." She'd fallen asleep on the couch. As usual.

"So then I sent you a text this morning."

"I was on a phone call." Their white-water rafting supplier had raised prices on this year's equipment without letting them know. She'd been negotiating for the sake of their business. *You're welcome.*

Jace cleared his throat, announcing his arrival as he exited the saddle room. Of course it hadn't taken him that long to store his saddle. He'd been giving them space. But the man couldn't stay in there forever, and that was how long it would take for Mackenzie and Luc to work this out.

Jace crossed to stand next to Luc. Like the two of them were a team in gym class Mackenzie wasn't invited to play on. He wrenched his hat from his head in a contrite gesture she didn't believe for a millisecond, sending honey-brown hair loping across his forehead.

"Luc." Bea popped her head into the barn. "Ruby took

a tumble and scraped up her leg. She's screaming for you or Cate."

"Coming." Luc strode toward the exit, slowing as he passed her. "We'll talk more," he said for her ears only. "Just…behave yourself. Please."

Well. If he wanted results like that, he shouldn't leave her with the enemy.

But then again, he'd *hired* the enemy.

Whoo-ee. The amount of loathing streaming from Mackenzie was enough to heat the town of Westbend in the dead of winter.

Jace hadn't forgotten what a powerful force the woman was, but over time the memory of her had softened. He'd remembered all of the good. Had clung to it. But there was nothing muted about the live and in-person version of Kenzie Rae. She practically vibrated with intensity.

Looked like she hadn't forgiven and forgotten with time. Hadn't decided that him up and leaving town was no big deal. Bygones. All in the past.

But then, she didn't understand why he'd done it. And knowing her, she'd rather kick him in the shin than listen to any explanation he had to offer.

"What are you doing here?" The woman could sure make her voice hiss and spit fire when she put her mind to it.

Jace definitely preferred being on Mackenzie's good side. A position he'd ruefully given up seven years ago.

"Working. When I ran into Luc last night, he told me what you guys need for help and asked if I'd consider it." Taking a job at Wilder Ranch was better than being worthless while his body healed enough for him to go back to riding bulls.

Jace had messed up so many parts of himself over the years that he couldn't remember what all had been broken or crushed. But this time had been the worst. He'd bruised his spleen and his ribs. Gotten pounded so badly in the head that he was currently rocking the concussion to top all concussions.

But none of that would have kept him from the sport he loved.

A broken riding arm had cinched his demise. His *temporary* demise.

Her eyes narrowed. "Why aren't you off riding bulls?"

He rolled up his shirtsleeve to give Kenzie a better view of his cast. Eight weeks casted and then some rehab. Maybe more, the doctor had said. Maybe less, Jace had thought.

Was that a flash of sympathy from Mackenzie? Maybe even concern? The whole thing passed so quickly, Jace couldn't be sure.

"I suppose I didn't notice your cast earlier because of the dark red haze of anger and annoyance at your very presence clouding my vision."

Jace laughed. He couldn't help it. She might hate him, but he didn't reciprocate the feeling.

"I've no doubt you've been injured before. Why'd you come home this time?"

"My mom's not doing well." Her emphysema had worsened over the last few months, but she was still working two jobs. Taking medicine and pretending that the disease wasn't killing her. The woman wouldn't slow down. Jace could appreciate that, but he also hoped to convince her to give herself at least the chance for more time.

But he wouldn't have taken a break from bull riding

just for that. He wasn't sure what that said about him. The injuries had forced him out. For now. And not one part of him wanted to admit to Mackenzie that his body was falling apart on his watch.

"I…" Her gaze softened. "I'm sorry to hear that about your mom."

"Thanks." The woman might be mad enough to breathe fire, but she was still concerned about his mother. Jace appreciated that.

"You know what I'm really asking." Her words clipped out—bitter, heavy and dripping with suppressed frustration. "Why are you *here*?" Translation: "Why are you at Wilder Ranch? *My* ranch."

Because I have to work. Jace couldn't handle inactivity. Laziness. Ever since he'd been fifteen and made a decision he was still paying for. He refused to sit around this summer, while he healed… And no one else was going to offer him a job that would interest him in the least for such a short amount of time. Plus Wilder Ranch—and Mackenzie's family—had been a haven for him during the worst time in his life. If this place needed him, Jace couldn't say no to that.

Even if Mackenzie wanted to drop a sledgehammer on his bare feet and then shove him across red-hot embers.

"Why not here?" His trite answer earned a flood of silent responses. First anger. So much that her cheeks turned a distracting shade of pink. The pop of color highlighted her striking features, rocking him like a gale-force wind. But before he could deal with his unwelcome surge of attraction, her look changed to resignation, then hurt. The last one didn't stick around long, but it was enough to *whop* him in the chest. To make his heart hiccup.

Jace had never wanted to hurt Mackenzie. Not in a million years. He'd tried talking to her about his plans. He *had* talked to her. She just hadn't listened.

Leaving her had been the hardest thing he'd ever done. He'd hated it. Had even hated himself after.

It had been about so much more than the two of them. It had been about his brother, Evan, who'd lost the chance to chase his dreams because of a stupid, lazy choice Jace had made.

So Jace had done it for him. He'd had to. There really hadn't been a choice.

But it was seven years too late for explanations, and Mackenzie would crush them under her boot if he offered any up.

"You can't do this job with a broken arm." Her chin jutted in challenge.

"Exactly what can't I do?"

"Ride a horse."

He chuckled at that silly idea, and she stiffened so quickly that he was shocked steam didn't shoot out of her ears. Jace really wasn't trying to provoke her, but the idea of a fractured arm keeping him from riding a horse when he still had one good one was ridiculous.

"My arm won't prevent me from doing this job, and you know it."

A strangled *argh* came from her. Sweet mercy, she was mesmerizing when she was angry. All alive and mad and sparking.

"Jace." His name on her lips shot a strange thrill through him. "Please don't do this." Gone was the burning fire. Now she was deflated. Edged with sharp steel— the deadly stab-you-through-the-heart kind. "I get that

Luc thinks we need you. And yes, we need someone. But *I* need it not to be you."

She packed a lot of punch into her spiel. And the fact that she'd shown him any kind of emotion—that she was practically pleading with him not to stay... Jace would like to grant her that wish. He really would.

But he couldn't. Because he needed this ranch. And this place needed him back.

It would be the perfect situation if so much hadn't gone wrong between him and Mackenzie.

"I'm sorry. But I can't."

"Can't? Or won't?" Her arms crossed over her Wilder Ranch–logoed shirt, forming a protective barrier, and a scowl marred her steal-his-oxygen features. Man, she was gorgeous. Tall, long and strong, with petite curves. Jeans that hugged her. Worn boots. She was—had always been—a walking ad for all things casual and country and mind-numbing. She hardly ever wore makeup. Didn't need it. And her wild dark blond hair had most certainly air-dried into those relaxed waves, because she would never take the time to blow-dry it or spend more than five minutes in front of a mirror.

And yet she could take down most of the guys Jace knew with just one piercing glance from those gray eyes of hers. They weren't blue. That was too simple of a description. They were storm-cloud eyes, so striking and unusual he'd yet to find another pair that had rendered him as helpless as hers did.

"Won't." She was already upset with him. He might as well fuel it. At least that would keep him from thinking she'd ever forgive him for leaving. From thinking that there could ever be a second chance between them.

Not that he wanted one. Because once Jace got the all

clear to go back to rodeoing—despite the doctor's recent warning that he shouldn't be doing anything of the sort—he'd be long gone again.

Chapter 2

"I'm not doing it. I'm not training him." Mackenzie winced at her petulant declaration, which was reminiscent of the tone her four-year-old niece, Ruby, used when she threw a fit. When the girl wanted to watch a show *right now*. And then usually ended up losing that very privilege because of her attitude.

Luc shook his head, his sigh long and ranking at a ten on the what-am-I-going-to-do-with-you scale.

The two of them sat on the corral railing as a gorgeous Colorado sunset showed off with pink-and-orange streaks kissing the mountains, and the cool air offered a respite from the warm late-spring day.

They'd been watching, encouraging and directing as the wranglers had practiced for one of the nightly performances they'd put on once the guests arrived. The first week might be rough, but it would come together.

It always did.

Ever since she'd been a little girl, Mackenzie had loved everything about Wilder Ranch. The guests who came back year after year. The wide-open land. The hot springs, the fishing, the shooting, the short drive to glorious, unfettered white-water rafting. This place just made sense to her.

Unlike Luc, she'd never had to run off for a time to figure out that this was where she wanted to be. She understood now why Luc had gone to Denver the fall after they'd graduated high school. But at the time she couldn't have said anything of the sort.

After Luc's return to the ranch, when their parents had decided to move to a different climate for their mom's health, it had been a no-brainer that Mackenzie would stay and run the ranch with her siblings.

She'd never struggled with being here—until Jace's appearance earlier today.

"If I give in on him staying…" Mackenzie still didn't say his name. Couldn't. "Then I should at least not have to train him."

If. Mackenzie clung to the word even though that option was slipping through her fingers. Luc was as sturdy and dependable as tree roots that sank into the ground and held tight for centuries. He wouldn't renege. If he'd hired Jace, Mackenzie didn't have much hope of upending that offer.

But maybe she could avoid him. Not run away—that was too weak. But just happen to never work anywhere near him for the rest of the summer.

That sort of impossibleness.

Please, please, please.

"Okay. I will. But then you have to do my job."

She groaned. She loathed bookwork. Paperwork. Life-sucking monsters. "I can't believe you hired my ex." That title was too formal. "My high school boyfriend." That was a little better.

"I really didn't know things ended badly between you, or I wouldn't have. I can't believe you hid that from me."

Mackenzie didn't defend her actions, because what he'd said was true. And hiding things from Luc was no easy task.

"I always just thought he'd left to ride bulls," her brother continued. "I didn't know you were so angry at him about it."

Ouch. That smarted. "He left—" she swallowed, but it didn't add any moisture to her mouth, which felt as if she'd been hiking for a week without provisions "—in a jerky way. Things didn't end well."

And then you left me, too.

Mackenzie hadn't admitted to anyone how hurtful Jace's departure had been. She was supposed to be strong, tough, solid—physically, yes. But also mentally. Emotionally. And Jace's disappearance had cut so deep, she'd been petrified that she'd never recover.

And then, before she'd even had a chance to begin doing exactly that, Luc had decided to move to Denver.

Both of them had abandoned her. It wasn't the first time Mackenzie had been left behind. Nor, she doubted, would it be the last.

"My to-do list is long right now. There's a stack on my desk of insurance issues and bills. Plus we're having a website problem, so I need to call about that."

"Can a person be allergic to paperwork?" Mackenzie rubbed a hand across the front of her neck. "I think my throat's closing off."

Luc snorted.

A fresh chill skimmed along Mackenzie's arms as the quiet night expanded with chattering crickets and a slight breeze rustling new leaves.

"You know you'll probably have to help out some when the babies come. I mean, I'm still planning to work, but Cate will need me. I promised her that she wouldn't be on her own."

This time. Mackenzie clenched her jaw. She'd gotten over what Cate had done in not telling Luc about Ruby until the girl was three years old. And it wasn't even her business. Cate was really great. Luc loved her—that much was clear. And Mackenzie had gotten on board. Had forgiven her now sister-in-law for doing what she had done.

But Mackenzie was still protective of Luc. She always had been. When they were kids and he'd needed open-heart surgery, it had felt like she was on that operating table with him. Like she was being cut open, too.

Luc had always been her person. When he'd left the ranch, she'd been so mad. Mostly because she'd missed him so much. The day he'd decided to come home, his truck kicking up dust down the long ranch drive, it was as if she'd been taken off life support and her lungs had kicked into functioning mode again.

Now that Luc had a family, she still missed him sometimes. It only made sense that he'd spend most of his time with them. And yeah, she saw him plenty because they worked together. But he'd been her closest friend for most of her life. She wasn't girlie. Didn't have any desire to go shopping with Emma and Cate when they went on one of their marathon trips—she just…wasn't built that way. Mackenzie had always hung out with the boys. She and

Luc had shared friends. And pathetically, now that he had a life and she didn't, she missed her brother. A mortifying confession she'd go to her grave denying.

"Hopefully the babies will sleep like champs and not fuss, but there's no guarantee of that. I missed so much with Ruby, and I just can't do that this time."

Knife to the heart. Luc was right, and she should jump on the supportive-sister bandwagon and…support him. "Do you have to be so logical? Can't you take a day off once in a while?"

He laughed. "You're usually right there with me. But Jace has you messed up. I've never seen you so…shaken over a guy."

Ho-boy. She didn't like that description of her one bit. She was acting like a train wreck.

Mackenzie had to pull herself together and stop letting it show how much Jace got under her skin.

And really, why should he have that much of an impact on her? It had been so many years since he'd hightailed it out of town that she should be long over these jumbled, intrusive feelings.

Mackenzie didn't think about Jace all of the time anymore. Not like she had when he'd first run away.

But she did have questions. Like, why had he called her the week after he'd left? And the next week, too? Two phone calls, no messages.

She'd been consumed by what she would do if she happened to catch his call. Would she answer or not?

Turned out her uncertainties hadn't mattered, because the attempts to reach her had stopped.

Maybe Mackenzie's issues were more with things left unsaid—undone—than the fact that she was still affected by Jace.

Maybe she was truly over him, but those whys remained.

If that were the case, she'd feel like far less of an idiot. Because that would mean she wasn't still hung up on *him*. Just on how things had ended.

"I'll train him."

Luc's head cocked to one side, as he studied her, analyzing her sudden change of mind.

"What? I can do it and be professional." *I think*.

Mackenzie had to prove to herself that she could handle being around Jace without letting him affect her. Had to prove that he didn't still have a hold on her.

And there was a secondary hidden agenda to her offer. If Luc were to train Jace, he'd be so thorough that Jace would be able to run the guest ranch himself in a week's time. But if Mackenzie trained him…she could brush over things. Hurry along. It wasn't like she had a bunch of extra time on her hands anyway.

Despite Luc's confidence in Jace, the man had no idea what he was doing. He'd fail before long, and then he'd leave on his own.

Just because she refused to let Jace affect her anymore didn't mean she wanted him anywhere near her or involved in her life.

So yes, Mackenzie would train him. Because the faster he failed, the faster he'd go away.

Jace would figure out how to make himself useful this summer if it killed him.

And this staff meeting might do exactly that.

Well, not the meeting so much as the ice-cold gusts rolling off Mackenzie. The ones giving him frostbite despite the sunny, seventy-degree weather outside.

"Jace will be helping out this summer." Mackenzie spoke to the staff, who had gathered. The first full-week summer guests arrived tomorrow, and the group had been wrapping up last-minute details. "Especially with Luc and Cate expecting the babies. We're not sure how all of that will go. So…" Mackenzie swallowed. Took about twenty years to continue. "Let's welcome him."

Let's. Meaning everyone except for her. Mackenzie might be spouting one thing, but her body language said, *Pack up and get out of here.*

Jace had hoped that she'd calm down overnight and accept that he was planning to stick around for a bit. He'd thought maybe they could actually forget the past and get along for the summer. But if anything, Mackenzie was even chillier than she'd first been. At least yesterday she'd showed some emotion, asking him not to stay. But now? It was like she'd built a wall between them.

She'd offered him a clipped "good morning" earlier, when she'd told him which room in the guys' lodging would be his and tossed him a key, but other than that, she'd avoided him as if he were a pest or a varmint or some kind of beauty product that she wouldn't touch with a ten-foot pole.

And really, Jace didn't expect anything else from her. He'd been a jerk leaving the way he had. Yes, he'd loved her. But he'd also *had* to go. The pull had been so strong, it hadn't been a real choice. Not when his brother's dream had become unattainable for him. Not when he'd told Jace to go, to live it for him.

Mackenzie dismissed the meeting, and the staff dispersed, their conversations light.

"I'm Boone. Good to have you here." A young man offered his hand, and Jace shook it. The staffer didn't look a day over sixteen. Was it even legal for him to work here at that age? Or perhaps he was still growing into his body. Either way, Jace didn't plan to ask for details. When Luc had said they were low on veteran staff this summer, he hadn't been exaggerating. Everyone seemed so young. Like puppies. No wonder they'd wanted to hire a lead. Jace might not have experience working a dude ranch, but he knew horses and livestock and pieces of ranching from working one during the summers in high school. People, he could do—he'd always had a way with the human species. So maybe this whole idea wasn't so crazy after all.

"I follow bull riding. Saw a clip of the Widow Maker ride."

Just the name of the bull caused Jace to break out in a flu-like sweat.

He'd watched the ride after the fact… He'd had to see it to know what had happened to him, because he didn't remember any of it. His body had been tossed and trampled like a rag doll in a terrorizing toddler's hands.

It was amazing he'd survived the ordeal. He'd only watched the video once, and that had been enough.

"That was quite the ride."

"You can say that again. You ride?"

"No. Did some mutton busting when I was younger, but nothing since."

"You could always get back to it." Possibly. Maybe. Though the kid was scrawny. "Let me know if you ever need any lessons."

Boone grinned. "Not sure I'm willing to risk my life like that, but I'll keep it in mind." After a nod, he took off.

A girl—maybe around nineteen or twenty—was talking to Mackenzie, and their conversation was quiet. Everything about the girl was thin. Her body. The hair barely filling out her ponytail. Was she okay? It looked like the world had chewed her up and spit her back out. In contrast, Mackenzie glowed with health and strength.

Jace wasn't trying to overhear, but their chat filtered in his direction. The girl was asking for an advance on her paycheck.

Mackenzie nodded, listening. "I'll talk to Luc and Emma, and we'll let you know." She squeezed the girl's arm in a reassuring gesture, and then the little mouse scampered off.

Mackenzie was supposed to train him today. At least that was what Luc had said. Jace wasn't sure how that would work when she was treating him like a rat in the gutter, but he was game if she was.

The day was sure to be a barrel of fun. Especially since his head was teetering on the edge of a cliff, deciding, without his input, whether to calm down or throw a fit.

Which could be because he'd had a hard time falling asleep last night. Jace wasn't sure which had caused that symptom—the concussion or the woman in front of him. It was a toss-up. Thoughts of Mackenzie—of the relationship they'd once had—had been resurrected like vivid movies. To the point that he'd finally slept and dreamed about her. Dreamed that he'd stayed in Westbend. That she didn't hate him.

Things that had consumed his mind when he'd first left to ride bulls and had holed up in an apartment with a few other guys in Billings. And then the rodeo had fully distracted him. And finally, finally the part of him that had been screaming that he'd made a mistake had lightened up. Quieted.

Until now—until seeing Mackenzie again. The need to work, to not spend his days lazing around, might not be worth this headache. And yet the challenge of something new, of helping out Luc and Mackenzie and Emma, still pulled at him.

Jace wasn't ready to give up a qualified ride yet, even though that was probably exactly what Mackenzie hoped and prayed he would do.

But since Jace's prayers were the opposite, that left them in a spiritual tug-of-war. Because, as far as Jace knew, God didn't pick sides. He loved both of them. And the Man upstairs was going to have to work this out. Because Jace didn't see Mackenzie calling a truce anytime soon.

"Well." Mackenzie shuffled papers on the table, which held her attention like her favorite pair of boots. Finally she glanced up, regarding him with as much contempt as she might a door-to-door salesman peddling high-priced skin-care products. "I should show you the trails. You might lead some rides, and either way you'll need to know where the groups are in case of an emergency."

"Don't I already know them?" They'd been all over this land together in high school. Had ridden more times than he could count.

Jace had preferred time with Mackenzie over the agony of watching his brother try to figure out how to live after losing part of his leg. It had been pretty awful around his house for a while. When Jace had been eleven, their father had been killed in a bar brawl. Drinking had always been his most important relationship, and his presence in their lives before that had been sporadic. Four years later Evan's foot and part of his leg had been amputated because of a lawn-mower accident. Mom had struggled—working constantly to support them and pay for Evan's medical bills.

Jace had escaped to Wilder Ranch all of the time in high school. Kenzie Rae had been his escape. The truth of that made every bruised, broken and sprained muscle or bone he'd experienced riding bulls roar back into existence.

"You'll know some. But a few are new." She strode to the door and then paused inside the frame, tapping the toe of her boot with impatience when he didn't immediately sprint after her. "You coming?"

"Right behind you."

And that was how it was on the trail, too. Mackenzie led. Jace followed. There was no riding next to each other. No conversation.

Only him trying—and failing—not to notice everything about her. Being relegated to the back seat on the ride gave him the chance to drink her in, to catalog the slight changes that had come with time. Jace had left a girl behind and had come back to find a woman. One who didn't need him. Didn't want him. Didn't know why hc'd done what he'd done.

With her dark blond hair slipped through the back of a baseball cap, and wearing a simple gray V-necked T-shirt, jeans and boots, Mackenzie turned casual into a heap of trouble.

They rode enough of the new trails that he gathered what he needed to know between her directions and the hand-drawn map she'd tucked into her back pocket.

When they reached a wide, smooth path that carved through open pasture, she didn't give him even the slightest heads-up before urging her horse into an all-out gallop.

The smart thing to do would be to let her ride. Enjoy the view. But Jace had never been one to take the easier road.

He nudged his horse into action.

If he'd thought Mackenzie was distracting earlier, seeing her fly wasn't helping matters.

The flat-out run was worth it—gave him a hint of that risking-it-all feeling—but by the time Mackenzie slowed Buttercup and eased her back into the trees, the dull ache in Jace's head had ramped up from barely noticeable to jet-engine-roar levels. And his ribs were on fire.

Probably not his best move, since he was supposed to be taking it easy. But not joining Mackenzie would have been painful in other ways. For a few seconds he'd felt young and free. Like they still had their whole futures ahead of them. He missed that, especially now. If Jace couldn't go back to rodeoing, what would he do with himself?

He'd never been any good at school. Or any job other than the one currently dangling out of his reach.

"You weren't lying when you said you could ride with one arm." Mackenzie tossed the comment/compliment over her shoulder as they reached the hot springs and she dismounted. It registered in Jace's chest, warm and surprising. *Getting ahead of yourself, Hawke. She didn't say she was crazy in love with you, just that you could handle a horse.*

Jace mimicked her dismount, needing a second to steady the wavelike motions crashing through his noggin. He'd give a hefty sum of money for an ice pack to press against his wailing ribs, which were none too pleased with his recent activity.

Mackenzie must have realized her mistake in leading

them to the hot springs, because her vision bounced from the water, to him, then back.

Yep, you sure did deliver us right back to the past.

They'd been out here plenty of times when they were young. Had stolen kisses in those very waters.

Back then she'd welcomed an advance from him. Even initiated.

Jace wobbled and managed to right himself while Mackenzie was thankfully looking in the other direction. He was far weaker than he should be, which only added to the angry rhythm inside his skull.

He hated being sidelined. Benched. Hated it even more that he didn't know when or if these concussion side effects would go away or get better.

The arm, the spleen, the ribs—none of that bothered him, because he knew they'd heal. But his noggin had a mind of its own.

He dropped to sit on a rock in the shade and settled his head in his hands. He sensed Kenzie moving but didn't look up. And then a canteen appeared between his arms.

"Thanks." He took it, meeting those stormy eyes. She walked toward the hot springs as he drank. The water was cool, crisp and, if he wasn't mistaken, the faintest taste of her mint Chapstick still coated the lip. He plucked a pill out of his front pocket and shot it down before Mackenzie turned back in his direction.

She studied him as she neared, stopping about five feet away. Enough that he could feel her intense observation, but not so close that she actually stepped foot into his world, his space.

"You okay?"

"I'm fine. Just hot, I guess." He took another swig.

"Your arm hurting?"

He hadn't even thought about that slight discomfort today. "Nah. I'm good."

Except he wasn't.

Mackenzie was a deer in the forest. Still. Analyzing. Eyes morphing to slits. She'd have him figured out in two seconds flat if this kept up. And for some reason he didn't want her to. If she knew about the ribs or spleen, that would be fine. But his head felt too…personal. No one knew that Dr. Karvina had advised he quit riding.

I'm going to level with you, Jace. If this were me or one of my sons, I'd quit now. I can't tell you how many concussions you can survive without permanent damage. It's not worth the risk. I've seen too many lives taken or changed forever by this sport.

His doctor's advice haunted him. Concussions were a big deal these days. Last year a young rider had committed suicide after one too many. After his death, the autopsy had confirmed he had CTE, a terrible disease that came from repeat trauma to the brain.

Head injuries had messed with his moods, his memory, even his personality. Gunner's last hit had been a whopper though. But still, no one knew the exact number of concussions that would be okay. Or how many would push a guy over the edge. Ever since the young cowboy had taken his own life, the rules had gotten stricter for all of the riders. It was logical—Jace could admit that. But that didn't make it easy to think about losing everything.

Which was why so many guys still did what they wanted—still rode when they shouldn't.

And Jace understood that, too. He wasn't done riding. It was his life. His people. He'd done it for his brother, but it had become his, and he wasn't going to quit now.

And he certainly wasn't going to discuss any of this

with Mackenzie. The woman who constantly wanted to kick him in the shins and then slug him.

Maybe he should just explain why he'd left. Get it all out in the open now. She could still hate him then, but at least she'd have answers.

"Kenzie Rae."

She'd begun pacing back toward the water but now whirled around.

"I have something to say—"

"Don't." She bristled, and her finger jabbed in his direction. "Just don't."

"You don't even know what it is!"

"Is it about Wilder Ranch?" Her tone snapped as fast and furious as a snake's strike.

"Nope."

"Then I don't want to hear it." She mounted up—the equivalent of a kid placing their hands over their ears. "We should get back."

He didn't move. Just glued himself to her until she called uncle and wrenched her gaze away.

"I've got things to do, Hawke." The reins twitched in her hands. He'd made her uncomfortable. He wasn't sure why that ignited a flicker of happiness in his gut. Probably because it meant he still affected her. And since she was under his skin like a chigger, yeah, that eased the sting a bit. "You know your way from here." She turned her horse. "I'll see you when you get back."

And then she left him. Sitting in her dust, her canteen still in his hands, words dying on his tongue that had needed to be said for seven years.

Huh. So that was what that felt like.

Chapter 3

Seven days at the ranch, and nothing had changed.

Mackenzie still didn't want him here. And Jace still refused to go.

Though he was starting to doubt his decision. Kenzie's disdain for him was beginning to seep into the cracks of his confidence.

Should he give in and quit? Crash on his mom's couch for the next weeks or months, instead of his room at the ranch? Go absolutely crazy from boredom and live suffocated by the fear that he'd never heal and return to his career?

He just couldn't function that way. No matter how much he'd like to not torment Mackenzie. Besides, he liked it here. Liked leading trail rides, the weather, the views, the wrangler competitions they entertained the guests with at night. Guest ranch life was busy—so full of people and staff and horses that his mind hadn't gotten bogged down with what-ifs about his injuries and the future.

Definitely not the worst job he'd had.

Except for the woman who hated him.

Oh, *hate* might be too big of a word for how Mackenzie felt about him. He was a pebble in her boot. An annoyance that she planned to ignore.

And then she approached the table where he was eating lunch with guests and other staffers and did exactly that.

She asked the guests how their day was going. She made sure to acknowledge each of the staff. And then she left the dining room. Didn't she realize that completely ignoring him was more noticeable than treating him like she did everyone else?

Jace popped up, cleared his dishes and then chased after her. He caught sight of her in the lodge living room—an inviting place with high ceilings, comfortable furniture and a massive fireplace that begged for snowstorms and cold winter nights.

Mackenzie's hair was down today—long and wild, and bringing him back to high school and the memory of what it had felt like to thread his fingers through those waves and kiss that mouth that had once been receptive to his.

Even in her jeans and a simple Wilder polo, the woman could cause a freeway pileup. She had on turquoise boots today—the third different pair he'd seen her wear since he'd arrived at the ranch. Mackenzie had hated shopping back in high school. Her only girlie addiction had been boots. Apparently that infatuation had continued.

No guests occupied the lobby at the moment, so Jace called out to her, "Kenzie Rae."

She turned to face him, upset heating her cheeks. At his presence or the use of her nickname?

Either way she'd have to adjust.

He stopped in front of her, ignoring her obvious irritation at his interruption. "What do you need me to do tonight?"

Being that this was his first week, he was still learning the schedule. Mackenzie might not want him here, but while he was, he planned to do a good job of whatever they asked him to do.

The glint in her eyes was quick as a bullet and disappeared just as fast. "The square dance is tonight."

Huh. He wouldn't be much of a help with that.

"Why don't you lead it?"

Jace snorted. "Ha. Very funny." She didn't laugh, didn't join in. "Wait. You're serious?"

"Why not? Luc seems to think you're so qualified to be working here. Not that anyone asked me. So, if that's the case, you can be in charge tonight."

"So that's how you're going to play it? I don't have any idea how to square-dance. You know I'm a pathetic dancer." The only real rhythm he'd ever had was on a bull. When he'd competed on the weekends in high school, Mackenzie had always come to watch him ride when she hadn't been working herself. After, there'd often been a dance, a band, a crowd. A few times they'd attempted the steps, but never with much success. Once or twice he'd just held her. Held on as if his life had depended on it. On her. He supposed it had in a way. She'd been everything to him. The future he'd denied himself when he'd chased Evan's dreams.

"I haven't seen you in seven years, so I know nothing of the sort."

Silent accusations brimmed, and Jace understood them. Had she wondered what he was up to over the years? If he was dating anyone? Because he'd wondered those things about her. It would have destroyed him to find out she was in a relationship or married, even though he didn't have any right to her anymore.

"I didn't take you to be vindictive, Kenzie Rae." He dropped the name on purpose now, goading, a little of her anger seeping over to him.

"Really? Maybe *you* don't know *me* at all anymore. I'm not sure you knew me then either."

Sweet mercy. The woman's punches were fast and furious and vicious and deserved. Jace rubbed a hand over his certain-to-be-gaping chest wound before that same traitorous hand snaked out and latched onto her arm.

The heat between their skin sizzled as much as their rising irritation. "I knew everything about you back then and vice versa."

"The Jace I knew would never have left like you did."

There would be no closing the wound today. Not with Mackenzie hitting the same spot over and over again. "I tried to tell you." His voice dropped low, aching with remorse. "So many times. But the words always got stuck." He swallowed. "And when I did manage to get some of it out, you didn't listen."

For a split second she'd softened during his speech. Those mesmerizing eyes had notched down from bitter to curious, *tell me why* shooting from them. But at his *you didn't listen*, everything in her hardened and lit like fireworks.

"I'm not doing this." She shook his hand loose as if he were nothing more than dirt—or worse—hitching a ride on her boots. "This is exactly why I was so mad that Luc hired you. Wilder Ranch is my family business, Hawke. My life. And you're not in it anymore. As far as I'm concerned, your time here is strictly about work. I don't want to hear any of this. It's too late to make apologies…if that's even what you're doing. It's too late to try to blame me for what *you* did. So if you want to be here, figure out how to lead the square dance, because as your *boss*, that's what I'm directing you to do."

Before Mackenzie could take off or Jace could process his jumbled thoughts enough to respond, the screen door to the lodge opened and Emma walked inside. Thankfully it was her and not a guest. She was all sunshine in a yellow shirt, jeans and rain boots as she paused to study them—probably taking in their irritated body language or analyzing whatever she'd just overheard.

Emma bravely continued in their direction. "Everything okay in here?" A faint curve of her lips attempted to diffuse the negative energy that surely radiated from them.

Kenzie's gaze slit and slid from him to her sister. "We're great." Fake perkiness punctuated her answer. "Jace and I were just discussing his duties for tonight. And he was expressing how excited he is about them. I mean—" her sarcasm ramped up "—since this is the perfect place for him to work, and Luc seems to think he's so qualified, I thought I'd give him some more responsibility."

Vicious woman. Jace willed himself not to find her attractive in the middle of her feisty little speech.

It didn't work.

If Emma wasn't watching them like a spectator at a UFC fight, Jace would seriously toy with the thought of kissing Mackenzie just to get her to stop spewing venom.

An action that might very well leave him as messed up as stomping through a field of rattlesnakes.

"Of course. I'm happy to do anything I'm assigned." Square dance? Fine. He'd figure it out. Somehow. There had to be another staffer who had a clue about what to do.

Mackenzie's determination to boot him out of here only increased his resolve to stay. She should know better than to challenge him, to turn this into a competition. His whole livelihood depended on him besting a two-thousand-pound bull.

Emma's strangled sigh was filled with exasperation, and a tinge of remorse lit in Jace. He shouldn't have engaged with Mackenzie at all. Certainly not in the lodge lobby, where guests could walk through at any second of the day.

"Feel like you two could use a mediator. Or some workplace counseling. Is that a thing?" Emma beamed, finding her own joke amusing. Jace's lips twitched, because the idea of Mackenzie and him sitting on a couch, trying to figure out how to work together when she couldn't stand the sight of him, *was* funny, but he couldn't let Mackenzie win the third-grade angry-staring contest they'd somehow begun.

"Um, so…listen." Emma was made of velvet—a stark contrast to Mackenzie's most recent tone. "I need people to get along. I can't handle all of this." Her nose wrinkled, and she waved a hand, encompassing them. "What can I do to help you guys? Because I get the past mattering and all that. Trust me—I understand how much that affects things. But you two have to figure out how to work together and not do this—" another hand motion "—anywhere guests or staff can see you."

She was right, of course. But Jace had been trying. For the most part.

"Maybe we could schedule in special argument time after everyone else has signed off for the night. Or get up early and duke things out." Jace let the retort slip, hoping it might earn the faintest shadow of humor—like the old Mackenzie would have offered up.

New Mackenzie released a growl/wounded-animal screech of frustration. "Actually, Emma, the best scenario would be for Jace to realize he's not welcome at Wilder Ranch and leave."

Emma's mouth formed an O shape as Mackenzie made a U-turn and strode toward the front office, her boots pounding as strong and fierce as she was.

Attraction swallowed Jace up. Confounded woman.

"That is not true." Emma's light brown ponytail and silver hoop earrings bobbed back and forth with her shaking head. "Of course you're welcome here. You always have been. I'm sorry for her—"

"You don't need to apologize for Mackenzie. I'm not surprised. And I deserve everything she's throwing my way."

The woman only seemed to reserve direct hits for him. Jace had learned that the Wilders had extended the paycheck advance to the girl asking for it. They were gracious like that. Even Mackenzie was. Just not with him.

"Oh, Jace." Emma softened. "It has been a long time. I was never sure exactly what happened between you two, but I didn't believe things ended well, like Mackenzie tried to spin it."

Mackenzie had kept the way he'd left under wraps? Sounded like something she would do. The woman was too tough for her own good. She needed to let people in. But then again she'd let him in, and he'd bailed on her.

"Over the years I kept thinking you'd contact her. Make things right."

"But I never did." He scraped his noncasted hand along the hair at the nape of his neck. "It wasn't like I didn't want to. I just didn't know what to say. How to say it."

Emma offered him an understanding smile. At least she didn't consider him a varmint. But then he hadn't left her high and dry. And Emma had always been homemade apple crisp with ice cream melting into the nooks and crannies, while Mackenzie was the kind of spicy dish that tore up your taste buds and still managed to leave a person wanting more.

If only a little of Emma's sugary demeanor would rub off on Mackenzie. Maybe then she'd actually hear him out. But Jace couldn't deny that the challenge of Mackenzie was exactly what had attracted him to her in the first place.

Which could turn out to be quite the problem this summer. Since he planned to go back to riding. Since he was an invalid, with all of these sidelining injuries. And since no matter what he did, Jace couldn't tame his attraction to the woman who wanted nothing to do with him. All because he refused to leave like she wanted him to… All because, the first time around, he'd left when she hadn't wanted him to.

But Kenzie Rae wasn't the only one who had issues and wants and demands. Jace had a few of his own. And if he didn't occupy himself with something useful this summer—like working at the ranch would provide for him— then he'd lose his mind even more than he already had when it had been demolished by the Widow Maker ride.

He'd worked hard this week to make himself useful, to stay busy, to help things run as smoothly as he could from his limited knowledge of the ranch. And Mackenzie refused to recognize that. All she could see was the trail of dust he'd left behind seven years ago.

Emma was studying the front office door Mackenzie had disappeared through, and Jace couldn't help wanting to ease the turmoil creasing her face. She wasn't in charge of fixing his and Mackenzie's past or current issues.

"I heard a rumor that the reason I haven't seen much of you is that you keep running off to spend time with your fiancé."

Just like that, her demeanor flipped and she turned all sparkling Emma, hands racing to cover pink cheeks. "It's true. I'm crazy about him. Can't seem to get enough. Thankfully, Mackenzie and Luc have been turning the other way when I keep sneaking off to meet him." Her lyrical laugh bubbled up. "That makes it sound so untoward. But it's not! I'm just..."

"Crazy in love."

"Exactly."

"I'm happy for you, Emma. If anyone deserves to be noticed and appreciated and cherished, it's you. Love looks good on you."

"Aw." She playfully shoved his arm. "You always were a sweet-talker." Her attention bounced over to Kenzie's wake again. "She's probably going to lose her mind if she comes back out here to find me consorting with the enemy." Her hand paused on his arm. "Be gentle with her, Jace. After you left..." She faltered and grew silent, her head shaking. "Did you know Luc left, too, shortly after you did?"

Oh. That wound opened up again. "I did not know that."

"He moved to Denver and came back eventually, but between the two of you, I wasn't sure what to do with Mackenzie."

Jace had so many questions. Like whether Emma thought Mackenzie would ever forgive him. Not to restart their relationship. He really couldn't do that when he planned to leave again. But he wouldn't mind getting along with the girl he'd once thought he'd marry.

"I really can't say more." Emma's hand squeezed his but dropped away. "Hang in there. If I know my sister, you're in for a fight if you plan to stick around."

Fight, he could do. And Mackenzie was worth it. Even if Jace was only here to right the wrong of their past. She deserved the truth from him—whenever she'd finally let him say it. His earlier doubts vanished. While his arm—and the rest of him—healed, he didn't have anywhere else to be.

Emma dropped into the chair across from Mackenzie's desk. The front office was surprisingly empty this afternoon, with everyone out with the guests, and Mackenzie had hoped to buckle down and get some work done—especially now that she didn't have Jace trailing her every move.

She'd only managed to train him Saturday, Sunday and Monday, and then she'd cut him loose. It wasn't enough. Of course, she should have done more for the sake of a well-run guest ranch.

But Mackenzie couldn't bring herself to continue.

She just kept hoping and praying that Jace would give

up on his outrageous idea to work here for the summer and leave already. Preferably yesterday.

"How're you holding up?" Emma's question was soft and caring, but Mackenzie wasn't willing to go anywhere near the meaning behind it.

"Fine. Why wouldn't I be?"

Emma rolled her eyes. "Really? You might be able to get away with that attitude with the staff or a stranger, but I'm your sister. I know that Jace being here is killing you slowly."

"I can't… I just…don't want to talk about it. Him." Mackenzie didn't want to deal with the thought of Jace at all. That had been her plan for the week, and for the most part it was working.

Except she was exhausted.

Not being affected by Jace took all of her energy. Not letting the man crawl under her skin and set up camp was hard work. Not yelling at him for the way he'd left was, too.

Not caring about any of it like she'd hoped? Utterly impossible.

"You want me to beat him up for you?"

A laugh escaped. "Kinda, yeah. I'd like to see that."

"Hey, I can be tough when I need to be."

"I have no doubt about that, sister. So…what's going on with you?" Mackenzie motioned to Emma, desperate to change the subject. "I heard you come home late last night. I don't know how you're functioning on so little sleep, heading over to Gage's whenever you can."

"Nice conversation turn." Emma raised an eyebrow.

Mackenzie waited her out. Emma wouldn't push too much on Jace. She was too sympathetic and patient and understanding—qualities Mackenzie only possessed in small amounts.

"All right. I give. But I'm here if you need to talk to someone. Or vent. Okay?"

"Okay. Thanks." She might take Emma up on that offer if she had any idea how to deal with the jumbled, frustrating emotions Jace created in her.

"In answer to your question about me...I'm tired. I'm overwhelmed. I don't know how this summer is going to work. I miss Gage and Hudson so much already and this is only our first week. And on top of that, Hudson is sick."

Gratefulness at the turn in topic swelled, but then concern for Hudson took its place. "What kind of sick? Is he okay?" Emma's fiancé had become a guardian to the one-year-old boy recently, and Emma already loved the tyke as if he were her own.

"Nothing serious. At least I don't think so. Just a nasty cold. He's congested and has a runny nose. He's miserable and I didn't want to leave him or Gage to come home last night." A grin surfaced. "No offense."

"Ouch. You want to see your fiancé more than your sister? I'm wounded."

Humor tugged at the corner of her mouth. "It's just so hard not being there. Gage is doing his best, but he's drained. I am, too, from going back and forth. From trying to find a couple of minutes in the day or evening to sneak over there and see them. And then just when I get there it feels like I have to come home. And with Hudson sick, I'd like to be there to help. He was clinging to me last night." Her hands formed a self-hug, rubbing along the skin of her arms. "That's why I got home so late."

"So why don't you stay?"

"Ah, that's not really an option, as you know."

Mackenzie snorted. "Not like *that*. I mean, are you ever going to change your mind about marrying Gage?"

Emma's head shook slowly. "No. Of course not."

"You don't have any doubts about him or Hudson." Mackenzie didn't say it like a question, because it wasn't. She already knew what Emma's response would be.

"No doubts about either of them. Of course not."

"So get married."

Confusion flickered. "We're planning to."

"I know you were thinking fall." Gage and Emma had tossed that idea around because both ranches slowed down and the schedule switched at Wilder Ranch. But that didn't mean they couldn't change their plans. They didn't have to follow some wedding protocol. "I'm saying get married sooner. What are you waiting for?"

Emma's mouth hung open wide enough that Mackenzie could toss a popcorn kernel into it without a problem—a game they'd played often as kids. One Mackenzie had always been the reigning champ of, much to Luc's frustration.

"Wait… What?"

"You want to be with Gage. That way you could be. After you're done with work, you'd go home and stay."

"Oh." Emma's eyes pooled with tears. "I want that."

"So get it. What do you really need to make a wedding happen?"

"Dress, pastor, flowers, food, people, place." Emma ticked items off on her fingers. "Mom and Dad. Gage's parents and his sister."

"You already have your dress picked out, right?"

She nodded, worrying her lip.

Of course, Emma had her dress picked out. The girl had probably been planning her wedding since she was five. Just like she probably had a Pinterest page filled with rustic, shabby-chic wedding ideas, like candles in mason jars and string lights, and the perfect shade of bridesmaid dresses. If anyone could pull a wedding together fast, it would be her.

"So, the biggest thing is family. And Pastor Higgin. Or you can always find another pastor to stand in if you need to—like the new assistant pastor at church."

"Actually…now that you mention it, Gage's parents are already coming at the end of July. I wonder if Mom and Dad could come, too. And his sister."

"That's a great idea. You could do a Saturday-evening wedding. The staff would rally to take care of things and complete the turnover for guests arriving Sunday. And you have so many friends you've helped over the years. You've been there for everyone. Let them be there for you. Mrs. Higgin could probably be convinced to make the cake. She's a fantastic baker. And you can ask for help with flowers and decorations. The only issue would be where."

She lit up. "I always imagined getting married here. Setting up chairs and a trellis in the grassy open space behind the lodge, with the mountains in the background. Casual and pretty."

"That makes it even easier if you don't have to find a venue."

"True." Emma bolted out of the chair and enveloped Mackenzie in a tight hug. "You're so right. This is the best idea you've ever had. Seriously, the best. Thank you, thank you, thank you." She let go and stood in a burst of energy. "I need to call Gage." And then she was off, with her phone in her hands. Mackenzie listened to the excited timbre of her voice for a few seconds before it faded away.

Emma had always been a bundle of cheerfulness. But Gage made her absolutely glow. Mackenzie didn't want to lose her sister, but she loved seeing her even happier than normal.

And really, shouldn't one of them be? Because ever since Jace had marched back into her world, Mackenzie wasn't confident she remembered how to get back to that feeling.

Probably wouldn't until he left again.

She'd been waiting all week for the man to hurry up and fail. For him to flounder. But he hadn't. So yeah, she'd thrown the square dancing at him as sabotage. If Jace couldn't figure it out, if he couldn't catch on, then he'd just have to leave.

And unlike the first time, that was exactly what Mackenzie wanted him to do.

Chapter 4

Mackenzie stood on a platform that towered above the forest floor. Gorgeous blue Colorado sky stretched above her. Bright green foliage spread out before her. It was a perfect day. Just the right temperature of warm but not too hot. Just the right everything.

She relaxed her legs and pushed off, her zip-line harness holding her as she flew through the path in the trees. Wind whipped by as she attempted to capture everything around her.

She reached the next tower and came to a stop, adjusting her T-shirt and shorts before taking off again. If only Luc and Emma would consider her idea to build a zip-line course at Wilder Ranch. But Mackenzie would have to wait, because the next project they'd decided to undertake would be the ice-cream parlor and small store Emma had proposed. In the meantime she counted on a friend's offer to let her use their course whenever the desire struck.

And today she'd needed to soar.

She'd needed to escape Jace and everyone at the ranch.

And Luc had known it. Having someone attuned to your idiosyncrasies wasn't the worst thing in the world.

This morning he'd shown up at the door to the cabin she shared with Emma. "Why don't you get out of here for a bit today?" he'd said.

"But what about the turnover?"

"I can handle it. We'll survive without you. Take a break. For everyone's sake." He'd infused teasing into his tone, but fear had sent her body into a panicked sweat.

Had the whole world witnessed her agitation over the last week? Did everyone know how torn up she was about Jace working at Wilder Ranch?

"Is it that noticeable?"

"No," Luc had responded. "I just know you."

She'd almost burst into tears—proof that she was a hot mess in need of some Jace-free time in a Jace-free zone.

Thankfully Luc knew her well enough to rescue her from herself. When she'd tried to protest, to say that she'd stay so that he could spend time with Cate and Ruby, he'd simply hugged her. "I'm sorry I hired him without talking to you first."

And then he'd left before she could argue more.

Bless him. The offer—or command—had been a huge answer to her prayers. The past week had left Mackenzie frayed and on edge. With Jace invading every portion of her life—living in the guys' quarters at the ranch, present at every meal—she'd been unable to find her footing.

Mackenzie had heard enough "Jace is so funny," "Jace is so great," "Jace did this" and "Jace did that" from both guests and staff that she wanted to cover her ears like a toddler.

He'd even come through with flying colors on the square dance last night. She'd arrived early, planning to save the evening and make sure the guests still had the experience they'd been promised, and there Jace had been—working out details and steps with the other staffers.

Things had gotten jumbled a few times during the night, but the guests hadn't cared. They'd loved every second. They'd loved Jace.

How come no one else saw through him to the man beneath that charming grin and those soulful chestnut eyes?

Mackenzie certainly did.

Clarification—she did now. In high school she hadn't. Back then she'd been intrigued by him. Jace probably still didn't know that she'd observed him for a few months before he'd talked to her. He'd been good at switching gears—one second sporting sad and serious, the next entertaining friends as the center of attention.

Once Mackenzie had gotten to know him, she'd realized it was his brother's accident that had broken him. Slowly but surely, as they'd hung out, Jace had shed that lost look. He'd bloomed back to life, and she'd fallen so hard for him.

No one had ever really gotten her the way Jace had.

They'd talked about getting married someday. Having kids. Where they'd live—somewhere near Westbend, because even back then Mackenzie hadn't wanted to leave Wilder Ranch. She'd somehow always known it was where she belonged.

She and Jace had been inseparable, and she'd had no

reason to doubt him. That was why the fact that he'd left, and the way he'd done it, had been such a shock.

Why it had hurt so stinking bad.

What Jace had said to her in the lodge lobby yesterday had rattled around in her mind ever since. Was he right? Had he tried to tell her he wanted to continue competing at the next level after high school? She remembered maybe one instance like that and nothing more.

But maybe she hadn't been listening, like he'd claimed.

Still, if that were the case, he should have made his plans more clear. He should have made sure she understood.

And now the man should really stop expecting her to somehow get over his callous departure just because he'd decided to grace Wilder Ranch with his presence.

Last night, after the square dance, when she'd been trying to quietly escape, Jace had caught up to her in the hallway. He'd had the audacity to wink. And then he'd toggled his eyebrows and said, "One word. YouTube."

YouTube. That was how he'd figured out the dance? The man had to be kidding. Except he wasn't.

A crease had split his forehead. "You're irritated that I handled tonight well, aren't you? Still don't want me here, do you?"

"Nope." The truth had just skipped right out.

"You could take a minute. Think about your answer. Give the illusion of grace."

"Nope." Mackenzie had wanted nothing more than to flee, but then Jace had wrenched the conversation up another level, while his voice had dipped low and meaningful.

"You ever going to forgive me for leaving the way I did?"

She hadn't spoken. There'd been no need to repeat the word that still fit a third time.

Jace's fist had clenched, and his lips had pressed tight. And then he'd turned back to the guests, to the staff, to what was supposed to be her world. He'd left her standing there, wrestling a supersize hissy fit into submission.

Composure was usually her thing. Nothing ruffled Mackenzie unless she let it.

But Jace Hawke broke all of her rules.

Mackenzie finished the rest of the zip-line course quickly. The temptation to fly through it a third time was herculean strong, but she couldn't.

She should really get back to the ranch and make sure everything was going smoothly with the turnover for the guests that would arrive tomorrow. Mackenzie had fit in a hike before zip-lining, so she'd already been gone for hours.

She probably shouldn't have left in the first place, but Luc had been right—she'd needed it. Time away from the ranch—from Jace—had been good for her. She already felt lighter, better.

The drive back went way too fast.

When she turned down the ranch drive, agitation rose up and choked her. Mackenzie loved this place. Always had. But Jace was ruining that for her, too.

Was she crazy to be this upset with him for sticking around? With the way he'd left… How much he'd hurt her… Nope. She had a right to be mad. But holding on to that anger was draining her.

Mackenzie parked at the lodge, planning to head inside, check on how things were going. But before she could even open the door of her little pickup truck, Jace stood next to it.

She ignored him and took her time switching from her tennis shoes over to flip-flops, then tossed the hiking shoes to the passenger floor of her truck.

Jace must have swallowed one of her impatient pills, because he hauled open her driver's door.

"What do you want, Hawke?" Why did he have to be the first person she saw when she returned? Hadn't God heard her prayers this week? She'd been requesting less Jace, not more, but the opposite kept happening.

Concern radiated from him, tightening his features. "You have your phone with you today?"

"Yes, but it's on Silent." Otherwise it would have been going off the whole time. Mackenzie had known Luc would handle things, so she'd gone off the radar. "I forgot to check it when I got back into my truck." She winced. That hadn't been smart of her. "Why? Is something wrong with the turnover?"

"No." Jace rubbed a hand over the slight stubble on his cheeks and chin. His eyes—they stayed tender. Sympathetic. Something *was* wrong.

"What is it? What's going on?"

"It's Cate. She went into early labor. She and Luc are in Denver."

"Wait, what? But isn't it too early? Are they trying to stop the labor?"

"She was too far along to stop it. Luc just talked to Emma. Cate had the babies."

"Already?" How was that possible? Mackenzie had only been gone for a handful of hours.

"The girls are tiny but getting good care. But Cate…"

Dread wrapped talons around her windpipe. "But Cate what?"

"She's having complications. She's losing blood. Luc

didn't tell Emma much. He had to go. He just said to pray."

Oh, God. I take it all back. How could I complain about such trivial matters like Jace being back in my life? I promise I'll be better. I'll be more mature. Please don't let anything happen to Cate or the babies. Luc would never recover. None of us would.

Mackenzie stared out the front windshield of her truck. "This can't be happening. Everything was fine when I left this morning." How could the world just tip upside down like that?

"Since the staff knows about Cate, Emma took Ruby over to Gage's to prevent her from hearing anyone talk about…any of it. No need to scare the girl. Then she'll take Ruby to see Cate and the girls if…*when* Luc gives the okay."

"That's good." *Breathe, Mackenzie. Breathe.* "Emma's the best with her."

"Ruby would have been good with you, too. You just weren't here as an option."

Mackenzie was certain Jace hadn't meant that comment the way she'd taken it. But it was still true. Her brother had needed her. There'd been an emergency, and she hadn't been here, because she'd been too busy being immature and running away. Sure, Luc had told her to, but she shouldn't have listened. She should have handled being around Jace better, so that hiding wouldn't have been necessary. She should have stopped throwing toddler tantrums and done her job.

"I need to go. I need to be there." *I need to see my brother, to know he's okay. And in order for him to be okay, Cate needs to be okay. Okay, God? Please.* But how could Mackenzie leave the ranch with no one in charge?

"But I can't leave the staff with the turnover. If Luc's not here, Emma either—"

"It's taken care of," Jace interrupted.

"How? You've never even been here for it before."

"Your staff, although new, has been well trained, and you have lists written up for everything. We knocked most of it out, and they know what else is left to do. They wanted to help. This is all they've got right now, and they're on it."

Sounded like Jace had been on it, too. Guilt rose up. They'd needed him already. Luc had been right to hire Jace without her consent, for the sake of the ranch. And if things were taken care of, that gave Mackenzie permission to go see her brother. And Cate. Because she was trusting that Cate would be all right. She was clinging to that.

"My keys." She checked the ignition. Not there. Where had she put them?

"I'll drive you." Jace held her keys in the palm of his hand.

What? How and when had he snagged them?

Maybe she'd dropped them when she'd first arrived. Who knew? Who cared?

"I'm fine, thanks. I can drive myself."

Jace's fist closed around the metal. "You're a mess right now. I'm not letting you drive."

Puh-lease. She wasn't some baby who needed to be coddled. "I'm fine. Give me my keys." The demand came out clipped and desperate. "I need to get going."

"No." Jace's arms crossed. "I can drive you or we can stand here and waste more time fighting. Can you just trust me on this? You're shaking right now."

"I am *not*." She held out her hand to prove it, and it

vibrated before her like a cup of coffee on the dash of a car. *Great.* How nice of her body to betray her.

"You're not driving my truck."

"Okay. I'll drive mine." The man strode across the gravel, to his vehicle. "Come on, Wilder, you're wasting time."

He had her keys. She wanted to scream and kick and throw a fit, but he was right. It would just waste time. If Mackenzie wanted to see her brother right now, which she did, she didn't have a choice.

Jace had never seen Mackenzie so shaken. And rightfully so. The news from Luc had been sporadic. Only that the babies were small and early. And that Cate had lost a lot of blood—had still been losing blood when Luc had talked to Emma. He'd said that the doctors were trying to stop the hemorrhaging, and that was all of the information they had.

Jace didn't know how to help or comfort. So he'd settled for getting Mackenzie safely to where she wanted to be.

They'd been in his truck for ten minutes, and the woman had yet to make a peep. He'd asked her to let Emma know they were headed to Denver. She'd texted, then let her phone fall to the truck bench seat. Since then she'd been staring out the window, like her whole world had crashed down around her. And it had. Mackenzie was incredibly close to her brother. Her twin. She was likely kicking herself for not being there today, when Cate had gone into labor and things had progressed so quickly.

Maybe he could get her talking, get her to focus on something else.

"Where'd you run off to today?"

Her wince was quick but noticeable. "Luc told me to take some time off, so I did. I hiked and then zip-lined. A friend owns a course, and he lets me go for free whenever."

He. Was this *he* young or old? "Boyfriend of yours or something?"

She snorted. "He's nineteen. Actually, his parents own it, but he runs it most of the time."

"And gives out free passes to gorgeous women."

Her face pinked, accompanied by an eye roll and a shake of her low ponytail. "No. That's not how it is."

She was getting riled now, but at least some color was rushing back to her skin and her breathing wasn't so shallow.

"I mean, he's asked me out before, but he's too young for me. I've told him countless times."

Jace narrowly avoided sprouting a smile. Young pup was probably smitten with Mackenzie. He didn't blame the kid.

"Do you normally take off on Saturdays?"

"No. After the staff is well trained, I could. I don't technically need to be there if they can handle things."

"But you usually are."

"Why not? Luc tries to spend time with Cate and Ruby after the guests leave. I don't have anywhere else to be, so I make sure things run smoothly. I should have been there today, especially with all of our new staff. But I just…" Her vision tracked out the window again, and she didn't finish her statement. Didn't elaborate.

"It's me, isn't it? You were escaping from me." Luc had told him that Mackenzie had taken part of the day off, that she'd needed to blow off some steam.

More like blow off some Jace.

A huff of air filled the cab. "Let's just let it go, okay? It doesn't matter. I wasn't where I was supposed to be, and now my brother's wife is having serious complications."

"That has nothing to do with you and where you were, Kenzie Rae, and you know it."

"I know nothing of the sort. What if I could have helped? What if—"

"Stop it." Jace softened his command by giving her arm a quick squeeze. His thumb etched across her skin before he let go and moved it back to the steering wheel, to keep from driving with his casted arm. "You couldn't have changed a thing. They left quickly. He didn't wait for you, if that's what you're worried about."

A hurt-animal noise tore from her throat. This woman.

"I didn't mean it like that. Just meant that he didn't waste any time. You don't get to blame yourself." Was that what had Kenzie so upset? That she wasn't needed? That Luc had left without her being there? "Emma... She told me Luc left not too long after I did."

Jace watched the car in front of him change lanes as Mackenzie studied him. At least the concussion hadn't stolen his peripheral vision from him.

"He did." Her body gave a telltale tremor. Like a secret admission she would never give away herself. Jace hated that he'd hurt her. That had never been his intent. And yes, he wished he would have handled things differently after high school. But the truth was, he'd been so in love with the woman across the seat of the truck from him, he would never have been able to walk away from her if he'd said goodbye.

The hold would have been too strong.

And Mackenzie was built for Wilder Ranch. He

couldn't picture her anywhere else. It fit her the way riding did him.

They were made for two different worlds, and a hefty chunk of time hadn't changed that.

"Feels just like when we were kids." Mackenzie spoke quietly, then rubbed her arms like she was chilled. The reaction had to be emotional, because his truck was toasty with the sun cascading in the windows.

"What do you mean?"

He didn't expect an answer from her. Kenzie wasn't in the business of telling him anything lately. But today's trauma must have messed with her tongue, because she kept going.

"When Luc had open-heart surgery, they forgot about me."

His gut clenched. "Who did?"

"Mom and Dad. They had to be up and out of the house early, and my aunt was staying with us, but I'd said I wanted to see him in the morning. Before they left. I don't know if they didn't believe me or what, but I woke up and they were gone. Luc was gone." Her sadness swelled and filled the cab of the truck. "I was so haunted by the thought that I might never see him again or that he might not make it through the surgery. I was a mess that whole day, until we heard the surgery went well."

Jace pictured her at that young age. Left. Alone. Missing her twin. She and Luc had always been close. Connected.

For him to be gone without her getting to say goodbye—for her to wonder about his well-being during openheart surgery. Ouch. That was a lot for a kid to bear.

It hurt just hearing her talk about it. And for her to still be holding on to that this many years later…that moment, that pain, must have remained all of this time.

Jace couldn't believe she was telling him this. He wanted to reach out and touch her again. To ground himself and her. But there wasn't anything he could do to stop the flow of blood from that particular wound.

Because when he'd left town, he'd only added to it. And then Luc right after him.

Turns out the most un-leave-able person Jace knew had been left on repeat.

Chapter 5

Jace transported them to the hospital as fast as his truck and traffic would allow. They didn't receive any updates on the way, and he was afraid to ask. If there were good news, Luc would have contacted them.

Mackenzie must have felt the same, because unease and fear radiated from her, sending currents bouncing off the metal framework of the cab.

"Have you heard from Emma?"

Mackenzie picked up her phone. "No. I'll ask if she knows anything new." Her thumbs flew over the keys. Her phone chimed almost immediately. "She hasn't heard from him either." She dropped the phone into her lap. "Do you still believe in God?"

Why would she ask him something like that? The woman kept assuming he'd changed with time, but he hadn't. And no one knew him like she did. Not his mom. Not his brother. Not even his rodeo buddies.

"Of course I do." Kenzie could question all she wanted, but Jace was still the same. He'd even prayed for her through all of these years. For her happiness, her success. That someday she'd be able to understand why he'd done things the way he had. That someday she'd forgive him for it. "I've been praying nonstop about Cate and the girls, if that's what you're asking."

Again with that study of him from the side. Jace let it slide, let her look, thinking maybe she'd finally see him for who he really was. Who he'd always been, minus the blip of leaving her after high school.

"Me, too." She found a piece of thread on the bottom of her shirt and twisted it round and round her finger. Mackenzie normally wore jeans and boots at the ranch, but today she was casual in a bright blue T-shirt, shorts and flip-flops. Her feet and legs were tanned, her toe-nails unpainted. She was the kind of pretty that couldn't come from a jar or a tube. It simply was. "Emma said they called the church prayer chain. The whole town of Westbend is probably on their knees."

"Then let's believe God is listening."

Jace parked in the hospital lot. He hopped out and then waited by the front of the truck for Mackenzie, not about to open her door or help her in any way. He wasn't that daring.

She met him near the still-heated engine. "You don't need to come in, you know." Her stormy eyes landed everywhere but on him. "I'm fine. You can head back home if you want." She motioned as if he were a fly she could shoo away. "Or go do something else…fun, in Denver. I'll get a ride back."

Fun? Was she nuts? Like he would go anywhere else right now. Mackenzie might not want his support, but it was hers anyway.

"Stop it. Please." He placed his hands—the left bulky with the cast—on her shoulders. It was the closest they'd been since his arrival at the ranch, but Jace no longer cared about whatever barriers Mackenzie had built. Those pretty grays, crammed with upset and worry, finally met his and held. "What happened between us in the past doesn't matter right now. This is bigger than that." She didn't move away, didn't disconnect from him.

"Okay." Her shoulders eased down under his grip, her chin jutting in agreement.

She'd given him an inch, and Jace wanted ten miles. The craving to haul her close and hold on was almost impossible to resist.

But he managed to. She was letting him in the slightest bit, and he refused to ruin that.

They walked toward the entrance, Kenzie's strides sure and strong. But that didn't hide the fact that whatever they were about to face inside the hospital walls was scaring her silly.

Him, too.

The woman behind the information desk directed them. When they reached the correct floor and stepped out of the elevator, Kenzie gave a quiet gasp as the door slid shut behind them. Luc was sitting on the floor outside a room about halfway down a long florescent-lit hallway. His knees were bent, his head crashed onto his arms.

It didn't look good.

For the whole drive Jace had been telling himself that when they got to the hospital, everything would be okay. That the news would be encouraging. That maybe Luc hadn't contacted Emma or Mackenzie because he'd been busy with Cate or the babies.

But now? Jace's theory was in question. Big time.

Helplessness suffocated him. He was worthless here. He didn't have the right to comfort Mackenzie anymore. Not like she would need if things had worsened.

She might not want him in her life, but he could be strong for her.

Jace could at least do that.

He'd failed her in the past. Maybe he could figure out how to make that up to her now and in the future.

Mackenzie's overcooked-noodle knees buckled at the sight of her strong brother crashed to the floor in the hospital hallway. With his head dropped to his arms, he didn't see them. Didn't know she'd faltered so hard that Jace had cupped her elbow and now held her steady.

She wanted to shake Jace off, but she was frozen and immovable. A mess. Mackenzie had never felt so helpless and woozy and worthless, and it was embarrassing. *Enough. This moment isn't about you. Go be there for your brother.* But what if things were worse? What if Cate…?

A boulder clogged Mackenzie's throat, making it impossible to swallow, to suck in oxygen. Numbness buzzed through her limbs.

"Breathe." Jace jiggled her arm. "In and out."

She obeyed like a weak, pitiful kitten who needed to be bottle-fed.

Her brother was in a heap, and she was so cemented and freaked out that she couldn't make her legs work in order to go to him. She was supposed to be the strong one. But the crown no longer fit.

"You don't know what's going on. Don't jump to conclusions." Jace nodded toward Luc, his voice quiet and annoyingly calm. "Go find out, and then you can deal with it, whatever it is. You can handle this. You're the strongest person I know." Mackenzie wanted to be mad at Jace for driving her here. For forcing her to ride with him. For not leaving her alone.

But she was pathetically grateful he hadn't let her get away with any of that.

The temptation to turn into him for just a second, to let those strong arms of his tighten around her and that familiar voice whisper in her ear that everything was going to be okay, even if it wasn't… Mackenzie wanted that like she'd never wanted anything before.

And she hated herself for that weakness.

You've been just fine without him for seven years. Jace Hawke does not need to carry you through this. You have God and your family, and they're enough. Those sources are trustworthy, and the man next to you is not.

Not anymore.

"I'm going to find a waiting room and some bad coffee. I have no doubt you'd rather me not be with you right now, and I get that. So go check in with your brother. I'll keep praying."

Stop it! Stop being so good to me.

It wasn't fair. Jace's support only reminded her of what could have been. If he hadn't left Westbend. If he hadn't left her.

She didn't want to give him the satisfaction of seeing her unravel, so Mackenzie filled her lungs and pushed her shoulders back.

Jace watched her, assessing. Probably checking to see if she was going to fall apart right in front of him. Again.

"I'm fine, Hawke."

"You're going to have to trademark that phrase pretty soon, Kenzie Rae."

"Don't *Kenzie Rae* me."

"But it's so much fun to make you mad. How can I resist?"

The faintest hint of normalcy, of humor, edged in with his teasing. But the heavy unknown future loomed bigger, and they both knew it.

"Thanks." That was all she said, all she could muster. Jace accepted it with a nod, then walked in the opposite direction.

He's not the worst guy in the world.

And that was exactly the problem. He'd been the best guy in her world once upon a time, and she hadn't wanted that to change.

But sometimes Mackenzie didn't get to make the decisions. They were made for her.

She could only pray this wasn't one of those moments and that what she was about to find out from her brother would be the good news she and Jace and countless others had been praying for.

Even though her brother's body language shouted the opposite of that.

It took Mackenzie ages to cross the speckled, bleached tiles.

When she finally made it to her brother, she didn't speak. She was so afraid to ask what was wrong and find out the answer was horrible that she just dropped to the floor next to him and mirrored his bent-knee position.

His head came up from his hands. His eyes were wet. Red-lined. The only memory Mackenzie had of Luc getting emotional was on his wedding day. When Cate and

Ruby had come down the aisle together—then his Adam's apple had bobbed, and he'd had to work to keep himself in check.

But that was about it.

"How is she?"

"She's okay." Luc rubbed his hands over his face as if trying to wipe clean a chalkboard. "She's okay now. She made a turn for the better. Finally. They thought they were going to have to do a hysterectomy. But at the last second the bleeding stopped." He choked back a sob. "The nurses are in there now, helping her, and I was in the way, so I came out here to pull myself together."

Mackenzie grabbed him and held on.

A half groan, half cry wrenched from Luc, near her ear. "What would I have done…? What if she hadn't…?" His anguish was palpable, registering in her bones.

"It's okay. It's okay. She's all right now." *Thank You, thank You, thank You, God.*

Mackenzie didn't know what else to say or do to comfort Luc, so she just hugged him and prayed silently, praising God that Cate and Luc's story got to be one of the good ones.

They released each other, and Luc inhaled, deep and relieved. His mouth opened and then closed as if he couldn't form words.

"You don't have to say anything else. I get it." Luc might not be able to express himself at the moment, but Mackenzie could read him loud and clear. She'd always known what Luc was thinking or feeling. It had been unnerving at times to be so connected to another human being. But then it had also felt completely normal, because she'd never known anything else.

They sat silently for a minute, Luc stitching himself together, Mackenzie giving him the space to do that.

"You have to see the girls." He lit up, dissolving the stark pain from only moments before. "They look so identical, I'm worried I'm not going to be able to tell them apart. And they're so tiny and perfect that I'm afraid I'm going to break them if I pick them up. Not that I've had much of a chance to do that yet. They're in the NICU now."

"I can't wait to see them. Are you finally going to reveal their names? It was incredibly annoying that you didn't tell us before they were born."

Her brother obviously found her impatience amusing, because he waited a few beats before finally spilling. "Everly Jane and Savannah Rae."

"You used our middle names? Emma's going to flip. Oh, I love the names. So sweet. I'm honored."

"The babies will be here for a while, gaining weight and developing their lungs, but it sounds like they're doing well, considering."

"Emma's going to kill me for getting to them first. She took Ruby over to Gage's. Since everyone at the ranch knew about Cate, they didn't want her to overhear anything. She's waiting for the all clear to bring Ruby to see the babies and you guys."

"That was a good idea. I need to call her and let her know Cate's through the worst of it."

"I will."

"That would be great. Thanks. So, how did you even know what happened? I tried to call you earlier today, but your phone must have been off."

"It was on Silent. I'm so sorry. I wish I could have been there for you guys." It might take Mackenzie a few weeks or months to stop kicking herself for being gone during an emergency. Jace's statement in the car that her presence wouldn't have changed anything might be logical, but she still didn't like that she'd gone off the grid. Or that she'd let Jace affect her so much that avoiding him had been the immature reason she'd needed to escape at all. "Jace told me when I got back to the ranch. And then he insisted on driving me here. I guess he thought I was too upset to drive. I don't know what that was about. I was fine." *Or I would have been. Somehow.*

"Ah, Kenzie. You're a stubborn piece of work—you know that?"

"You mean I'm fabulous? Irreplaceable? A true superwoman?"

Luc groaned and stood, then tugged her up. "Right. All of those things." She even earned a quarter smile. "Maybe you shouldn't be so hard on him."

She wrinkled her nose.

"I have a favor to ask of you."

A switch in subject matter? Yes, please. "Of course. Whatever you need. Coffee? Food? Clothes?"

"I'm sure it will come as no surprise that our bags were packed by Cate, and we have every possible item we might need, here with us. Except car seats. But we won't be needing those for a while."

Mackenzie grinned. "I should have seen that one coming." Cate was nothing if not organized. "So, what is it?"

"I get that I ruined your life by hiring Jace without talking to you first." Oh, boy. So, they were continuing down the Jace road. "And I love you enough that if I could change that and find someone else, I would in a heartbeat."

Her own heart bogged down like a boot stuck in mud.

Luc wouldn't have hired Jace if she'd just been honest about how things had ended between them. How much he'd hurt her. It was more her fault than anyone's that the man was working at Wilder Ranch.

"But I can't," Luc continued. "He's all we have right now. And I need to be here for Cate and the girls. We're probably going to be driving back and forth between the ranch and Denver plenty. I'm not sure when the girls will get to go home. Cate either. I need you to buck up for the summer and accept Jace's help. Train him."

"I did."

That look he gave her. It was *I know you better than that* and *you're digging a hole* all in one. "I mean train him all the way this time. And quit trying to get him to leave."

"But—"

"Do you really think I don't know what you've been up to?"

Well. "This is all making me feel like a huge idiot." She huffed, humiliation and regret wrapped up together. It was like when she'd been a kid and thought she was getting away with something only to find out that her parents had been onto her the whole time.

And she'd definitely been childlike about Jace.

"I'm sorry I've been a big ole baby. I get it. And you're right. I'll stop. Promise. You don't need to worry about a thing with the ranch. We'll handle it. I'll even force myself into your office to make sure people and bills are paid and the lights stay on. Don't worry about a thing. Seriously. I've got it covered." She swallowed the bitter truth of her next statement. "I mean, Jace and I have it covered."

"Good. Thank you." Luc nodded just as the nurses

came out of Cate's room. "I'm going in to see my wife. You coming?"

"In a minute." She wanted to give Luc and Cate some time together without her intrusion. Plus she needed a second to deal with the mortification she was currently drowning in.

Luc strode into the room, shutting the door behind him, and Mackenzie barely resisted banging her head against the wood.

How embarrassing! She'd been a scheming toddler about Jace, and the whole world knew it. Well, maybe not the whole world. But her brother was bad enough.

Why had she been so immature about the man? They were long over and done. There was no need to stay tangled up in the past. In a should-have-meant-nothing high school relationship.

Mackenzie hated admitting she'd been wrong in how she'd been acting. And it was like chewing sand to think about being civil to Jace, to think about welcoming him and not just tolerating the guy who'd once made her feel so trivial that she hadn't even been worthy of a goodbye.

But for her brother's sake—for the ranch's sake—she would do exactly that.

If she were truly over Jace, there would be no harm in letting him back into her life. Professionally speaking, of course.

Chapter 6

Jace had been summoned by his *boss*, Mackenzie, and he wasn't about to be late.

The two of them had been running, heads down, since the babies' arrival nine days ago. After Cate's discharge from the hospital, she and Luc had stayed in Denver for a few days, to be close to the girls, who still needed to reach some milestones before they'd be allowed to come home. Now Luc and Cate were spending nights at the ranch and driving to the hospital during the day.

Thankfully Mama Wilder had come to help watch Ruby for a few days, because Jace didn't know how Mackenzie and Emma would have added that to their full plates.

He'd jumped in with both boots since the twins' unexpected early arrival, trying to be a help, hoping that his being here somehow made it easier for Luc to be there for his wife and daughters.

At least that would lessen the sting of not being able to compete. A couple of Jace's buddies had texted him about what he'd missed, updating him, asking how he was. Jace hadn't responded yet. If he didn't soon, they'd come knocking on his door. But it was hard to be out of the loop, not earning points. At least the guys would understand that.

Jace had just gotten back from supervising the afternoon shooting-range session, and Kenzie had said to meet him by the corral, but she wasn't there when he arrived.

Sable, the buckskin quarter horse who'd caught his attention last week, approached, meeting him at the railing.

"Hey there, pretty girl." She whinnied, then nosed around, looking for a treat. "You think that I'm going to bring you something every time I say hi?"

Her head bobbed in answer, and he laughed. "Fine. I give." Jace had popped into the kitchen on his way over and snagged an apple for Sable.

He offered it to her, and she chomped the treat. After, she nuzzled his shirt and his shoulders. "You're not nearly as stingy with your affection as some women I know." One woman in particular. Not that Jace was trying to win Mackenzie's affection.

But even though they'd worked together all week and done a good job of it—at least according to him—there was still a line in the sand. One Mackenzie had drawn and didn't dare cross. There'd been no talk about anything personal. Just business. It made sense, but at some point the two of them were going to have to stop pretending they didn't have a past.

"I guess the timing's not right yet. I can be patient."

With Luc's absence, there hadn't really been an opportunity to discuss anything outside Wilder Ranch.

It had been trial-by-fire learning for Jace, because while Mackenzie had attempted to train him more in the last week, their time was often cut short or interrupted.

But it was working. Jace was figuring things out. So he had no idea why Mackenzie had called this impromptu meeting with him.

Maybe she still wanted him to leave, though she hadn't given him that impression since the hospital. Mackenzie had been on her best behavior. He wasn't sure whether to be grateful for that or concerned about what she wasn't saying.

Jace brushed his free hand down Sable's neck, her coat gleaming in the sunlight. "You could rub off on her, you know. You're as sweet as they come." She held his gaze, those deep, dark eyes seeing and understanding more than anyone probably gave them credit for. "You're right. That wouldn't be nearly as interesting, would it? I always did like that Kenzie Rae was made of spice." Sable pawed the ground. "You have some sass in you, too, girl. No need to get in a huff about it."

That seemed to placate the horse, who burrowed her nose into his shirt in search of another treat. "I gave you all I've got. And don't tell the other horses that I'm sneaking you contraband. Pretty sure the *boss* would be upset about that." Jace's cheeks crinkled at the picture of Kenzie taking him to task. Her spunk was exactly what attracted him to her. Kenzie Rae could rule the world with one glance. When Jace had first noticed her in high school, it hadn't taken him long to "happen" to walk by her locker just as they were both headed to shop class— as if her signing up for shop class hadn't been enough of a reason to fall in love with her right then and there. And it hadn't taken her long to challenge him to a competition at the Wilder Ranch's shooting range.

The first day they'd hung out had stretched, morphing from shooting to riding the ranch and then dinner with the Wilder family.

Jace had fallen for all of it—her, her family, her world. They'd quickly become inseparable.

Maybe they'd moved too quickly into a relationship for their young ages. But it hadn't felt like it. It had felt like he'd found the one for him and age didn't matter one hoot.

And kissing the woman? It was like watching a fireworks show from five feet away and somehow managing not to get burned. "She can kiss. I'll give her that." Those lips held just as much spark as the rest of her. There might be one thousand off-limits signs between him and Mackenzie, but Jace wouldn't mind a quick refresher in that area. "Not that she wants a kiss from me these days. So I guess we don't have to worry about that, do we, Sable-girl?"

"You're not slipping the horses treats now, are you, Hawke?" Mackenzie startled him, and Jace jumped like he was guilty. Since he'd been thinking about kissing his boss, he supposed he sort of was.

"Of course not." He turned and flashed an innocent grin. Mackenzie was about ten feet away and still approaching. Had she heard his earlier comments? Should he ask...or no? A glint registered in those storm-cloud eyes for just a second before it was gone.

Even in her Wilder Ranch gear—polo, jeans and boots—Mackenzie was the picture of summer. Her wavy hair shifted in the breeze, and Jace's mouth turned to sand at the sight of her. He was once again the high school version of himself, smitten with the girl who'd breathed life into him after Evan's accident.

"I see you're playing favorites." Mackenzie's nod encompassed Sable, and Jace barely resisted snorting at where his mind had gone instead. He'd really never had another favorite—or another girlfriend—besides Mackenzie.

"Well, she's hard to resist." If Mackenzie had any inkling he was referring to her, she didn't let on.

"Sorry I'm late. Mom's here, as you know, and Emma had to talk to us. She'd decided that with the added stress of the twins still in the hospital, Luc and Cate going back and forth all of the time, and the strain that creates on the rest of us, she and Gage should postpone the wedding or just get married at the courthouse instead of having it here, at the end of July like they'd planned."

"Sounds like Emma."

"Doesn't it? Mom talked her off the ledge. She reminded her that they're planning to have a simple ceremony and reception, and that everything would calm down soon and work out like it's supposed to. And that Luc and Cate would be incredibly upset if she changed her wedding because of them or the girls."

"Sounds like Mama Wilder handled everything just fine."

"Oh, man." Mackenzie's head shook. "I haven't heard that name in so long. I forgot you used to call her that."

He sure had. He'd practically been a Wilder family member those last couple of years. Another reason it had been so hard for him to leave. He hadn't just torn himself away from Mackenzie; he'd ripped his heart out by leaving all of them.

"So, what's up? Did you ask to meet me out here so you could fire me? Or kill me and hide the body?"

Her eyes crinkled at the corners, and her level of pretty about knocked him over. "No." Her head tilted. "Though you are giving me ideas."

"Very funny."

"Honestly? I was desperate to get outside. I hate being in the office on a gorgeous day like this."

Jace couldn't agree more. "Luc's work driving you crazy?"

She waved a hand. "Nah. It's been all right."

He raised questioning eyebrows and waited.

A reluctant shrug followed. "Okay, so it's not my favorite. But after everything that happened with Cate and the babies, the last thing I'm going to do is complain. And in regard to your earlier remark, I'm pretty certain I've been on my best behavior around you. I haven't said one unkind thing to you in the last week."

"You been keeping track?"

"Maybe. Maybe I'm rather proud of myself."

This woman. "You're a piece of work—you know that?"

"I've heard that before, yes." A smile. An actual full-fledged smile followed, along with a jolt of attraction from him. *She's your boss, not your girlfriend. Cool it, Hawke.*

"Luc said that you could teach the wranglers some things, even if you can't do them yourself because of your arm. Is that true?"

She was asking what he could add to the ranch, not pressuring him to leave yet again? Jace willed his jaw not to fall open in shock.

"Sure. We could do steer wrestling. Cattle roping. Not

sure exactly how to teach those with the arm, but I'd figure it out." Jace glanced at the intrusive cast. He'd been taking every supplement he could find that promoted faster healing. And something must be working, because when he'd checked in with Dr. Sanderson this week, he'd shown improvement in all areas.

Even his noggin had calmed down over the last few days, giving him hope his symptoms were finally subsiding.

"I should be able to talk some of the guys through it. Not like they'd be competing in a real rodeo. Just against each other."

"As long as it's something the wranglers can do without getting hurt, I think the guests would love it."

"As for team penning…" Jace scanned the corral. "I'm not sure we can swing it. Usually it's culling certain cattle from a herd. So we'd need livestock for that. But we could do a makeshift version where the wranglers just have to corral three cattle. Something simple like that. It would probably still be entertaining for the guests. We could have them compete against each other for fastest times."

"That would work."

"Does this conversation mean you're accepting that Luc hired me and you're going to stop trying to get rid of me?"

A dash of *don't push me too far* mingled with a faint smile. "Seems like it."

"Does this also mean we're going to get along now instead of all of that angry sassiness and chilly ignoring me?"

Her thumb traced the scar on her arm that had come from attempting to sneak through a barbed-wire fence as a kid. "I haven't done that in forever." She paused. "At least not for over a week."

"True." A weak and yet somehow amusing defense.

"And my answer is maybe. If you'll do one thing for me."

Warning sirens blared. "And what's that?"

"Teach me to ride a bull."

"What?" No way, no how would Jace put the woman he'd once loved up on one of those bucking beasts. "You're joking, right?"

"Nope. I don't see why the boys get to have all the fun."

"That's what will help you get along with me?"

She huffed. "Luc already commanded me to do that. But let's just say the bull riding lesson might bring to life my more…generous, patient, forgiving side."

Jace hadn't known she had one of those. Only Kenzie Rae. And despite understanding the appeal of riding a bull, he couldn't do it. He'd never forgive himself if she got hurt. And she would. Everyone did eventually.

"I'll teach you something else. What about cattle roping?"

"No. I want the real deal."

"Ah, no. That's way too dangerous."

"You do it."

"I'm a man."

Fire lit her features, and Jace threw his head back and laughed deep and long. "I'm kidding." He tried to catch his breath, slapping a hand against his sternum. "I'm joking." His arms formed a protective barrier in case she attacked him for the chauvinistic reply. Of course he hadn't meant it in the least. He'd just wanted to get a rise out of Mackenzie. "I knew your reaction to that would be hilarious."

"Har-har." She was all annoyance, but he was positive her lips held the slightest curve.

"Kenzie Rae, I have no doubt you can do anything you put your mind to, and that being female doesn't change what you can accomplish, but I'm not teaching you to ride a bull. I can't. It's too dangerous and I'd never forgive myself if you got hurt."

"You're hurt right now!" She motioned toward his arm.

"Exactly my point."

A strangled *argh* came from her. "Fine. I'll find someone else to help me."

"No, you won't. You certainly wouldn't be asking me if you had any other options."

That punch-him-in-the-gut mouth angled up at the corners. "True."

"You already said we were going to get along now. You can't take that back just because I refuse to get you injured on a bull."

"Don't tell me what I can and can't do, Hawke."

He groaned. She laughed—actually laughed. The sound was painful and delicious all at the same time.

"Come on." Mackenzie strode toward the barn. "Let's go see what supplies we have and what we'll need to get."

Jace jogged after her, and out of nowhere his head spun and reeled.

Seriously? He'd barely moved at all. How could something so simple cause such a reaction? Frustration choked him. Just when he'd thought the dizziness and headaches had packed up and left for good, the symptoms reared up again.

He hadn't even put medicine in his pocket, because the last couple of days had been great.

He slowed to hopefully combat the vertigo, and Mackenzie paused to wait for him, confusion at his snail pace puckering her brow. "You okay?"

"Yep." Nope. Not in the least.

Jace might have just made the slightest hint of progress with Mackenzie, but the rest of him was still barreling downhill.

Jace walked with Mackenzie as they entered the barn, but something about the last few seconds niggled and latched on. What had that been about? It had almost looked like Jace had swayed after he'd jogged in her direction.

But that was impossible. The man rode bulls for a living. He jumped to safety when his eight seconds were up—or got thrown before that, if the bull bested him. So the idea of him wobbling after a few steps didn't make sense at all.

Maybe she'd imagined it.

Except…that wasn't the first time Mackenzie had noticed him acting strange. There'd been the day they'd ridden the trails and he'd claimed he was overheated, out by the hot springs. And the day the twins were born…on the way out of the hospital, that night, Jace had tossed her his truck keys and told her to drive. Mackenzie had assumed he'd been offering her an olive branch—making up for his churlish behavior earlier in the day, when he'd insisted on driving her to the hospital. But then on the ride home, he'd let his head fall back, resting it against the seat. He'd claimed he was tired and closed his eyes, but Mackenzie had noticed him rubbing his temples…

almost as if he were in pain. When she'd asked him about it, he'd said that he was "fine" and then grinned, a hint of teasing in his response because of all of her I'm-fine retorts earlier in the day.

Those instances, along with the one from a few seconds ago, made her think there was something going on with Jace. Something he wasn't telling her. Maybe wasn't telling anyone.

When they'd been young, he'd never hidden things from her…or at least that was what she'd thought. Until the day she'd found an envelope addressed to her and slipped in with the other ranch mail. One that detailed how Jace *had* to go. *Had* to choose the rodeo over her. One that told her he was sorry.

Not as sorry as she'd been.

She led Jace toward the storage area connected to the back of the barn that held all of the seasonal equipment. She wasn't sure if they had anything usable or not, but it was worth checking before they spent money.

The ranch did well, but they were all frugal and careful to keep it that way.

She stepped into the storage room, and two figures in the corner jumped apart as if they'd been Tasered. Nick and Trista. The young couple had come on staff this summer, already dating, and had obviously just been caught, attached at the lips.

Certainly it was a kiss that no one was meant to see.

But at a guest ranch, there was no privacy.

Emma had warned Mackenzie before she'd hired the wrangler that he was already dating Trista, one of the Kids' Club staffers. So before offering him a position, she'd talked to the two of them about exactly what kind of protocol would be expected from them. What behavior was not acceptable.

They'd just blown through the details of that conversation.

"You guys." Disappointment sucked the oxygen from the room. "We talked about this when I hired Nick. You knew the rules when you came on staff."

Nick and Trista shared an embarrassed glance.

Jace stiffened at the encounter, his shoulder brushing Mackenzie's. Was he biting his tongue? Or staying out of it? Either way she felt strangely supported having him stand next to her. Having him be a witness to the situation. At least then it wouldn't be Nick and Trista's word against hers if things went further south.

Nick squared his shoulders, regret evident. "It was my fault. I'll take the blame."

"I'm so sorry." Trista teared up. "We didn't mean to. I was just putting some things away and we ran into each other in here. It wasn't calculated. I promise."

"If you give us another chance, it won't happen again." Nick added. "I love working here. Trista does, too. We both need to make money to cover our college expenses."

Mackenzie was torn between sympathy for the couple and concern for the ranch, for the livelihood of her family. If a guest had run into these two…that would have been a whole different scenario. So unprofessional. "We can't have you meeting up, accidentally or on purpose, during work. And we definitely can't have a guest—adult or child—running into you like this. Personal time should be spent together outside the ranch. Not here."

Trista covered her face with her hands. "I'm mortified."

"Keep her and let me go if you have to. I don't want Trista losing her job because of me."

Well. Mackenzie's heated upset notched down. They were just young and in love. And it wasn't like she'd caught them doing anything more...thankfully.

Normally Mackenzie would talk to Luc and Emma before making a decision about what to do in a situation like this, but things were too busy this summer. She'd have to go with her gut. And her instincts said they were just kids who'd made a mistake.

"I'm going to write this up in your employee files, and then I'm going to give you another chance. But if this happens again, you'll both be let go. Okay?"

Nods answered her, their fearful expressions subsiding.

"All right. Please go back to whatever you're supposed to be doing."

They scampered off after expressing their thanks for the second chance.

"Well, well, well." Twinkling eyes accompanied Jace's teasing. "Look who has a big ole softy heart."

"I do not."

He let loose with a deep laugh, just like he had outside, when he'd told her she couldn't ride a bull because she was a girl.

Of course he'd been joking. Jace had never been the type to say anything derogatory about women. Quite the opposite. He'd thought his mama was strong for overcoming all she had, and Mackenzie had always considered that one of his attractive qualities.

Not that she needed to dwell on any of those.

"We have to write them up. If we don't, and there's a

next time, I won't have any proof. Though hopefully it won't be needed."

"Sounds good, boss."

"You can quit with the boss stuff now."

"Oh, Kenzie Rae." His scratchy drawl lowered and strung out like honey. "I'm just getting started."

Her sigh expanded to fill the room. "That's exactly what I feared."

Chapter 7

"We keep the employee files in Luc's office," Mackenzie explained to Jace as they entered the room. She unlocked the file cabinet and removed the two folders she needed. "We use a standard form. It's on the computer." She was about to drop into Luc's chair behind the desk when she realized there wasn't a second seat. And she had promised Luc that she'd actually train Jace. "Hang on."

She went down the hall and stole a chair from the front office. When she finagled it through Luc's doorway, Jace strode over. "Let me."

"I've got it. It makes no sense for you to take the chair with only one arm. Now, scoot so I can get this thing in here."

Jace moved out of her way, grumbling under his breath. She only caught *confounded* and *stubborn*.

Her lips pressed and bowed. Fine. Mackenzie would

take those descriptions any day. She maneuvered around Jace and situated the second chair so that it was squeezed behind the desk, with hers.

After she took a seat in the rolling chair, Jace dropped into the one next to it with an agitated—and rather pouty—huff.

"I don't like being useless."

Mackenzie understood that. She'd been a much-bigger baby about a broken leg when she was a kid and had hated every cooped-up moment. "You're not. You just need a little time…to come to terms with the fact that a girl is stronger than you." She flashed him a victorious smirk. It was nice to have something up on the man—at least more than that quarter of an inch that shrank down to nothing when she went toe-to-toe with him.

"I've never doubted your toughness, Kenzie Rae. You are most certainly a force to be reckoned with."

She wrinkled her nose and rocked back in surprise.

"You don't like it when I agree with you, do you?"

"I don't know that I don't *like* it. It just surprises me."

Jace's low chuckle reignited something long forgotten and buried inside her. Attraction. Definitely the kind that should remain off the table.

The space behind the desk shrank even more when Mackenzie began clicking through folders on the computer and Jace leaned in to catch what she was doing.

"It should be in the employee-form folder… There it is. So we'll just print it off and fill it out. And then I'll have the two of them sign copies for their files so that they know what's expected in the future."

The *zip-zip* of the printer filled the quiet. Jace grabbed the sheet and handed it off to her—he wouldn't be able to fill in much with his casted hand.

Mackenzie wrote in Trista's and Nick's names, then drew a blank when she got to the part about describing the incident, because Jace had inched even closer to her, and her brain cells had taken a hike the second his shoulder had grazed hers. He smelled like high school Jace. Soap and deodorant with a hint of sweat from the day—he'd supervised the shooting range this afternoon—but that scent wasn't unwelcome. And if that wasn't the strangest thought she'd ever had...

"Trying to figure out what you're going to say?" Jace questioned.

"Um...yeah." Something like that. "I'm not exactly sure what wording to use."

"I have a few suggestions."

His humor transferred to her amused lips. "I'm sure you do." Mackenzie could only imagine what he would come up with. "I do not think Human Resources would approve."

Jace studied her profile, and she willed her skin not to react, not to overheat, not to notice. None of which worked. "Does HR care if my boss was sabotaging my work when I first started?"

"HR doesn't take complaints like that."

Jace laughed, rich and loud and delicious, just as banging on the office door—which had a tendency to swing shut—interrupted.

"Come in," Mackenzie called out.

Jace didn't scooch back, though everything in her was screaming for him to do exactly that. They weren't doing anything wrong, but her sympathies flared for the awkwardness Trista and Nick must have felt in the storage room.

Bea poked her head inside the office. "Mackenzie? Vera sliced her hand open, and it doesn't look good."

"Coming." She popped up from behind the desk, and Jace moved to let her out.

Mackenzie jogged with Bea across the lodge lobby and into the kitchen. Red splattered the floor, the countertop, the towel wrapped around Vera's hand. She hadn't been expecting all of *this*.

"Vera, are you okay?"

The silver-haired woman was seated on the stainless-steel kitchen countertop, with her hand elevated. "I'm guessing you're not going to believe me if I say I'm fit as a fiddle?"

"Ah, no."

The woman's favorite answer to "how are you?" wasn't going to work at the moment.

"I'm sorry about this." Despite her pluck, Vera wobbled on the edge of tears. "I was cutting an avocado and the knife just went…" She shuddered.

Vera was in her early fifties and had ended up at the ranch this summer because she'd recently made some life changes. She'd told Mackenzie during her Skype interview that after living timid and afraid for a long time, she'd started taking risks—like quitting her job of twenty years to pursue new things and choosing gratefulness instead of negativity. She wanted to explore, she'd said. To stop people-pleasing and grab each day by the horns.

Probably hadn't imagined this as part of that scenario.

Joe, head chef and Wilder family member since Mackenzie had been young, brought an ice pack and applied it to Vera's wrapped hand. "This is just a war wound, honey. Every good chef has a few." He lifted his weathered, arthritis-burdened fingers, showing the white scars in his rich black skin. But after the display of calm for Vera's benefit, his eyes toggled to Mackenzie's. They held alarm, and his head gave a quick shake.

Jace stepped into the circle. Mackenzie hadn't realized he'd followed her. "I've been around my fair share of injuries and blood. Gotta be honest, Vera, I'm not sure you're even above a four on the scale for the worst stuff I've seen."

His teasing earned a watery chuckle from Vera. "Thanks a lot, bull rider. Way to kick a woman when she's down."

"Mind if I look?" Jace asked.

Mackenzie waved him forward. "As long as Vera's okay with it."

The woman inhaled and then nodded.

"Look over my shoulder and count the bins on that shelf, okay?" When she followed Jace's directions, he unwrapped the towel, quickly, efficiently, so that they could see the cut.

It was deep and gaping.

Unfortunately Vera saw it, too, and she let out a squeal of horror and swayed from her seated perch on the countertop. Jace rewrapped it quickly and then situated himself next to her, tucking a friendly arm around her shoulders as if they were two buddies, hanging out, even though he was probably keeping her upright.

"Looks like you've earned yourself some stitches. Kenzie, you driving?"

Mackenzie was in shock herself, from the amount of blood, from Jace's ability to jump in and handle the whole thing like he was a medic. From the fact that Jace…belonged. He fit. Even after she'd tried so hard to tell him he was a round peg and Wilder Ranch was a square hole.

"Kenzie Rae." Her name wasn't a question; it was more of a command.

"Yes, of course. Let's go."

Jace kept an arm around Vera as they walked to the front of the lodge, just in case. Vera was handling the injury well at this point, but he didn't need her crumbling to the floor and adding another.

Mackenzie had jogged over to Luc's office to grab her keys. Her small Ranger pickup was parked at the lodge, which worked out well, since Jace didn't think Vera was up for one of her enthusiastic speed walks.

"You're a trouper, Vera. You're going to be just fine. Although I don't see why you have to create such a fuss over a little cut." Jace waited to see if she'd take the bait.

"You're just jealous that I'm getting all of the attention. You can't be fawned over all of the time, bull rider."

He laughed. "That's my girl." If he kept her engaged, they'd have her fixed up in no time.

Jace had liked Vera right away when they'd met. She was quick-witted, funny, positive. She'd told Jace that she used to live a painfully solitary existence. She'd been a complainer. Sad. Bitter even. And then, about a year and a half ago, she'd had an aha moment and flipped everything upside down. She'd transformed her life in gigantic, hard steps. The scariest of which had been quitting her job. She'd begun roaming, traveling, taking odd jobs as they came. And according to her, they always did. That was how she'd ended up at Wilder Ranch for the summer—on a whim.

Jace wished the woman would become friends with his mom. She could use a bright light like Vera in her life. Everyone could.

Outside, he assisted Vera into the middle seat. Mackenzie showed up with her keys and buckled Vera in. The three of them squished into the pickup like sardines, but it was probably for the best. That way they could hold Vera up without admitting they were doing exactly that.

She kept her hand elevated and iced while Mackenzie drove.

The local hospital was very small and should probably be classified as more of an urgent-care center. No wonder Cate and Luc had driven to Denver when she'd gone into labor. Jace shuddered to think what would have happened if they hadn't.

Mackenzie dropped Jace and Vera by the entrance, then parked. When Jace offered Vera an arm to lean on, she took it as if he were escorting her to a play or the opera, all regal and proper.

Mackenzie caught up with them just inside the sliding doors. The waiting area was empty. There was no one—literally not a soul—occupying the chairs or the desk. They were open, right? It wasn't much after five o'clock. They had to be.

"You two sit and I'll see if I can find someone." They got situated while he strode to the desk and checked behind it. He had no idea what someone would be doing down there, but really, where was everyone?

"Hello? Anyone here?"

"Coming," someone called out from behind the wall flanking the reception desk. Seconds later a woman wearing scrubs covered in kittens rounded the divider.

"Ms. Silvia?"

At Jace's recognition, she went from scowl to melting. "Jace Hawke? Is that you?" She dropped items on the desk and then reached across for a hug. "It's about time you came home to visit."

"It's good to see you, Ms. Silvia."

"What are you doing here? Your mama okay?"

"She's fine. I brought in one of my coworkers. She cut her hand open pretty bad."

"Oh, sweetie. Poor thing. We'll get her fixed up. Just need you to fill out some paperwork."

"I'll do that." Mackenzie popped up and took the clipboard from the woman. "It will be workers' comp."

"I see." Ms. Silvia's narrowed gaze swept down Mackenzie as if she'd taken the knife to Vera herself, and Jace squashed a smile. It was good to have someone on his side. His team. And Ms. Silvia had always been that.

When things had been rough as a kid, he'd ridden his bike down the street to her house. She would give him a cookie or a glass of lemonade. Sit on the front step with him. She'd even hired him for odd jobs and paid him for them.

She'd been a saving grace in his childhood, especially when Dad had fought with Mom. Evan had been partial to disappearing from the house during those spats, too—or at least hiding behind loud music and headphones.

Mackenzie returned to the seat by Vera and began filling out paperwork, asking the injured woman for details as needed.

Jace leaned across the desk. "Is there any way we could get Vera back quickly? It's a pretty deep cut." Not that Jace had gotten that great of a look with all of the drama in the kitchen. But he'd seen enough to know she needed medical attention.

"I'll have our medical assistant bring her back. Dr. Bradley is just finishing up with another patient, and he's all we have on tonight. We're short-staffed." Ms. Silvia patted his hand. "You just hang tight, sweetie."

"Thank you," Jace called out as she took off, then rejoined Vera and Mackenzie, taking the seat across from them.

"Thanks for checking if they could get her in faster." Mackenzie quirked an eyebrow. "Sweetie." She added some sugar to her tone.

"You're welcome, honey." Mackenzie could bring it, as far as he was concerned. She'd been holding back from any real conversation with him. Acting as if they didn't have a past.

If she wanted to play, he'd play.

"Good thing you were here. If Vera and I would have been alone, it would be tomorrow before she got treated." Vera's eyes were closed, but a small laugh came from her. "Ms. Silvia have a crush on you?"

Jace had accused Kenzie of as much with the zip-line kid, but really… "Why? You jealous?"

She rolled her eyes.

"Silvia used to take pity on me as a kid. Throw odd jobs my way and then pay me for them. I'm pretty sure I did a horrible job at each one, but she never stopped asking me for help. And there was usually a treat of some sort involved, too. I'm sure she knew I wouldn't have had any money if she hadn't shoved some my way. But she always made me work for it."

"My opinion of Ms. Silvia is growing."

"As it should."

"What is it with females and you? In high school Mrs. Beign used to give you a hall pass all of the time, and you'd just mess around and not go to class."

Curved lips—sure to annoy Kenzie—sparked and

grew. "What can I say? Women love me." He followed the quip with an I-can't-help-it shrug.

"Not all women." Mackenzie tossed him one of those sassy smiles she kept in her pocket for parting shots.

"Trust me, honey." He dropped the endearment again. "That is information I do know."

Whoops. Mackenzie had traveled into uncharted territory during this conversation with Jace, and she wanted out. Now.

"How are you doing, Vera?"

The woman's eyelids were shuttered, her breathing even. "Fine. I'm just sitting here, listening to you two bicker and flirt, wondering how I never noticed anything between you before."

Jace hooted, and humiliation consumed Mackenzie. See how quickly things got out of hand when Jace was involved? She was far more professional when the man wasn't in tow.

Ms. Silvia bustled back to the desk, and a young girl who looked annoyed to be alive met them in the waiting room. "Follow me." The deep organ notes of her greeting screamed, *I'm bored* and *I want to go home* all at once.

Vera stood. "I want you guys to come with me. That way, if I faint, you can pick me up off the floor."

"You're not going to faint." Jace popped up and wrapped an arm around her as they began walking. "You're way too tough for all of that."

"I'm not so sure about that, bull rider."

Mackenzie dropped off the paperwork with Ms. Silvia, and the three of them entered the exam room. After the medical assistant took Vera's vitals, she scampered off to hide until her next torturous human encounter.

Five minutes later a man with salt-and-pepper hair and wearing a white lab coat came in. "I'm Dr. Bradley." His teeth were perfect and oh-so-bright. His smile was AARP-commercial-worthy.

And a very single, never-been-married Vera looked as dazed as if she'd just walked into a wall. How could the handsome doctor have more of an impact on her than her sliced-up hand?

Dr. Bradley motioned to the exam table. "Have a seat. Let's get your hand checked out."

Based on the next few minutes, it was more like the two of them were going to check out each other. If Vera thought Mackenzie and Jace had been flirting, it was nothing compared to the current doctor-patient vibe. Plenty of gazing, smiling and gentle shoulder touches were exchanged. At the current rate it would take days for Vera's hand to get stitched up.

Jace leaned close enough that he could whisper under Dr. Bradley and Vera's conversation. "I feel like we're on their first date with them."

Mackenzie snort-laughed, and doctor and patient turned to investigate. "Sorry. Nothing to do with you, Vera." Although…guess that hadn't exactly been the truth.

She slugged Jace on the arm after the two turned back to their conversation. "Stop it! HR does not approve of your shenanigans."

Jace just grinned, and annoyingly her pathetic cells swooned. *Enough, traitor body. This man wrecked you once, and he can do it again far too easily.*

Dr. Bradley was telling Vera about his grown children now and his first grandson. Vera seemed to have forgotten about her hand. And maybe Dr. Bradley had, too.

Jace sank down in his chair, letting his head fall back against the wall.

"Searching for a comfortable position, Hawke?"

"Yep. Considering that we're going to be here for a while…" He studied Dr. Bradley and Vera through squinted eyes. "Weeks maybe. He's going to tell her she needs a hand replacement and lots of follow-up visits. You may want to warn your workers'-comp insurance things are about to get expensive."

Mackenzie managed to keep her amusement quiet this time. She leaned in Jace's direction, her voice a whisper. "What if Dr. Bradley has three wives, all in different states?"

"I don't," the doctor answered. "I'm widowed, actually."

For real? He'd heard her? How? Did the man have bionic ears? Of course it was Mackenzie's comment that he'd caught, not Jace's.

At least Dr. Bradley didn't look upset with her.

"I'm so sorry. Really." Could Mackenzie fit under her chair? The temptation to crawl under something was strong.

"Thank you." Dr. Bradley was gracious, nodding to accept her apology.

In her peripheral vision, Jace shook with laughter. "Stop it," she hissed, which only increased his enjoyment of her blunder.

"I'm sorry to hear that, too." Vera touched Dr. Bradley's arm with her uninjured hand. "So…you're not married…or…seeing anyone?"

Dr. Bradley's pristine white teeth flashed. "No, I'm not seeing anyone."

Go, Vera! The woman was not afraid—Mackenzie

would give her that. At least Mackenzie's humiliating moment had been used for good. Vera was a woman on a mission today. She hadn't been kidding about living every moment to the fullest—no regrets.

And why shouldn't Vera go for it? If nothing came of her flirting with Dr. Bradley, she'd be on to her next adventure and job before long, and would probably never see the man again.

She had nothing to lose.

Unlike Mackenzie, who, since Jace's arrival, felt like she had everything to lose. Her sanity. Her peace. He kept inching into her space—physically and figuratively. Currently his arm was dangerously close to hers, on the armrest between them. Just that caused her skin to tingle with awareness.

The man made it too easy to remember how good it had once been between them. And way too easy to forget how he'd left.

Chapter 8

Thirty minutes in the exam room, and Dr. Bradley and Vera were still enthralled with each other.

Jace leaned closer to her chair, still willing to risk conversation that only he could get away with. "We could be doing the chicken dance over here and they wouldn't even notice us."

"Mmm. Chicken." Mackenzie should never skip lunch like she had today. It wasn't safe for anyone when she didn't eat on a regular schedule. Like a toddler or a baby. "Trust me when I say that no one wants to see you do that."

"Afraid you'll find my moves too attractive to resist?"

"I'm afraid the doctor will think you have something wrong with you medically and want to admit you."

His mouth formed a confident, distracting arch. "I know you're laughing underneath that iceberg veneer, Kenzie Rae. I always could make you laugh."

"Could not." *Impressive comeback.* Mackenzie barely resisted an eye roll at her elementary maturity. "I can't believe I said that about—" Mackenzie nodded toward Dr. Bradley in lieu of using his name. He'd probably overhear again if she did. "You bring out the worst in me, Hawke."

"No, ma'am. I believe I bring out the best."

Maybe he had once upon a time, but not anymore.

Without warning, Jace grabbed her hand and hauled her up from the chair. "Vera, we're going to hit the vending machines. Do you want anything?"

Vera shook her head, and then Mackenzie was dragged out of the room by Jace. She should say something, do something…but before she could get her lax vocal cords functioning, the aggravating man severed their contact.

"Sorry." He stared at where their joined hands had just been. "You implied you were hungry, and…old habits die hard, I guess."

She ignored the flash of muscle memory and her on-fire fingers, reaching into the trough of hurt that this man ignited instead. "You know I'm still—"

"Don't say it," Jace interrupted her. "You're still mad at me, and I get that. You can be. But at some point you and I are going to talk. When you're ready. At some point we're going to work this out."

Mackenzie's body ached from discussing their past, even in such loose terms. "I'm not ready."

"Okay." Jace's chest deflated. "Then I'll wait. You tell me when."

"What if I never want to talk about it?" Mackenzie hated that what had happened between them still had its claws in her.

For so long she'd wondered why he'd left the way he

had. But now that she had the opportunity to find out, Mackenzie was afraid to know the truth. "I loved bull riding more than you" or "I didn't love you anymore" weren't things she could survive hearing. Even now.

"I hope that's not the case, because there are things I need to say. Things you need to understand." Jace held her gaze for a hot minute—as if driving his point home—and then turned toward the vending machines.

They walked the rest of the way in silence. He slipped money inside the snack and beverage machines, pressed some buttons, then handed her a sweetened iced tea and a package of Reese's Peanut Butter Cups.

What? How did he *do* that?

Jace scooted to the left and pressed a few buttons on the coffee machine, making a cup of brew to go with his Junior Mints, while Mackenzie reeled from the simple gesture.

He took a tentative sip, testing the temperature as he faced her. "What's wrong?" He touched the package in her hand. "Did I get you the wrong thing? I didn't even think to ask. I just…"

And there was the problem—not the lack of asking, but the fact that he knew her like he did, even after so many years of separation. That he remembered something simple like what she ate or drank.

It was painful to think about what they'd once had—where they'd once been in their relationship—and where they were now.

"No, it's fine. I'm just…" And then—ugh—her turncoat eyes filled with moisture.

Jace didn't ask for permission, he just enveloped her in a hug, his coffee and candy held around her back, her peanut-butter cups and drink tucked between them. "I'm

so sorry, Kenz." He held her tightly, and she let her muscles sag for just a minute. Just one minute. "I'm so sorry."

Mackenzie beat tears back with a stick while crushed
against this man, who'd held her heart for so long. She
really needed him to let her keep it whole this time.

"Me, too, Hawke." She forced herself to push away
from him. To break the contact that had felt like home.
"Me, too."

Jace had been right about the length of time they
were at the hospital with Vera. The visit had lasted for
hours—though thankfully not a week—because another
emergency had come in. Dr. Bradley had split his time
between the two patients, but eventually Vera had gotten fixed up.

In more ways than one.

She also had a date planned with Dr. Bradley for Saturday night.

Someone might as well find love, because it certainly
wasn't going to be Jace anytime soon.

He was married to his work. And the only girl he'd
ever loved was still angry with him.

Rightfully so.

Mackenzie parked as close to the female staff's lodging as she could get, and they unpacked themselves from
her pickup. The two of them sandwiched Vera on the
walk to her room and up the stairs.

"The stars are gorgeous tonight!" Vera waved her uninjured hand at the sky. "So beautiful." Reverence with
a side of pain meds.

Jace shared an amused glance with Mackenzie over
the woman's head. Vera's rose-colored view of the world

tonight was only a smidgen more than her everyday positivity.

He waited outside the door to her room while Mackenzie settled Vera inside and made sure she had her medicine and water for the middle of the night. "Call me if you need anything. I'll keep my phone turned up." Mackenzie shut the door behind her. "Do you think she's going to be okay for the night?"

"Yep. The medicine should knock her out." They walked down the stairs. "Plus you told her to call if she had an issue. And I'm guessing you keep your phone on every night, in case of an emergency."

Mackenzie's lips quirked. "Maybe."

"You're a pretty good boss, Wilder."

They paused near her truck. "Now you're just kissing up."

The phrase sent his mind happily skipping down memory lane. Jace definitely hadn't been doing any of that. He would have remembered.

Outdoor lights emphasized the red skin flaming at Mackenzie's obviously regrettable choice in wording. Jace wanted to jump all over that. Question if she was extending an invitation. But he knew better—Vera might get to fall in love on a whim, but he and Kenzie didn't have that luxury this time.

Not when their careers were on two different paths. Not when he was bound and determined not to hurt her again.

"I've never seen anyone fall in love that fast, and in an emergency room to boot."

Jace welcomed Mackenzie's shift in conversation. Anything to get him away from his current outlawed thoughts. "Me either."

324 *The Bull Rider's Secret*

"She's so happy. To think that maybe she just met her match for the first time at fifty-four years old... That's pretty cool."

Vera and Dr. Bradley had moved fast—Jace would give them that. But then again, life was too short to wait around and see if something happened.

Life was also too short to delay explaining to Mackenzie about why he'd left the way he had, but he couldn't push her much faster. She needed time and he had to respect that.

"Agreed. You headed to bed?" It wasn't that late, but he was exhausted. Mackenzie had to be, too.

"Yeah. In a minute. Need a ride?" She opened the driver's door to her truck.

"Nah." The guys' lodging wasn't much past the women's. "It's a nice night for a walk."

"Okay. Good night, Hawke. Thanks for your help today."

She was thanking him? Would wonders never cease? Jace didn't wreck the good moment by letting any of his thoughts tumble out. "You're welcome. Night."

He watched her pickup as she drove back to the lodge, the brake lights turning red as she stopped and then parked. Why wasn't she headed to her cabin? Was she planning to leave her truck at the lodge and walk?

Mackenzie got out and took the lodge steps two at a time, then disappeared inside.

What was she doing? It was late enough that anything she had to do could wait until tomorrow, wasn't it?

Except they'd never finished the paperwork. And Mackenzie had said she wanted to follow up with Trista and Nick tomorrow. Have them sign it. And her days were so jam-packed right now, covering for Luc, that she probably wanted to get it done tonight. Cross it off her list.

Mackenzie worked harder than anyone Jace knew, and due to the toughness in his profession, that was saying a lot.

Jace followed the path to the lodge and found Mackenzie exactly where he'd expected to—hunched over Luc's desk.

"Trying to avoid training me again, Wilder?"

She flew inches off her chair, surprise quickly morphing to confusion at the sight of him. "What are you doing here?"

"My job." He joined her, taking the chair still next to the rolling one she occupied. "Sorry if I startled you there. I should have given you some indication it was me." Even though the ranch was completely safe, a woman still had to watch out for herself. Had to keep her intuition on high alert. After the late shift stocking shelves at the five-and-dime, his mom had always walked to her car with someone else. It just made sense to be careful. "Sometimes I can be kind of an idiot."

Mackenzie's lips twitched. "I hadn't realized." She motioned to the paperwork with the pen in her hand. "You don't need to be here. I'll handle this. Just wanted to get it done tonight because tomorrow things will be crazy again—"

A loud growl interrupted her.

"Was that your stomach or a bear?"

Her laughter made Jace's previous exhaustion fade. "Guess that candy didn't count as dinner for you either. I'm starving."

She set the pen on the desk, and it rolled to the edge of the papers and stopped. "We could sneak into the kitchen.

See if there's anything left from dinner or make a sandwich."

"Sounds good to me."

They abandoned the paperwork. In the kitchen, Mackenzie flipped on the lights. Thankfully the staff had cleaned up the mess from earlier. The strong smell of bleach permeated the space.

Mackenzie opened the fridge and poked her head inside. "No leftovers." She shuffled some items around. "But there's deli meat." She backed out with a couple of packages.

Jace scrounged for bread and located some choices. They each added what they wanted, including lettuce and sliced cheese they found in the fridge. Jace retrieved the mustard for himself and the mayo for Mackenzie.

"Thanks." She looked up momentarily when he handed the condiment over, almost as if she were wounded or concerned or...who knew what. Just like her expression earlier by the vending machines.

"You don't like mayo anymore?"

She squeezed it onto the bread. "I do. It just surprises me how much you remember about...me."

Like he could ever forget. All of her likes and dislikes, quirks and habits had set up camp in his brain years ago, with no plans to relocate. Jace returned the condiments to the fridge when they were finished, and retrieved the jar of pickle spears.

He turned. "Still need a pickle, too?"

"That definitely has not changed. A sandwich without a pickle is a crime." Mackenzie retrieved a spear for herself and didn't even ask if he wanted one. Because he didn't. Never had, never would. See? She knew him, too.

They cleaned up after themselves and then took their

plates back to Luc's office. This time Jace dropped into the rolling chair.

"What do you think you're doing, Hawke?"

"Learning." He took a bite of sandwich and set his plate to his right so that Mackenzie had room for hers on the left. "Let me try this. That way I can help if someone else needs to have a warning added to their file." Jace took the pen and began detailing—very horribly, due to his cast—what had happened this afternoon.

Found employees canoodling in the barn. They were warned that if this happened again, they would be let go.

It looked like a four-year-old had scribbled across the paper by the time he was done. Although Ruby would have probably done a better job.

Mackenzie wiped her hands on a napkin and snatched the sheet to read what he'd written. It took her a second to decipher his handwriting. "What? No. You can't write that." A chuckle followed. "There is nothing professional about what you just wrote, Hawke."

"Why? What's wrong with it? It's true." Jace ate his sandwich while Mackenzie stole the pen and scribbled out *canoodling*. Then she must have decided the form was too messy, because she leaned over him and clicked Print on another.

And she smelled good doing it, too. Mackenzie had always rocked simplicity. Her nails were always unpainted and short, her hair wild and free. And in high school she'd smelled like that baby-powder deodorant, soap and freedom. But she must have started using a different lotion or hair product or something since he'd left, because she was this strange mix of new and old and sweet and fresh.

Jace wasn't opposed to the change.

After the printer spit out the form, she began writing,

her head shaking, a smile hiding beneath the tug of her teeth against her lip. "An improper physical proximity for a work environment." She spoke as her hand scrawled much-neater letters onto the page.

"Canoodling. Exactly."

She laughed again, and something warm and forbidden rose up in Jace. He used to make her laugh all of the time, just like she used to make him. He missed that.

Mackenzie added a few more sentences between bites of her sandwich, while Jace finished off his.

"There. Good enough." She slid the paper toward him. "Can you sign on the bottom as a witness? And then I'll have them do the same sometime tomorrow."

Jace scrawled his jumbled signature, and Mackenzie's followed.

"Anything else, boss?" Jace wasn't leaving if she had more work to do.

"Nope." She finished off the last of her sandwich and brushed her fingers. "Now I'm going to crash."

"Me, too."

They returned their dishes to the kitchen, washed them and added them back to the stack. On the way out of the lodge, they flipped off lights, leaving the outside one on when they got to the front door.

"Did you have any plans tonight that were disrupted with Vera's stuff?"

Jace shut the lodge door and made sure it latched before following Mackenzie down the steps. "Just my job." He winked to show he was teasing. No need to get Mackenzie all riled up when she'd finally stopped wanting to kick him in the shins. At least that was what he assumed, based on her recent behavior. "Although, I do need to swing by and see my mom sometime. I haven't been able to check in on her as much as I'd originally thought I would while being home."

Mackenzie paused at the bottom of the steps. "The ranch is definitely greedy with a person's time. Are you sure you should be spending all of yours here?"

"Trying to shove me out again?"

"No. Just asking honestly if your time home wouldn't be better spent with your mom."

"She's working constantly anyway. The woman's almost never at her house. Even though I've sent her enough money that she could have quit at least one of her jobs ages ago."

Mackenzie's eyes softened in the outdoor lodge lighting. "You're a good son."

He shrugged. "Not really, but I do love her."

"That counts."

"I sure hope so. I'll find a way to see her soon. And she said she's going to church on Sunday, so that will work, too."

"In the last year I've seen her at church a lot. Before that—not so much."

"I'm glad to hear that. I prayed for her over the years. She was the type to say she believed in God, but that was about it. I'm really glad to hear she's coming around." Especially with her emphysema. The disease was an eventual death sentence, though thankfully some people survived well with it for many years. And Jace was determined, somehow, to make that his mom's story.

"Thanks for your help today with Vera. And the paperwork." The last bit was laced with humor.

"I'm happy to lend my HR expertise anytime. Are you leaving your pickup at the lodge?"

She nodded. "I'll just walk to my cabin."

"I'll walk with you."

She studied him, and then her head slowly shook. "I don't think that's a good idea. Would you do that for another staffer?"

"We just did with Vera."

"That's not the same and you know it. It's better if we're careful. Platonic."

"Boss and employee," he filled in.

"Something like that." The corners of her mouth sank like they were weighted. "Good night, Jace." She turned and walked up the hill.

She'd used his name, but it had been chock-full of sorrow and sadness.

When Jace had left town, he'd assumed that he was doing the right thing by pursuing Evan's dreams for him.

But maybe he'd been wrong. Maybe Mackenzie had been the right choice. But it was too late to fix any of it now. Too late to go back and change his mind.

And if that didn't make his head ache with remorse, he didn't know what would.

Chapter 9

"Burning the midnight oil?" Luc greeted Mackenzie as he walked into the front office, which was empty because everyone was watching the wranglers compete. Shovel races, a game in which one person would ride on an overturned shovel pulled behind a horse, and wrangler pickup, a game in which rider and horse race down to pick up a second passenger and then gallop back to the starting line, were both scheduled for tonight.

They'd even incorporated some of Jace's activities in the past couple of weeks—steer wrestling and cattle roping. Things hadn't gone perfectly, but the guests didn't know that. The wranglers had pulled it off and entertained the crowd.

"Burning the eight o'clock oil for sure." It was nice having her brother back—albeit part-time. Cate had been driving home at night and heading back to Denver each day to be with the babies. Luc had been alternating days between the hospital and work. Mackenzie had tried to tell him they didn't need him, that he should go be with his wife, but the truth was, they did. She hadn't done a very good job of covering his work, and they both knew it. It just wasn't the same without Luc, just like the Kids' Club wouldn't be the same without Emma.

Mom had only been able to stay a week, so Mackenzie and Emma had been helping out with Ruby, or she'd been attending the Kids' Club during the days Luc was gone.

Supposedly the twins were going to be discharged soon, and it felt like everyone was holding their breath until that finally happened.

Luc dropped into the chair at the desk, next to hers. "Did you hear about tonight?"

"No. I've been holed up in here, trying to get these last-minute reservations for August confirmed."

"We haven't had an injury around here in forever, and now all of a sudden we had Vera's, and tonight we almost had another."

"What? Who? What happened?"

"Nothing, thanks to Jace. A toddler sneaked through the railing tonight. It was so quick. He was so quick. The wranglers were racing, and they didn't see him. Jace had been sitting on the railing—because, of course, he can't compete with his broken arm—and he hopped down and scooped the boy up before he got trampled. Ran him out of harm's way. I couldn't believe it." Luc rubbed his fingertips into his forehead. "The guests were grateful and not upset. Which is great. I can't even imagine what kind of nightmare that would be if he'd gotten hurt. They said Titus is just one of those boys who moves so fast, they have trouble keeping tabs on him."

Mackenzie's stomach revolted at the thought of a child getting injured or worse on their watch, their ranch. "I'm so thankful he's okay. How would we ever live with ourselves if…?" She couldn't finish the sentence.

"I don't know. It would be horrible. I'm sure glad Jace saw it happening and rescued the kid."

"Me, too."

Luc stood and slapped a hand on her desk. "Go home, Kenzie. Get some rest. You've been working enough to cover for three people. And I'm thankful for it." He flashed a grin. "Cate just got back from the hospital, so I'm headed over to the house to see her and find out how the girls are doing."

"Okay. Let me know if there's an update."

"I will. Are you good if I go with her tomorrow?"

"Of course. It's no problem."

"Thanks, best sister in the world."

"I'm telling Emma you said that!"

His laughter echoed back to her as he exited the office.

Mackenzie finished the email she was writing and hit Send, her mind stuck on Jace the Hero. She would love to get the lowdown from him, but marching over to the guys' lodging and pounding on his door didn't appeal.

No need to draw any more attention to her relationship with Jace. The hospital visit with Vera had been bad enough. Who knew what the staff had been saying about them in the weeks since?

Mackenzie had managed to keep things between them at an employer/employee professional level since that time. And whenever a thought regarding Jace popped into her head that wasn't compliant with that plan, she followed it up with a silent he's-just-another-staff-member mantra.

Mackenzie let the computer screen go dark. If it was any other employee, she *would* contact them to see how they were and thank them. So maybe a short text to Jace wouldn't be a crime.

She snagged her phone from the desk. Mackenzie might have stopped following Jace's career years ago, but she'd never been able to force herself to delete his number from her phone. His new-hire paperwork had confirmed it was still the same.

Heard you rescued a toddler tonight.

She added some clapping emoji.

Trying to get a raise or something? Because we can't afford your kind of hero salary, Hawke.

She hit Send and then began another text.

I'm kidding, of course. I'm very thankful you were there to rescue little Titus.

"Did you hear about tonight?" Bea popped her head into the front office, startling Mackenzie. The phone slipped through her fingers, clattering against her desk.

"I did. I'm so thankful the little guy is all right."

"Definitely. Glad I'm not over here as the bearer of more bad news."

"Hey, do you know where Jace is? I wanted to talk to him."

"I think he was heading over to his mom's. Said he needed to check on her."

Sounded like something a hero would do. And Mackenzie was sounding awfully wobbly on keeping her thoughts about Jace professional only.

"Okay, thanks."

With a wave, Bea took off. Mackenzie definitely wasn't going to drive over to Mrs. Hawke's house and stalk Jace, so she'd have to talk to him tomorrow.

Her phone rang, and she plucked it from the desk. Jace's name filled the screen.

She swiped to answer. "Things are turning to hero worship around here."

No chuckle filled her ear. "Mackenzie? This is Carleen Hawke. Jace is here, and he's sick. He says there's some pills he needs from his room there. I wasn't sure what to do, so I called you. Can you get them and bring them over?"

"Of course." Mackenzie popped up from her desk and grabbed her keys. "Tell me what they look like, where they are." While Mrs. Hawke described what Jace needed, Mackenzie hopped into her pickup and tore across the ranch toward the guys' lodging.

She took the steps two at a time and barged into Jace's room. It wasn't locked—no one bothered locking their doors, because it wasn't necessary. On the nightstand, Mackenzie found numerous pill bottles. Prescription and over-the-counter.

So the man was in pain… He just hadn't thought to mention it to her.

Mackenzie spotted the bottle Mrs. Hawke had described, and then, at the last second, decided to bring them all, just in case she'd gotten the details wrong. She made a basket with her shirt and scooped the medicines into it, then held the bundle close as she hurried down the stairs and over to her pickup truck.

"I'm on my way. Do you need to call for an ambulance? How bad is he? What's going on?"

"He says it's just a migraine, and he won't let me call anyone. I'm not even sure he's coherent enough to know I'm talking to you right now. Just come."

They disconnected, and Mackenzie raced into town.

Jace's mom lived just off Main Street, in a little yellow house that usually begged for a coat of paint and some yard maintenance, but when Mackenzie arrived, all of that had changed. The house had been painted—a nice buttercream—the bushes were trimmed and the grass had been recently cut.

Jace had been busy—or more likely, with his broken arm, he'd hired the jobs out.

Mackenzie parked and gathered the bottles again as Jace's mom came outside. "Hey, Mrs. H." She rounded the front of her vehicle.

"I'm so glad you're here. He's pretty messed up right now."

She followed Mrs. Hawke up the steps and into the living room. The scent of roast mingled with old house and what was likely an imitation version of some potent perfume.

A long flowered couch perched under the front window, and Jace was stretched out on it. He had a washcloth over his forehead and eyes.

He looked... Mackenzie didn't like it. His color was gray. He didn't remove the washcloth, didn't greet her. No teasing. Nothing. She dropped to the floor next to him.

Jace lifted the corner of the washcloth so he could peek out. "What are you doing here?"

"I brought your meds." *And I'm going to excuse your*

snarl because you're in pain. "Is this the one?" She held up the prescription bottle.

"Yeah," he rasped.

She fished out a pill and took the water glass that his mom offered. "Can you sit up enough to swallow this?"

Jace moved the washcloth up to his hairline and began the slow and tedious process of lifting himself into a semisitting position with one good arm. It was strange to see him so weak. Hurting so much.

Once he was halfway upright, he froze and slammed his eyelids shut. He didn't take the pill or the water. Mackenzie stayed silent, praying for relief for him.

Jace moaned, and she scooted out of the way as he dropped from the couch, onto one hand and two knees. Then he crawled—using his elbows—into the bathroom. The door kicked shut behind him, and then she heard him lose everything in his stomach.

Mackenzie wanted to be sick with him. What was going on? She'd never had a migraine herself, so she didn't know much about them. But she hadn't realized they could take down a man like Jace and render him so helpless, so tormented. Should they call someone? Jace had mentioned seeing Dr. Sanderson for his follow-up care while he was home. Mackenzie could try him, but was that the right thing to do? Or did Jace just need to get this medicine in him?

"I've never seen him like this." Carleen sank to the armrest of the couch.

"Me either."

The seconds turned to minutes as they waited, and Jace didn't return.

"What do we do with him? I'm no good at this stuff. I never was very maternal."

"That's not true, Mrs. H. You raised two great boys."
Mackenzie stood, holding on to the water and pill. "I'll
check on him. Why don't you make us a cup of tea?"

Carleen's hands wrung and shook. "I can do that." A
hacking cough racked her small frame, and she held on
to the armrest until the fit subsided. So, the emphysema
had worsened like Jace had said. Mackenzie's heart split
in two. Over the years, she'd checked up on Jace's mom—
dropped off some extra ranch food or a dessert when she
thought of it. But in the last few months, she hadn't been
by. Now she was kicking herself for that.

Carleen moved into the kitchen as Mackenzie slipped
off her black-and-brown cowboy boots by the front door,
then padded quietly back to the bathroom in her socks.
She touched the door softly, a slight tap with the pad of
her finger.

"J, can I come in?"

A groan answered. She'd take that as a yes. Inside
the bathroom, he lay sprawled out, head resting on the
tile. The old bathroom fan revved and then settled, its
rhythm erratic.

Mackenzie sank to the floor, next to him, with her
back against the wall. There really wasn't room for the
two of them in here, but moving Jace right now wasn't
an option.

"Think you can keep one of these pills down?"

"I'm going to try." Jace managed to raise his head off
the floor, and she supported it while he popped the pill
and downed a quick swig of water.

Mackenzie took the glass from him and set it on her
other side. When he shifted back down, his head landed
on her legs.

"Sorry." He attempted to move, but she stopped him with a hand to his forehead.

"It's okay. Just stay still." All of those don't-touch, stay-professional and don't-dip-into-the-past warnings flew out the window. And truly, they'd never really had a chance.

Mackenzie had tried so hard to view Jace as a temporary employee, but her plan most definitely had not worked. Because her concern for the man was nowhere near a platonic level right now.

Seeing him in pain flattened her. Made her want to punch a hole in the wall or call every doctor on the planet until someone offered him relief.

And those were strong feelings for a staff member. She hadn't felt any of those things for Vera when she'd sliced open her hand. Just a lot of concern. But nothing like what was roaring through her right now.

Mackenzie traced two fingers along one of Jace's eyebrows, then the other. She repeated the motion on the agony lines that were etched into his brow, while wondering how she'd gotten here…and what it would take to climb back out.

Wherever Jace currently was—and his mind was so hazy, he wasn't quite sure—he never wanted to leave. Fingers slid through his hair, past his ears, across his forehead.

He squinted, taking in the tiny square beige tiles in his mom's bathroom and Mackenzie's concern peering back at him.

"How long have we been sitting here?"

"Awhile. Long enough that your mom brought me some tea and offered me a refill." She lifted the mug in a salute and took a sip, her fingers regrettably no longer on duty.

"You hate unsweetened tea."

"*Hate*'s a strong word for something like tea. And I asked her to make it. She was so upset, I was trying to occupy her with something to do."

He let his eyelids fall shut again. The black felt cool and calm now that the terror in his head was subsiding. "She's probably cleaning the kitchen right now. That was always her go-to when she was upset. She'd scour everything and make us pull our weight, too."

"Smart woman, when she had two capable boys. And yes, Evan was still that after the accident."

True. Evan was a world traveler now. After a few rough years, he'd stopped letting the amputation hold him back. And while that was great, Jace would never be able to completely let go of his guilt over what had happened to his brother. Because mowing was supposed to have been his chore that day, not Evan's. Something he'd admitted to no one ever. Something he'd never talked to Evan about. It had been too painful. He'd been racked with remorse and shame for years. Jace had worked through some of it with time, but that core had always remained. It was part of why he'd followed Evan's dreams for him. Because Jace was the one who'd stolen them in the first place.

Mackenzie looked so serious as she studied him. He reached up to smooth the pucker splitting her brow. "You're beautiful even when you're upset." And he didn't like being the one who'd created those worry marks.

Her head shook, but a faint smile crested. "You're crossing the line, Hawke."

"No. I would never do that." But of course he was.

"Don't make me drop your head to the floor."

He winced. "I'm sorry. I didn't mean it. I take it back."

Mom appeared in the open bathroom doorway. "Are you feeling better?"

"Yeah. I'm okay now."

The exhale she released was haggard, and she leaned against the wooden frame. He was supposed to be helping her, supporting her—not the other way around.

"Need anything? Water, food?"

"Nah. I don't even want to move yet. Don't want to mess anything up with my head, so I'm just going to chill here another minute." *On the bathroom floor, with the girl I once loved with everything in me supporting and comforting me.*

Maybe Jace would never move at all.

"Just holler if you need anything." She pushed off the door frame. "Oh, I almost forgot. Mackenzie, hon, I found a dish when I was cleaning that I think is one from the ranch. From when you dropped off food. So I'll just set it by the front door."

"Okay. Thanks, Mrs. H."

"Call me Carleen, dear. How many times have I told you that before?"

His mom left. Mackenzie studied the floor, the bathroom cabinet, the ceiling.

"You visit my mom?"

"Sometimes. Not lately, unfortunately. That's why I didn't know her symptoms were getting worse."

"Kenzie Rae." He reached up and slid a hand along her cheek before letting it fall back to his side. "What am I going to do with you?"

She destroyed him. She was so caring, so sweet and yet so feisty. She was everything he'd ever wanted and still couldn't have. Not if he wanted his life back. Jace couldn't abandon Mackenzie a second time. Couldn't hurt her like that again and live with himself. And he did want his life back. He loved the rodeo—and his brother—that much.

"I think the real question is what am *I* going to do with *you*?"

"I have a few suggestions."

"Hawke!" She whacked him on the arm, and he chuckled.

"I didn't think you'd go for that."

"I can't believe you've been having migraines like this and you didn't say anything." She'd ignored his flirting, which was good. At least one of them was keeping their head on straight today. "Is that what was going on the other times you acted strange, too? What's the deal? Is this a riding injury of some sort?"

"That was a lot of questions. I think my brain hurts again."

"Argh!" Her fingers raked through her hair, an action he'd happily take over for her.

There was no point in trying to hide anything from Mackenzie now. She'd already seen him at his worst. "I have a lingering concussion from the ride that broke my arm—" he paused "—and bruised my spleen and ribs."

"What?" She actually squeaked. If he wasn't supposed to be resisting the magnet that was Kenzie Rae, he'd tell her how cute she was.

"The head stuff… It's not going away like it has before. But then I've never had a concussion this bad. I'm fighting some vertigo. And the migraines are unpredictable."

"I wonder if tonight's was because you rescued that little boy. From the movement?"

"Maybe."

She was quiet for a good long while. "Why didn't you tell me?"

"I didn't want to give you any extra reasons to kick me off the ranch."

"Can you ever be serious?"

"I am being serious. Kind of. I suppose I didn't want you to know how messed up I was. It's easier if people just think it's the arm. That's visible. That makes sense. I hate that the concussion isn't getting better. At least not fast enough for me. It makes me feel like a wuss. Guys don't quit for a concussion. They don't quit for anything. Some of them have a busted Achilles tendon and they keep riding. We all do it."

"Well. That's just dumb."

He laughed.

"Aren't concussions a really big deal? Isn't there some disease that can come from too many?"

"Sometimes. Chronic something or another. CTE for short. But that's not what's going on with me."

"Good. Says who?"

He grinned, crossing his casted hand over to latch onto her arm and rub a thumb along her soft skin. "Worried about me, are you?"

An eye roll answered.

"Doc Karvina is my rodeo doc, and he's never implied its anything close to CTE." *Just that I should stop competing before that becomes a reality for me.* "And I saw Dr. Sanderson in town, and he said I'm making improvements. The spleen and ribs are pretty much good to go. The arm still needs time." Waiting was the worst part. Instant healing would be so much more preferable. "Overall I'm a specimen of health."

"Did either doctor say they could do anything about your sassy mouth?"

Humor surfaced. "They did not mention that."

"Just…" Mackenzie huffed. "Take care of yourself, okay? This sport… It isn't worth your life."

"I will. I always do. I'm not going to do anything stupid." Jace would wait until he healed before he got back up on a bull. Or at least until the majority of his symptoms subsided.

"Good." All of that concern written across her pretty features almost did him in. Wasn't he supposed to *not* be causing the woman pain and suffering this time around?

"You going soft on me, Wilder?"

Mackenzie studied him, those mesmerizing gray depths full of all kinds of emotion he no longer had the right to. "Maybe. And if that's not a problem, I don't know what is."

Chapter 10

Mackenzie stowed the rafting supplies in the storage area at the back of the barn. She'd just returned from taking a group, and it had been glorious to get out of the office and outside. But while her favorite activity usually energized her, today she was dog-tired.

In the last two weeks she hadn't been off duty for more than an hour or two at a time. Even her Saturdays had been filled with Wilder Ranch work—issues, planning, the big Fourth of July celebration last week that was always a hit.

The only escape she had managed was for church on Sundays. At least she'd had that. And she'd needed it. She'd needed that break, that minute to remember that taking care of everything at the ranch wasn't all on her shoulders.

Because it had begun to feel that way.

Why, she wasn't quite sure. Emma was doing her job and more, even with her wedding being only ten days away. And Jace had been a huge help, too. But somehow Mackenzie still felt…alone in all of it.

The twins were finally being discharged tomorrow, so Luc's world was going to get even busier. Emma was about to get married and become a wife and a mom all in one instant I-do moment. And once Jace healed, he'd most certainly go back to bull riding.

Mackenzie couldn't shake the notion that she was being left behind once again. And she didn't like feeling sorry for herself. Didn't like this weight strangling her.

At least the campout was tonight, and many of the guests had signed up for it. Which meant that she should have a night to relax, since she wasn't in charge of that. Sure, she'd be around in case of any emergencies, but at least the evening would allow her to chill.

After organizing, she walked over to the lodge. Jace was sitting on the front steps, almost as if he'd been waiting for someone. Her? Strange. They'd been so well behaved since the migraine encounter. No more touchy-feely. No more diving into the depths she'd promised herself she wouldn't go near.

He hadn't even pressured her to talk about the past. If this was the calm in the middle of the storm, Mackenzie wanted to rent a room and stay here.

"Anyone ever tell you that you work too much, Wilder?"

She dropped down beside him. "Anyone ever tell you that you stick your nose in other people's business too much?"

His head cocked. "Nope."

"Well, they should. If you must know, taking guests

white-water rafting does not qualify as work to me." The icy-cold splash of water misting her, the thrill of the next big drop. She loved every second of it.

"I feel the same way about the shooting range. I just got back from supervising that." He nudged her shoulder with his. "You look like you could use a night off."

"Maybe."

"Definitely. So you should be thankful I finagled one for you."

"Huh?" She glanced at him. "What do you mean?"

"I mean I talked to the boss—"

"I am the boss," Mackenzie interrupted, pathetically relishing Jace's chuckle.

"Don't I know it. I meant your twin. And he's on my side. He's home tonight and agrees that you need to take the evening off. He said, and I quote, 'If Mackenzie takes a night off, it will lessen my guilt for how little I've been here lately.' Luc said he'd be on call, in case of emergency, for the campout tonight. And I have just the thing planned."

If Mackenzie was getting a night off, she intended to sleep. Well, first she'd put on a movie—*Pale Rider* or another one of her favorite Westerns—and then she'd conk out on the couch. Who said her life wasn't just as exciting and full of new adventures as the lives of everyone around her?

"I'm tired, Hawke." She barely resisted closing her eyes and dropping her head onto his shoulder. And that was saying a lot, since she'd been nothing but careful around the man.

He switched to the step behind her and began rubbing her shoulder with his noncasted hand. Her neck lagged forward, her head barely hanging on. "You're really going to put me to sleep now."

He switched shoulders. "I know how tired you are. Maybe we should do it another night."

Her curiosity perked. "What's 'it'?"

"A thank-you."

"For what?"

"For checking on my mom all of these years."

What would that be? "You got me boots?"

"No, ma'am." His drawl stretched out, and his fingers continued to dig into her tired muscles. She moved his hand an inch to the left, and he blessedly continued. "Something you asked me about."

"Hmm." Mackenzie couldn't think. Didn't really want to right now. After this little massage, she'd crawl into bed and not come out until morning.

"Something involving a bull."

Her senses woke up, and she flipped around, causing his hand to drop. "You're going to teach me how to ride a bull?"

"Not a live one."

"What other kind are there?"

"Mechanical."

Mackenzie analyzed. If she said no, she wouldn't get to try at all, because she didn't think Jace was going to let her do the real deal. Unless…! Unless she proved that she could handle it. Then maybe she could convince him.

"A little wussy but I'll take it."

He laughed, and it registered in her stomach like comfort food. "Are you sure? If you're exhausted, it's probably not the best timing."

"My energy has suddenly returned to me."

"Okay. But the offer stands if you'd rather reschedule."

Mackenzie suddenly wanted nothing more than to get out of here. "I'm game. Let's go make me a champ."

Jace had wanted to thank Mackenzie, not make her pass out cold on the drive to his friend's place. Her head had fallen back against the seat during the drive, her shoulders drooping lower with each mile. She'd changed into jeans, along with boots and a vintage T-shirt that had a black-and-white cow's mug on the front wearing a red bandanna. Equal parts cute and distracting. The woman was like a baby lulled to sleep, and now he didn't have a clue what to do with her.

He'd heard of the advice not to wake a sleeping baby, but a sleeping Kenzie Rae was a tad more confusing.

Jace had parked at the end of Colby's drive and not headed in yet, trying to figure out what to do, kicking himself for not knowing better than to have waited and taken her on another day. Kenzie had told him she was exhausted, and she hadn't been lying.

If he turned around and drove back to Wilder Ranch, would she be upset? What was more important? Sleep? Or a night away?

The woman had been working so hard lately, and the Fourth of July holiday last week had been even busier than usual, with all the ranch had done to celebrate that. Wilder Ranch kept Mackenzie running. Jace, too. When he'd first gotten injured, he'd assumed that waiting to heal would just about kill him. But the fast pace of his temporary job had fixed that for him.

In exactly one week his cast would be coming off. After that he'd be hitting physical therapy at a run. And then he'd be back to bull riding by September for sure. Hopefully before.

He was more than ready. But a good chunk of him was going to miss Wilder Ranch. Miss the woman next to him whose heavy, openmouthed breathing was edging toward a snore.

Maybe that should turn him off, but it didn't. He liked seeing Mackenzie relaxed. He liked it even more that it was with him.

A month ago this scenario would never have happened.

"Hawke, are you watching me sleep?" Her steel-gray eyes popped open. "Creepy!"

"More like I was watching you drool and snore." She hadn't done either, but her look of horror and panic made the jab worth it.

"I do not drool when I sleep." She swiped a hand across her lips, checking, and his gaze stalled and stuck.

He'd edged closer while analyzing whether to let her sleep, and now it would only take the slightest lean to test out his theory about her kisses and whether they were as good as he remembered.

You're thanking her, not taking advantage of her tired, vulnerable state. Jace forced his body back to the driver's seat.

"Where are we? What are we doing sitting here?"

"We're at my friend Colby's. I was trying to decide what to do with you."

"Where to hide my body?" She scanned their surroundings. "The middle of that field over there would probably work."

He laughed. "Do you want to go home? I feel bad dragging you out here when you're so exhausted."

"Actually, the nap helped." Her shoulders inched up sheepishly. "I feel rested. Sorry I conked out though."

"The two-hour ride was pretty boring without anyone to talk to."

"Two hours?" She sat up straighter, took in the rock formations and evergreens that lined the drive. "Where exactly *did* you take me? I've been asleep that long?"

"I'm kidding. It was only about forty-five minutes."

"Oh." She whacked him on the arm. "If you're trying to thank me, you should probably tone down the jerk and up the doting, adoring admirer."

"Noted." If only sparring with Mackenzie was a full-time career. Jace would have job security for life. "You ready, old woman? Or do I need to get you home in time for *Wheel of Fortune*, *Jeopardy!* and a TV dinner?"

She flashed a sassy smile. "I'm ready. You're going to be sorry you ever started this with me, Hawke."

He had no doubt she was right.

Mackenzie climbed out of the passenger seat of Jace's old beater truck. It was funny to her that he didn't get a newer vehicle. Based on his career successes, he should certainly have the money. But then again material things had never appealed to him. At least not to the younger version of the man.

Take today for instance—his boots and jeans were worn, his T-shirt advertising some rodeo, his baseball cap perfectly broken in. And Mackenzie was not, for one second, going to admit those things looked good on him.

At least not out loud.

Colby had a simple but well-kept spread. A ranch house and two outbuildings were on the property, some bikes and other toys outside. The front door opened, and a young man bounded in their direction. "Ace, how's it going?"

"Ace?" Mackenzie questioned.

Humor twisted Jace's mouth. "An announcer coined the unimaginative nickname once, and the guys never let it go. It's stuck ever since."

Jace and Colby shook hands and did that one-arm-man-hug thing.

"Mackenzie, this is Colby. He retired from riding a few years back and now gives private lessons to kids, along with raising a brood of his own."

She shaded her eyes against the sun. "It's nice to meet someone who's part of Jace's life since he left Westbend. I assume you have some stories you can tell me."

Jace groaned. "I'm regretting this already and you're not even up on the bull yet."

"Yes, ma'am." Colby's full-of-mischief grin promised plenty of dirt. "That I can do. We can discuss over dinner. Les has some food in the Crock-Pot for tonight. She's working right now."

"Colby's wife is a nurse," Jace explained. "Not sure what she saw in his sorry hide."

"Me either." Colby chuckled and slapped Jace on the back. "Come on." A smattering of kids flew out the front door and chased after them as they made their way to one of the outbuildings. Two blonde girls and one blond boy, and they all looked under the age of four—maybe five.

Colby and his wife had their hands full for sure.

"Whacha doing?"

Mackenzie slowed her steps to match up with the little boy who had sidled up next to her. "I'm going to ride a mechanical bull. What are you doing?"

Two fingers slid between the boy's lips, and he spoke around them. "I'm thwee. I don't know what I'm doing." He took off like a shot and caught up to his sisters.

Cute kid.

Colby slid open the large doors on the gray building, and the three of them stepped inside. The mechanical bull was in the middle of a ring, with padded cushion surrounding it.

"Where's the real bull?"

"Out in the pasture." Colby glanced at Jace, amused. "You've got your hands full with this one."

"I already told you that's not happening, Wilder."

"Fine." She gave an exaggerated huff. It had been worth a try. Maybe there was a chance in the future, if she behaved herself. Or now that she'd met Colby, she could always go around Jace and ask him. "I'll take what I can get."

"Sure hope you know what you're doing, Ace. She's a firecracker. I gotta go make sure the kids haven't gotten into any trouble in the last minute, so I'll see you two later. Hopefully with all of your limbs intact."

Colby's parting statement didn't fill Jace with confidence. He still wasn't sure exactly what he was doing here with Mackenzie. He'd wanted to thank her for checking up on his mom over the years. With most women that would be chocolate or flowers. With Mackenzie? Something that could break her neck.

And since there was no way he was putting her on a live bull, this option was second best. If he didn't teach her, didn't help her, she'd go find someone else, out of spite, and then really get herself injured. At least he had that thought to comfort him.

But the woman had better not get hurt on his watch.

Mackenzie had hopped over the perimeter of the floor mats and was now touching the mechanical bull as if it were a live animal. "Let's do this." She climbed on and shot him a let's-go-already look.

"You're crazy. I'm going to teach you some things first so that you don't get booted right off and hurt yourself."

"Okay, but how hard can it be? Just…stay on. Right?"

His jaw unhinged, and then she pealed with laughter. Her head tipped back, hair flowing with it. Gorgeous, horrible woman.

"That was even better than your girls-can't-ride-bulls comment!"

Jace shook his head, lips twitching. Mackenzie was definitely a force to be reckoned with. And seeing her happy, teasing him… He liked all of that a bit too much.

"What's first, coach?"

Jace approached. "Put this on." He'd gotten her a glove that would fit her smaller hand so that her knuckles didn't blister or bleed. Because knowing Mackenzie, she wouldn't quit if things didn't go her way the first time. "Then slide your hand under the rope, palm up. Line up your pinkie finger along the backbone." Mackenzie did everything he said like an old pro. "Good. You want to stay up on the bull and use your legs to hold on. Make sure you stay centered."

Mackenzie scooted toward the rope, got situated.

"Use your free hand to stay balanced, and try to keep your upper body relaxed. When the bull tips down and forward, push your knees and heels into the bull and lean back. You want to shift your weight opposite of the movement. If the bull dips back, then lean forward." That was generalizing things, but he had to start somewhere.

"Makes sense."

"We're probably just going to have to try it so you can get a feel for it. Then we can work out the kinks."

Right now Jace didn't even exist to Mackenzie. She was in full-concentration mode, full-experience mode. It only upped her attractiveness. He'd always loved her adventurous spirit.

"I'm going to start you off slow so you can get the feel of it."

Mackenzie raised her left arm. "Okay. I'm ready."

Jace's gut sank to his boots. Why had he started all of this again? After a quick prayer that the woman wouldn't get hurt, he manned the controls. Mackenzie handled a few dips, but then a spin knocked her off. She popped up quickly and climbed back on before Jace even had the chance to check on her.

"You okay?"

"Yep. I just lost it on that spin. How do I stop that from bucking me off?"

"Keep your legs tight and shift the opposite way, but then you have to be ready and adjust for the next move or it will still toss you."

"Okay." Mackenzie nodded and raised her arm. "Let's go again."

The next ride was much better. Jace increased the difficulty as she went again and again, stretching her time, her skill. The woman was fierce. Every time she got thrown, she climbed back up immediately. There was no complaining. No lollygagging.

"Keep your legs tight. It's easy to focus on just the upper body, but your legs are where your strength is."

She stayed on the longest for the next ride. Just shy of eight seconds.

"Argh! I was so close." Mackenzie remounted. "Make sure you make it hard enough to count."

Jace was controlling the speed and variation of the mechanical bull. "Trust me, I have not been taking it easy on you." He'd known she would never put up with that. Watching her get pummeled over and over again was torture, but at least she was getting better with each ride.

At her nod, he started the machine again. The mechanical bull dipped forward, back, then spun, and Mackenzie shifted with each movement. She stayed balanced and up on her rope.

"You're almost there. Six, seven, eight." Jace whooped in celebration just as Mackenzie went flying across the padding like a plastic bag caught in a gust of wind.

That had been a hard hit. He switched the bull off and scrambled over to her. This time she didn't get up immediately, didn't make much noise at all.

The glove she'd been wearing was five feet away from her, and she was flat on her back, with a hand over her forehead. Had it knocked her out?

He moved her arm to her side. "Are you okay?"

"That was amazing." She sat up, eyes wide and bright. "Let's do it again."

Jace crashed from his kneeling position to sitting on the mat. "You're going to be the death of me, Kenzie Rae. I thought you'd gotten hurt, and I was kicking myself for letting you do this."

"Don't kick yourself. This was a good thank-you gift." Mackenzie looped arms around her bent knees. She was the kind of pretty that hollowed him out and made him want the life he'd given up for good. Jace might be leaving town again, but Kenzie Rae would always own a piece of him. There was just no one like her.

"You're welcome. I think."

"This isn't the real thing, but it's pretty addicting."

"It is. And the real thing is so much better."

"Huh. Crazy." Her tone was dry. "That must be why I asked you for that."

"Maybe someday." What? Absolutely not. This woman made him say yes to things that shouldn't even be considered. "I take that back."

"Too late! You can't take it back."

Jace tugged his baseball cap lower in lieu of digging an even bigger hole.

"I can see how you'd have a hard time giving this up." She nodded toward the mechanical bull. "If your concussion doesn't improve… Well, I can't imagine how awful that would be for you."

"It would kill me to give up riding." Not that Jace was going to worry about that. His head would get better. Not competing wasn't an option for him, so it had to. He wasn't perfect yet, but he was improving with time, and that gave him hope.

But with the way Mackenzie was talking… She knew he was going back no matter what, right? She'd asked him to be careful, and he'd said he would. Surely she didn't think—

"Ace!" Colby bellowed from the doorway as he strode their way. "Is she still alive?"

"And kicking." Mackenzie answered Colby, popping up as if she hadn't just been beaten down by the machine numerous times. As if she hadn't slept like a comatose woman the whole drive here.

Adorable weirdo.

"She did okay…" Jace pushed up from the mat, adopting the most serious face he could muster. "But she needs a lot of work."

"Hey! I did amazing!"

"And she needs to tone down her overconfidence."

"Jace Hawke, you're just upset that I did so well because you don't want to let me ride a real bull."

True.

"Let's get some dinner in you two."

At Colby's suggestion, Jace wiggled his fingers. "Sounds good. I could use a break. I'm getting sore from running the controls."

"Hawke! You're a jerk." Mackenzie poked him in the chest. "Just for that I want another go after dinner."

Great. He'd just started relaxing that she'd survived unscathed, and the woman wanted to get back up on the bull.

But then again Jace couldn't exactly blame her, since all he wanted to do—despite his uncooperative body— was exactly the same thing.

Chapter 11

"Who hasn't had their makeup done yet?" Emma's friend Abby scanned the cabin living room—currently being used as wedding-prep central for the women—hungry for her next victim.

Mackenzie had been standing—okay, hiding—near the wall next to Emma's bedroom. Leaning against it like the beams would crumble without her support. Praying she didn't spill something on her rust-orange bridesmaid dress while snacking on the fruit and other appetizer items filling their small dining table. Laughing when it fit. Smiling at the right parts. Generally trying to become one with the wall and avoid notice from The Primpers in the room.

Emma had two friends helping out with hair and makeup—Abby and Kim. They'd been working tirelessly, and Mackenzie had been avoiding them with just as much effort.

"Mackenzie!" Abby zeroed in on her.

Avoid eye contact! Avoid!

"I'll go light on you. I promise."

Mackenzie's noggin shook like a bobblehead on a car dash. "I'm good, really. I don't think anyone is expecting me to wear makeup, when I never do."

Abby rounded the couch and curled a hand around her biceps, dragging her to the makeup-torture zone. "But that's exactly why we *should* do it. At least a little. Just to highlight those gorgeous cheekbones. I've been dying to get my hands on you for years. You're so naturally beautiful, you'll hardly need a thing. Just a few touch-ups here and there. Trust me. This won't hurt a bit."

Abby gave Mackenzie a slight nudge to get her to drop to the couch cushions, then sat on the coffee table, facing her. She picked up a fat makeup brush and went to work like some kind of master painter.

What was wrong with her face the way it was? Mackenzie swallowed her protest. *For Emma. I'm doing this for Emma.* Not that Emma cared one iota what she looked like today. Her sister's eyes would be on Gage and Hudson—with cartoon hearts spilling out, no doubt.

Abby worked quickly—Mackenzie would give her that. Lip gloss, eye shadow, mascara. The items came at her like bullets.

"Oh, I have the perfect idea for your hair!" Kim's squeal came from behind the couch.

Mackenzie winced. She'd been hoping to at least avoid the hair station.

After Abby finished, Kim directed Mackenzie over to a dining room chair so that she had better access. Bobby pins scraped her scalp as the sound of women filled the room. Emma, being herself, had invited most of the women in the county to get ready with her.

Okay, that might be a slight exaggeration. But with the photographer, and Gage's mom and sister in the cabin, along with their mom, Cate, the twins, Ruby and The Primpers, things were crowded.

Everly and Savannah didn't mind though. They'd been passed around plenty and had slept through most of the commotion.

The girls had been home from the hospital for nine days, but Mackenzie had only held each of them for a few sporadic minutes in that time. They were tiny rock stars and had a following of groupies—both friends and family—vying for their attention. Mackenzie had stayed back regarding that, too, because she wasn't the baby-whispering type. But those moments connecting with her new nieces had still definitely been good.

One day she'd take them out on rides like she did Ruby. Or they'd climb trees like she and Ruby had sneaked off to do this week, during the hubbub of the babies' arrival. Usually Emma was the aunt who spent more time with Ruby, but she'd been busy with wedding prep lately, so Mackenzie had quietly stepped into that role. She'd made sure Ruby wasn't forgotten, checking in on her, stealing her away when work allowed.

And Mackenzie had enjoyed every second. Turns out her niece liked to adventure as much as she did.

Another bobby pin tore off a chunk of her scalp. "Kim, I could probably do my own hair." *Since I've been managing it for the last twenty-five years.* "I'm sure you have other people to help." *Please.*

"I don't actually. You're the last one!"

Mackenzie resisted another argument. Instead she

closed her eyes, straining to find some peace in the midst of the attack on her skull.

Hopefully Jace had been able to do the same after completing the guest turnover this afternoon. He'd been up late last night with another migraine and had been disgruntled about it this morning because it had been the first in a long while. Every time he thought he had them beat, another appeared out of nowhere to derail him. And the vertigo still plagued him at times, too.

Despite those setbacks, he'd begun physical therapy once his spleen and ribs had healed, and now that his cast was off, the arm was included, too. He was obviously preparing to go back.

But at the same time, he'd told her he wouldn't do anything stupid. Which, in her mind, meant he'd heal fully before returning.

So what did that mean?

If his concussion hung around, would he retire? No one could fault him for that. He'd had a long, successful career. He could easily move on and do something else. Find a new passion. No one could ride bulls forever—their bodies would eventually give out.

Would he stay if he didn't get better? And if he did... what did that mean for them?

Was there a "them"? Mackenzie wasn't sure she was okay with that term popping into her brain. Though the man had certainly been sneaking into her thoughts and her world a lot lately. It was so easy to lapse back into old habits with him. To remember why she'd fallen for him the first time around.

Mackenzie still didn't know why Jace had left the way he had. And she still both wanted and didn't want to know. Though the first option was gaining momentum.

Oohs and aahs caused her to open her eyes.

Emma had come out of her bedroom in her wedding dress. The living room of ladies highly approved, based on the exclamations and tears.

Rightfully so.

Emma's dress had delicate spaghetti straps and flowers along the bodice that dripped onto the long, flowing skirt. She was a woodland creature with her hair curled and loosely pulled back on the sides, sprays of flowers tucked into the do.

She was a vision. Striking and glowing and gorgeous.

Mackenzie might not love all of the changes happening around Wilder Ranch, but seeing Emma so happy made the growing pains worthwhile. She couldn't imagine a better match for her sister. Gage's world revolved around Emma, and she'd brought him back from the land of cranky and stoic after his ex-wife had done a number on him. The two of them were a perfect pair.

"Aunt Emma, does your dress twirl like mine?" Ruby was in a white flower-girl dress, and she spun in a circle, enthralled with the way the skirt flared.

"Let's see." Emma's eyes twinkled as she joined in. The moment was sweet, and the photographer must have agreed, because her camera sounded repeatedly as she captured each frame.

Emma handled the attention that came with her wedding day like a fairy-tale princess, all calm and gracious. If Mackenzie were in her shoes, she'd need boots, first off, and then a large boulder to hide behind.

If the right match existed for her, Mackenzie hoped her someday wedding wouldn't include all of this...fussing.

"All finished," Kim announced.

"Thank you." Mackenzie forced the appreciation

through clenched teeth and then slunk off to the bathroom to investigate the damage.

"I don't even look like myself." She pressed over the sink, leaning close to the mirror. There she was…underneath all of the shiny, glimmery concoctions. With a tissue, she dabbed away some of the lip gloss, lightening it, then swabbed gently at the eye shadow—which, thankfully, was a soft color. Mackenzie didn't want to mess anything up so much that she ended up back in the makeup hot seat, so she quit meddling. The slight adjustments helped. She used the small hand mirror to check her hair. It was actually cute—not that she would ever take the time to do it again. Waves were caught up at the nape of her neck, casual and stylish.

She set the mirror down and met her reflection again. "It's a wedding. You're supposed to be dolled up. And this is all for Emma." The affirmation made her mouth quirk. Hopefully no one could hear her crazy talk through the door. Mackenzie squared her shoulders. She could manage to wear the makeup and leave the hair through the wedding and reception. And then after she'd reward herself with a T-shirt, sweats, pizza and a Western with lots of gunfights.

She exited the bathroom to find everyone getting ready to either walk or ride down the hill to the lodge.

"I can walk." She volunteered to let some of the others hop in vehicles, since she was wearing cowboy boots with her dress—*thank you, Emma, for that saving grace.*

"I'll go with you," Mom said, also taking Ruby's hand. "Come with us, kiddo, but let's lift up your dress while we walk, so it doesn't get dirty."

The perfect summer-evening temperature drifted along Mackenzie's skin as they strolled, and Ruby chattered excitedly about her "fruffy" dress and light-pink-painted fingernails. Scents of grass and dirt and ranch swirled, comforting. The wedding had been scheduled for after dinner because they'd needed time to set up and get ready, but that meant a cooler temperature and twinkle lights—Emma's favorite. Both wins.

When Ruby spied Luc near the entrance to the lodge, she dropped the skirt of her dress and took off at a run.

"So much for keeping the hem clean." Mom's wry comment was spiked with humor, taking years off her already young-looking features. Her hair was a shade darker than Mackenzie's—more of a light brown—but it held some of the same wave. If not for her mother's autoimmune disease that flared in Colorado's fluctuating climate, Mackenzie had no doubt that her parents would still be living here, running Wilder Ranch. "Reminds me of another little girl I once knew."

"Except I would have thrown a fit about the dress."

"True. I didn't know how amazing grandbabies were. Didn't realize what I was missing until Ruby and Hudson came along. And now we have the twins, too."

And none from me. Not that Mackenzie was overly maternal. She wasn't. And maybe that was why no one thought she had that ache inside her, too—for a husband, for kids, for a family of her own.

But she did. It was dull and distant, but there. And ever since Jace's reappearance, that dull, distant ache had been making itself known with troublesome throbs and sharp, shooting pains.

Jace slipped into a seat for the ceremony at the last second. He and the other staff had handled the turnover today so that the Wilders could prepare for the wedding.

A few small issues had sprung up throughout the day, leaving him running behind. But they'd figured things out and managed not to bother any of the Wilder clan.

Thirty minutes ago he'd hustled over to the guys' lodging to get ready. He'd jumped in the shower and then thrown on his best jeans and a short-sleeved button-up shirt. His hair—too long and in need of a cut—was still slightly damp.

Emma had made it clear that the wedding was to be casual, and he'd taken advantage.

Music started, and Jace swiveled with the rest of the crowd, toward the back of the grass aisle. *Sweet mercy.* His windpipe closed off so fast, he barely managed not to hack and cough, and cause a scene.

There was most definitely nothing casual about Kenzie Rae.

She walked down the aisle with Luc, confident and relaxed, stunning times a million. The color-of-changing-leaves orange dress she wore accentuated slight curves, and her muscular legs tapered into cowboy boots. She turned at the front, a small batch of flowers in her hands, and watched for Emma.

Mackenzie had on makeup. The effect sent Jace bumping into the back of his chair. She was a knockout. And yet…he was partial to the girl underneath all of that sparkle and shine.

The one who rode faster than him and could probably beat him at most anything. The one who managed to siphon the oxygen from his body with just a glance.

Tuck away her jaw-dropping beauty, and Mackenzie was still a force to be reckoned with—strong and funny, vulnerable and loyal.

And Jace was the idiot who'd let her go. The same idiot who planned to repeat his actions all over again soon.

Not that Mackenzie was anywhere near *his* this time around.

Ruby came down the aisle next. She paused to wave at Jace, and he winked at her. She'd quickly wormed her way into his heart. There was something about Ruby and her bubbly personality that drew people in. Jace had only lasted a few days at Wilder Ranch before joining her fan club.

She took her time heading down the aisle, doling out precisely three flower petals to each row. When she finally reached the front, she high-fived Mackenzie. When the guests laughed at the gesture, Ruby took a bow.

Charmer.

Next came Emma on her dad's arm.

He must have said something to Mackenzie after releasing Emma's hand, because she looked like she was fighting amusement.

Mackenzie had always been a daddy's girl. What had the man thought when Jacc left town after high school? He was afraid to find out. Jace had always respected Wade Wilder. Always wished his own father had been even a quarter of the man.

Things progressed quickly once Pastor Higgin began the ceremony. When they repeated the vows, Gage choked up numerous times while promising to love Emma forever. And then again when she promised the same back to him, her voice clear and strong, her tender gaze glued to the man holding her hands in a grip so tight, it looked like it might hurt her.

Jace didn't know Gage very well, but if ever there was a man in love, who desperately needed the person across from him and looked as if he'd been granted a second chance in life, it was him.

Mackenzie discreetly attempted to wipe under her lashes, but Jace caught the movement because he couldn't keep his attention from wandering in her direction over and over again during the ceremony.

After Gage and Emma were declared husband and wife, they kissed, then scooped up one-year-old Hudson on their way back down the aisle.

An instant family, just like that.

But families like the Wilders didn't grow on trees. Jace knew. He'd practically forced himself into theirs in high school. He'd loved everything about the way they operated as a unit. Teased each other. Worked hard, played hard.

After everyone had been dismissed from their rows and began mingling, Jace sought out Mackenzie. She was a magnet for him. He couldn't resist being near her, even if the end of that was too close for comfort.

"Kenzie Rae." At her name, she turned from the punch bowl, a dainty glass cup in her hand that was in stark contrast to the strong, tanned woman. The dress she wore— no doubt while grumbling—only accentuated her toned arms.

"Hawke." She sipped her punch. "How did it go this afternoon?"

"Fine. A few issues, but we handled it."

"What went wrong? Was it something with the McBanes? Because she said she wanted to talk to me yesterday, and with all of this going on, I totally forgot."

"No. Mrs. McBane only had good things to say. She wanted to rebook for next year. She didn't realize that we give everyone the opportunity to do that before they head

out. So she was fine. You just can't handle not knowing everything that's going on around here, can you?"
Or was it that Kenzie didn't trust anyone but herself to
manage things?

"That's not true." Mackenzie tried to take another
drink of punch, but she'd already emptied it, since it
held about as much as a thimble. Jace took it from her,
refilled it and then returned it to her. She thanked him.

"It is true," he continued. "There was a chip in the
tile in Cabin Nine. Boone and I finagled a fix as best as
we could. It should hold through this week, but then we
probably need to get a maintenance check on it." Evan
was the one who had any fix-it skills in their family, but
Jace had muddled through.

He could have called his brother to ask for advice,
but he hadn't because he'd been avoiding Evan lately.
Pretty much since the injury. Evan had called a number of times, but Jace had either missed the attempts or
dodged answering.

He just wasn't sure what his brother was going to say…
or if he was going to tell Jace to quit. To retire.

And Jace really didn't want to hear it right now. Not
when he was bent on getting better. Positive attitude went
a long way, and he refused to entertain any other thoughts
right now.

"That's not bad. So everything went okay, then?"

"Yes. Everything went fine." Only Mackenzie would
be talking shop at her sister's wedding. "If I thought I'd
detected some tears from you during the cere—"

"You'd be wrong." Her reply was quick, humor flar-
ing so fast, he almost missed it. "Allergies. They were
really kicking up tonight."

"Ah. And yet they seem better all of a sudden."

Those glossy, distracting lips of hers broke into a curve. "Amazing, right? What were you doing watching me anyway, when Emma's the bride? She looks so stunning, I'm surprised everyone wasn't blinded by her beauty."

"She does look beautiful. But she's no you." Jace didn't temper his words. He should be able to speak the truth at a wedding, shouldn't he?

Based on the confusion and softness cresting Kenzie's features...maybe not.

"J." Mackenzie's eyes shimmered—with tears or "allergies," he couldn't be sure. "That was sweet."

He waved a hand over her hair. "I like what you've got going on here."

"Thanks, though you'll probably never see it this way again. Emma's friend did my makeup—" she motioned to her face "—and I didn't have the heart to fuss. I was trying to be all Team Emma for the wedding. No complaining. Whatever she wants."

"You look like a celebrity. Like I should be standing in line to get your autograph. But I'm actually partial to the girl who treats makeup like a venomous snake and doesn't know what to do with the smoky-powder stuff covering your eyelids. I like that Kenzie Rae a whole lot."

"I—" She faltered. "That's the nicest thing you've said to me in a long time." Her voice hitched, tender and low, sweet and concerned. "But shouldn't we be..."

Careful? Yes.

Kenzie's warning was spot-on. Jace *was* traveling into unchartered territory. Places they'd been careful not to go since he'd shown up at the ranch.

And for good reason, too. It was just...with Mackenzie looking at him like she was, softening like she was...Jace couldn't remember what any of them were.

Chapter 12

How long were weddings supposed to last? The reception had been in full swing for an hour and a half, and Mackenzie was as drained as if she'd been moving cattle all day.

"You're not supposed to show up the bride, you know."

Dad approached, smooched her cheek and hugged her. Just like that, all of her strung-tight muscles and nerves from having to be "on" tonight and engage in endless amounts of small talk unraveled.

"Thanks, Dad." His hair had grown grayer since the last time her parents had visited. His mustache, too. The man was the quintessential cowboy. Rugged and strong and dependable. "And thanks a lot for making me laugh at the beginning of the ceremony." After Dad had given Emma away, he'd turned and flashed a goofy expression at her before retreating to his seat next to Mom.

"I did nothing of the sort." His attempt at innocence failed and fizzled.

She motioned to her face. "Did you see they put all of this goop on me?"

"You look pretty with it and without it."

"Well, aren't you diplomatic today?" She looped her arm through his and watched as the guests mixed and mingled, leaning on him, wondering when she could trade all of this in for a movie and pajamas.

"What's on your mind, Kenzie-girl?"

She straightened. "What do you mean?"

He glanced sideways at her. "I mean, I know when something is going on with you. And something is. I'm just not sure what. With all of the wedding madness, I haven't been able to figure it out." He scanned the wedding guests, landing on Jace, who was talking to Vera and some other staff members. "Wouldn't have anything to do with a certain bull rider, would it?"

Was she that transparent? "No."

Her dad's low chuckle warmed and comforted.

"Maybe." A golf ball lodged in her throat. "I tried to pretend like everything was okay when he left. That I was happy for him. And I am—was—happy he could chase his dreams. But his leaving broke me, I think. And I'm not sure if I can…" *If I can… What? Get over him? Move on? Let him back in?* All of the above.

Dad patted her hand. "I'm not partial to anyone who hurts my kids. Any of them. Because of course I don't have favorites." He winked at her. "The last thing I want is for you to be hurting, baby girl." The endearment stemmed from when she and Luc had been in the womb—described as baby girl and baby boy—but her brother's nickname hadn't stuck like hers. "I think maybe…" Dad's exhale held sorrow "…maybe Jace was just a kid doing his best back when he left for the rodeo. His dad sure didn't set much of an example for him."

"True." Victor Hawke had drunk himself into an oblivion for most of Jace's upbringing, and then that same vice had brought about his demise when he'd been killed in a bar fight. Nothing like the childhood Mackenzie had been granted. But her sympathy and compassion for Jace didn't make him safe. "I'm afraid to find out…" *Why he really left.* "I'm just…afraid." A bitter taste swamped her mouth.

"You've never been afraid of anything. As a baby, you climbed everything you could. Finagled a way out of your crib at a year old. I found you on the countertop more than once. You scared the living daylights out of me on more occasions than I can count."

"So you're saying I've turned into a wuss?"

Humor swept over her dad's features. "I'm saying maybe this is important to you for it to matter this much. For it to scare you like this."

A sigh escaped. "I don't like this conversation anymore."

He shifted to face her, his warm, strong hands squeezing her arms. "My girl can tackle anything. That much I do know. Especially with God by your side." He gave her a pointed look—one that said, *Dive all in. Go for it. Grab a little of Vera's mind-set and leap.*

After another hug, he left her standing alone. No doubt so that she could follow through and stop chickening out.

His message was right on, and Mackenzie knew it. She could handle the truth with God's help, no matter what it was. And if what Jace had to say was horrible, at least that would give her a reason to steer clear of him, to stop falling for him all over again.

Ever aware of Mackenzie's whereabouts, Jace watched her approach from across the crowd. She beelined for him, and his heart gave a big ole thump in his chest, so loud he was surprised wedding guests didn't turn to see what had caused the ruckus.

Kenzie stopped a step behind him, as if she didn't intend to break up the circle of conversation he was a part of but wanted his attention.

She had it. He eased back from the group, entering the Mackenzie zone that sucked him in like a black hole. "You okay?"

"Can I talk to you for a minute?"

About more work stuff? Why not. "Sure. What's up?"

Skittish. That was what she was, with her eyes flitting this way and that. Her hands wringing. "We might have to talk somewhere else. I'm not sure this is the best spot."

"Okay. Why? What's this about?" Alarm bells clanged, his intuition on high alert.

She released a pent-up breath. "I'm ready to know."

Jace angled his head. "Ready to know what?"

"Why you left the way you did."

Mackenzie's declaration blindsided him like a hoof to the back of his skull. All this time he'd tried to talk to her, to be open and honest with her, and now she wanted to have this conversation here? After he'd basically given up on forcing her to discuss anything regarding their past?

"You want to talk about this now? At your sister's wedding?"

She shrugged. "Why not? Gage and Emma are so enthralled with each other, I'm surprised honey isn't leaking from their pores. They won't notice if we take off for a few minutes." Her eyebrows arched. "Why? Do you need more time? It's not like you have to get your story straight. I want the truth, Hawke. I can handle it."

She might be able to, but what if he couldn't?

When Jace had first tried to tell Mackenzie his reasons, she'd still been white-hot-ember mad at him. Any confession of how much he used to love her would have been safe because neither of them were remotely close to those feelings at that time.

But telling her now that they were getting along... It felt like restarting something they were working very hard not to go anywhere near.

Despite his stumbling earlier tonight, Jace's plans still hadn't changed.

Still...he owed Mackenzie an explanation. So he'd just have to figure out how to be careful with her—with both of them—and speak the truth at the same time.

Two hours later Mackenzie dropped onto the couch in her cabin and used the remote to turn on the TV, then the DVD player. She'd fallen asleep during *Tombstone* the other night, so she cued it up to around the spot she'd dropped off. Not that it mattered. She'd seen the movie so many times she had it memorized.

Earlier her conversation with Jace had stalled before it even had a chance to start, because Boone had interrupted them, panicked.

Mackenzie couldn't decide if she was relieved or annoyed by that.

Probably a bit of both. Relieved that she didn't have to hear the truth, especially if it was hurtful. Annoyed that they hadn't just gotten the whole thing over and done. That she still didn't *know*.

But at some point it would happen. Jace would tell her his whys, and she'd either break or...not break.

Boone had been rattled because he and some of the other staff had been—unbeknownst to Mackenzie—decorating Gage's Jeep Grand Cherokee for the bride and groom's departure.

Someone had decided they should fill the inside with balloons.

Someone had sneaked Gage's key fob from his bag inside the lodge, planning to return it without anyone being the wiser.

And then *someone* had lost the key fob during the decorating.

At first Mackenzie had thought the whole thing was a bunch of drama over nothing. Emma was happy and married, and if she and Gage had to leave in another vehicle, the smitten girl would barely even notice.

But then Mackenzie had realized that Emma's overnight bag was in the locked Jeep. She and Gage were staying at a bed-and-breakfast for the night, and Gage's parents were watching Hudson at his place.

The overnight bag being inside the Jeep turned the situation into a wedding emergency.

Thankfully Emma and Gage had been—and still were—blissfully unaware of the crisis.

Jace, the man who kept surprising her, had taken the lead for finding the key fob.

He'd collected flashlights and directed them all in a methodical manner. And he'd been the one to finally find the fob—which had been buried in the grass underneath the vehicle, near the front-passenger-side tire.

And just as strange as Jace taking over…Mackenzie had let him. Which for her was…big. Like it or not, she was letting him back into her life.

The whole night had left her feeling abnormally emotional.

Coming home to a cabin void of her sparkly, happy sister hadn't helped anything. Emma's things had been moved over to Gage's earlier this week, and now with the snap of her fingers and a marriage certificate, she was gone for good.

Having the two-bedroom cabin all to herself should be more appealing to Mackenzie, but it wasn't. "Buck up, woman. Seriously. You're turning into a whimpering fool."

This sentimental stuff was for the birds.

But even with the changes, for the first time in a long time, Mackenzie still felt comforted. At peace. Her dad's words tonight had hit home for her. *With God by your side.* The short phrase had reminded her that even when she felt alone, she never really was. Sure she'd been left behind a time or two, but never by God. He was her constant. Her strength.

Rap-rap-rap. At the knock on her front door, she jolted upright. Who was still up? And what emergency was she needed for now?

Mackenzie had changed into gray yoga pants and a T-shirt that read Country Roads Take Me Home after the wedding reception, removed the bobby pins, tossed her hair into a ponytail and scrubbed the goop from her face. She might not be ready for another wedding, but she was presentable enough.

She opened the door to find Jace on her step. He had

an Angela's pizza box in his hands, and her taste buds clanged like symbols.

He'd changed out of his button-up shirt, crisp jeans and boots into a more casual T-shirt and worn jeans. The earlier outfit... Well, she'd noticed him in it. That was for sure.

This one had the same effect.

The front porch light shone into his eyes, which were full of something Mackenzie couldn't name if she tried.

"What's going on?" Everything from the wedding had been cleaned up. It was late and she was tired.

He shifted from one foot to the other. "We didn't get to have our conversation."

"It's fine. Really. We can another day." Mackenzie didn't have it in her to do this right now.

Jace raised the box. "This is your bribe. We walk and talk, then food. I had to call in a favor to pick it up late. Last pizza they made tonight."

Low blow. She was a sucker for Angela's. And just like he seemed to know and remember all things about her, Jace had her figured out.

"Either get some shoes or you can go barefoot."

Should she claim a headache? Aunt Flo? That second one would really scare him off. Or she could snatch the pizza box out of his hands and slam the door.

Humor surfaced.

"Oh, boy. Do I even want to know what you're thinking?"

"Probably not." The pizza won her over. "Can you put that in the oven on low while I find some shoes?"

"Put it in the oven still in the box?"

"Sure." She was already halfway to her room. "It will be fine. It's just to keep it warm." Mackenzie fumbled through her disorganized shoes. She found one rubber flip-flop, and it took her another thirty seconds to find the other tucked under a boot. She slid them on and walked out to find Jace fiddling with the oven.

"Know what you're doing there, Hawke?"

"Think so."

"You've got it too hot." Mackenzie dialed the knob back.

It was a small appliance because of the lack of space in the cabin, but he'd managed to slide the box inside. "What kind did you get?" The garlic, tomato and other spices were begging her to steal a piece right now.

"Hawaiian."

Her favorite. Of course.

The two of them stepped outside, shutting the door, trapping in the Italian aroma. Dry grass crunched under their steps as Mackenzie inhaled the scent of pine. Rain had been sparse this summer. Not an unusual occurrence for Colorado, but they could use some moisture.

They took the lane that led through the trees and past various empty cabins, small landscape lights casting a warm glow on the path. Everything was quiet. Deserted.

What would Jace confess? That he'd fallen out of love with her and hadn't known how to admit it? Maybe there'd been another girl. Her list of guesses for why he'd left the way he had was long and imaginative.

And about to be answered.

"Did you know that I was supposed to mow the lawn the day Evan was injured?" Jace shuddered at the revelation that had owned him for so long. Nothing like diving right into the past.

Mackenzie's brow puckered, and her footsteps mo-

mentarily hesitated. Her head shook slowly as they re-
sumed walking. "No. You never told me that."

"I'd been hanging out with a friend that morning, and
Evan had been working at the feed store. But when I came
home, instead of mowing like I was supposed to, I started
playing video games." Jace had saved up his money for
that stupid game console that he hadn't known would
cause so much trouble. "Mom was at work. She wasn't
there to nag me, so I let the chore slide. Figured I'd do
it later or the next day. When Evan came home, he must
have realized I hadn't gotten it done. Instead of hound-
ing me about it, he just...did it. I'm not sure if Mom had
asked him to or if he just thought I was skirting it like a
little brother. Which I was."

"Oh, J." Mackenzie's fingers brushed against his. And
then her hand slid inside his and squeezed. He held on,
silently begging her not to let go. He needed her support
in order to continue this conversation.

Jace had assumed it would get easier with time, but it
hadn't. Maybe it never would.

Mackenzie kept pace and didn't pull away from him
as they walked past cabins and pines, the deserted spaces
blurring as the regret of that time consumed him.

"Evan mowed for a number of the neighbors, and one
of them let him use their riding mower on our lawn. I
didn't have permission to borrow the rider, so I would
have used the simple push mower. But Evan..." He'd bor-
rowed the monster that had turned on him.

Mackenzie's swift intake of breath was burdened. "I
wish you would have said something."

"What would it have mattered? What happened
couldn't be changed."

"Maybe. But that's a lot for a kid to bear."

"I was fifteen! I should have known better." Images of his brother in the hospital flared. The flat sheet, the leg that should have continued below his knee but didn't. His brother's eyes, so bloodshot, so panicked.

"Evan had always loved bull riding. He had posters of famous riders in his room. He followed the sport religiously. When he lost that chance… I think it shattered something in him. I know it shattered something in me watching it all happen. Knowing I could have prevented it."

"But—"

"I get that my theory may seem unreasonable." Jace cut her off before she could go on about how illogical it was that he shouldered the blame or believed he could have changed things. "And if it were someone else telling it, I'd be able to say the usual stuff—of course, it's not your fault. Things happen. But emotionally…that just doesn't ring true. The what-ifs and the blame… They've become a part of me, and I don't think they're ever going to let go."

"I want to disagree with you. To repeat the truths you just listed—that you couldn't have changed things, that it's not your fault. But I also get what you're saying. I'm sure I'd be the same way if I were in your shoes."

They followed the lane as it turned toward the barn and corral. "There was a horrible day after the accident, when Evan started tearing apart his room. He ripped down the posters, threw his winning belt buckles against the wall. He basically raged, and I didn't blame him. He slumped against the side of his bed, sprawled out on the floor and pointed at me. Told me to live. To chase his dreams for him. So that's what I did."

Jace stopped to face Mackenzie, and their hands disconnected. He missed her contact instantly. Trees surrounded them, the forest a blanket with the moon and stars sprinkling through. "That's why I left. I had to follow his dreams for him because he couldn't." Unwelcome emotion closed off his windpipe. "I tried to talk to you about competing at the next level a couple of times, but it wasn't easy to bring up the conversation because... I didn't want to leave you. We talked about the future so much. And I wanted that, too. I was torn, confused." He held her gaze, willing her to believe him. "So I took the coward's way out. I left you the note because if I would have tried to say goodbye, I would never have been able to walk away from you."

Her arms had crossed during his speech, and her hands now rubbed up and down her skin, which rippled with goose bumps. She looked to the side, gathering herself, her emotions, maybe even her anger. Jace wasn't sure what all was rolling through that pretty head of hers.

"I didn't think dating long-distance or between rodeos was an option, because I was afraid I'd never commit to bull riding. That I'd always be homesick for you. So I thought it was best to cut all ties."

"Why did you call me? After?"

Those first few weeks rushed back. Jace had been nauseated over leaving. He'd missed Mackenzie with a physical ache he hadn't known was possible. It had been so hard not talking to her, not knowing how she was. Twice he'd tried her, both praying she'd answer and praying she wouldn't. Torn over the need to hear her voice and the need to make a clean enough break that he'd actually find a way to compete, to do well at the sport Evan had loved so much.

"Because I missed you like crazy."

Mackenzie pressed the toe of her flip-flop into the ground and twisted. "I thought…" Storm clouds brewed in her eyes when she lifted her chin. "I always thought you didn't love me anymore and you weren't sure how to tell me."

"Impossible." The word slipped out before Jace could stop it or temper it or downgrade it. They weren't supposed to be entering this territory in the present, but he couldn't lie about the past. "That was never the case. It was the opposite. I loved you so much, but I also *had* to follow Evan's dreams."

Mackenzie had stepped forward, into his space. Her fingertips scooted along his jaw, and Jace's lungs quit on him. Neither of them spoke. Neither moved. Mackenzie just explored him for a minute. Touching his hair, his shoulder, the blank space his cast had recently occupied. He let himself slide hands up her arms and drink in her soft, smooth skin. And then they were kissing. Jace wasn't sure who had started it. He really didn't care about unimportant details like that, because they were wrapped up in each other, her hands looped behind his neck, his raking up her spine. He would swallow her up if he could. Jace's theory and memories of kissing Kenzie… They didn't do the real thing justice in the least.

"Kenzie Rae." He tried to pull back, to be the logic.

"Shut up, J." And then her mouth was on his again, and he was drowning in her. She was all spice and fire and energy. How was a man supposed to resist?

The kiss softened and slowed, and the two of them parted but stayed close, his pulse as dramatic as a teenager.

There'd been a moment at Colby's place when Jace had wondered if Mackenzie had gotten the wrong impression from him. If for some reason she'd begun to think he might not go back to bull riding. Since then, whenever that particular worry had popped up, he'd quickly dismissed it. Of course Mackenzie knew. He'd never led her to think anything else.

But then…why had she kissed him?

"You know I'm leaving, right?" The truth tumbled out, not at all how he'd meant to say it. He'd wanted to be honest, protect her.

By the spark of pain he'd just witnessed, he'd done exactly the opposite.

"I know if you heal, you're leaving again." Her brow furrowed. "But your head, the concussion… I thought… if it doesn't improve, you can't go back to riding."

"It will get better." His hands dropped and formed fists. "It has to. And either way, when I'm done with physical therapy, I'm going back."

Anger, frustration and confusion flitted over Mackenzie's features. "But that's dangerous. You said you wouldn't do anything stupid. Which translates into not going back if your brain hasn't healed. What if you get another concussion on top of this one? What does that mean for your future? What about all of the athletes suffering from CTE?"

"There are risks, yes, but there's no guarantee I'm going to get another head injury. No one knows the future. And even if I do, doctors can't predict how the brain will respond." Though the thought of living with CTE made his saliva take a hike. The disease was torture.

"I don't understand." Mackenzie heaved in a deep breath and pushed it out slowly. "I did some research online." She'd gone from heated to trying for calm. "Did you know there's something called post-concussion syndrome? I wonder if that's what you have going on."

Dr. Sanderson had already said as much. Mackenzie didn't need to go playing doctor or researching his issues. Especially since he was showing improvement.

"I'm getting better. Before last night I'd gone almost two weeks without a migraine."

"But that doesn't mean you should jump back on a bull. I don't get it. Why can't you let this go? What do you have to prove?"

What did he have to prove? Everything. "Would you give up this ranch?" Jace raised his arms to encompass the place.

"That's different."

"It's not."

"This ranch isn't going to kill me." Mackenzie's volume escalated, and some small animal scrambled in the forest near them, skittering off to safety.

"Bull riding isn't going to kill me either."

Her hands formed a self-hug, protecting. "Actually, you don't know that."

Chapter 13

Three weeks out of his cast, and Jace was doing absolutely everything with his arm. Mackenzie couldn't fathom how that was safe or right or how the man wouldn't reinjure the fracture, but it wasn't her business.

He wasn't her business.

At least he hadn't gone back to bull riding yet. And he was obeying Dr. Sanderson's orders for physical therapy. Jace had gone into town for it twice already this week and had three appointments planned for next that he'd let Mackenzie know about for scheduling purposes.

Tonight he'd participated in the shovel races like a boy who'd been waiting for exactly that all summer. And he probably had been.

If anyone understood the need to compete and play and adventure, it was Mackenzie.

But the changes also meant he was beginning his departure all over again. He'd made it clear that was his plan, and while he hadn't told her a specific date, Mackenzie sensed it was fast approaching.

Now that the twins were home and Luc was back to work full-time, there wasn't as much demand for Jace at Wilder Ranch. They could survive without him.

But Mackenzie didn't want to.

And she hated that. How had she developed feelings for him again? Or had they never gone away? The answers didn't matter. Because Jace was leaving. And nothing she felt about it would change his mind.

Mackenzie certainly wasn't going to try to convince him to be logical and not go. No, sirree.

The man had to figure that out on his own.

Baby screams pierced the darkness as Mackenzie walked from the corral to the lodge. Luc carted the twins in a double carrier that attached to his chest and back as he paced the gravel path in front of the lodge.

"You been pinching the girls again?"

He laughed, the picture of calm despite the ruckus happening under his nose. "What's Everly doing back there?" He turned so that Mackenzie could peek inside the carrier.

"She's asleep."

He fist pumped. "One down, one to go."

"Want help? I'm no Emma but I can take one."

"It's okay. Cate's in the shower." He spoke over Savannah's continuing cry. "And these two wouldn't settle, so I decided we'd walk until they did."

"Ruby okay?"

"Yeah, she's in bed with white noise blaring so she can hopefully sleep through any late-night interruptions from her sisters. All of a sudden she feels so old compared to these two."

"I thought the same thing yesterday when she came with me on the ride. Never complained once. Maybe I could take her into town Saturday night for ice cream. She's probably feeling a little misplaced with the twins demanding so much attention." Grandpa and Grandma had done their fair share of doting on the girl when they'd been back for Emma's wedding, but now they were gone, and so was Emma. She was at Wilder Ranch for work during the day but quick to scamper home at night to her new husband and baby.

"Ruby would love that. It would make her whole week."

"Consider it done."

Savannah's cry escalated, and Luc bounced up and down. "I hear you, baby. I'm working on it. Now, don't wake your sister while you're at it."

"Savannah Rae, you're going to give us a bad name." Mackenzie rubbed a finger across her niece's cheek. Savannah captured the finger and wrapped her tiny hand around it. Her wail stopped.

"Freeze. Don't move. Don't—" Luc's directions were interrupted by another howl. "Never mind." He grinned. "This one always has a pea under her mattress. Must take after her namesake."

"Ha. Just for that, I'm going to pinch Everly."

His eyes grew wide, laugh lines creasing. "You wouldn't." He backed away, his next words almost drowned out by cries. "I'd better walk with her before she wakes up the whole ranch."

"I'm just turning down the lodge and then I'm headed to bed. Hope the walk works."

"Thanks. Me, too."

Mackenzie checked the offices first. Luc's was locked, and there was no light slipping under the door, but the front office was illuminated like a football field on a Friday night. She grabbed the glass of iced tea she'd left on her desk earlier and cleaned up the condensation it had left behind. Then she flicked off the lights and headed for the kitchen. After loading her glass in the dishwasher, she proceeded to check that the appliances were off. Joe had already put everything to bed, so she did the same for the room and tromped upstairs.

Everything was good there, but on her way back down she heard music. Mackenzie paused at the bottom of the stairs. A sliver of light spilled into black inkiness from the small exercise room at the end of the hall. Her boots clicked lightly as she approached. The room had a handful of machines in it, weights and other items that the occasional guest chose over hiking and exploring Wilder Ranch.

Not that Mackenzie understood that.

She peeked through the crack. Jace balanced in a squat while on an exercise ball. He jumped forward, off the ball, then jumped backward to land on it again, all while staying upright. And then he began to do squats while still on the ball. How was that even possible? She would end up in a cast from one attempt.

"You just going to stalk me out there, or are you planning to come in?"

How had he even noticed her through the narrow gap? She pushed the door open. "Trying to break your neck this time?"

Jace was dressed in workout shorts, tennis shoes and a sleeveless shirt that held a ring of sweat. She didn't recognize the music coming from the speaker hooked up to his phone. He jumped down, walked over, thumbed the volume low.

Mackenzie had done her best to be normal with Jace since their kiss, to tell herself over and over again it had simply been that—a kiss. But no matter how many times she convinced herself, fear kept rising up that it had been about so much more.

Especially after Jace had confessed why he'd left the way he had. That hurt she'd felt for so long had dissipated, and buried feelings for him had sprouted and tumbled out of control.

Stupid.

She should have known better. Mackenzie still wasn't sure what had come over her that night, kissing him like that. And of course he'd thoroughly kissed her back before telling her he was planning to return to riding even if it harmed him.

Even if it killed him.

She wanted to rage at Jace for that, but she was harnessing all of her self-control not to.

He's not mine to worry about.

If only her brain would listen.

He picked up a small metal bar, which had a weight attached by a chain. Arms held straight out, he rolled it up and then down on repeat.

"You come to join me, Wilder? Get in a workout?"

Funny…they'd both switched back to calling each other by their last names over the last three weeks. As if by mutual agreement, they'd tried to separate. To be careful with their feelings for each other. Because yeah, Mackenzie got the impression Jace was fighting the same pull she was.

And that neither of them knew what to do about it.

"I was just shutting things down. Didn't realize you were back here."

"Gotta get in shape if I'm planning to be back for the Miles City Rodeo in two weeks."

"Two weeks?" Oh. She hadn't expected him to go quite that soon. Mackenzie dropped to the wooden bench that lined one wall, a shelf with stacks of small white towels hanging above it. "I thought you'd need more time. More physical therapy."

"Supposed to be six to eight weeks, but I'm going to cut it a little early." Shocking. Why would he make such an unwise decision? Was being at Wilder Ranch—and around her—that horrible? "I talked to Luc about it earlier today," Jace continued. "With him back now, you guys don't have as much need for me. He thinks things will be fine for the short remainder of the summer, after I go."

"Of course. We can handle Wilder Ranch without you." Mackenzie had known he was leaving, and that small blip where she'd wondered if he'd retire hadn't lasted very long, so why did it hurt so much? What was it about Jace that drew her in? Why couldn't she just decide not to want him, to like him, to need him?

"I did the wrangler competitions tonight. And the shovel race." He set the weights on the floor and picked up a jump rope. "Finally. I've been jonesing to all summer." The whirl of the rope joined the quiet music.

"I saw." He'd looked happy and carefree and out of her grasp. "Just don't get hurt on our watch."

"I'm not planning to, boss."

"You probably consider it physical therapy."

"I do." The rope tangled around his feet and he re-situated, starting again. "Even got approval from Dr. Sanderson."

Wait. What? "You did?"

"Ah, no." He let the rope go slack and flashed her one of those killer smiles. If they were together, she had no doubt it would be followed up by a smoking kiss. But since they weren't—and since that last lip-lock had been foolish on her part—that most definitely wasn't going to happen.

Because he was leaving her. Again.

Despite everything Jace had told her—about his brother, his reasons for going back to riding, why he'd left the way he had—Mackenzie couldn't shake the wounding that history was repeating itself. That she still wasn't enough of a reason to stay. The future plans they'd once dreamed up together weren't enough either. The man would choose the thrill of riding a two-thousand-pound beast over having her in his life. Again.

Mackenzie didn't even know how Jace's migraines and vertigo had been lately, because she'd stopped asking. And he'd stopped telling her.

After finishing with the jump rope, he switched to a small ball and balanced again, weights in his extended hands. Once his sets were done, he grabbed a towel and dropped to the bench, next to her, leaving space between them. "I stink."

"I noticed." Actually, she hadn't, but his cheeks, crinkling with amusement, made the jab worth it.

Jace scrubbed the towel over his hair, leaving it around his neck. Even with a recent cut, the locks stuck out in a hundred directions at once. "I'm sorry I stayed for the summer. I should have listened to you." He uncapped his water bottle and drank. "You were right."

"Why? Because it was so awful here?"

"No." Those soulful chestnut eyes met hers. "Because it was so good. Wilder Ranch has always felt a little bit like home for me. I basically lived here during the waking hours in high school. Being here has been good for me, but also…"

"Also, what?"

"Hard."

"How so?"

He shrugged. "Because of you."

"All of these compliments are so sweet. Continue."

Jace ignored her sass. "Being around you reminds me of all of the reasons I wanted to be with you when we were younger."

"But they aren't enough. They weren't enough then, and they're not enough now." Mackenzie was revealing way too much.

"That's not true." Jace tossed the towel into the hamper in the corner. "It's not about you or me. The rodeo is my job, Kenzie Rae. I have to go back to it."

"You don't have to. You're choosing to."

Exasperation leaked from his lungs. "Fine. Say it however it makes you feel better."

"But it doesn't make me feel better." She popped up from the bench and began pacing the small space. "This is why I didn't want you to stay, J. Because this—" she motioned between them "—doesn't just go away. At least not for me."

He frowned. "Not for me either."

Mackenzie ached like the flu had taken over her body. "Then don't go." *No.* She'd vowed to stay out of his business. She'd promised herself she would swallow the words and keep her head down and not try to stop

Jace from leaving. But the remorse of last time—of how things had ended between them—was too intense. And if her asking prevented that same thing from happening again…she had to try.

"Stay."

Mackenzie's suggestion choked Jace. Never had he wanted to grant her—or himself—anything more. And the fact that the toughest woman he knew had said that to him? Had opened herself up like that?

It slayed him.

"Don't." He dropped his head into his hands, elbows on his knees. "Please don't." His temples throbbed with pain, but not of the migraine variety. This was heartbreak, pure and simple.

"Why not?" Exasperation peppered the question, seeping from Kenzie's pores, sending angry currents bouncing off the walls. "We're just skirting around the truth, and at least this time we get to talk about it."

Ouch. Unlike the last time when he'd abandoned her.

"You could live in town. You could buy a ranch, do what your friend does and train other bull riders. There are so many options. Even if it's not to be with me, then you should be doing this for you. It's time to be done, and I think you know it. You're just fighting it."

She might believe that, but it wasn't true. Not for Jace. There were no other options for him. Bull riding was his life. He loved it. And then there was Evan and all that his brother had missed out on because of his choices, his laziness… Even after so many years, he couldn't let go of that.

"You're wrong." The defense came out strong and confident, neither of which he felt.

"I looked up your last couple years of competition."

That stung. "Why? So you could prove that I'm not good enough anymore?"

"No. I would never do that. But you've been injured numerous times. It's not worth it. Your brother wouldn't want you to do this for him. He wouldn't want you to risk further injury. Have you even asked him? Does he know you carry all of this guilt? That you think his accident was your fault? Because it's not." She crouched in front of him, close. "It was an accident, J. That's all it was."

"It was my fault." Jace erupted from the bench, blowing past her. "And yes, he knows, because he's the one who told me to do this."

Mackenzie groaned and dropped back to the seat. "What did he say to you exactly? Do you remember?"

"No." He couldn't quote Evan's tirade. But he'd never forget the gist. "I was young. I couldn't tell you exactly what he said."

Defiance sparked in her stare. "I think you should ask him."

"And I think you should mind your own business." Jace winced. He was a jerk. He was snapping at Mackenzie for no reason. None of this was her fault. Sure, she was pushing him—trying to get him to consider quitting—but she wasn't the only one on that bandwagon. Dr. Sanderson had expressed the same concerns at Jace's appointment yesterday.

He crossed over, knelt in front of her like she'd done with him. "I'm sorry." Jace laced his fingers through hers. "I didn't mean it. I'm just… I'm a mess. Leaving you was the hardest thing I've ever had to do, and I hate that I'm doing it again." Her sadness slammed into him, rocking him back. What he wouldn't give to make her laugh instead of causing this.

"I hate that you could add another injury on top of not being fully healed. I'm really struggling with that, J."

"I get that. But I just…have to go. I'm sorry."

"I tried so hard not to say any of this to you. But now that it's out, I'm not sure I would have forgiven myself if I hadn't."

There should only be one of them who couldn't forgive themselves, and Jace had already taken the crown.

She disconnected from him physically, pushing off the bench and scooting around him. "I've got to go. I can't…" She toggled a finger between them. "I can't do this right now. But we're good, okay? We'll be fine until you go."

Liar.

She left the room, and his heart splintered.

So much for not wounding her. So much for doing things differently this time around.

Chapter 14

Jace carried the last bag of his stuff down to his truck and tossed it into the back. It was time for him to get on the road, and anticipation had him jittery.

He'd had his last follow-up with Dr. Sanderson—who wasn't pleased he was cutting short physical therapy on his arm—and Doc Karvina would clear him to compete when he arrived in Miles City. They'd already Skyped, so there should be no surprises there.

His ribs and spleen were good to go. He'd trained hard with his riding arm, and it was holding up nicely. His headaches and vertigo might not be nonexistent, but they were slowing down.

Jace should have gone over to Colby's and ridden one of his bulls before today. He'd told himself he couldn't take more time away from Wilder Ranch, when he was supposed to be helping out, but the truth was, he didn't want to know how his body would react to riding. He'd been clinging to positive thoughts and prayers instead. Choosing to believe he'd have good results and no trouble.

Even if his week had been filled with horrible nightmares that had shouted otherwise.

Luc had returned to working full-time, so Jace didn't have to shoulder guilt about leaving the Wilders in a bind. The ranch was almost to fall season, when things would slow down.

There was nothing else holding Jace here.

Except for Mackenzie. Always Mackenzie.

"Hey, bull rider." Vera walked in his direction. She had on her bright pink tennis shoes and a turquoise shirt along with multicolored shorts. Her arms flailed back and forth like propellers.

"Getting in your workout?" Vera's new lease on life also included a twenty-minute speed walk every day.

"Yep." She paused in front of him, continuing to march in place. "We're going to miss you around here."

"I feel the same." Vera had become one of his favorite people this summer. Her teasing and zest for life were going to leave a hole in his.

"I'll be following your career now, so you'd better make it good."

He laughed. "For you? Anything. How's that doctor of yours?"

"Amazing." She lit up, knocking ten years off her age. "Joe seems to think I'm not too much of a mess in the kitchen, so I'm going to be staying on for the fall season."

"I'm glad you're happy."

"Thanks." Her head quirked, and her chin-length, reaching-for-silver hair shifted with the movement. "And you? Are you happy?"

"Of course." He was going back to riding, wasn't he? Except…even with that spurring him forward, Jace felt strangely glued to this place, these people. Especially to the woman he still had to find and force himself to say goodbye to one more time.

Vera's arm and leg movements halted. "That was a mighty quick response, bull rider. You might want to think twice before you tear out of here."

The slightest hitch of anger rose up at Vera's intrusion. Everyone had been chiming in with opinions Jace hadn't asked for. Even his mom had questioned the logic of him returning to rodeoing. But just as quickly, his upset dissolved. Vera was in love, and she wanted that for everyone. How could Jace fault her for that?

"Mackenzie's in the barn, by the way."

"How did you know I was looking for her?" Earlier he'd checked in the front office, then Luc's, the rest of the lodge, even her cabin.

No sign of the woman.

But the barn? Was she hiding from him? Or actually working?

Probably the first.

"I saw how much you tried to keep your attraction to each other under wraps this summer. I knew she'd be your final destination before skedaddling out of here today."

Vera could add "truth speaker" to her list of attributes. "It's not worth trying to deny, is it?"

"Nope."

"Mackenzie would be mortified to know that you have us all figured out."

"Then don't tell her…that. Though I'm guessing there's a few other things you could say to her." Oh, boy.

Vera leaned closer. "If you could make any choice you wanted to right now, what would it be? The one you're making? Or something different?"

That sitting-in-front-of-the-church-pulpit, being-called-out feeling descended on Jace. "Vera, you should be a life coach. Or a counselor."

"It's not difficult, bull rider. It's just… What would you do if no one held you back? If it wasn't about pleasing someone else? What do you actually want?" She emphasized each syllable of the last sentence.

Kenzie Rae. Bull riding. A time machine to go back and keep my brother from getting injured while covering for me.

All easy peasy, of course.

White teeth flashed as if she'd read his mind, and then she hugged him. "You can do it, bull rider. You're as genuine and strong and good as a person gets."

His throat cinched tighter than a bull rope. Jace didn't say anything more, and Vera didn't require it of him. She was off, limbs swinging, humming to some song in her head.

Jace strode toward the barn, not giving himself the space or time to overthink. This conversation with Mackenzie had to happen. He refused to leave without saying goodbye to her this time. He simply could not repeat that mistake.

He found Mackenzie with Bryce, the vet, who was examining Jethro. The horse had been temperamental lately, and that was a huge liability, since Wilder Ranch horses were counted on to be consistent and cart around new riders each week.

"How's his appetite been?" the vet asked Mackenzie as Jace approached.

"Low. And he's had other gut issues, too." She scrubbed a hand down Jethro's forehead. "But we're going to get you fixed up, boy. You hang in there."

Jace's gut dipped. He'd always been a sucker for Mackenzie's soft side. "Hey, Doc." Bryce greeted him and continued with his examination. Jace sidled up to Mackenzie. "Can I talk to you?"

She kept comforting Jethro and didn't turn to look at him. "I'm busy."

"It will only take a minute." Unfortunately. *Just enough time to say goodbye. Break both of our hearts one more time.* "Please." His low pleading registered in the plunge of her shoulders.

"I can't." Her wounded whisper cut through him. She couldn't leave the horse? Or she couldn't talk to him? Her storm-cloud eyes flashed with lightning as they met his for the faintest second. "Why don't you leave me a note?"

Frustration ripped from his chest. "Kenz." He kept his voice quiet. "I'm begging. I won't drag you out of here, but we are having this conversation. It can happen right here or somewhere else."

Jace was surprised she didn't respond by stomping on his boot or slugging him. Instead she simply seethed with wordless anger and resignation. "Doc, I'll be back in a minute."

"Okay."

Mackenzie took off like a shot, and Jace followed her into the saddle room.

Once he'd closed the door behind them, she whirled in his direction, all heated upset and impatience. "Fine. I'm here. What do you want, Hawke?"

The smell of leather filled the room, and it brought Jace back to the first day he'd shown up at the ranch and camped out in here while Mackenzie and Luc had discussed his arrival.

Back when he had naively thought he could be around Mackenzie and not love her.

"You're not going to make this easy, are you?"

"You're the one who's not making it easy. You're the one determined to ride when you could seriously injure yourself."

"Kenzie Rae." Her name was heavy on his tongue. Jace *really* didn't want to fight with her. "That's always been the case with bull riding. It's no different this time around." He'd been repeating the same to himself. Only... it felt different. He was equal parts excited and fearful over returning. He might be playing it tough, but he'd give a hefty sum of money not to get hurt again.

Mackenzie had been right—in the last two years, he'd sustained his fair share of injuries. With his recent time off, Jace had buried all of that. But now that he was about to go back, the doubts and fears were clawing their way out of the ground.

Riding scared would no doubt mess with his ability to compete, so Jace had to find a way around it. He had to get back up on that bull.

Mackenzie straightened the saddle next to her, then shifted the oil on the shelf for no apparent reason. "Which bull did you draw?"

"Gnarly."

"What's he like?"

"He's a spinner. Why? You have some coaching advice for me? Or did you just take a sudden interest in my career?"

She rolled her eyes. "I have to do something with all of this jumbled worry and concern that's built up inside me."

"You could trust and pray that I'm going to be okay."

His suggestion was met with a crinkled brow. "I'm working on it."

He was, too.

"You should get out of here. You're going to be behind if you don't take off soon." Her eye contact was sporadic at best. Mostly she was inspecting saddles and the ground. Anything but him.

"I would have left already, but I couldn't find a certain someone."

"The vet's here. I was working!"

"And avoiding."

"No."

"Yes."

She released a pent-up *argh*, with a few extra letters and syllables added on. "This is a fun little argument we're having, but I should get back out there." Her hand snaked out. Patted him on the arm twice. "You have a good drive. Be safe, okay?" And then she pushed past him, as if he was going to let that be their goodbye. As if they didn't mean far more to each other than that.

"No. We're leaving things right this time." Jace caught her arm midstride and tugged her close, wrapping her up tightly. She didn't struggle to break away, and the slightest shiver raced through her. *I love you, Kenzie Rae. Always have. Always will. I'm sorry I have to do this. I'm sorry.* Saying any of it out loud would only wound, so he didn't. Jace just held on.

How was this pain "right"? There was no right in this scenario. Jace had made his decision, and Mackenzie didn't get a say, just like the last time.

She was mad at him about that. She was mad about a

lot of things right now. For the past few days, she'd been determined to hold herself together. To survive Jace's departure the second time around. To fight the belief that she wasn't enough of a reason for him to stay. To trust that it was about Evan and not her.

So far she was failing miserably on all counts.

Mackenzie buried her nose in Jace's shirt and inhaled—soap and deodorant and something inexplicably him. Everything about him was comfort.

And everything about him leaving was torture. A huge part of her had hoped he would just up and leave like the last time. Spare her the pain of this goodbye.

"You need to let go of me." And yet she didn't loosen her hold of him. "Someone is going to come by and find us like this."

Jace laughed as he released her. "Like Trista and Nick? They'd have to write you up."

She pointed. "They'd write you up. I didn't start this."

Jace caught her hand, threading his fingers through hers. Mackenzie's logic screamed that she should untangle from him, but the rest of her wishy-washy self confirmed the truth—it was too late. Too late not to love him again. Too late to save herself.

"You've got some good staff around here. I'm going to miss them and this place."

"They've come far this summer." And a number of them had already asked about returning next year, so they wouldn't have another rebuilding season.

They wouldn't have another summer of Jace either.

Mackenzie was trying to believe that was a good thing. That maybe when Jace left this time, she'd actually be able to let him go for good.

"I'm going to miss you more."

"Stop it. Don't go there." Her head shook, and her heart—it bogged down in her chest, lodging between her ribs, each beat sending out new shards of glass that pricked and bled and tore up her insides. "Now I understand why you left a note last time."

"I'm sorry for leaving." Jace's Adam's apple bobbed. "You could wait for me, you know."

Disbelief flared, irritation turning her skin to flames. "You're going back to rodeoing when I completely disagree with that plan…you're leaving me a second time after I begged you not to stay at the beginning of the summer…and now you want me to wait for you? For how long? Until you can't function? Until you develop CTE? Until you break something for good or get paralyzed? How long, Jace?"

He didn't have an immediate answer for her tirade. "You're right." His hand scraped the hair at the base of his neck. Where her fingers used to go whenever they pleased. But everything about this man was off-limits. If he was going to injure himself further, she couldn't take part in that. Couldn't support him.

And she definitely couldn't wait. Mackenzie had realized something earlier this week, when she'd been gearing up for him to leave all over again—she'd already been waiting for seven years. Waiting for Jace to come back to her. Waiting to know the truth.

And both of those things had happened, but it wasn't enough. Not unless he chose himself over this sport. Not unless he put aside his guilt over Evan's accident once and for all.

"I can't wait for you, because I'm afraid you'll never return." Not in one piece. Not without the kind of injury that would keep him off a bull forever. Because what else would get the man to quit? He'd already been riding for seven years—and that didn't even include competing in high school. That was a long time. A lot of injuries. "There's nothing wrong with being done, you know. It's not quitting or failing. It's just being smart."

The brown pools of his eyes were mournful. "I can see how you'd think that, but we've already had this discussion. I've already made my decision. I have to go back."

"Fine." Mackenzie crossed her arms, thinking maybe if she did, they would keep her body from crumbling into pieces. "Then go."

A sigh wrenched from Jace, and then he cradled her face with his hands. His eyes held a message, but he didn't speak. Didn't explain or confirm or deny the love written there.

He just kissed her. His lips were familiar and warm and strong, and inside she was breaking into tiny chips of stone. It was the most painful kiss Mackenzie had ever experienced. Her hands itched to reach out and grip his T-shirt, but she fisted them instead. She couldn't hold on to him right now. It hurt too much. Her body smarted and stung in places she hadn't even known existed.

Jace finally let go, and then his departure was swift. He strode out of the saddle room, and she stayed put, unable to move. She waited, picturing him leaving the barn. Jogging over to his truck. Tearing down the ranch drive. Walking out of her life. Leaving her behind. Again.

Five minutes later she was still glued to the same spot, unable to make her boots move, worried her beaten and bruised body was just going to give up and quit on her.

At least if it did, all of this would hurt less.

Chapter 15

Jace parked in front of his mom's house. Another good-bye to check off his list, and he was still reeling from the last one. From seeing Mackenzie so upset and knowing he was the cause. Why had he stayed on at Wilder Ranch?

He should have listened to her from the start. She'd been right. There was no "just friends" when it came to the two of them. He didn't have that button with Kenzie Rae. It was all or nothing.

Jace wanted all of her, but she wanted nothing to do with him if he planned to keep riding. They were at a stalemate.

After knocking on his mom's door, Jace tried the knob. It twisted in his grip, so he stepped inside. "Mom." His bellow echoed and slammed against the walls of the small living room.

"Back here," she called out from down the hall, appearing a few seconds later in pink-and-green-plaid pajama pants and a robe, her shoulder-length hair disheveled.

"You okay?"

She waved a hand. "I'm fine. Just had a tough night—that's all. You know I have trouble sleeping sometimes." Her lungs clamored for air, the wheezing taking a knife to Jace's already weighted-with-guilt chest. "I'm going to make a cup of tea. Warm liquid usually helps calm things down. Do you want anything?"

It was at least ninety degrees out, so no, Jace didn't. "I'm good, thanks." He followed his mom through the doorway and into the kitchen. Her hands shook ever so slightly as she got out a mug, warmed up water and decided which kind of tea to have.

"Mom, you've got to take better care of yourself." Jace tempered his scolding with a quiet tone and hopefully some grace he didn't feel. "I've been talking to you about this all summer. It's part of why I came back to Westbend." And now he was leaving and obviously hadn't accomplished anything. Not if her symptoms were still keeping her up at night.

She bobbed the tea bag in the water. "I'm fine, honey. You don't need to worry."

"What has the doctor told you recently? Because I can tell your symptoms are worsening."

"Dr. Sanderson said I'm doing fine. As fine as I can be while fighting this disease. You can call him yourself and ask."

And wasn't that the worst of it? The emphysema had a mind of its own. Jace couldn't prevent it from worsening. He could only push her to slow down, and hope and pray it helped.

Mom opened the fridge and added a squeeze of lemon to her tea. "Are you really going to get after me when you're planning to hightail it out of here and go back to the very thing that injured you?" She let out a huff. "Jace, I don't think you get to suggest I make changes unless you make some, too."

This was not how he'd wanted this conversation to go. He'd been hoping for *you're right* and *I'll slow down.* "My stuff is different."

Smile cresting, she picked up her tea and patted him lightly on the cheek. "Okay, honey." She moved into the living room and sat on the sofa, and he paced in front of it.

"You could at least quit one of your jobs, Mom."

"Which one? I like both of them."

Jace barely resisted rolling his eyes. "Keep the one that's less stressful and pays you more. Quit the after-hours stocking at the five-and-dime."

She took a sip of tea and shrugged. "I actually like working, Jace. It keeps me busy. Gives me something to live for. People to see. What do you want me to do? Hole up in this house and die?"

Jace was beginning to grow a headache, and this time he had no doubt as to the reason for it. "I want you to live, Mom. Take a walk. Volunteer somewhere, if that makes you happy. But there's no need to continue working two jobs. I've sent you enough money that you shouldn't have to."

She plunked her mug onto the side table and squared her shoulders in his direction. "I've never used any of that money."

"What?"

"I put it aside. It's yours, and I never wanted it. I put it into a separate savings account. It's been earning pretty good interest."

No way. Jace dropped onto the other end of the couch. "The whole point of me sending that money was to alleviate some of your stress." He stopped to swallow, to will his voice down from angry to reasonable. "Allow you to work less. Heal. Give your body a break."

"I know. But I really didn't need it. And it *was* nice having it in case of an emergency. It did provide that comfort for me." Mom cradled her tea and shifted so that she leaned back against the armrest and faced him on the couch. "I love you for watching out for me. You and Evan both. You're the best sons I could ever ask for. And you're not one thing like your father, either one of you. I'd love to take credit for that, but I'm starting to think it was just the grace of God. That He watched out for and protected you two. Kept you from bad choices. Even with Evan's accident, I can look back and see so many ways that God was in his recovery details. For a long time I thought God had abandoned us. But now I know He didn't."

It was so good to hear his mom talk about God like this. To know she'd found her way back after the hard stuff she'd endured. Jace wasn't sure how to respond about the money, but he did know that.

"I was thinking the money would make a nice down payment on a place for you one day. I thought maybe… maybe you'd come back to Westbend."

Jace had considered buying a place near Westbend, once or twice over the years. But at the time, coming home with Mackenzie still angry at him hadn't exactly been a draw.

And now he was right back to square one with her.

He winced thinking about how he'd asked her to wait for him. Her reply had been spot-on. For how long? He didn't know. And he shouldn't expect her to sit around, pining for him, after all of this time.

"You don't have to tell me what you do with it. But it's yours. It's there when you need it."

"Fine." What was the point in arguing? "But will you just consider going down to one job? Just…pray about it."

Her eyes crinkled at the corners. "Pulling out the big guns, are ya?"

"Maybe. I'm not saying you have to use the money. But if you do decide to slow down a little, it could still be there as a backup. And you should keep any interest, because that was all you."

Her head shook as her smile grew. "You always were very convincing, even as a kid." The home phone rang, and she pushed up from the couch, snagging it from the top of the TV cabinet. "It's your brother."

"Don't answer!" Missed calls from Evan had been piling up on Jace's phone, more so in the last two weeks. "I don't want him to know I'm here. I don't want to talk to him." More like he didn't want to hear what his brother had to say.

"Are you crazy? Of course I'm answering. He's usually someplace where he can't call." She switched the receiver on and greeted Evan.

Jace stood. He should really get going. Things—like that goodbye to Mackenzie—kept stretching out, taking up extra time. But he couldn't exactly sneak out while his mom was on the phone, could he?

"He wants to talk to you." She held out the receiver, and Jace muffled a groan.

How could he say no? The phone was being jiggled

under his nose. Evan could probably hear if he so much as inhaled.

Jace would just have to make it quick. He palmed the receiver. "Hey, E. What's up?"

"Heard you're a big ole mess, little brother." Evan's teasing came through the line clear, and with it a slew of childhood memories. Times his brother had stood up for him. Protected him. Times they'd played army as boys. Rode their bikes until the mountains swallowed the sun.

"Nothing I didn't learn from you." Their exchange felt like home, and Jace's shoulders notched down as his brother's familiar laughter sounded. "Where are you this week?"

"Appalachian Trail. I'm about to take out a group."

"That's great." Evan had found a way up and through his handicap and now led trips for others who were recovering from various traumas. He'd done amazing things with his life, and what did Jace have to show for his own?

Not much at the moment.

"Mom says you're going back to riding and she thinks you shouldn't."

Jace stepped outside and copped a seat on the front step. So much for getting out of town quickly.

"Mom is just overconcerned."

"Really? No one else is? What's your doctor say?"

I'd quit now... I've seen too many lives taken or changed forever by this sport. Jace didn't want to lie, but he also didn't plan to share that information with Evan.

"That bad, huh?"

"No. It's just… He gave me some advice. But you know bull riding. It's a guessing game. I could come back and have my best season yet."

"Or the worst."

"Thanks for the vote of confidence."

"That's not what I meant, and you know it. It's not about you or your skill level. Things just happen in bull riding that are out of your control. What is it that's pulling you back to riding? The money? Competing? Because you don't know what else you'd do? I'll help with Mom if you level with me."

All of the above and more. Discomfort shimmied up Jace's spine.

"And if you can't tell me why you have to go back now, then help me understand why you picked up the sport in the first place. I've always wondered…" Quiet tension expanded. "J, did you start competing because of me?" His brother didn't tiptoe into an awkward conversation; he leaped.

That scene from their childhood flashed back—Evan sprawled out on the floor, his face red with frustration. "You told me to, remember?"

"*I* told you to? When did I ever say something like that?"

"After your accident. You were upset. Tearing down the posters in your room. You told me to live your dreams. To not let anything hold me back."

"Huh. That's not how I remember it."

A golf ball jammed Jace's throat. "How do you remember it?"

"I was angry."

"I've got that part down."

"Grieving a childhood dream. You walked in on your two legs, and I was upset at the thought that you didn't realize what you had. No one really does until it's gone. I may have said something about being thankful for your abilities or chasing your dreams. Or even mine. I'm not sure. But I didn't mean for you to ride bulls because of me. I was still a kid, J. I was mad at the world, and my rampage really didn't have anything to do with you." A sigh rang in his ear. "I'm sure I just wanted you to live, to take advantage of what you had."

The ball of worry slid into his gut and expanded. Evan actually made sense. Jace had never been able to remember the exact words his brother had spoken. Only the way they'd been fired at him. The heat behind them. The guilt he'd felt. Jace had seen the posters, the loss of his brother's dream, and he'd wanted to make that up to him somehow. As if pursuing riding would wipe out his part in what had happened.

"Your accident was my fault, you know."

A beat of silence followed his declaration. "Really? How do you figure that? Did you give the mower a shove?"

"Of course not." Jace swallowed, wishing it would add some moisture to his dry-as-a-bone mouth. "It was my job to mow that day. If I would have done my—"

"Then maybe you would have lost your leg instead of me?"

"I wouldn't have, because I wasn't allowed to use the riding mower."

"Oh, J. I knew it was your job. But you were a kid. I also knew it would take me half the time on the neighbor's mower, so I did it for you. It shouldn't have been a big deal. Dad was such a jerk when we were growing up. Never around and worthless when he was. I probably felt some sense of responsibility regarding you. We're all messed up in our own ways, brother. Just because you didn't mow doesn't make the accident your fault. I'm the one who was completely distracted that day. I'm the one who didn't turn the thing off before checking why it wasn't running right. If I could go back and do things differently, I would, but it happened. I can't change that, and I'm not about to sit at home and cry all day. At least not anymore. I have a life, and I'm living it. Are you living yours? Or are you living mine?"

Yours died on the tip of Jace's tongue. But was that true? He did love bull riding. The sport had become his somewhere along the way.

"I'm not going to tell you to quit," Evan continued.

"You'd be the first, then."

"But just…think before you go back. You've had a great career. There's nothing wrong with retiring before it takes you down for good. I know this sport. I know what it does to guys, how it messes up their bodies. If continuing is about what happened to me in any way, it doesn't need to be. Because you and I… We're good. If there's anyone to blame for my accident, it's me. I knew better than to handle anything the way I did. It was stupid. A fluke. But it wasn't your fault."

Jace's cheeks were damp, his heart pounding as his brother signed off.

After Jace left and the vet finished up, Mackenzie sent her brother a panicked text that she needed a minute—or more like an hour—and escaped.

But her escape wasn't from Wilder Ranch; it was to it.

The earthy smell, the crisp, clean mountain air and hot summer breeze had all unwound her. Going for a ride had, like nothing else would, righted her world.

Mackenzie couldn't give up this place. And if Jace loved riding as much as she loved Wilder Ranch, then it made sense that he couldn't quit that dream. Even for her. Even with his head injury. She should be able to accept that and realize it wasn't about her.

But it felt like it was.

Big-time.

All of these years she'd been wrong—it wasn't the note that had caused the most pain. It was the fact that Jace had left in the first place. Because this round was just as painful. Maybe even more so because she'd realized that she still loved the man.

He was the one. And yet…he couldn't be. Not when he was determined to risk life and limb for a stupid sport. Mackenzie couldn't wrap her brain around that.

She led Buttercup back to the corral and removed her saddle. Sable came to check her out, nosing around her shirt. "I didn't bring you a treat, girl. I'm not your boy. He left us for greener pastures."

The ride had helped, but it hadn't dissolved the wretched war wound of Jace's departure. It was still there, pulsing inside her, cramming her throat.

She needed something good, something pure and full of hope to wash away the encounter she'd had with Jace an hour ago.

God, if You have any comfort to send my way, any wisdom, I'll take it.

Gladly.

"Hey." Luc's voice came from close by.

She turned. "I didn't hear you coming this way."

"Called your name twice."

Oops. Mackenzie exited the corral and placed her saddle on the ground. Luc had Everly with him—her hair was darker and fuller. A good thing since it helped in telling the girls apart.

"Can I hold her?"

"Of course." Luc handed the baby over immediately, and Mackenzie snuggled Everly into her arms like a football. Dark chocolate eyes peered up at her. This would work for something pure and sweet to ease the pain thrumming through her veins.

"I can't get over how much they look like Cate."

Luc's cheeks creased. "And we're all thankful for it." He nudged her saddle with his boot. "How was the ride? Did it work?"

"Fine. Yes and no." She was still drowning, even though there was no water in sight.

"How are you feeling about Jace leaving?"

"Like I don't want to talk about it." Mackenzie stared at Everly's perfect little features instead of her brother. Pink lips formed an O shape and then slid into something close to a smile. Probably gas, but Mackenzie would take it.

"I'm shocked."

A short laugh escaped.

"Are you done being angry at me for hiring him?"

"Nope." If Luc hadn't hired Jace, then her body wouldn't currently be registering at trampled-by-a-herd-of-cattle levels.

"I thought the two of you were finally going to figure things out, make it work. And then you'd owe me forever and ever because it was all my doing."

Mackenzie attempted a smile, the movement slow—like creaky old hinges that barely budged. "You'd like that, wouldn't you? It's hard to be with someone who won't stick around."

"That's what you're upset about? Jace going back to riding? Why? That's his job. Of course he's going to go back."

Mackenzie barely resisted a groan. Men. "I know that. But he had a pretty major head injury when he got here, and it's not fully healed. And I doubt his arm is ready to go either. Partially rehabbed seems to be good enough for him. What if he gets tossed from a bull again? Another concussion right now would cause even more damage. How much more can he take before it affects him forever?"

"I'm assuming you said all of that and he didn't listen." She nodded.

"Then you tried. He made his decision, even if it is a poor one in your opinion. So why don't you just love him through it? You already do. Might as well let yourself."

Everly made a sweet complaint, so Mackenzie switched the baby to her shoulder and lightly patted her back. "I don't…" What was the point of fighting it? Had she ever not loved Jace? It had been seven years, and no, she'd never fallen out of love with the man the way she'd fallen in. Last time she'd thought he didn't love her back when he left. But this time she knew better. He'd been keeping his feelings in check, just like she had been.

He'd asked her to wait…and she'd said no. No, because it wasn't convenient for her to live without him in the waiting. No, because she was afraid he'd hurt himself.

She should have said yes.

"Is Jace getting injured again going to change how you feel about him?"

"No." It wasn't. But it could hurt like crazy. "Since when are you such an expert on love?"

"Since I almost lost Cate for the second time, and you didn't let me. You fought me on that, and you were right."

Her mouth bowed, this time fluid, easy. "Wait. Say that again. I was what?"

"You were right. And now I'm right. Because I have never seen you even remotely interested in someone else the way you are with Jace. There are no comparisons, because there hasn't ever been anyone else for you. *Amiright?*"

"Did you just mush that together like a teenager?"

"Yep. Nailed it, too."

"You are such a dork." She didn't want to give Luc the satisfaction of finding his lame joke funny, but humor surfaced.

"Now's when you can admit how right I am."

Not out loud. Definitely not out loud. "Nope." Her eyes were wet, her smile wobbly. And her brother just let it all slide.

He hugged her. "Okay, stubborn." Everly was tucked between them, so Luc left room for her. She twisted her head to figure out what was happening, and Luc pressed a kiss to the baby's hair before letting go, backing up.

"Even if things don't work out with Jace, you've got us, Kenzie. And God. He's consistent. Even when we don't *feel* like He's with us, He still is."

That was the truth that gave her the most hope, the most peace. "Thanks. I'm doing better at remembering that."

Everly fussed and sucked on her hand.

"I should get her back. Think it's time to feed them. Cate's been sticking to a pretty tight schedule, or we all lose our minds."

Mackenzie handed the bundle over to Luc, immediately missing Everly's comfort and the scent of her fruity baby shampoo.

"Are you going to be all right?"

"I think so." Maybe. Hopefully. Especially if she figured out the answers to a few other questions. Like…did she *really* believe that Jace loved her? That the man had legit reasons holding him captive, making him choose the rodeo over her all over again? And that loving him through this hard time might be one of the best things she'd ever done?

Mackenzie thought maybe yes.

Definitely yes.

"Think you can live without me for a couple of days?"

A knowing grin ignited. She didn't have to explain anything more. Luc understood. "We can probably make that work."

Chapter 16

After the conversation with his brother, Jace could hardly see straight. The highway stretched in front of him, seemingly endless, and he was barely past Denver.

When he'd first started rodeoing, he'd loved the long drives. Anticipation had always burned inside him. Today it was more apprehension.

A word he usually didn't go anywhere near.

But his head—his stupid head—was aching. Would it erupt into more? Or would it calm down? It never really gave him a choice in the matter. Jace popped a pill and took a swig from his coffee cup, using the lukewarm liquid to send what would hopefully bring relief down his throat. He kept his foot heavy on the gas pedal. Heading away from the woman he loved and missed. The desire to call Kenzie, to hear her voice, even though he'd only left her two hours ago, was huge.

He stomped out the idea. He'd done enough damage the second time around, hadn't he? No need to cause more.

Sweat beaded on his skin. It was sweltering today, warming more as the sun rose higher. Jace had both windows open in his truck, and the blistering air swirled around, making a weak attempt to diffuse the heat. He should really get a truck with air-conditioning in it. And he could. But he'd just figured, why not drive the thing until it died?

Jace had done well with bull riding over the years—until the last few bouts with injuries—and after his first year of blowing through his successes, he'd learned his lesson and begun putting chunks away.

And sending some to his mom.

Crazy to think she'd never used a dime of it. No wonder he'd had to hire the painting out on the house when he got back. And the yardwork. The irony of that one stung. The chore that had once been his that he'd failed at. And had again as an adult.

If she wasn't going to use the money, then he'd hire some lawn-maintenance place to take care of things. And maybe get someone on retainer for repairs on the house, too. At least that way he wouldn't feel like such a deadbeat son, leaving her when she was sick.

Sure, she'd been sick for years, but she was getting worse. Anyone could see that.

Would Mackenzie still check on his mom like she used to? Jace's gut said yes. Which only increased the guilt and upset churning in his stomach.

He should be there to check on her.

He should also feel that old eagerness to return to riding growing with each mile that ticked over on his odometer. That jonesing to see the chute, the bull he'd ride, his friends.

But that was sorely lacking today. Mostly he just felt… like he was driving in the wrong direction.

A *bang/hiss* boomed, and the truck lurched and swerved. Jace gripped the steering wheel and tried to combat the careening motion, but he overcompensated to the left. The front of the truck veered and dipped. He must have blown a front tire. The air in his lungs evaporated as he wrestled for control of the vehicle.

He let the truck idle down before tapping lightly on the brakes. Amid more turbulence, he managed to slowly come to a stop, off to the side of the road.

Thankfully no one else had been near him, because he'd traveled into both lanes during the aftermath.

Jace turned on his hazards and made sure he had the space to check out his vehicle without getting run over. Sure enough, the left front tire of the truck was blown. He hadn't checked the tire pressure before leaving town. Must have had a slow leak or something he hadn't realized wrong with it.

Toss some extra hot weather on top and the tire didn't stand a chance. Stupid. That was what he was. He knew better. He'd been taking care of vehicles around their house since he'd started to drive.

"Perfect." He kicked the wreckage. "Just perfect."

Everything was working against him today. He'd left the ranch late because of his goodbye with Mackenzie, and his mom's late because of the conversation with Evan.

He was starting to wonder if he actually wanted to leave at all.

I have to go. At least that was what he'd always believed. But talking with Evan had rocked him, made him deal with things he'd left buried for years.

Evan had known it was Jace's job to mow...and he didn't blame Jace for the accident. He'd extended grace. Would Jace have done the same in his brother's position? He didn't know. He'd like to say he'd do anything for his brother, for his mom, for Kenzie.

But he wasn't staying in Westbend, even though Mom was sick.

And Mackenzie... She'd asked him to stay, to not go back, and he'd refused. She'd pleaded with him to recognize his physical limitations for his own good. For his own health. And he'd refused to listen.

Sun scorched the back of his neck like licking flames, and his skin sizzled.

All of this time he'd dreamed of getting back up on a bull, and now that he was about to, he was petrified that his head would explode with pain and never recover if he did. Or that he'd get tossed and break something else. Something worse this time that couldn't be fixed as easily.

How lame was he? How could he not finish what he'd started now? What he'd been fighting for?

Jace went to the back of his truck and fished out his lug-nut wrench from under his things. He'd start by loosening the lug nuts before raising the truck. His hand curled around the metal wrench just as something hit him on the top of the head.

He looked up. The sky was mostly clear. A few wispy, puffy white clouds dotted the blue. Only one dark cloud held even a remote potential for rain, and it was stationed directly over him like something out of a Charlie Brown cartoon.

"You've got to be kidding me."

He'd thrown his things into the back of the truck because the drive was supposed to be clear. Jace hauled the large duffel, his saddle and a few other items over to the passenger door of the cab and tossed them inside.

More drops joined in, catching him on the back of the neck, the shoulders. He briefly considered getting in the truck to wait it out, but rain was so sporadic in Colorado. If he did, it would probably turn out to be nothing.

He returned to the tire and began working the lug nuts loose. One was so tight he gave up on it and switched to another. While he worked, the sun beat down and random raindrops pelted him at the same time.

"How is that even possible?" He directed his question to the sky and earned a wet *plunk* in his eye. Jace blinked to clear the moisture away. "All right, all right. I'll stop asking questions."

Traffic had been cruising along at a pretty steady pace while he worked on the tire, and no one had stopped to offer help, which was fine, but Jace heard the slowing of an engine approaching now.

He kept working on the last stubborn nut. Didn't look up until he heard a door open and footsteps crunching.

The woman coming at him was a tall drink of water. *His* tall drink of water. "Kenzie?" He dropped the wrench and popped up from the ground. "What in the world are you doing here?" There was no way she could just be driving past. He'd been headed for Miles City. Last he'd checked, she didn't have any business heading north.

Which could only mean one thing: she was looking for him. The woman either had good news...or something was horribly wrong.

* * *

Luc had told Mackenzie not to come back until Sunday morning. Which gave her more than enough time to drive to Jace's rodeo, watch him compete…and tell him she loved him, that she would wait for him—however long it took. And patience was not, by any means, her strongest attribute.

But she'd figure out how to get good at it, because Jace was worth it. Worth that and more.

The words she'd practiced while gunning toward Montana had fled the moment she'd recognized Jace's truck on the side of the road. About the same time she'd begun wondering if God was in the business of orchestrating flat—or more like blown—tires.

"You okay?" Jace closed the gap between them, meeting her by the tailgate and then directing her to the other side of the truck, away from traffic. "Is everyone all right?"

"Everyone is fine." Mackenzie nodded toward his injured truck. "Just thought maybe you needed a girl to come along and change a tire for you. Wasn't sure you were capable."

A wedge split his forehead, questioning, while that grin she loved sparked and grew. "Girls can't change tires." His familiar voice, soaked with humor, nestled in her gut, warm and right. Jace reached out and squeezed her arm. "I'm not sure why you're here…but I'm glad you are."

"I need to know something before I say my piece." Her heart was pounding so hard, she was certain it was going to skip right out of her rib cage.

"Okay." He angled his head. "What do you need to know?"

"Do you love me?" Still? Again? She wasn't sure what to add onto the end of that.

Jace's jaw loosened, and he rubbed a hand across it. His eyes, full of confusion and hope, held on to hers. And then he nodded. "Yeah. I do." He didn't elaborate. And why should he? That was what she'd needed to hear.

"Then I'll wait." He stared at her, mouth gaping. Did she need to be more clear? Fine. "I love you. So if you need to be a big idiot and get yourself hurt, then I'll stand by you while you do it. Because you're it for me. Loving someone else isn't an option. I don't even like other people half the time."

Jace laughed, and man, did he look good doing it, too, with his eyes crinkling at the corners, his smoking smile turning her stomach inside out. "I love you, Kenzie Rae—always have, always will." He kissed her then, burying his fingers in her hair, the scrape of this morning's lack of shave against her lips, moving into her space like he was meant to be exactly there. And he was.

The sky, which had only been sputtering up until now, opened up, pelting them. Jace grabbed her hand and directed her to the passenger door of his truck, then ushered her inside. Mackenzie scooted over the saddle and other items, and slid behind the steering wheel, leaving Jace room to crawl in behind her. After climbing in, he slammed the creaking door shut and they both cranked the windows up, fighting the sheet of rain flooding the cab.

The driver's window stuck halfway up, and Jace stretched over her. "Here. You've gotta—" He slammed the side of his fist into the door near the handle and then finished the job.

Mackenzie brushed the moisture from her arms, but

without a towel, plenty remained. "You really need a new truck, Hawke."

"And *you* really need to stop calling me Hawke. Especially since that's going to be your last name pretty soon, too, and continuing to call me that would just make things confusing and awkward."

Her stomach curled into a warm little ball. "Oh, really?"

"Absolutely." He invaded her personal bubble again—hadn't really left it since reaching over her to get to the window—swooping in for another taste, which she was just fine giving. Jace kept hold of her hand as he eased back from kissing her, and all of her doubts and worries and fears vanished. Whatever came, they'd figure it out together. Mackenzie would start her in-sickness-and-in-health vow now and carry it into forever for this man.

"I was planning to watch you compete. The boss—" she grinned when one of his eyebrows arched "—gave me a couple of days off so that I could drive to Miles City and talk to you. But then I found you stranded on the side of the road." Mackenzie wasn't even going to question how that had come about. And she'd never been happier to see someone have car trouble.

"You like that, don't you? Think you came along to rescue me?"

"I did, didn't I?"

His mouth sported a wry arch. "You did. I have a lug nut I can't get loose. You could probably handle that for me." He sat back against the seat, facing forward, toying with her fingers. "So…"

Had he turned shy all of a sudden? "What?"

"I'm not sure I want to go back anymore."

"Where don't you want to go back to?" Wilder Ranch? Westbend? Montana?

"The rodeo." Jace met her gaze, his earnest, and her heart broke and stitched back together at the same time. "All I can think about is screwing up the rest of my life for this sport." She'd thought the same so many times, but it still killed her that Jace would have to give up something he loved so much. "I talked to Evan. We figured some things out."

"It's about time."

"Kenzie Rae." His head shook, but the twinkle in his eyes told her he wasn't offended by her being…her.

"Evan doesn't remember asking me to live his dreams for him. And I'm sure he's right. He probably didn't. But that was all I could see and hear that day, the only way I knew to somehow try to make it up to him." Jace smoothed his thumb across her knuckles, making her stomach spin cartwheels the length of a football field. "He told me not to let that dictate what I do anymore. My choices. And I think…*you've* always been my dream. I just never allowed myself to ask and answer that question before. You're what I want." He said it steady and strong and sure. "And the rest? I have to figure out."

"So you're not going to go back? Even this weekend? Not going to compete?"

"Nope. I think I'm going to retire. At least for now. Maybe God will change that for me in the future. But currently? I'm done."

Everything in her erupted in celebration, her nerves tingling, face heating. "I'm so glad. Not that you have to give up something you love, but that you'll be okay."

"Me, too." He kissed her softly. Mackenzie took her time, enjoying every second of the feel of Jace under her fingertips, letting her hands scoot up his arms, which were still damp with rainwater.

Jace tucked a piece of hair behind her ear. "So, you don't have to be back until when?"

"Sunday morning. Why?"

"Any chance you're interested in going to a wedding tomorrow?"

"Whose?" He'd been planning to attend a wedding? How had she missed that detail?

"Ours."

Mackenzie's shoulders straightened. "What? Are you serious?"

"I've never been more serious."

"But…" That was crazy. Right? Except…what else did she want? She already knew from being a spectator and participant in Emma's wedding that all of that fussing wasn't a fit for her. But this man was.

"We could get married tomorrow."

"How does that even work with a marriage license? Can we get one that fast?"

The slow curve of his lips was completely distracting. "Does that mean you're actually considering it?"

"Are you? You'd better not ask if you're thinking about backing out…J." She'd almost said Hawke again.

"Not a chance ever again. You're it for me, and you're never getting rid of me."

"A little stalkerish, but I like it." She couldn't believe she was actually considering marrying him tomorrow. But was that even an option? Mackenzie wasn't exactly up on the how-tos of eloping. "Isn't there a waiting period for a marriage license? Or blood tests?"

"I have no clue." Jace grabbed his phone from its perch

on the dash as thunder erupted. This storm had come out of nowhere. "I'll look it up."

They scrolled through the State of Colorado website as Mackenzie tucked her arm through his and leaned against his shoulder. "We'd get the certificate the same day. It says we can marry ourselves after we get the license. We don't even need someone else to do a ceremony."

"What? That's crazy." Mackenzie stole his phone and read. "I'm not sure how I feel about that. I'd like someone to do it. Pastor Higgin would be great, but then we'd have to drive back to Westbend, and not only are we closer to Denver, but if we go home, someone will talk us out of this. And I really don't want that to happen."

"That's my girl."

"We need a judge." She clicked. "But it almost looks like we have to call and schedule it with them. I thought people could just walk in and have a judge marry them. Who knows." She handed the phone back. "We can get the certificate and then ask questions when we're there."

Jace scrolled with the pad of his thumb. "They're open for a few more hours. Want to get it done today?"

Mackenzie should probably be experiencing panic at the idea of marrying Jace tomorrow, but she wasn't. Instead a steady thrum of excitement was racing under her skin. It felt right. He felt right.

And they'd choose each other for the future, just like she'd been quietly choosing him for years. After all she'd never been able to truly kick the man, or the memories of him, to the curb. Keeping him forever only made sense.

"Time's a wastin'. Let's go."

His face lit up, and his lips met hers, swift, sweet, a promise. "I think impatience may be one of your better qualities."

She laughed.

A line jutted through Jace's brow. "I still need to change my tire."

Pouring rain rolled down the windows without interruption and another crack of thunder rumbled.

"Any objections to leaving this—" Mackenzie tapped the dash "—lovely specimen here? We can call roadside assistance and have them change the tire, then swing back for it later."

Jace tugged her into his arms, and she crash-landed against his steady chest as he pressed a kiss to her hair, her forehead, the hollow of her cheek. "No objections from me."

Epilogue

It only seemed fitting that since she'd fallen for Jace Hawke twice, Mackenzie should marry the man twice.

But at least she hadn't been forced to plan the wedding reception at Wilder Ranch that she was about to attend.

Emma, Mom and Cate had seen to that.

When Mackenzie and Jace had returned to Wilder Ranch two months ago with simple wedding bands on their left ring fingers, giddy, unable to stop smiling at each other like lovesick fools and completely delighted with their decision, no one had mustered the heart to be upset with them for very long.

Even her parents had reacted well during the phone call, when she and Jace had spilled the news. Mom had quickly started plans for a reception. She'd asked if they would consider redoing their vows and letting Dad give her away as part of the evening.

Mackenzie hadn't always dreamed of a big wedding, but she had imagined her dad walking her down the aisle. She and Jace had quickly agreed to Mom's requests, though the night could never compete with their actual wedding.

Which, for being thrown together, had been absolutely perfect.

The day Mackenzie and Jace had decided to get married, they'd driven back to Denver, gotten the license, found a judge—the father of one of Jace's buddies. It had all fallen into place. Quick. Easy.

Jace had suggested they find outfits for each other. At first she'd balked. After all, shopping ranked close to hair bows and red lipstick in her world. But he'd convinced her it would be fun, and it shockingly had been.

He'd picked out a dress for her. Simple lines. A sundress, really. An ivory color with a delicate pattern sewed around the neckline and hem. It had spaghetti straps and a crisscross back. And then he'd declared that, most important, she needed new boots. The pair she'd been wearing that day definitely hadn't been fit for a wedding. He'd picked those out, too—camel brown with off-white stitching. It would almost seem as if the man knew her.

Mackenzie had selected new jeans and a button-up shirt for Jace, plus a vest. Because if he was making her wear a dress, she'd required the same level of fancy from him.

And oh, my, had he looked good in the outfit.

Judge Berg had met them at Lookout Mountain Park the next morning, and they'd said their vows outside, with the Rocky Mountains as a backdrop.

Mackenzie would never forget all of the little details she hadn't expected to remember about that day. Or the man who'd been consistently by her side ever since. They were still praying and figuring out Jace's next career steps. But in the meantime he was helping out at Wilder Ranch again. She secretly hoped he'd stay on. She liked working with him. But whatever he figured out, they'd make it work, because they were stuck with each other now.

"Kenz, you ready to head upstairs?" Jace bellowed from the other side of the lodge's bathroom door. She'd been trying to fix the zipper on her dress, which kept edging open, but she couldn't get the clasp done without help.

She cracked open the door. "And people say romance is dead. Come in here. I need help with my dress zipper."

Jace stepped inside the bathroom with her, shutting the door behind him and letting out a low whistle. "You don't even give anyone else a chance, woman. It should be a crime to look as good as you do."

They were both wearing what they had chosen for their elopement, and again the man was ad-worthy. He rezipped and clasped the back of her dress in two shakes, and she turned, adjusting his vest, lingering for the faintest of seconds near his abs. Retiring from bull riding hadn't changed his physique, and Mackenzie didn't have any complaints. By the way his brows toggled with amusement, she'd been caught.

"I just got a text they're ready for us." But instead of leaving, Jace wrapped his arms around her, and Mackenzie let herself fall. He felt so good. So right. Warm lips pressed against her neck. "You smell good."

The continued embrace unraveled her muscles one at a time. "You do, too."

"What do you say we get out of here?"

She laughed and eased back. "We already stole the

wedding from them. I'm pretty sure we have to give them this."

"True." He gently pressed a kiss to her cheek, as if she was some sort of delicate doll that could easily be broken. "I don't want to muss you up before everything starts."

"You don't have to be so careful with me." Her hair was natural—down in loose waves. "I'm not wearing any makeup but mascara." Which had been her one concession.

"Which stuff is that? The eye goop?"

She nodded.

"That's why your stormy eyes look so striking. It's a good thing you don't wear it all the time. I already have trouble not letting you get your way all day long. Adding makeup when you're already so gorgeous is just unfair."

Warmth flared at the compliment.

Jace's heart was visible in the inky pools of his eyes. "I'm feeling kind of sentimental, being that I get to marry you twice."

"I was thinking the same thing."

The party tonight wasn't huge—family and friends. Most of the summer staff had come back for it, even though it was on a Tuesday. The fall schedule hosted groups every weekend, so a weeknight had been the only option. Jace's mom was present, of course, but Evan couldn't make it, because he was climbing some mountain. He'd sent a gift and expressed how happy he was to see Jace moving on with this new part of his life.

"Well, I suppose we should get upstairs." Jace's drawl was thick, exaggerated. "Time's a wastin'." Ever since she'd said that line to him in his broken-down truck, it had become a favorite of his.

He started opening the bathroom door, but Mackenzie slammed it shut. "Wait! Check if anyone is out there first. We don't want to be seen coming out of the bathroom at the same time."

Amusement and *are you serious?* warred for dominance in his expression. "You do realize that we're already married, right?"

"Yes. But it's still weird."

His sigh said, *You're crazy, but I still love you*, all in one swollen breath.

He opened the door an inch and made a big show of peeking out. "The coast is clear."

They sneaked out of the bathroom and then headed up the stairs to where her dad was waiting outside the square dance/multipurpose room. They'd opted to have the reception in the simple space, and Emma and Cate had been decorating all day.

Mackenzie was grateful to have two sisters on her team.

"Ready? I think everyone is all set." Her dad held out an arm, and Mackenzie slid her hand through it. "I hope you two were behaving yourselves." Mackenzie knew her dad was teasing, but by the way Jace's face lost all color, he didn't.

"Yes, sir. We were just—"

"Son," Dad interrupted. "I don't want to hear what you were doing. I'm joking. You do realize you're already married, right?"

"Right." Jace visibly relaxed, though his Adam's apple bobbed as if he were trying to swallow a rock.

"I understand why you asked for my blessing to marry my Kenzie-girl after the fact, instead of permission beforehand." Distress pulled Jace's features taut as her dad continued, "I want you to know, I would have deferred to er decision anyway. I trust her. And you. And I couldn't be happier to have gained another son-in-law. I think she picked well for herself."

Jace cleared his throat, no doubt fighting emotion. "Thank you, sir."

"You're part of this family now, son. You've become a Wilder as much as Mackenzie has become a Hawke."

Mackenzie had never been more thankful for her father's wisdom than right now. His gracious, wide-open heart somehow knew exactly what Jace needed to hear. The way her dad had cared for this husband of hers—first as a wounded teenage boy and now as a man—made her cup overflow.

The two men hugged, and then Jace stepped inside the room to stand with Pastor Higgin.

"Thank you, Dad." There weren't enough ways or words to express what his support meant.

"Anytime you need me, I'm here, baby girl. But I'm guessing that won't be as often, since you have a good man by your side."

True. Mackenzie had already noticed how her fears of being forgotten had faded lately. She'd stopped anticipating everyone rushing forward without her and started expecting to be included, in the middle, part of it.

Very Vera-like of her.

The music started, which was their cue. "You Look Good" by Lady Antebellum blared, and Mackenzie laughed. Jace must have arranged the song. She walked in on her dad's steady arm, and he whispered how much he loved her and how proud he was of her before handing her off to Jace.

They repeated their vows, with Jace's adoration and devotion radiating. Pastor Higgin pronounced them husband and wife—again and still—which resulted in laughter and cheers. They ate scrumptious barbecue that Joe had prepared and caught up with friends and family and staff. Mackenzie didn't get to spend much time with her husband throughout the evening, which only made her more thankful they'd gotten married with just the two of them back in August—when they'd been able to focus only on each other.

She was talking to some friends from church later in the evening when Jace approached. "Ladies, I'd like to steal my wife for a dance, if that's okay."

"What?" Mackenzie rocked back in surprise. "You don't dance."

In answer, Jace whirled her into the small area reserved for exactly that—a space Ruby hadn't left all night. She'd been twirling in her flowered dress, and Hudson had been with her for much of the evening, his diapered bottom—in baby dress pants—bouncing to the beat. Her niece and nephew both knew how to boogie when the occasion called for it.

Other couples were already dancing. Mom and Dad. Luc and Cate. Gage and Emma. Even Vera and Dr. Bradley, who were still going strong.

"You don't know everything about me, wife." Jace spun her out and then back, and she stumbled to keep up, mentally and physically. Who was this man? And what had he done with her husband?

"Is that so? And here I thought you told me just a few months ago that you didn't know how to dance."

"I didn't then." He pulled her close, guiding her. "When I found out we were going to have a reception, I learned. I thought you might actually let me lead if I surprised you."

She'd consider being offended if he wasn't so right. Not having a clue where to step next made her totally dependent on Jace directing her.

"And just where and when did you learn to dance?"

His head tipped back, and eyes filled with mirth held hers. "YouTube." She laughed, and his grin edged with mischief. "Actually, Vera taught me."

He tucked her close again, slowing their pace, their cheeks aligning. "It's almost like you don't want to let me go, Mr. Hawke."

"Ding-ding-ding, Mrs. Hawke. You've got me figured out."

Her heart was doing all sorts of mushy things inside her chest. "Thanks for not leaving when I tried to shove you out of here." To think…she could have missed all of this if she'd gotten her way at the start of the summer.

"Thanks for giving me another chance to love you. You're everything I've ever wanted, Kenzie Rae."

Sappy warmth rose up from her toes, cresting her skin along the way. It was almost as if she and Jace were meant to be. Almost as if Someone bigger than them had brought them back together. Almost as if the man holding her planned to be her constant, her forever, her place to belong.

And Mackenzie could get used to that. In fact, she planned to.

* * * * *

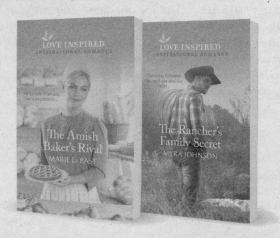

SPECIAL EXCERPT FROM

LOVE INSPIRED
INSPIRATIONAL ROMANCE

*After a traumatic brain injury, military vet
Behr Delgado refuses the one thing that could help
him—a service dog. But charity head Ellery Watson
knows the dog she selected will improve his quality of
life and vows to work with him one-on-one. When their
personal lives entwine with their professional lives, can
they trust each other long enough to both heal?*

Read on for a sneak peek at
The Veteran's Vow *by Jill Lynn!*

Ellery approached and held out Margo's leash for him. She was so excited he was doing better. The thought of disappointing her cut Behr like a combat knife.

Margo stood by Ellery's side, her chocolate face toggling back and forth between them, questioning what she was supposed to do next. Waiting for his lead.

Behr reached out and took the leash. If Ellery noticed his shaking hand, she didn't say anything.

"I want to teach her to stand by your left side. That's it. She's just going to be there. We're going to take it slow." Ellery moved to Behr's left, leaving enough room for Margo to stand between them.

A tremble echoed through him, and Behr tensed his muscles in an effort to curb it.

Margo, on the other hand, would be the first image if someone searched the internet for the definition of the word *calm*.

"Heel." When he gave Margo the command and she obeyed, taking that spot, Behr's heart just about ricocheted out of his chest.

This effort was worth it. Was it, though? He could get through life off-kilter, running into things, tripping, leaving items on the floor when they fell, willing his poor coordination to work instead of using Margo to create balance for him or grasp or retrieve things for him, couldn't he?

Ellery didn't say anything about his audible inhales or exhales, but she had to know what he was up to. The weakness that plagued Behr rose up to ridicule him. It was hard to reveal this side of himself to Ellery, not that she hadn't seen it already. Hard to know that he couldn't just snap his fingers and make his body right again. Hard to remember that he needed this dog and that was why his mom and sisters had signed him up for one.

"You're doing great." Ellery's focus was on Behr, but Margo's tail wagged as if the compliment had been directed at her.

They both laughed, and the tension dissipated like a deployment care package.

"You, too, girl." Ellery offered Margo a treat. "Do you want me to put the balance harness on her so you can feel what it's like?" she asked Behr.

He gave one determined nod.

Ellery strode over to the storage cabinets that lined the back wall. She returned with the harness and knelt to slide it on Margo and adjust it. Behr should probably be watching how to do the same, but right now he was concentrating on standing next to Margo and not having his knees liquefy.

Ellery stood. "See what you think."

Behr gripped the handle, his knuckles turning white. The handle was the right height, and it did make him feel sturdy. Supported.

Like the woman beaming at him from the other side of the dog.

Don't miss
The Veteran's Vow *by Jill Lynn,*
available March 2022 wherever
Love Inspired books and ebooks are sold.

LoveInspired.com

IF YOU ENJOYED THIS BOOK, DON'T MISS NEW EXTENDED-LENGTH NOVELS FROM LOVE INSPIRED!

In addition to the Love Inspired books you know and love, we're excited to introduce even more uplifting stories in a longer format, with more inspiring fresh starts and page-turning thrills!

LOVE INSPIRED

Stories to uplift and inspire.

Fall in love with Love Inspired—inspirational and uplifting stories of faith and hope. Find strength and comfort in the bonds of friendship and community. Revel in the warmth of possibility, and the promise of new beginnings.

LOOK FOR THESE LOVE INSPIRED TITLES ONLINE AND IN THE BOOK DEPARTMENT OF YOUR FAVORITE RETAILER!

LOVE INSPIRED

Stories to uplift and inspire

Fall in love with Love Inspired—
inspirational and uplifting stories of faith
and hope. Find strength and comfort in
the bonds of friendship and community.
Revel in the warmth of possibility and the
promise of new beginnings.

Sign up for the Love Inspired newsletter
at **LoveInspired.com** to be the first
to find out about upcoming titles,
special promotions and exclusive content.

CONNECT WITH US AT:

[f] Facebook.com/LoveInspiredBooks

[t] Twitter.com/LoveInspiredBks